J. A. Downes was born and raised in England and educated at Imperial College, London University, where he gained a B.Sc. in Physics.

A busy career in information technology provides just a little time left over to explore the mystery of history and, finally, to write about it.

He currently lives with his wife and her horses near the Rocky Mountains in Canada.

J. A. Downes

Predestination

The Bloodstone of Boiorix

Independently published.

20211208

ISBN 979-8-76736898-3

Visit www.jadownes.com to read more about the author, this book, and his other book projects.
Engage in the online discourse exploring the world depicted herein.

Cover art by JD Smith. See more at www.jdsmith-design.com
Cover art © JA Downes and JD Smith 2021

Prologue

Reformation England

Twelve years after King Henry VIII appointed himself head of the Church of England, he died, leaving his nine year old son, Edward, to inherit a religiously fractured, politically isolated and almost bankrupt kingdom.

Henry's will demanded that a Regency Council of sixteen leading men be convened to govern the realm during King Edward's minority. Within days a power struggle resulted in the King's uncle, Edward Seymour, being named Lord Protector of the Realm. Land and honours were claimed by Seymour and more were granted to those who supported him. Those who opposed him were at first excluded from the Council, then arrested. Foremost amongst them were Stephen Gardiner the Bishop of Winchester, and Thomas Howard the Duke of Norfolk. Both men were on the conservative side of the religious changes and vocal opponents of the continuing Reformation.

Seymour was perceived as supporting the common man against land enclosures and as being sympathetic to their general grievances, and so he enjoyed popular support. He rigorously implemented King Edward's Protestant agenda, but also prosecuted a ruinously expensive war against the Scots who were supported by France. Within three years the Council turned on Seymour and his disastrous management of the country, and John Dudley the Earl of Warwick emerged as the new leader of the Council.

As 1551 drew to a close, King Edward was fourteen years old, well educated, and fiercely Protestant, he had even written that the Pope was the anti-Christ. John Dudley was still Lord President of the Council, but ennobled as the Duke of Northumberland. Edward

Seymour was manoeuvring to regain control, and Gardiner and Howard were still in the Tower planning for the day they could turn back the tide of Protestantism and, more importantly, inflict revenge on their enemies on the Council. All the Catholic powers of Europe looked on the Reformation in England with horror and dabbled in its politics where they could, while the Pope schemed to reunite Christendom.

Dramatis Personæ

<u>Reformers</u>
- John Cheke, academic, tutor to King Edward VI
- Thomas Bowcer, manservant to John Cheke
- Dr John Dee, mathematician, astrologer, polymath
- William Cecil, Secretary of State
- William Herbert, nobleman, courtier, ex-soldier
- Sir John Dudley, Duke of Northumberland, President of the King's Council
- Sir Edward Seymour, Duke of Somerset, ex-Lord Protector
- Jack/Jacques Delauris, galley slave
- Jerôme Maurand, disillusioned French Catholic cleric
- Jakob Mierjewski, Hanseatic merchant
- Gerolamo Cardano, Italian doctor and polymath
- Kat Arden, assistant to Dr Dee
- Roger Cooke, apprentice to Dr Dee at Kingston
- Nikolaus, apprentice to Dr Dee at Mortlake
- Ed & Hal, twins in Dr Dee's household
- Tobias Inkbold, manufactory manager
- Allie Ward, daughter of innkeeper

<u>Catholics and Religious Conservatives</u>
- Reginald Pole, English Cardinal, papal legate
- Alberto, secretary to Cardinal Pole
- Pope Julius III, Pope
- Stephen Gardiner, Bishop of Winchester
- Sir Thomas Cheyne, Lord Warden of the Cinque Ports
- Gregory Ballard, yeoman warder
- John Hawkins, poisoner
- Sir Henry Bedingfield, Privy Councillor
- Charles of Guise, French Cardinal
- Simon Renard, diplomat and spy for Emperor Charles V
- Cristóbal, accomplice of Renard
- Tomás, accomplice of Renard

<u>Turks</u>
- Ariadenus Barbarrosa, Ottoman Admiral
- Suleiman, Sultan of the Ottomans

Part I

"Truth is within ourselves; it takes no rise
From outward things, whate'er you may believe
There is an inmost centre in us all
Where truth abides in fulness; and around
Wall upon wall, the gross flesh hems it in,
This perfect clear perception, which is truth.
A baffling and perverting carnal mesh
Binds it and makes all error; and to KNOW
Rather consists in opening out a way
Whence the imprisoned splendour may escape
Than in effecting entry for a light
Supposed to be without."

                      - Robert Browning. Paracelsus.

Chapter 1 - Underestimation

Wednesday the 2nd of October 1551
Epping Forest, England

Acorns

He paused at the edge of the forest and assessed the terrain with a critical eye.

Behind him all was quiet, just the scuffling sounds of his own troops disturbing the leaves and stepping on twigs. He confirmed that his flanks were secure, obviously. He scanned the ground ahead, where a single road snaked down the open hillside toward the valley bottom. There were no trees or hedges for concealment, just open grassland.

A crossroads was barely visible in the middle-distance, and well beyond that a smattering of thatched cottages nestled in the meander of a stream, one supporting a waterwheel that was lazily dipping its blades into the sparkling thread. Smoke rose languidly from the largest building, until, reaching the height of the surrounding hills, it was caught and shredded by the wind.

Idyllic.
Or was it?

He nervously tapped his baton against his thigh. Being commander was a lonely responsibility. The decision to advance could expose his whole army to a withering counterattack. He well remembered his tuition, especially that concerning Agincourt. A muddy field could slow down a superior force allowing it to be torn asunder by volleys of arrows.

Squinting into the pale October sunlight he saw a line of clouds that were rolling over themselves as they approached him like waves breaking on the seashore. He gave them a respectful, but wary, nod of recognition, because he had met their kind before. So he waited. This would be no Agincourt.

As he watched, the distant village blurred then disappeared behind a curtain of rain until he could no longer discern the houses at all, they were just a darker smudge on a darkling horizon.

Here it comes, he thought, as a gentle hissing intruded at the extent of his hearing. Using his baton he signalled that his troops should immediately take cover, although they ignored him as usual. He eyed a particularly large oak tree looming beside the dirt track. *That will do for me*, he thought.

The sound grew to an unmistakable drumming as the wall of rain advanced across the meadows. When it was an insistent roar he knew he had to move or be consumed.

He scrambled and gratefully ducked under the outer branches of the oak and made it to the safety of the old tree's protective bole before the torrent of rain hit. He realised he had dropped his baton somewhere out there.

"We will wait out the weather before our final advance on the enemy. Understood?" His army looked at him warily but made no reply.

He settled back against the trunk and watched as the first fat raindrops ploughed into the forest track where he had been observing. Within minutes the deluge on the leaf canopy was so loud that a strange serenity overcame him. The barrage from the rain was all-consuming and soon he could hear nothing else. Beneath the overhanging branches the view was opaque with bouncing raindrops. He settled down in some comfort, soon oblivious to the wider world with all its cares and sorrows. The sight and sound of the downpour were hypnotic, his head nodded and he dozed off. As morpheus overtook him a final thought crept through his mind, *An experienced commander lets his army eat and sleep whenever he can. You never know what will happen in the future…*

Time passed.

When he awoke a fine mist was rising from the soggy ground as the weak evening sunshine gave the last of its warmth.

He stood groggily, and yawned. Returning to the path he breathed deeply of the earthy forest smell after a storm.

His empty stomach grumbled loudly. His companions looked at him. Well they had slept, so why not eat? "Troops - Permission to forage!" The pair of piglets eagerly dived into the downed foliage and oinked with pleasure at the acorns they discovered. As for himself, he knew there would be no food until his father returned from the muster of the local militia, where we was leading a platoon of real soldiers. He would share exciting tales of soldiering and chivalry. But first his mother would have other chores for him; fetching water from the well, collecting logs for the fire, feeding the animals. And the same chores tomorrow. And the day after that.

He kicked at a mound of leaves in frustration, "It is no use. Nothing exciting ever happens here!"

He scoured the path looking for the whittled stick that served as his baton.

What was that noise? He swivelled in alarm and peered into the gloomy woodland, the shadows refusing to yield any secrets.

There it is again. Strange. Is it the rumble of distant thunder?

It had gone before he could place it. He hushed his pigs and stood still as a sentinel, straining his ears. *No, it is gone.*

Dejectedly he turned back to the path and kicked the leaves to and fro still hoping to find his baton.

Again. That was a definite rumble, and louder now!

He turned quickly, scanning the wall of trees, his muscles tense.

He recognised the thunder at last - it was horses' hooves!

The noise returned yet again, this time quickly rising to a crescendo as a trio of horsemen crested the ridge and galloped out of the woods. His pigs scattered, surprisingly nimbly, as the riders passed perilously close to them.

The central rider was clearly important, with a thick beard, fine clothes and a flowing cape. *A prince or a duke?*

The two beside him were hard faced men with swords at their hips. *Bodyguards!*

All three horses were steaming from their flanks and sported foamy spittle around their muzzles.

Despite their speed, time seemed to slow as the leader glanced directly at the boy, and threw an ironic salute by touching two fingers to his cap. And winked. Then he was gone.

He watched the riders as they plummeted down the winding road until they disappeared from view, hidden by a fold in the land.

He realised he had been holding his breath, and managed to breathe again only through an exercise of will.

Who were those men?

Their clothes were so grand and fur trimmed capes as well.

All carried swords like father when he goes to the militia. I wish I had a sword!

The horses were so fine and so fast!

Wait until I tell Thomas, he will be so jealous!

With feverish excitement he rounded up his piglets ready to make the final push toward home.

Then he noticed it. Hanging from a branch was a fine cap.

Knowing that the forest track was not wide, he supposed that one of the riders had ducked beneath the branch to avoid being unhorsed.

But not low enough.

He retrieved the hat and turned it around and around in his hands. His face broke into a brilliant smile. He had never held anything so fine, with two long pheasant feathers and a small badge pinned to the front. He looked closely at the badge and saw that it was a tiny shield with three red crescents on it. He balanced the hat on his head and, wiping splashes of muddy red clay from his face, he set off for home, whistling a jaunty tune he had learned when working at the village inn.

Thirty minutes later his smile was gone. The rain had returned and with no cover available to him this time, he got soaked to the skin.

He paused at the crossroads outside his village and tried to straighten the hat that hung limply on his head.

Hearing splashes he turned and looked back along the road he had just travelled and watched as two swarthy men, dressed in fine brocaded black riding clothes, galloped up. They stopped beside him, one on each side.

In one fluid motion the taller one dismounted and snatched the hat away. He glanced at it for a moment then threw it up to his companion, who seemed to check the badge then nodded, finally throwing the hat to the ground. Pulling a small coin from his purse, he leaned close and hissed out a question, "Leetle boy, tell me which way the horsemen went, the ones from whom you got that cap, and this coin is yours."

He eyed the coin that was being held tantalisingly close to his face. It was a shilling. Enough to buy a grown sheep from the market.

He would sell his grandmother for a shilling. Well maybe not. Unless it was one of those days when she droned on and on about how everything had been better when young King Hal was a lad….the sun shone more, the harvests were better, they always had food in their bellies…

Fingers snapped in front of his face, bringing him back to the present moment. His eyes refocussed, but this time on the small jewelled crucifix dangling at the man's throat. He paused for a moment, then blurted out, "To S'norbals my Lord."

The man looked confused, clearly unable to understand the accent.

So he turned and pointed west, toward the setting sun, "That way!"

The Spaniard looked where he was pointing, then checked the various town names on the fingerpost. He smiled, showing pointy teeth, and tossed the coin into the mud, remounted, and the pair rode off at a canter in the direction of "St Albans".

The boy scrambled in the mud for the coin and after a few moments his nimble fingers felt its cool sharp edge, and he held it aloft smiling, his good fortune had returned. A shilling.

He went over to the hat and pulled it from where it was stuck in the mud. In their excitement to continue the chase, one of the horses had reared in a powerful levade, sadly for the hat caught beneath the hind hooves. As a result it was a broken mess, the feathers snapped and the material torn. Sad at the loss of his prize, he took the badge which was undamaged and pushed it into his pouch, then laid the hat itself beside the fingerpost, almost reverently.

He looked down the road after the two foreigners, and made the same hand gesture that he had seen his father make to the backs of the local tax collectors. Then he turned north, towards the Cambridge Road, where the first three riders had actually gone. He stood up straight, raised two fingers to where his cap had been and imitated the salute of the bearded rider, and then, very carefully, he winked.

Chapter 2 - Accommodation

Friday the 4th of October 1551
On the Cambridge Road

Cambridge lights

Slowing his tired horse to a walk and shivering in the icy wind that was blowing in from the fens, John Cheke pulled his fur-trimmed cloak closer around him.

He regretted his decision to wear such a thin doublet for this trip. It was a fine garment of embroidered and coloured silk that he had recently purchased at great cost from a Hanse merchant in London, and there was no doubt that it looked well on him. But it wasn't keeping him warm.

He had set out from Richmond three days ago with two trusted retainers for protection.

He was convinced they had been followed by two swarthy riders, but seemingly their fast riding and skilful routing had shaken their pursuers on the second day, because they had seen no-one trailing them since then.

For the first few days the weather had been pleasant enough, cool with intermittent rain. However this fourth day had started cold and got steadily worse, with near constant drizzle turning the dirt roads into muddy streams. The weather bothered Cheke, but seemingly not his horse, who walked on through the gathering gloom of the evening, oblivious to the rain that was now turning to snow.

"Maybe I should have taken the new fangled coach from London", he mused, since they were following the coach road anyway, both for speed and relative safety. He could certainly have commanded a seat inside, but he knew the journey would have been intolerably bumpy especially while the roads were dry, and he would have been unable to escape the incessant chatter and inquisitiveness of fellow passengers. The constant noise would probably have caused an ague in his head. No, he was definitely better off on his own horse, with good company and an occasional swig of Dutch Cognac for warmth.

He briefly stood in the stirrups and stretched his aching body, feeling his tired muscles pull and his knees and hips crack. He tried flexing his arms, taking care not to jiggle the horse's bit, and found his fingers so stiff from the cold that he had to work them for several minutes before any feeling returned at all. Not surprising, he thought, given that they had been riding since five o'clock this morning according to the bells of St Michael's church.

He had spent the previous night at *The Crown Inn*, in Hockrell, where the ale, accommodation, and even companionship if you wanted it, were all of good repute. His men had lodged across the street at the Black Lion, an altogether cheaper and less salubrious establishment, although from the spring in Martin's step Cheke was pretty sure that he at least had found the evening entertainment to his liking. After a hasty breakfast he had paid the bill in the assumed name of Underhill, and with worried glances at the heavy grey cloud they had mounted up and continued north.

Cheke experimented by closing his eyes, and believed he could still taste the sage butter that had dripped off his breakfast of fine manchet bread. Unfortunately the pleasure he took from the memory was short lived as he heard Martin's stomach growl loudly, presumably complaining that in their haste to reach Cambridge before nightfall they had not stopped for dinner. Instead they had merely watered their horses, first at Saffron Walden, near the late Lord Chancellor's house, and then at Whittlesford. "Not long now lads," Cheke said, trying for an encouraging tone, although the sardonic look he received from Richard suggested he had missed his mark.

As his horse plodded on he was rocked into a gentle dreamlike state, and his mind drifted to thoughts of his father, who had lived all his life in the university town. Peter Cheke had held the post of Bedell in Divinity which was an administrative position at the University, and so he was a relatively important man in the town. He had required that his son John achieve even greater prominence, and had not been pleased when John followed his love of languages, thinking it a poor way for his son to achieve any kind of status. He had to grudgingly admit he was wrong a few years later when John was quickly elected a Fellow of St John's College and started to attract the praise of his colleagues. Now at 37 John had far surpassed that early honour,

Yes, father, you would have been proud, he thought, *had you yet lived.*

Sadly Peter had been dead some twenty years now, buried in the churchyard at St Botolph's, only a few yards from the rambling house that his University position had earned him.

His horse tripped on the uneven ground, shaking Cheke out of his reverie, and up ahead he saw the welcoming Cambridge lights glowing faintly through the sleet. "About time", Cheke muttered to himself through clenched teeth, and nudged his horse to increase the energy of the walk a little.

Their horses' hooves were muffled in an inch of snow as Cheke and his companions rode up Trumpington Street, past Peterhouse College on their left and Pembroke College on their right. Silhouettes of scholars could be seen in flickering candlelight as they passed their windows. Pausing briefly outside St Botolph's church, Cheke inclined his head and said a short prayer for his father's soul, then turned to his right into the narrow Botolph Lane, and finally under an arch and into the courtyard of his father's house.

"Domus meus" he said to his companions as he swept his arm toward the main structure, and in response to their blank looks he added "My house," and rode ahead towards the outbuildings.

It is pretentious of me to speak Latin, and not in keeping with our divergence away from the papist church. I should use my new Greek instead, he thought, acknowledging his current project, the introduction of a new Greek pronunciation, that he was working on with his friend and colleague Thomas Smith.

But Martin and Richard wouldn't understand Greek either.

He chided himself some more, *they have been good company and helped me feel safer on the journey. A pity Richard has been so grumpy since losing his favourite hat in the forest yesterday though.*

They had no sooner halted in the courtyard than his manservant, Thomas, came out of the house, flinging a cloak around his shoulders as he came. He bowed to Cheke, then reached out a beefy hand for the reins and steadied the horse. Cheke dismounted stiffly, almost falling as his frozen feet hit the slippery, snow covered cobbles.

The bells at St Botolph's suddenly rang out for Evensong, making Cheke jump involuntarily. While Thomas handed the horse off to a stable lad with instructions for its care, Cheke gave a murmur of thanks, introduced his companions, and, remembering to take the small satchel that he had carried from London, he hurried into the house through the same door that Thomas had used. The door gave directly onto the kitchen, not the normal entrance for a Gentleman, "To hell with propriety," he muttered, "the kitchen is ever the warmest room in the house".

Cheke strode into the kitchen shaking snow from his cape and startling the cook, Anne, who was Thomas' wife.

He reddened beneath his beard, embarrassed. Anne was clearly surprised to see the master of the house appear in the kitchen. She curtsied to him and muttered greetings, then bustled about preparing some warm Malmsey wine. He gratefully accepted a goblet, cupping it with both hands, then drinking deeply while warming his backside near the ovens. Between gulps, he asked after the health of Anne's youngest child, Luke. The boy had been taken with a fever in the summer and everyone had worried it was the sweating sickness, but the days had passed and the boy slowly recovered. Anne thanked Cheke for his courtesy and explained that the four year old was well again, and already causing trouble by getting under the staff's feet.

Passing his cloak, now wet from the melted snow, and the empty goblet to the kitchen girl, he asked Anne to send a late supper of whatever hot food she had available to his study, and the same to Martin and Richard out in the mews. With a nod he left the kitchen and plunged deeper into the house, through the main hall with its large portrait of the dour Peter Cheke thankfully barely visible in the gloom. *I should commission a likeness of myself to replace father's grim visage*, he thought, *or is that narcissistic?*

When he entered his study he found Thomas' eldest son, also called Thomas, already lighting a small fire in the grate. Newly added logs were popping and spitting as the heat drove moisture off the wood and into oblivion. Cheke ruffled the boy's hair and sent him on his way back to his mother in the kitchen.

Anne sent in some warmed wholemeal bread, together with a rich pottage that was pleasantly spiced and generously filled with tender lamb's meat. *How she manages to produce such good food at a moment's notice is a wonder to me.*

As he spooned the last of the pottage past his beard, and the fire crackled in the hearth, John found himself truly relaxing for the first time in four days. His eyes roamed the room and settled on his fine collection of two dozen books on the shelves opposite his desk. The most expensive volumes were bound in vellum, and two had embroidered velvet. His favourite four caught his eye; Aristotle, Plato, Proclus, Demosthenes. If only he could afford more! Despite the recent introduction of the printing press, good books were extremely costly.

He sighed as he remembered the times under the late King Henry, when Greek had flourished at the University. Shaking his head in pity he privately lamented how all studies were being disrupted by the high turnover of scholars now that Catholics were being suppressed in greater number. As Commissioner for Eton school, and for both Oxford and Cambridge Universities, his inspections had revealed the reduction in quality of studies, but it was a difficult topic to bring up with the King because it was his own policy toward Catholics that was the cause.

A discrete knock at the study door brought Cheke back to the present and Thomas entered with a courteous bow. "Sir. How may I serve you this evening?"

Lifting the leather satchel that he had brought from Richmond, Cheke gestured to the desk and Thomas tidied the debris of Cheke's supper to one side.

"Thomas, we need to plan for tomorrow. I have to recruit some trustworthy new tutors for his Grace, King Edward, and then…"

Thomas interrupted in concern, "You are being replaced as tutor?"

"Not at all, it is merely time to find supplementary tutors capable in mathematics, astrology and astronomy, who can enhance the King's education in areas that I cannot."

He paused and added, "But they will have to be willing to work at a cheap rate, as the court does not have the funds to be overly generous."

Thomas looked thoughtful for a moment, and then raised his calloused forefinger in the air with a conspiratorial look.

"If I may suggest, perhaps…", a little cough, "I know you thought him vainglorious when last you saw him, but I hear young Master Dee has just returned from his travels to Louvain and Paris, with many wondrous devices in his baggage, but also with an empty purse…"

"The magician John Dee!" Cheke exclaimed, then, stroking his beard, he said, "He had just pulled off that stunt with the flying beetle in his production of Aristophane's *Peace*, and was all puffed up with himself because everyone thought it fantastical." Nodding in acknowledgment he continued "That is indeed a cunning idea and no mistake. Dee is still young and so may not overly intimidate the King, and yet is already acknowledged as greatly skilled in all these arts. And one scholar is cheaper than three, is that not so? Your suggestion is as excellent and as welcome as your wife's cooking, Thomas!"

Thomas bowed at the compliment. "And the second task we must complete tomorrow?" nodding pointedly at the satchel.

Cheke tipped several thick letters from the bag onto the desk, and said, "This is altogether more serious, and what causes me to come with bodyguards. It concerns the King's business. These are privy correspondence from my Lord Archbishop Cranmer to Lutherans and Evangelicals on the continent. I am to find a suitable courier who can deliver them without raising suspicion. If these letters were to fall into the wrong hands a great deal of ill-will could befall the new reign."

"That sounds rather dangerous, why has the Archbishop troubled you with the burden?"

"He knew I was returning to Cambridge, and thought I would be able to find travellers who could secretly take the letters onwards. However he also thought I would not be suspected and followed by Spanish agents, and in that guess I'm pretty sure he was wrong, unless the local brigands have taken to wearing the latest continental fashions," glancing around as though remembering his peril he shivered despite the fire's warmth.

There was no doubt about his master's anxiety, so Thomas volunteered "I will walk through the ground floor of the house every hour tonight, and I'll let the dogs roam the yard, they will alert us to any trespassers. I will go and see to it now." And with that Thomas bowed again and retreated from the room.

Sipping some more of the wine, Cheke smiled grimly at the thought of Thomas patrolling the house with his cudgel. Totally loyal to Cheke, Thomas' experience in the army meant he wasn't afraid of anything less than a galloping, fully armoured French knight, and not even that if he had his war bow to hand. Yes, Cheke nodded to himself, he would sleep safely in his own bed tonight.

Chapter 3 - Compensation

Saturday the 5th of October 1551
Cambridge

The magician's candidature

Early the next morning Cheke headed up Trumpington Street in weak sunshine toward Trinity College. Thomas had insisted on accompanying him, after they discussed it, even though neither believed any harm would come to Cheke during daylight hours in the quiet university town.

Thomas carried the leather satchel under one arm, his long strides giving a slow, rolling pace to the large man. Towering over most people he was fully six feet tall and had a wide, powerful chest, with thick arms of corded muscle. Despite his forbidding presence Cheke could see that Thomas warily watched everyone that they passed, taking to heart the recent rumours that he had shared of increased knife violence in the town.

An archer in Henry's army at the siege of Boulogne back in '44, Thomas had been one of the 4,000 English soldiers left defending the town when Henry had returned to England and the Lords Norfolk and Suffolk had withdrawn to Calais. He had stayed in Boulogne until the end of the war when the Treaty of Ardres-Guînes was signed in June 1546. During that time his wife Anne, and infant son, Thomas, had been housed by Cheke in safety and comfort in Cambridge. Thomas was still profoundly grateful to Cheke for the protection given to his family while he had been at war, and now was a loyal and protective manservant in return. Plus, as he had admitted to Cheke, it was a far preferable position than begging in the streets of London, which is what many of his old companions were reduced to.

They passed St Catherine's and Corpus Christi colleges. Further up the street he saw a dozen scholars debating animatedly on the green in front of King's college, and worrying that it could be cover for an ambush of sorts he gestured to Thomas that they should cross the road, where they walked in the shadows of the rooming houses on the East side of the street.

Stepping on an unseen patch of ice Cheke's foot slipped from under him and he cried out "God's teeth! Aargh, now I have twinged my back."

He would have fallen if he had not been steadied by the attentive Thomas.

Another few hundred yards and they re-crossed the street and Cheke paused as they passed through the imposing gatehouse of Trinity College. He gestured to the buildings to cover the fact that he was massaging his aching back, and said, "You know when King Henry founded this college just five years ago he didn't want to spend from the Royal Treasury, so he merged two existing Catholic colleges, *Michaelhouse* and *King's Hall*, and several hostels". He reached out to the brickwork, "These buildings are already over two hundred years old. What will be left of us in two hundred years, eh Thomas?"

Taking the question literally Thomas replied, "Your Greek will survive sir, never fear. And the new religion will endure surely?"

"Vanity of vanities, all is vanity", and in response to Thomas' enquiring look he added "Ecclesiastes, Thomas, Ecclesiastes," and patted the wall sadly before shaking his head and continuing into the quiet courtyard.

Here Cheke looked around the variety of multi-storey buildings in confusion, and asked, "How on earth are we going to find Dee and conduct the magician's candidature?"

"Yon scholars might know," said Thomas, pointing to a half dozen young lads sitting idly on the grass near an open doorway.

As they started across the yard there was a blinding flash of light then an outpouring of black smoke from one of the third floor windows, and a roll of thunder that echoed around the buildings.

Crouching defensively Cheke looked at Thomas in horror before he heard derisive laughter from the group by the door. While Cheke's shock turned to embarrassment, Thomas was already striding over to the group in anger. They jumped to their feet with raised hands and stumbled over each other to escape the wrath of the big man, "We meant nothing by it master, but surely you know that Doctor Dee is always causing a disturbance by practising his dark arts?"

They continued by confirming that Dee was in residence, and indeed should be tutoring them in astronomy at this time, but he had made them wait while he finished his experiments.

Leaving Thomas to guard the door and ensure privacy, Cheke took his bag and went up three flights of stone steps, emerging on the top floor landing where there were just two doors. Pausing only for a moment he entered the room on his left, presumably the room the explosion had emanated from, and stopped in mid stride. The room was full of smoke that immediately stung his eyes and caused him to bend over coughing. He backed out and waited a couple of minutes until the smoke seemed to be thinning, and entered again, this time with his handkerchief over his mouth.

The room was total anarchy. Books and parchments were piled on every horizontal surface, and several large crates occupied one corner of the room. One of the crates was open, and a large bronze coloured lattice sphere was visible inside.

He heard a rattling intake of breath from the far side of the room, and saw a figure in a Fellow's gown half hanging out of a window, his chest heaving as he sucked at the outside air. The figure rose, steadied itself and before it had turned he heard a familiar lilting voice say "Pray, pass me that damp cloth from the table, John, for I fear my face may be as black as my name," followed by a chuckle as the magician enjoyed his own joke.

The man turned from the window toward the immobile Cheke, revealing a pale face smudged by the smoke, a fashionable goatee beard below a long straight nose and slightly hooded black eyes. As Dee walked closer his face split into a wide mischievous smile and flakes of soot fell from the creases in his cheeks. He reached past the still stunned Cheke and took a cloth from the table and proceeded to wipe most of the soot from his face.

"What in God's name is happening here?" spluttered Cheke.

Dee tossed down the cloth and clapped Cheke on the shoulder, Cheke stiffening at the over familiarity.

Dee walked around the room, weaving between the benches, boxes, and piles of books, "Early this morning I was using a Ptolemaic method to extract the Red Dragon, a chaotic energy of the First Matter, and an early step in the creation of the Philosopher's Stone." He paused and cast an amused glance back at Cheke and then continued more reflectively, "It was progressing well, but slowly, and my students would soon be arriving for their lessons, so to speed up the process I employed an optical accelerator of mine own devising. However it was more powerful than I expected. You see the results," he swept his arm around, gesturing to the room. The clearing smoke revealed overturned equipment, a charred tabletop, and parchments that were scattered around the room like leaves in an autumn wind.

Cheke knew that alchemists often coded their experimental descriptions in colourful language to hide the details from the uninitiated, and as a scholar of Greek not alchemy he was obviously uninitiated, so he deduced that Dee was having fun with him, *"Red dragon" indeed!*

Dee started gathering the parchments into a pile and weighted them down using a strange brass disc that was larger than a dinner platter. Meanwhile Cheke gawped at the numerous piles of books. He checked the nearest pile, the authors included Nicholas Flamel, Giordano Bruno and others. One especially heavy text caught his eye and he hefted it to read the author and title from the page opposite the frontispiece, "Summa Theologica" by St Thomas Aquinas. Cheke had heard of Aquinas of course, who hadn't? But he wasn't quite sure what he espoused. *Something to do with investigation into all of creation allowed one to better understand the mind and nature of the Creator,* he thought. *Heady stuff.* He replaced the book.

"Isn't it dangerous?" he asked Dee.

"No, not really. I sheltered behind that pile of boxes..."

"I mean politically," interrupted Cheke sharply, "You are practising alchemy in direct contravention of the guidance from the Master of the College. And you don't even seem very good at it."

A sing-song reply came from Dee, his voice gaining some Welsh-ness from his sarcasm,"Well, why don't yew just shout it all about so everyone can hear yew?"

"I should think they already heard your own explosive announcement. I certainly did, and from across the courtyard at that!"

"Fair point," chuckled Dee immediately genial again, as he reached over and took the tome from where Cheke had placed it, "Aquinas here, says we all have the capacity for rational thinking John, and that through grace we can grasp the truth. However the sainted Thomas doesn't really indulge in inquiry so much as special pleading, so let's leave this very Catholic work here alongside his inspiration, Aristotle, where they can think together without being at all practical. We can retire to my privy chamber while the foul air in this room blows clear. I might find some wine to cleanse the taste of smoke away, and perhaps a sugared almond to sweeten your disposition. Meanwhile you can tell me all about your urgent mission for the King. "

Cheke swallowed, ignoring the dig at his humour, "What are you talking about, 'my urgent mission for the King'?"

Dee exited the room and led the way into the smaller and tidier room opposite. He replied nonchalantly over his shoulder "You arrived late last night after a journey of several days, and you carry a satchel embossed with the seal of the Archbishop of Canterbury - How is Lord Cranmer by the way? - then you sneak over here afraid of the shadows as though the Pope's withered hand was groping to squeeze the new religion from your very soul."

He poured two large glasses of a ruby coloured wine from a carafe, and immediately half emptied his own as he drank deeply.

Cheke collapsed shakily into the chair that Dee waved him to. "How do you know all this - are you spying on me?"

"Come now John, don't ask questions that I would be forced to avoid answering. Tell me what's on your mind and how I can help."

Sipping the wine and clearing his throat, Cheke delayed replying for a few moments as his mind whirled, then with a resigned sigh and a shake of his head he launched into the same tale he had recounted to Thomas the previous evening.

"And so, I need to recruit three eminent scholars to act as tutor to the King, in areas where my own skills are weak, namely astronomy, astrology and mathematics," he glanced innocently towards Dee, "I thought you might know some candidates that might be suitable?"

"Do I know some candidates? I am the only candidate you need! But of course you know this. What does the position pay? For I am sorely over-spent after my trip to Louvain and the additions to my book collection," gesturing to another pile that must have had at least 8 thick books in it.

"It will pay £12 a year, to the qualifying candidate. But you have to prove your skill to the satisfaction of all three members of the appointment council, of which I am but one."

"Aha, a skill test, how intriguing. What is this test?"

"Each of us has asked a personal question, of great importance to us," he handed over three letters of stiff parchment, each fixed with a different wax seal. "Send your sealed responses before the end of this week to my manservant Thomas at my house in St Botolph's Lane. He will forward them to me."

Dee shuffled the letters and tossing one onto the table he held the other two up to the window so they caught a shaft of light.

"And who are the other two members of this appointment council, pray tell?"

"William Herbert and William Cecil"

"Mad Dog Herbert?"

Almost choking on his wine, Cheke corrected him, "William Herbert, Master of the Horse, Lord President of Wales and the Marches, Privy Councillor and one of the guardians of the young King. Yes."

"And William Cecil, who like us gained his Bachelor's at St John's, but has already risen to power as Secretary of State?"

"*Joint* Secretary of State, yes. The Master Secretary, who is also Chancellor of the Order of the Garter, and a good friend of mine."

Dee whistled, "Exalted company you keep these days John. I am indebted that you came to me first. I will attend to your little tests this very day, but have no fear I am sure I will excel.

"So now, tell me of your main mission and your problem with the Pope?"

Cheke glanced out of the door toward the stairwell, and whispered urgently, "Pray lower your voice, these are dangerous times. I have some correspondence from Cranmer that must be quickly delivered to learned men of the new religion on the continent, preferably without attracting the attentions of Spain or the Pope's intelligencers. I would send one of my own men but I fear I am being watched, and that descriptions of all my men are already on their way to Mary of Hungary in the Low Countries, and no doubt from there to her brother Charles V of Spain."

"Aha, it is as I thought", Dee sprang up and threw open the window overlooking the courtyard and leaning far out he yelled to the group below "John Cheyne, get up here right now, I need you to go to Louvain. Again."

"Sir Thomas Cheyne's son? Can we trust him? His father is as fickle as any that can be found at court these days."

"Can we really trust anyone John? But seriously young Cheyne is a straight arrow, I send him on errands to the continent quite often and thanks to his father's name no-one judges him ill." Winking, "Of course we won't tell him of the actual mission, that is an extra insurance against discovery. And finally, to guarantee his silence, I also have some evidence against him and the Master's daughter that he won't risk the release of.

"Here, let us place Cranmer's letters inside a letter to my good friend

Gerard Mercator, who is at Louvain University. I will ask for more astronomical instruments to be sent to me, that Cranmer will pay for," he cast a crafty smile towards Cheke.

"Mercator is a good Reformer. He will ensure the letters are forwarded safely to the intended recipients. Who are the recipients by the way?"

"Heinrich Bullinger in Zurich, Jean Calvin in Geneva, and Philip Melanchthon in Wittenberg."

Dee let out a low whistle, "Melanchthon? Why does Cranmer write to him? To ask for assistance in the creation of a new doctrine, or creation of an improved educational system? But wait, a revision of canon law is more urgent. Perhaps Cranmer is sounding out that most august Lutheran for his views? Yes, quite likely. Ah, that is bold. Our couriers will need to take care, the wearisome Schmalkaldic War takes no prisoners. These gentlemen will all be watched for certain. I begin to see why you are nervous my friend. Maybe I should be too! However, I assume Cranmer will be suitably grateful…"

"Indeed, indeed."

"Then let us cast our ship onto the tide," and with that Dee quickly wrote an explanatory letter, and enclosing Cranmer's letters inside, he sealed the bundle and tied it with red twine for good measure.

Humming some tuneless Welsh-sounding dirge to himself, Dee rose and fetched an inch thick manuscript from across the room and set it down on the table, saying "And now we need something to explain your visit here…."

He re-dipped his quill and added a dedication to William Cecil in a beautiful flowing script on the inside of the cover page, just as John Cheyne arrived at the doorway. Dee stood and handed the manuscript to Cheke, and very deferentially said "Sire. Please take this treatise and present it to Master Secretary and beg his patronage for his poor servant Johannes Dee", he bowed low and while his face was hidden from Cheyne he winked conspiratorially at Cheke.

Cheke rolled his eyes up in despair, *the man is incorrigible!*

As Cheke turned to leave he heard Dee instructing Cheyne on his mission to Louvain. As he started down the steps he acknowledged to himself, *Dee seems as skilled at subterfuge as he is in the magical arts. Maybe we will all survive this madness yet.*

Chapter 4 - Prognostication

Thursday the 10th of October 1551
Cecil House, London

Impressing an earl

John Cheke watched as William Cecil jogged off the tennis court wiping sweat from his red face with a large white cloth, smiling at the small group of friends and family in the gallery. "What a day!" he called. "Knighted by the King, and beating William Herbert at tennis, it could not get any better."

His wife, Mildred, swept towards him with a rustle of skirts and hugged him and he laughed out loud and exclaimed to all, "My best day just got even better, and methinks tonight will be better still." His daughters, Francisca and Anne blushed deeply and giggled into their sleeves.

Cheke shook his head and smiled, he didn't understand the passions that the game of tennis aroused, but he was happy to be in the company of his friends on this admittedly good day.

He could easily hear William Herbert, still at the far end of the court, ranting at the injustice of the dead cat bounce that had made the ball unreturnable, and how that surely couldn't be allowed to stand, especially after that final sneaky and rather intolerable bobble service from Cecil. Herbert was striking the hard ball again and again against the tambour that jutted out into the court, and the sound boomed and echoed through the court and the galleried surrounds, adding even more melodrama to his outraged ranting.

Cheke knew that Herbert was only feigning his anger, probably for the benefit of the two girls who he called nieces and who worshipped him, even though his volcanic temper had sometimes been heard roaring through the house for real when the men talked business. Or when they shouted business, thought Cheke wryly, as he smilingly recalled the all too frequent outbursts by the old warrior.

Ironically Herbert had made his name fighting for the French King, Francis, where his energetic violence and fierce temper had only been equalled by his courage and battlefield skills. Francis had then commended him to Henry VIII, who recognised his talents and promoted him in England. Despite being fifty years old now he was fitter than most younger men and revelled in beating opponents everywhere from the tilt yard to the chess board.

Herbert came into the gallery a few moments later still pretending to be angry, and standing hands on hips with legs apart he boomed, "Who agrees that I was robbed by a very rascal of a sneaky player." This provided more excuses for giggles from the two girls as they ran to him shouting "Me, me" and hugged him, one on each side, much to the amusement of all. After some more jokingly combative verbal exchanges the two combatants left arm-in-arm to wash and prepare for dinner.

Cheke pushed back his chair with a contented sigh after the large meal. The rest of the Cecil family had left after much merriment and laughter, and now a servant poured more of the fine Bordeaux wine for the three men, then retired discretely leaving them to talk.

William Herbert's short black beard bristled as he turned to Cheke and Cecil, "That so-called *magician* John Dee was completely wrong. His astrological reading foretold that I would be made an Earl this week, and yet here I am, merely *Baron* Herbert of Cardiff."

William Cecil patted the air to placate the old warrior and replied, "Calm yourself friend, he was pretty close. You were elevated to a Baronage which is a lofty post and shows that the King's favour continues, and that chief minister Dudley favours you too. And it is well deserved for you are steadfast in your service."

Herbert played with his goblet and then replied, "I suppose so yes. And you and Cheke were both knighted exactly as Dee foretold."

Cheke smoothed his beard and mused out loud, "How did he know that this would happen today do you think, exactly on the 10th of October 1551? After all, Dee has no special friends at court who could have slipped him some information. There must be some trick - we will have to discover it."

The men toasted their new found success and the talk turned to the King's business until the wine ran out, then Cecil stood up, slightly unsteadily, and proclaimed that his young wife Mildred was desirous of his company for the remainder of the night, and smiling through his beard he bowed and left for his chambers. Herbert watched him go, then turning to Cheke he said, "If my wife was a clever 25 year old I'd leave my guests and slip off to my bedroom as well, wouldn't you John?"

"Tsk, come now William, your wife the Lady Anne, is not so very old. And my Mary is only 26 and yes I would readily run to her. Unfortunately she's back in Cambridge with my two little boys", he sighed, "I will write to her tomorrow and give her our news, although she had complete faith in John Dee's astrological forecast so it will be no surprise to her. Apparently she buys some pamphlet of his every week, in which he provides general astrological forecasts, and she claims he is always correct in every respect."

The next morning a royal messenger summoned Baron Herbert back to the King at Hampton Court Palace. This was somewhat surprising and a little unnerving if truth be told, so Cheke and Cecil agreed to accompany him for moral support. And anyway they were curious.

The three men donned their best clothes again and added their warmest capes as a light snow was in the air, then walked with the King's messenger ten minutes to the Thames Stairs and boarded the King's barge. As soon as they sat under the brightly striped awning the rowers put their backs into their oars and the craft pulled away from the bank into midstream, scattering wherry men from their path, who all doffed their caps at the sight of the barge, though no doubt they muttered in annoyance as the waves created by the barge threw their own much smaller row boats about, causing upset for their passengers.

Nearly two hours later Cheke, Cecil and a nervous Baron Herbert climbed the stairs from the river, up to the landing stage at Hampton Court pier, where, flanked by guards with pikes, Herbert was marched quickly through the huge gatehouse and off to the Presence Chamber to see the King. Cheke and Cecil mixed with the other courtiers in the West Courtyard, and spent some time admiring the great astronomical clock on the tower of Anne Boleyn's gatehouse that led to the inner, so called, Clock Court.

It was fully two hours later when Herbert finally emerged from the direction of Clock Court, and almost jogged down the path to them. He was unusually giddy with excitement. He hustled them out of the palace and back to the barge and excitedly told them that Edward had just elevated him again. This time to Earl of Pembroke.

"The last person to hold Pembroke was Queen Anne Boleyn. She was made Marquess of Pembroke before her marriage to King Henry. And we all know what happened to her!" said Cecil, drawing a thumb across his neck.

Herbert took this in good spirit, saying "You know my father was the bastard son of the former Earl of Pembroke and his mistress, Maud. So now this title is back in my family and I have every hope of keeping it for a long, long time. And my head!" With pride and some small amount of wonder in his voice Herbert said "A Baron yesterday and an Earl today, now we shall see who has influence in this land".

Stroking his beard, Cheke wondered out loud, "Now you have me thinking of Dee again. He got it right after all, you have been made an Earl this week. How did he manage to foresee this, I wonder? T'is plain it was not even decided until last night, else the King would have done it yesterday."

The two Williams quieted their banter and looked seriously at Cheke while they digested this thought.

"Just a lucky guess perhaps," although from his tone it was clear that Cecil knew it could not be so.

With a tremor detectable in his voice Herbert asked "What do we know of this mage anyway?"

Glancing over, Cheke saw that Herbert's face had turned deathly white under his beard.

Perhaps realising he didn't sound like a fearless warrior Herbert quickly added "You know, we are considering him as a tutor to the King and just because he is impressing an Earl does not mean we can take it for granted that he is not a danger to the realm."

Cheke just continued to look at his friend, who continued in an even more agitated voice, "He cannot do *conjuring* can he? *Necromancy*?"

Cheke rolled his eyes at this last comment, "There is no such thing William. And yet…"

He recounted the story of meeting Dee in Cambridge just a week before, and then told them what he could remember of Dee's time at Cambridge. "Dee came to St John's College back in November of '42, a skinny youth, with but small grace and little means. I remember because it was the year my friend Sir Thomas Smith and I introduced our reform of the pronunciation of Greek - you'll remember Sir Thomas had just returned from gaining a degree in law at the University of Padua. Well anyway, our new pronunciation stirred up such contention in the college that the chancellor, Bishop Gardiner, issued a decree against it." Cheke snarled, unable to prevent the anger caused by the memory, "God curse his name. I'll not forget that insult very quickly my friends."

He removed his cap, rubbing his face briskly to help overcome his sudden emotion. "Anyway, Dee was about 15 years old. His father, who is named Rowland I think, is a Mercer and was a gentleman courtier to Henry, although now much reduced. That's how he could afford to send Dee to St John's." Then smiling, he said, "Dee claims to be a descendant of Rhodri the Great, Prince of Wales. He is definitely full of himself."

Serious again he continued, "But maybe he has reason to be. He was a remarkable student, reading everything he could find in the college library. His room-mates say he slept barely a few hours each night and he studied the rest of the time. He quickly gained a deep learning in many branches of the sciences: mathematics, astronomy, astrology to name but three. He got his BA after three years, and then was made a founding Fellow of Trinity College when the old King founded it the next year. There was always wild speculation surrounding his appointment at such a young age. How did the King even know of him?"

He continued, "There was also wild talk of Dee performing some conjuring when the Fellows at Trinity were putting on the play *Peace*, by Aristophanes. Somehow Dee made a large Scarabeus beetle fly high into the ceiling of the hall with an actor mounted on its back! He has said many times that it was but ropes, pulleys and mirrors, but all those who saw it swear it was conjuring.

"Since then he has been to Paris teaching Euclid to packed halls and much acclaim, and then working with Mercator and Frisius at Louvain. The French King Henri tried to keep Dee at his court by offering him a stipend of 200 crowns a year, but Dee said he was needed back in England. He is truly a genius. However he does believe deeply in God, and thinks the way to understand Him is through mathematics, which is a little unusual but not so dissimilar from St Thomas Aquinas apparently."

Cecil interjected excitedly, "John, you remember that manuscript you gave me from Dee last week? Did you read it?" As Cheke demurred Cecil continued, "In that manuscript Dee describes how he has measured the size of the universe by measuring the distances of all the planets, stars and clouds from the earth, complete with their directions and brightness."

"What's *the universe*?" asked Herbert, who did not have the academic background of his younger friends.

"The crystalline sphere that contains all the stars in the sky," replied Cheke absently, as he absorbed this new information, "I would not have believed that such a measurement was possible if you did not give it credence."

"Well I for one am convinced we can elect him as tutor in mathematics and astronomy based on that manuscript alone, and we have our own proof of his skill in astrology, thanks to him predicting our knighthoods" said Cecil.

"I do not disagree", said Cheke, "I vote *yes* as well".

The two men looked at Herbert, who was quiet and seemed deep in thought, although that was generally not his metier. When nudged by Cecil, he mumbled, "Yes, yes. I agree. Measured the universe eh? What else can that man do for me, for us all, and for England?"

It was Cecil's turn to grow thoughtful and he mused out loud, "We all know that England's might cannot compare to that of Spain nor of France."

As Herbert made to interject, Cecil made a placatory motion and continued, "I know that in the past we have won surprising victories against great odds, but that is my point. They were surprises and the foe was larger. Our only reliable leverage comes from acting with one of those countries against the other, or at least the threat of doing so. Now with the break from Rome and the establishment of our own Church we have managed to antagonise both of them at the same time, and will need all the help we can get to continue our independence. One day our careful balancing act might fail and either one of those mighty princes might turn their full attention on England, or, even worse they might join together against us. We would need a magician if that ever came to pass."

The barge bumped ashore at the King's Stairs, outside the Palace of Westminster, and Cheke looked around confused. Cecil apologised, "In the excitement I clear forgot to mention my summons by John Dudley, the Duke of Northumberland. As leader of the King's Council I cannot ignore him. Please, accept my invitation for supper at Cecil House, where I will join you anon."

Cheke heard the bells of St. Martin's church ringing out 5 o'clock while he and Herbert waited with Cecil's family for his return from

Westminster. Mildred looked worried about her husband's continued absence, and when Cheke tried to assure her that all would be well she whispered a confidence, "My husband thinks the Duke of Northumberland is an arch-schemer, and complains that service under him carries much risk."

Cheke was aghast. "Such thoughts should not be voiced out loud, my lady. Not even to loyal friends like myself."

Finally doors were heard banging and servants running throughout the house. Cecil had returned. Mildred flew to his side and after a brief embrace Cecil told them all to start supper without him, as he had one last task to conclude before he could join them. As they settled down and the meal was served Cheke nudged Herbert and pointed with his chin toward the window. Through the small leaded panes, in the gathering gloom of evening, a handful of men could be seen loitering outside by the stables.

Whilst Cheke distracted the family with his famously hilarious impression of Cicero, Herbert excused himself and exited the room.

A few minutes later he returned and whispered an explanation to Cheke. "I thought they might be threatening William in some way and was ready to draw my blade. But it seems he has everything in hand and was actually instructing them in some secret matter." He leaned closer still and lowered his voice yet further, "He mentioned a cache of weapons, and said that only two days remained."

"Curious!"

As he returned to the dining hall Cecil was pressured to comment by the silent looks of his two friends, so he hissed across the table to them "The less you know about this my friends, the safer you will be."

Then whilst he tousled the hair of his eldest daughter Cecil said aloud, "Now let's continue supper before Francisca eats all the best meats."

Chapter 5 - Education

Wednesday the 16th of October 1551
London

The risks of power

It was a Wednesday, almost a week later, when Cheke and Herbert followed Cecil and his son Thomas out of Cecil House into the morning sunlight, heading toward the river.

"Do you know where Cecil is taking us, John?" asked Herbert.

"I know not. Nor why the lad accompanies us," replied Cheke, gesturing to Cecil's eldest boy, Thomas. "Cecil did say it would be an education for the lad. But from what I can see Thomas has little interest in politics and even less aptitude."

The mischievous nine year old darted in and out of the group as they crossed the Strand, narrowly avoiding the freshest horse droppings, as they all threaded between several small crowds gathered around street preachers.

"He needs to be brought to heel," snarled Herbert as the lad darted in front of him causing him to side-step into a particularly deep puddle.

Cheke grimaced, but refrained from commenting on the lax parenting skills.

Ahead to their left Cecil pointed out Durham House, it's imposing stone gatehouse rearing up above their heads. "Thomas, see that house. Catherine of Aragon lived there before marrying King Henry VIII, and Anne Boleyn stayed there prior to marrying him too, but it has since been granted to the Princess Elizabeth."

Thomas ran over and peered through the gates into what was a large courtyard. Cheke himself could see horses being shod on one side whilst a wagon was being unloaded in the centre.

Cecil joined his son, and laying one hand on his shoulder he pointed with the other, "That large man on the wagon is delivering wine barrels by dropping them down from the wagon onto straw filled sacks on the ground, do you see? Then both the carter and an official of the house count them at the same time, so they can agree on the quantity delivered and ensure an agreed total and price."

As liveried servants rolled them away toward the house, Thomas slipped away from his father and ran on ahead.

Their little procession continued past the gatehouse and started down a sloping cobbled ramp toward the river, with the wall of Durham House on their left and another, lower wall, to their right.

Over that righthand wall Cheke could see fruit trees and beyond them Norwich Place, which he knew was one of the homes of Charles Brandon, Duke of Suffolk, before he died.

The smell of the river assaulted him as they got closer to the stairs, a mixture of fetid mud and a fishy tang. As he usually spent much of his time in Cambridge and the rest in Kingston, both of which were country towns, he wasn't used to the stench, and he wrinkled his nose in distaste.

Several gentlemen and their servants moved respectfully out of their path, recognising the entourage of Master Secretary, as they reached and descended the stairs toward a waiting wherry that had been reserved for them.

A short boat ride later they jostled for position with a dozen other wherries all of which were trying to deliver their occupants to the Parliament Stairs.

As they ascended the stairs Cheke pointed south-east across the river and said to Thomas, "Those towers rising above the trees in the parkland opposite, they belong to Lambeth Palace, home of the Archbishop of Canterbury, Thomas Cranmer." But the boy paid scant attention.

One of the guards recognised Cecil and called out to him, "Master Secretary. My lords. Please follow me," and led the way between several smaller buildings toward a larger hall.

As they strode through the highly decorated room Herbert tried to join in to help the boy's education, "This hall is called the *Prince's Chamber*." But Thomas made no sign that he had even heard Sir William.

They continued down dimly lit corridors that were richly hung with various tapestries. Thomas marched beside the guard, like a half-sized soldier, having to skip occasionally to keep his stride in unison.

They came to an arched doorway, and through that into another hall where a long table was surrounded by a dozen chairs and small sets of tiered benches were arranged on both sides.

"This room used to be the House of Lords, where Parliaments were held, but those Parliaments are now moved to a newer and larger building just to the west of here," explained Cecil to his son as they continued through and then up a long stretch of stone steps.

They emerged into a huge chamber containing numerous small groups of richly clothed men all talking animatedly.

As they entered the chamber Cecil was immediately dragged into hurried conferences with various small groups. Cheke could see him alternately shrug and shake his head. Assuming he had only been brought to watch over Thomas he did his best, but the lad was scooting around like a puppy in a henhouse. The last Cheke saw of him was when he raced toward one of the large and colourful tapestries hung on the walls, looking completely mesmerised.

Cheke acknowledged that they were indeed glorious pieces of art, though he doubted their authenticity. The nearest showed a battle scene with hundreds of knights carrying swords, and ordinary soldiers with lances that were tilting toward the sky like a forest of slender trees, and behind them all the tall pointed tents of the captains of the armies, and on the horizon a huge castle in white stone.

Cheke nudged Herbert and tried to speak over the hubbub to the taller man, "Can you fetch Thomas? He's over there by the tapestry, looks like he's starting to panic, maybe because he can no longer see us through the crowd."

"S'wounds. A baby-sitter now am I?"

Cheke chuckled into his beard.

Herbert weaved dextrously between the groups of nobles and finally stormed over to the lad. He grabbed Thomas' upper arm in his large calloused hand and half lifted and half dragged the boy back toward Cecil, who had finally made it to the far side of the hall himself and stood by the window, still conversing with two other nobles. As Cheke caught up with the fast moving Herbert he couldn't help leaning down and whispering an admonishment to Thomas, "You should pay heed young Thomas. Today we are in elevated company and will witness an important spectacle. You should mark it well, for it illustrates the risks of power, and one day your own fate could be decided just so easily".

As they rejoined Cecil, Cheke wondered who the other two men were. One was clearly a scribe of some sort, holding papers and nodding as the other, a grave, older man, with a thin face, wearing black robes and an unfashionably large hat, spoke with Cecil like an equal. As though reading his mind Herbert whispered, "That is Sir William Petre, Cecil's colleague as joint Secretary of State. A papist but yet a good man."

Petre was explaining, "...assure you the matter is completely in hand, for I wrote to the Lady Mary myself and informed her most straightly of the decision of the Privy Council, that she should refrain from the Mass in her household, on the forbearance of her brother the King."

"Excellent Sir William. And what of the other matter?"

"I meet the German ambassadors next week, and will propose an alliance of our Reformer states. It is in all our interests, and yet, as ever with these things the outcome is not certain, for the very existence of such an alliance could cause great heat in both the French and Spanish courts, and thus perhaps cause more danger than comfort. So, mayhap the overall result is not so suitable for any of us?"

"Then I bid you godspeed on your errand Master Secretary", Cecil bowed briefly, and turning to his companions he gestured to one of the large arched windows that was, as yet, not thronged with men.

Herbert nudged Cheke and bent to whisper urgently in his ear, "See yon baby-faced craven over yonder?" He gestured to a puffed up little man in an over-large fur, "That is Lord Chancellor Richard Rich. Beware of him John. Rarely have I met such a grasping weasel with an evil streak a country mile wide. It was he, along with that dog's backside Thomas Wriothesley, that personally tortured the fair Anne Askew in the Tower. I'd like to pluck his eyeballs, to teach him some decency, but he switched from the Protector to Dudley a couple of years ago, and may well see the graves of all of us yet".

Cheke was alarmed as he saw Rich's gaze sweep over the crowd and pause to stare impassively at him. He felt his soul shrivel beneath the malignant gaze. Herbert, true to form, was not so easily intimidated. He gave a low growl and straightened to his full height and with what must have been a huge effort he softened his face and smiled, giving a familiar wave, though Cheke believed he could hear Herbert's teeth grind as he did it.

Suddenly, the mood in the hall changed from collegial gathering to something altogether darker, and everyone turned to the windows.

Cheke peered out and saw a pleasant square lawned garden with several small groups of men engaged in conversation. The left and right hand sides of the garden were flanked by covered walkways, with the square being completed on the side opposite them by the wall of a huge building that towered even taller than the hall they themselves were in. Decorated spires rose from each corner of that building, and thick stone buttresses that reinforced its wall jutted into the garden. He assumed it must be the famed Chapel of St Stephen, a wonderful looking building, although it was no longer a church, it now housed the Parliament of the Commons when they sat.

Cheke was about to ask when the next Commons Parliament was going to be, when a glint of sun caught his eye to the left of the square under the cloister. A double column of soldiers, with steel breastplates and armed with pikes, marched out of the cloister toward the centre of the garden. At their head was a captain with a sword, who directed them toward one group of men on the green. As the soldiers approached them they turned as one and in their midst Cheke could just make out the famous features of Edward Seymour.

Seymour stepped forward and gestured that his colleagues should not draw their swords. "Who is that man?" asked Thomas, finally paying attention.

Cheke answered for all of them, "That is the Duke of Somerset, Edward Seymour. He is the King's uncle, and was until recently called the Lord Protector, the most powerful man in the land."

The captain and Somerset spoke a few words and then the eight soldiers formed up in two columns around Somerset and led him away toward the river. "He is being taken to the Tower I suppose," said Herbert, "Again".

"And this time he will find his release is less than certain," said Cecil.

At this comment they all glanced at Cecil who said in a low voice, "Dudley needed evidence against Somerset, and I...found it. You remember those men in my courtyard last week? When Somerset is safely in the Tower he will be accused of treason and this time he will not escape. Somerset does not forgive those who cross him, so I have made it as certain as possible."

Cheke had barely noticed the awed silence that had descended on the room as the arrest had taken place, so intent was he on the scene unfolding before him, but now as the soldiers disappeared though an archway toward the river the room erupted into animated chatter.

Herbert raised a quizzical eyebrow, "You have done what?"

"I found evidence of a plot by Somerset and his affinity. You remember when we and the rest of the Privy Council, absent Somerset, were celebrating the King's birthday a few nights ago at that private banquet? My men were entrusted with the safety of the event. During a security sweep they found several stashes of weapons hidden around the hall and a series of unlocked doors down a corridor to an outside door. Beyond the door a group of Somerset's men had gathered and so were apprehended. They claimed they had been lured there separately, but no one will believe such a fanciful story. They were all arrested of course, and are currently confirming their parts in the plot when we explain it to them, and implicating Somerset as they go, so they might avoid the rack."

Herbert gasped, "Your men kept the arrest very quiet then, for I saw and heard nothing to indicate there was aught of concern!"

"Yes they are good men. As indeed are Somerset's men really, that is why they will all be forgiven and will but pay a modest fine each. But Somerset himself must go, before he divides the kingdom with his plotting to overthrow Dudley. He is a good and competent man in many ways, and well liked by the population, but he just does not know when to let go of power. With the Spanish circling and the French stirring we cannot afford the division that he is causing."

As the soldiers and Somerset disappeared from sight Cecil turned his little group back toward the door they had entered through and, with occasional quiet comments to noblemen who approached, they slipped out and retraced their steps to the river.

Chapter 6 - Disembarkation

Early November 1551
Off the Norfolk coast

Hail Mary, full of grace

Simon Renard, Lieutenant of Aumont, watched nervously as the sailors lowered his travelling cases to the waiting row boat which rose and fell with alarming violence in the heavy chop of the North Sea night. He wiped rain and sea water from his face one more time as the lashing rain drenched everything he had brought with him from France. Turning to the Spanish captain he thanked him courteously and received nothing but a grunt in reply.

He seethed inwardly, but to the captain he just nodded and turned back to the ship's railing.

As an accomplished Burgundian diplomat (and spy), he reported directly to the Count of Burgundy, also known as the Emperor Charles V of Spain. But to Álvaro López de Duranto, Marquis of Tortosa, captain of the Spanish galleon San Felipe y Santiago, he was just cargo, and dangerous foreign cargo at that.

Finally, his last bag was lowered to the waiting boat and with a quick glance to confirm the dim lamp was still shining from the shore, he clambered down the netting to join his belongings. The motion of the small boat was much worse than it had looked from the deck of the warship and he regretted acquiescing to the captain's insistence on immediate disembarkation despite the poor weather.

The sailors were soon heaving strenuously at their oars and cutting through the swell, hopefully toward the shoreline, but he had long since lost all sight of that. Finally, with a last heave over breaking surf the small boat grounded on the sandy beach. Sailors immediately jumped out and hauled the boat further ashore, and started dumping his property on the beach, none too gently either. He made sure his money chest was safely on the strand, then clambered out himself. As soon as his boots touched the ground the sailors whisked the boat back into the surf, hopped in, and started pulling hard for their ship. The whole landing had taken no more than five minutes, and no words had been spoken.

He turned inland and faced the empty beach, suddenly afraid. A foreigner, sneaking into England, during a period of heightened political tension, in the middle of the night. If the local watch caught him he would probably be dead before he could give any convincing explanation for his appearance.

Within a few minutes two men staggered over a grass covered dune. They waved, then slogged their way down through the soft, deep sand, onto the beach. They greeted him in Latin with the pre-arranged code phrase, "Hail Mary, Full of Grace, The Lord is with thee," and he dutifully replied, "Blessed art thou among women", although he doubted anyone else would be standing on an isolated Norfolk beach in the middle of the night with more luggage than they could hope to carry.

With the codes exchanged appropriately, they greeted each other more warmly and soon transferred the baggage and Renard to a horse and cart the other side of the dunes. They travelled swiftly and surely on woodland paths for over an hour until they reached a small cottage hidden in a forested valley.

As he collapsed onto a straw mattress and pulled a thin blanket over himself Renard realised he had never once glanced back to check on the fate of the San Felipe y Santiago. Shrugging he thought to himself, *best of luck evading the English patrol ships, captain*, and he fell into a deep sleep.

Renard spent two days at the cottage, drying his baggage and recovering from the trip. His new colleagues had introduced themselves as Tomás and Cristóbal. They shared all their newest intelligence and insisted he share the latest news from home, although all his news was second-hand at best as he had been on assignment in Paris, France, for the last few years.

The most important intelligence had been delivered cautiously by Tomás, because it was incomplete, and spoke of a failure by them. Four weeks ago the men had been following a courier, an academic called John Cheke, suspected of having letters for Reformers on the continent from the Archbishop of Canterbury, Thomas Cranmer, but they had lost him in a minor town called Saint Albans.

"Future failures will not be tolerated," he said firmly, "fortunately for you we intercepted a courier as he landed in Antwerp, and we made copies of the letters he was carrying.

"Those letters make it clear that the Archbishop is trying to convene an ecumenical council and to unite European Reformers with England at its head. That cannot be tolerated by our Master, so we are charged with disrupting the enterprise. But first, I have to visit the Lady Mary, our Master's cousin, to assure her of our fidelity and support. How far is it to her residence?"

"She has several residences, and is allowed to use many of the royal palaces. But we are in luck, she is currently in Barsham Manor, which is but one day's ride from here. She is likely to stay there a week or more, so that she can visit the remains of a nearby shrine to Our Lady of Walsingham."

"Good. Cristóbal, ready the horses. And Tomás, we will need proper accommodations. A house in London and others close to each of Mary's main country residences. Do you have sympathetic Englishmen who can covertly arrange leases?"

"We have several, but for fear of reprisal they will do little more than that to aid our cause."

"I shall recruit more, never fear," stretching to his full height and with a zealot's gleam in his eyes he continued, "I shall create a network of informers and supporters so great that when I am done we will know more about the plans of this young King and his nobles than they do themselves. We shall drive fissures in their society and holes in their defences, and be ready to rain hellfire and purgatory upon them at our Master's slightest command."

Tomás and Cristóbal exchanged a nervous glance as they realised that their cozy assignment had now become part of the front line of the undeclared war by Spain against England and its heretical King Edward, and that the man now leading them was so full of energy that he would ensure that front line advanced and extended until victory was achieved.

Chapter 7 - Rumination

Late November 1551
Cecil House, London

Foreign exchanges

The fashionably dressed courtier strode through the lashing rain with one hand firmly holding onto his hat as his cloak swirled wildly about him in the gusty wind. His head bowed, he concentrated on avoiding the worst of the puddles and didn't see the young woman until the last moment. He would have knocked her clean off her feet had she not grabbed at his doublet to arrest her backward fall at the same moment as he instinctively reached out both hands and caught her.

For the briefest moment their faces were just inches apart and William Herbert found he was looking directly into the unmarked face of a rare beauty, with bright red hair and vivid green eyes. He apologised profusely and helped her stand upright, just as his cap was blown from his head. Cursing, he turned and watched it somersault down the road and into the distance. When he turned back the woman was already several feet away and climbing into a closed carriage that rapidly pulled away heading towards the City.

Muttering darkly to himself he reached the relative calm of the entrance to Cecil House and within a moment was admitted by the waiting servants. Leaving his wet cloak with the maid he brushed the other servants aside and showed himself into Cecil's study.

Throwing a rough greeting to Cecil he went straight to the roaring fire to warm himself, "So what is so important that you drag me away from my own hearth and home on a miserable day like this?"

"I appreciate you coming so quickly William. The King's debt problem has escalated into a crisis and I need your counsel. Our position with the Dutch and German lenders is acute and has left me with a dilemma. I have already forced Sir William Dansell out of office as you suggested last week, he was so ineffective it was embarrassing," said Cecil, "Now I need to find a replacement to send to Antwerp in the role of Royal Agent.

"It has been suggested to me that the best answer is to appoint Master Thomas Gresham, and let him go and perform the delicate negotiations on the foreign exchanges. What do you think about that?"

Still rubbing his hands together for warmth, Herbert said, "Gresham was one of Dansell's junior assistants wasn't he? From a decent family, but not noble. Why would you think he can influence the lenders sufficiently to resolve this?"

Cecil had poured two glasses of wine, and handed one to William while taking a careful sip from his own. He stayed silent for a few moments, then decisively put down his glass and strode over to a desk littered with documents. Selecting one he unfolded it and passed it to William.

He immediately recognised the elegant script as belonging to Dr John Dee, newly appointed tutor to the young King, and prognosticator extraordinaire. After a few minutes William looked up at Cecil with interest. "You went to John Dee and asked him who should replace Dansell? And he recommends letting Gresham take the position of King's Agent in Antwerp and predicts that he will settle the debts at far below the currently expected cost? Are you mad? You can't possibly tell the King that you suggest placing the financial future of his realm in the hands of a commoner, however skilled at finances he may be, all based on an astrological prediction. He'll laugh you out of the court, or more probably throw you in the Tower!"

"I don't intend saying any such thing. I have not lost my wits. Indeed to the contrary I have a rare plan," and at this Cecil smiled.

"I plan to present a selection of leading merchants, including Gresham, to the Privy Council for them to interview, and will lend my recommendation to Gresham because he was an assistant and has done some small financial business already for the King, so they will have some knowledge and good opinion of him. This way whoever is chosen I can say it was their choice, or if Gresham succeeds as Dee says, then I can say it was my recommendation."

"Ha. Crafty. And after all, if Dee has already predicted a good outcome then all should be successful anyway.

"Although, supposed knowledge of the future is not always a blessing," Herbert paused, "Did you know I asked Dee whether I was wise to keep my wife Anne in Norfolk, waiting on Lady Mary, the King's sister?"

Cecil looked up from sorting papers on his desk, "You didn't tell me that, no. And you already have my counsel on the matter: it is dangerous to keep her there where she might be corrupted by Mary's Catholic devotion, or alternatively might incur the King's displeasure to you."

"Well Dee goes much further than that. He claims Anne will catch a fever in Norfolk and not live to see next summer!"

Cecil was shocked, and gazed openly at Herbert for several moments.

Herbert continued, "I was mad as hell I can tell you and wanted to beat the impertinent whelp to a bloody pulp where he stood, but," Herbert sat and held his head in his hands, "I had been having dreams where I saw Anne as a phantom with arms stretched out pleadingly to me. So I stayed my hand from striking Dee. The man has been right so many times already that I believe he will be right now as well, whether I will or no." A small cry of anguish escaped his lips, "What of our children, Henry, Edward and baby Anne who is not even one year old?"

Cecil laid a hand on his friend's shoulder and squeezed slightly, "Then return your wife to London and quickly. Maybe your intervention can change this fate."

Light fingers

Herbert replenished his own glass and took a deep draught, while Cecil called for a light meal to be served. Even though Herbert was still wallowing in a degree of self-pity he recognised that Cecil had tried hard to improve his spirits.

When the servants retreated and they were left with a bottle, Cecil asked about Herbert's other errand.

"Ah, that I have done, in fact I have brought the list of names with me as you requested." He reached inside his doublet and, not finding what he expected, he searched the other side, "Strange, I could have sworn I had the list with me."

Suddenly his nostrils flared and with a curse he leapt from his chair, "God's wounds, I don't believe it. I have been robbed!"

He stormed across the room and kicked at a chest that stood near the window, causing no small pain to his foot, then returned chagrined and, sitting once more, told Cecil the story of the woman he had almost knocked down in the street who must have had light fingers.

Cecil recognised the import of it immediately and went very pale, "Did the cutpurse take your money as well, or just the list?"

Herbert checked and found that his purse was safe.

"William, this was no random robbery. She must have targeted you for the papers you were carrying. Now some enemy knows all our plans, and we don't even know who they are. You have been a fool!"

Herbert exploded with anger, knocking his chair over as he stood, "Don't presume to call me names Master Cecil, for it was not my idea to go about town carrying this information. It was yours."

Cecil immediately backtracked and tried to defuse the situation with placatory words and gestures, asking for forgiveness for his rash and poorly directed anger.

In fact Herbert was already calm. Warriors didn't get to be old warriors by failing to control their temper, but he didn't choose to show his returned composure, instead he maliciously let his friend continue to grovel for forgiveness for several minutes. But then he suddenly grew tired of the game, and interrupted him with a powerful swatting of his hand.

Cecil stopped his apologies, realising it was a game, and that it was over. He hesitated briefly to channel his thoughts, then started talking about how they would need to warn all the potential recruits who were named on the list.

Herbert suddenly laughed out loud and slapped his leg in merriment. He took a long drink from his glass and set it down again in satisfaction.

Cecil sat very still and studied Herbert for several moments, clearly thinking the aged knight's mind had snapped. Seeing no more odd signs, he shook his head and asked, "Alright, I give up. What has made this betrayal of our colleagues a thing of amusement?"

"Dee."

Cecil looked confused, "I don't understand. What has Dee got to do with it?"

"He suggested I write the list in a special code that only he and I had the key to. I thought him ….frankly I thought him overzealous at least and possibly mad. But by God I am mighty glad he had me do it so. The rascals who took the list will never be able to read it! The Brotherhood is safe."

Chapter 8 - Auscultation

One Year Earlier, 6th of June 1550
Toulon, France

Jerome Maurand

Jacques climbed up a few steps and ducked through the hatch, blinking as he emerged into the bright sunshine of a perfect Mediterranean afternoon. He squinted toward the port city he knew to be Toulon.

Across the harbour to his right he could see a squat, circular and forbidding stone fort.

"It's called *Tour Royale* that is," commented his friend, Nicholas, from behind him.

He shivered as he looked at it, and quickly tore his eyes away in case its malignant force would somehow become aware of his attention.

"Apparently they started building it forty years since, they did, at the command of Louis XII. Well, he's long gone isn't he? Moulding in his grave that one. Well they continued building the *Tour* anyway and finished it a while back now. Dedicated to Francis I. Mind you, he has never seen it as far as I know," continued Nicholas conversationally.

The fort had a commanding view of the approaches to the harbour, and bristled with cannon of various sizes. *Heaven help anyone trying to sneak into the harbour past that colossus. Or trying to sneak out of the harbour either*, thought Jacques.

The dockside to his left was thronging with people busy provisioning the many ships at anchor with necessary goods, and beyond the quay were a jumble of inns, taverns, markets, houses of the town's folk, and of course, lots of churches. Surrounding them all was the city wall, and beyond that the majestic rise of Mount Faron and its companion mountains.

"Home," sighed Nicholas wistfully.

Sarcastic bastard, thought Jacques.

"Well, home port of our galley *Réale*, and in fact home port for the entire bloody French Navy in the Mediterranean," said Nicholas.

"That's why there eez zo many military ships in the harbour?" asked Jacques in broken English.

"You got it, mon frère. Although the *Réale* is the heart of Francis' fleet of course," amazingly Nicholas puffed out his chest with pride as he said this, "Manned by over a hundred slaves it is. Mostly French of course."

Like me, thought Jacques.

"With a few Englishmen like me to teach you the meaning of stamina."

Jacques shuffled forward a few steps across the deck, his manacles clanking with each step. A swish, and an unseen baton thudded into his chest, to stop him moving forward. The baton wielding sailor grunted as the baton bounced off the solid muscle of Jacques' pectorals, and in an uncouth accent told him to wait. A few moments later, "Allêz", and he was pushed forward by the same baton, to the port side of the galley, where another slave with a small hammer and practiced strokes, released both his leg shackles, and the shackle from one wrist, leaving the final one in place. He was then pushed down the gangplank toward the quay.

On the quay, Jacques waited as the little group assembled. He and the other dozen men were reminded that their "shore leave" had been granted due to good behaviour and their completion of five years service. They were expected back before nightfall the next day. Each was given a couple of small coins and laughingly told to enjoy themselves. But not too much.

"Come on Jacques, what are you waiting for?" asked Nicholas.

"I haven't decided what to do - I didn't believe they would actually let us off the galley, so I never thought about it."

"You don't need to think lad, just follow my lead and you'll have a night that'll bring a smile to your face whenever you think back to it", pointing with his chin toward the nearest brothel.

"But how do they know we will stay in the town and not just escape into the hills?"

Nicholas slapped a calloused hand onto Jacques' bare shoulder and scraped his thumbnail over the letters 'GAL' crudely branded onto his upper arm, then lifted his right wrist with its still attached iron manacle. "These are their guarantees lad. The city guard is stationed at every gate out of the city, and checks everybody's wrist for manacles. If you are found trying to sneak out you will be executed without trial. Your severed head will be decorating a spike over the gate before the day is done. Now come on, before all the best girls are taken."

"You go, I'm going to find a tavern and have a quiet drink." Jacques was actually terrified by the idea of lying with a woman, although a little excited at the same time.

The big man shrugged, and ambled away. After a couple of steps he turned back and shouted, "Just remember, back here by tomorrow evening, else the Guard will search the town and when you're found, *and you will be found*, you'll be executed on the spot."

Jacques looked about the quayside. All around him were piles of provisions, in boxes, bales, and barrels. Teams of men loaded the provisions onto carts using small A-frame cranes, and other men led donkeys that pulled the carts. Further to his right lay rows of cannon, with uniformed men inspecting them. Near the cannon were thousands of cannonballs in pyramid shaped piles and more men counting and inspecting them. Jacques had seen the port many times before, but it had never seemed this busy.

He walked toward the waterfront bars, but quickly saw that they were all full of sailors, not the best place for a galley slave to get a quiet drink. So he angled off toward a dim alley, ready to head deeper into the town, but had to wait while a column of soldiers marched past. They didn't look very experienced, but their pikes and halberds looked polished and sharp enough. There were even a couple at the rear carrying the long and clumsy arquebus firearms.

The tavern he finally chose was in a poorer part of town, well away from the waterfront, and even this was fairly busy, although with locals not sailors. Women carried bottles of wine and flagons of ale to crowded tables, where they were passed from man to man and finally scurried away with their dignity barely intact.

Jacques sighed and went further into the gloom, hoping to find a quiet table where he might merely avoid the stink of his fellow man for a few hours.

Beyond a low dividing wall he found a quiet spot, and sat, closing his eyes, finally relaxing. He let his mind contemplate the knowledge that he wasn't chained like a dog, hauling on an oar in time with a booming drumbeat. The smells, sights and sounds of the last five years would be with him for a long time, but here they dimmed and were replaced with stale wine, sweat, and wood smoke. So better, but not a lot better.

A hand on his shoulder shook Jacques out of his reverie, and he reacted with the speed of a striking snake, by grabbing the wrist and twisting hard enough to tumble the hand's owner onto a stool, where he almost dropped the wine bottle and cups he was holding in his other hand, "Merde!"

Now fully awake Jacques realised the old man was no threat and let go of his arm, but he still watched carefully as the man, presumably a cleric, straightened the stained, black Soutanne that was draped over his thin body, and placed the wine and two cups on the table. Muttering oaths to himself, the man poured wine into each cup and pushed one toward Jacques, slopping some onto the table. He crossed himself, and quickly drank off his own wine. He immediately poured some more. "My apologies friend, I meant no harm. I am Jerôme Maurand. I recognised you. Please, share my wine before you die," he gestured at the untouched cup, "Go on, it won't bite."

"What do you mean you 'recognised me'? I am sure we have never met."

"Hmm? Well. Not *you* as such, no. But your sort."

"My *sort*? What do you mean, my *sort*? And drink *before I die*? You are an offensive person indeed!"

"There, there, don't take offence. I just meant someone from the galleys. I have been aboard a galley, I know the conditions. I know they do not release slaves, therefore I know you are going to be found soon, and will be executed, and will die. That's all. Nothing personal."

Jacques glowered, still offended, but drank a mouthful of wine anyway, and immediately choked on the strong taste. When he was younger he had been allowed watered down wine, but that was over five years ago. Since then it had been brackish water ladled by the galley's cook. He slowed down, and sipped the remaining wine while he regarded Jerôme. "What were you doing on a galley, priest?"

"What? Hmm. Well, I was going to ask you similar questions. Perhaps this will be a long night." Jerôme waved over a serving woman, muttered something too quiet for Jacques to hear, and a few minutes later she returned with a small basket of bread, cheese and more wine, in exchange for a coin from the priest.

Jacques eyed the basket, then looked at the priest, who nodded and pushed it closer. Needing no further encouragement he broke off some bread and cheese and with small bites he savoured them, then crammed more into his mouth as though he hadn't eaten for a week. Which was nearly true, as the gruel served on the Réale hardly counted.

Presently the priest began his story:

"Seven years ago I was newly arrived here in Toulon and ministering to the officers of the Réale in their barracks, and their Captain saw me writing in my journal afterwards. He invited me to travel with them on their next diplomatic mission, and to publish a story of their heroics afterwards.

"I was flattered and foolish, and so I agreed.

"Oh, the horrors and injustice I saw on that voyage - I fear they will haunt me forever."

Jerôme drank deeply from his cup, shaking his head sadly.

After a long pause he continued.

"We left harbour with four other galleys, and only when we were underway did Captain Polin tell me that our mission was to rendezvous with the heretic, Ariadenus Barbarrosa. This of course, was a name all men knew and feared. What good could come of meeting this Muslim fiend, this Ottoman Admiral, this scourge of Christians throughout the Mediterranean?

"But worse still, after meeting Barbarossa we were to continue on to see Suleiman, Sultan of the Ottomans!

"I was appalled. What were French Christian sailors doing on a diplomatic mission to the Muslims? I was repelled by the whole concept, but what could I do?

"We sailed for weeks, through calm waters and through storms, until we met Barbarossa's fleet of two hundred ships, near Sicily.

"There we jointly attacked city after city of honest, god-fearing Christian folk on the Italian coast, and after each battle we watched as the Turks took hundreds of prisoners from the surviving citizenry. They must have had six thousand captives by the time we left them, and many tens of thousands more were left dead or dying. Any prisoners who struggled were stabbed and thrown overboard into the sea, there to float amongst scores of other bodies. The sea foamed red with the blood of innocent Christians."

Jerôme had closed his eyes, and now he shuddered at the memories. Tears ran down his face and mixed with the wine in his cup as he fortified himself to continue his tale.

"We left Barbarrosa in Sicily and our little fleet sailed on to Constantinople.

"Our ships were allowed passage through the sea of Marmara, and into the Golden Horn. As we entered the Horn we could see a magnificent palace on the headland, with dozens of domes and spires and a great tower. I later learned it was called the Topkapi Palace, and it was the home of Suleiman. We continued past the sea walls, navigating between dozens of small sailing craft, but only the Réale was allowed past the inner harbour defences and to the quayside on the left bank.

"I could see a great mix of peoples thronging in the town and down to the docks. There were many Moslems of course but also Jews and Greeks who I assumed to be slaves, but later found that they lived free!

"We drew up alongside a great wall of white stone, and Captain Polin took me and twenty officers and men, and we were led past highly decorated beautiful buildings by a large host of robed Muslim officials.

"After twenty minutes of progress up clean, paved streets, we reached tall, decorated walls, and were led past a couple of guards and through an open gate into the first of two great courtyards, and finally we were received by the Sultan himself in a magnificent throne room.

"Captain Polin gestured to some of his men and they stepped forward and presented a box of some treasures that I did not see, and the Sultan seemed pleased.

"Then Polin told the Sultan, through an interpreter, how we had met Barbarossa's fleet and we had jointly attacked several coastal towns of Italy that were held by the Holy Roman Emperor, Charles V.

"Suleiman seemed satisfied with the tale, and after some grand statements of common enemies, joint conquest, and lasting amity, he withdrew with a large retinue of princes and functionaries.

"We relaxed and feasted on exotic fruits and meats, but no wine, for the Moslems do not drink it. After two days with more such meetings and feasting we returned to the ship, which had been provisioned during our absence, and we departed for our return journey to Toulon.

"I was mighty disturbed, because the Sultan and his realm seemed fair and just, the population clean, healthy and safe, and yet were they not the same filthy Mohammedans who fed like jackals on the body of Christ after they had murdered men, women and children? How could this be? I did not know. I was sleepless for many nights as I wrestled with the contradictions."

Jerôme's tears had left trails in the grime on his face as he had recounted his tale, and now he wiped the dirty sleeve of his Soutanne across his face smearing it further. Clearly he had not forgotten, nor recovered from his ordeal.

"We returned safely by October 1544, and I spent the next six months writing my account of the journey for Polin as we had agreed. Then I quit his presence and lived in solitude for several years while I wrestled with the guilt of working with the enemies of Christ. I have not cleansed myself of the shame yet, but I try to make amends by doing good works," and with another sniff he emptied his cup.

He was a pitiful wreck of a man to be sure, of good heart, but clearly broken by his inability to live with his conscience after the journey.

Jacques busied himself eating some bread and cheese to give the priest time to pull himself together and regain his dignity.

After several minutes Jerôme gestured, "And so, what is your sad story friend, how did you come to the galleys, how did you escape, and how are you planning to leave the city alive?"

Jacques drank more wine, and felt heat rise to his cheeks. Was this a trap? His stomach flipped from anxiety. He looked around, seeing other folks drinking in small groups, laughing and talking and shouting and eating, and generally not paying any attention to the slave and the priest. Jerôme waited patiently, putting no pressure on Jacques, just occasionally sipping from his own cup.

Jacques was undecided and swirled the dregs of wine around the bottom of his cup and watched them form the shaky shape of a cross. He gasped and blinked, and the dregs scattered again and finally lay quietly at the bottom of the cup. He fought his doubts, but then with a shake of his head he finally set the cup down, drew in a deep breath and resolved to tell his own tale.

He cast his mind back to that fateful day, 20th of April 1545, in his native village of Mérindol, France. He clearly remembered the feeling of the early morning sun on his face, casting long shadows across the cobbles. The smell of boiling woad leaves, and horses. And the joy in his heart as he played carefree with his sister, while his parents worked nearby…

Waldensian customs

Emée giggled, and ran haphazardly in the walled courtyard, chased by her older brother, Jacques. He was holding a squawking hen in his outstretched hands as he ran, and as the bird flapped its clipped wings in alarm they brushed his laughing face. Jacques slowed a little to let his sister have some measure of safety, then launched the bird up and out toward her. It partly flew and partly fell down to the cobbles, landing near her feet with feathers flying, then quickly strutted away under a cart and across the yard toward the other chickens. Emée shrieked with joy and ran behind her father's bulky form.

Henri Delauris was dealing with the first woad delivery of the day, directing a farmer to unload his crop into the rear corner of the yard. He beamed with joy as he scooped Emée up into his arms and playfully cuffed Jacques around the ear. "Now Jacques, time to be useful. Go and help the good Monsieur Goulart unload his crop."

"Yes, Papa".

Reaching up, Jacques tried to pull a sack off the cart, but it was a little too high and heavy for him to move. Goulart watched, smiling, for a minute, then helped the boy by pulling the first sack to the floor. Working together they quickly emptied the cart. Upon a nod from Henri, a sour looking worker called François started emptying the fresh green leaves from the sacks and tipped them down a chute into the darkness below the barn, where they fell into a mill to be crushed and then added to boiling water. The smell of boiling leaves wafted out after them.

Henri invited Goulart to join the family for breakfast below a shady tree in the yard. Madame Delauris brought out bread, honey, water, and a dark red wine, and they all sat at the trestle table. After a short prayer of gratitude to God for their blessings, according to their Waldensian customs, they ate their simple meal together.

Goulart told them of his eldest daughter's betrothal to a boy from a merchant family in Mallemort, the town across the river from Mérindol. He spared no detail as he excitedly explained the celebration plans and invited the whole Delauris family to the feast at his farm next month.

Henri bent and whispered to Jacques, who excused himself and left the table. The family listened to Goulart's news, enjoying the man's evident pride and excitement.

Jacques slipped into the storeroom and took a small, but beautifully decorated jar from a shelf. He carefully cradled the valuable jar of blue-green powder in his arms, knowing that his father would normally send a batch of the dye every few months to Toulon for sale, where it was much sought after and fetched a high price. Before returning to the gathering he paused, and saw the grumpy François throwing the empty sacks onto Goulart's cart. The worker cast a surly glance at the group under the tree, then spat on the ground by the cart's wheel, and left the courtyard muttering to himself. Jacques didn't understand why the man was always so angry and resentful, he had a good job and was paid and treated well by Jacques' father.

Jacques took his seat again, whilst his father stood and clapped his hands to get the group's attention.

"Claude, your family and mine have known each other for nearly twenty years now. Your girl, Marie, is like a daughter to us. We would like to give you this gift for her marriage, with our blessings." He handed the jar to Goulart, who sat for a moment, too surprised to respond.

Jacques nudged Emée and they giggled with their heads together.

Struggling to his feet, and with a catch in his voice, Goulart held up the jar and started to respond to the unexpected generosity, "Henri, Annette, you are the best friends a poor farmer like me could wish to have, …"

The clattering of hooves outside and the clinking of metal on metal interrupted him.

Three riders entered through the main archway into the courtyard, their breastplates shining and their swords drawn. Following the horses came a dozen soldiers, jogging in with long pikes held in front of them, their faces hard, lacking any emotion.

Henri started to rise from the bench with his hand held up in a stopping gesture, but before he could even speak the nearest running soldier had thrust his pike into his chest, the momentum driving it all the way through so the bloody tip appeared behind him. He coughed bright red blood and with glassy eyes staring wide he lurched backwards, kicking the table over as he went. Annette screamed and started towards her husband, but was grabbed by two of the soldiers and dragged off behind the tree. She struggled violently and continued screaming until one of the men stuffed her own apron into her mouth. Jacques held Emée tightly and together they cowered behind the table, as one of the mounted soldiers slashed down at the gaping Goulart, splitting his face diagonally from ear to chin, spraying blood and pieces of sticky flesh over the children. The gifted jar flew from his hands and shattered on the cobbled floor, the bright blue powder it had contained was spilled over a large area. Another soldier brought his weapon down on Goulart repeatedly, nearly hacking his head from his body, crimson splashing over the innocent blue of the powder. Death imitating art.

Peeking from behind the bench, Jacques saw the loathsome François entering the courtyard behind the soldiers, laughing and pummelling the air with his fist as though joining in the massacre. His laughing startled one of the soldiers who span around in fright, the sharp blade of his long pike ripped through François' throat, and arterial blood spurted over the soldier who grimaced as he wiped his face, and kicked at the fallen worker's body.

Jacques pushed his sister toward the house telling her to run, and grabbing the knife from his father's belt he lunged toward the nearest soldier. The man laughed and easily caught him in a choke hold, and looked toward his mounted Captain for instructions. The Captain shook his head. The last thing Jacques saw was another soldier picking up Emée and throwing her onto the back of a horse like a sack, before the back of his head exploded and everything was darkness.

Aix-en-Provence

The line of prisoners stumbled to a halt beside a derelict barn, and one by one were allowed to use the water trough to quench their thirst. Jacques was in the middle of the line of perhaps forty young men. While they shuffled forward and drank they were idly watched by the Provençal troops and the mounted officers. Jacques glanced at the officers and saw that the Captain was the same man who had led the attack on his home. He lunged forward without thinking, as anger overcame his weariness, but before the troops even noticed his movement the men either side of him had reeled him in with the chains that bound them together and forced him to turn away. It was partly self-preservation, and partly helping one of their own.

Soon the soldiers ordered the line forward again, and they trudged on for many more hours.

Jacques shoes were ruined and his feet were bloodied by the time they reached the large town of Aix-en-Provence. The sun was starting to set behind them as they trudged through the wide cobbled streets, first passing warehouses and single storey houses, then stone built merchant houses, and finally emerging into the town square.

A small crowd of townspeople were jeering and gesticulating as the prisoners trudged into the square, but while some troops formed the prisoners into two lines facing the Hôtel de Ville, other troops held the crowd back. A few minutes later a large man wearing a tricorn hat and a bright blue sash appeared at the balconied window, and flapping his arms he called for quiet so he could speak.

"Mes Amis, we have long desired to see an end to the heretics who have been living amongst us like a worm in an apple. For years we have waited for the appeals to end, and finally by the grace of God, King Francis agreed, and so I, Jean Maynier d'Oppède, the President of your parlement of Provence immediately raised an army to crusade against them. And here you see the results before you. Let's see if five years in the galleys will teach them to follow the teachings of the Mother Church." He raised his voice so he could still be heard over the crowd's excited murmurs, and with spittle flying he shouted out, "Captain Escalin, take them away to the galleys!"

Jacques stood in shock. *What is the man saying? Where are the heretics? My family was clearly Christian, my parents were totally pious. How could the King of France send a crusade against Christians? This makes no sense.*

He was pushed by the man behind him, and so staggered forward, his mind a whirl of confusion and anger.

To the docks

Maurand, slack-jawed, continued to stare at Jacques as the young man concluded his tale.

"So, here I am five years older. I have survived the galley this long through the aid of my fellow slaves, but barely."

Downing the last of the wine, the priest seemed to come to a decision.

He rose unsteadily from his chair and glanced around the tavern, then gesturing urgently he turned and scuttled toward a door almost hidden in the dark panelling at the rear of the building.

He hustled Jacques out of the tavern's rear entrance, through a seemingly endless series of alleys, and finally into a courtyard of whitewashed buildings. It was an obviously poor area, but several artisans were cheerfully at work, and women were washing clothes in a large water butt and chatting contentedly. The priest led Jacques to a single story building and through a stout wooden door, into a single room house. Telling Jacques this was his house, and to wait, he hurried out again.

Jacques nervously paced around the room, his unease increasing as the moments passed. Was Maurand going to the City Watch to claim a reward for finding a runaway slave? He wasn't even sure he was really running away yet, and he certainly didn't want to be given over to the Watch. He retreated into the rear of the room and looked for another exit, but there was only a single window and it was clearly too small for Jacques to squeeze his shoulders through.

Before he had time to plan any escape the door squeaked open, it was Maurand and a blacksmith. The fellow had a huge barrel of a chest and arms thick with muscle, and he carried a mallet and a chisel. Gesturing toward the cold fireplace he waited while Jacques laid the manacle on a flat stone, and then with just two strikes from his hammer he removed the securing pins and the manacle fell from Jacques wrist. With a brief nod to the priest the man gathered the pieces of ironwork and left as quickly as he had arrived.

A gnarled old woman came in next and gestured that Jacques should sit. She bustled around him and within a few minutes had shorn his long, ragged hair, and scraped his face with a sharp blade in a passable imitation of a shave, so all he had was stubble.

Maurand thrust a bundle of clothes toward Jacques, "A pair of Dutch sloppes made of canvas, a woollen doublet with long sleeves that will cover the brand on your shoulder, a leather jerkin, and a pair of worn leather shoes. Put them on quickly."

As Jacques dressed, Maurand continued, "The clothes were donated by the widow next door. Her husband was a dutch sailor who died after returning from a long voyage last year."

As they left the house Maurand handed Jacques a small knife in a wooden scabbard, "Tie this to your belt so that it dangles between your legs," Jacques raised an eyebrow, but Maurand just shrugged and said, "This is how the English sailors wear their knives".

"Where are we going?"

"To the docks," then seeing Jacques alarm he continued, "Not the military docks, the commercial ones. There are several ships in port today and we should be able to get you onto one as a deck hand."

"But I know nothing about sailing," cried Jacques, "I was a galley slave for five years, pulling on an oar, and before that a child. I don't know one end of a rope from the other."

"Most of the men know nothing when they first go aboard, you will learn as quickly as them, maybe faster."

Jacques walked in a daze, not really believing he was going along with this wild plan.

They turned into a quiet alley, close enough to the docks that they could hear the cries of the teamsters shouting orders to sailors loading supplies. Jacques, his eyes wild, grabbed Maurand's shoulder and pulled him around, "What are we doing? I can't run away, they will catch me for sure. They'll kill me. The next time you see me I'll be nailed to the city gates and my head will be on a spike."

Maurand pulled him into the shadows and spoke quickly but soothingly, "Non, non, you will be fine. Already you look completely different than an hour ago, in these clothes no one will suspect you for a slave. They can't see the brand on your shoulder, and you do not have the shackle on your wrist. Just take deep breaths and be calm. Speak in English like your friend Nicholas taught you, not in French, and no one will suspect anything."

"But why are you helping me like this?"

"I did not lift a hand to help my fellow Christians when I was on that ship with Polin. I have lived in shame for many years, now it is time to help others who are persecuted. Now quickly, pull yourself together. We will get you aboard an English or Dutch ship and when you are at sea no one will care whether you were once a slave."

Chapter 9 - Personification

February 1552
London, England

Narratio Prima

Jacques climbed down from the crow's nest of the *Stanislav von Danzig*, the three masted Hanse merchant ship that he had boarded with the old priest's help back in Toulon nearly two years ago.

Hungry after his four hours as lookout, he was hurrying to the galley when the first mate, Georg, stepped away from a small group of sailors and, catching his shoulder, pulled him aside. Leaning too close, with his breath smelling of spicy Polish sausage, he leered, and said, "The merchant wants to see you Jacques, as soon as possible." Georg's hand lingered uncomfortably long on his chest. Squirming with discomfort Jacques twisted away and almost ran along the corridor toward the merchant's cabin in the stern of the ship, with Georg and his cronies' laughter following him all the way.

Jakob Mierjewski greeted Jacques with a broad smile, and eagerly called him into the cabin. A large and prosperous merchant from Danzig, he had taken a shine to Jacques after learning the lad could do arithmetic. He had extended Jacques' education by teaching him how to maintain a ledger of trading accounts, how to navigate by the sun, moon, and stars, and how to invest his gambling winnings in the commodities that were carried on the Stanislav as it plied its several trading routes from Gdansk, Poland, to England and back.

Jacques had been on board twenty months now, and this was the tenth voyage in which he owned a tiny share of the cargo, and he anticipated a good profit when they docked in England. So far he had been nearly doubling his money on every trip. This time they were carrying honey and furs, and they expected to load up with good English broadcloth for the return trip.

Jakob also let him use a small chest in the cabin for storage of any especially valuable personal trading items, and on this trip it contained two books. The first was a new book called *De Revolutionibus* by Nicolaus Copernicus, a clerical administrator from a small town called Warmia in Poland, near Gdansk. The second book was a related work by Georg Rheticus, printed in Gdansk, called *Narratio Prima*. Jacques loved to read, and trading in books gave him the double pleasure of reading a book and then selling it, usually for a profit.

Jacques had bought both books very cheaply from a bookseller in Gdansk during one day of shore leave when the *Stanislav* had docked there. The rear of the bookstore had been on fire and was seriously damaged. The remaining brick walls were propped up by lengths of timber jammed at an angle. The bookseller desperately needed to reduce his stock while he made repairs. Jacques had proudly showed his purchases to Jakob, but rather than congratulating him on finding more bargains, the merchant had gently smiled and shook his head, telling him the low purchase price didn't matter because Jacques would probably never be able to sell them. He had gone on to explain that although they were fairly recent books, they were commonly known to contain seditious subject matter, and such books were usually avoided by all but the adventurous.

Jacques had been reading a few pages every night, and had so far discovered that the *Narratio* was a summary version of the *De Revolutionibus*, and that they claimed that the Earth travelled around the Sun once every year. This explanation of planetary motion directly contravened the teachings of the Church which said the Earth was the static centre of the universe, with the sun and all other heavenly objects circling around it on celestial spheres.

Jacques had groaned when he learnt this, realising the merchant was right, and that he'd have a tough time selling these books, even if he took them all the way to England where the Reformed religion had broken ties with the Catholic church. Still, he had them now, so he struggled through a page or two of the dense latin text and complex mathematics every night. Late one night during a protracted philosophical discussion over several glasses of Polish vodka he had commented to Jakob that the Church teachings of a static Earth must be right and the books wrong, because if the Earth was moving around the Sun then surely people and ships and in fact all loose things on land or sea would be flung outwards into the air. He demonstrated his idea by spinning the plate of hard biscuits that was on the table in front of them, and yes sure enough the biscuits were flung outward off the plate, some landing in Jakob's lap, some on the floor where the ships cat enjoyed the unexpected snacks. Jakob, had snorted in derision, and said that the instructions of the Church always benefit only one thing, and that thing was the Church itself.

Jakob pulled a familiar map of the English coast from a chart locker and laid it across the table. He explained how he and the Captain had been asked to modify their destination by the Hanse representative in Hamburg where they had stopped for supplies. So instead of putting into King's Lynn, the small trading port on the Norfolk coast where Jakob's brother, Andrus, was the principal merchant, they would go south and follow the broad tidal estuary of the Thames and go all the way into London, and sell their cargo through the major Hanseatic Kontor in England, called the *Steelyard*.

"I don't understand why you seem so happy about this, Jakob. You love meeting up with Andrus. Every return trip you have a blauer montag where you spend the whole day recovering from your weekend drinking games!"

"That is true", he nodded sagely, "but we will get a much better price for the cargo in London, and the whole crew will experience the hospitality of the Steelyard and the wonder of London - a most magnificent city."

"And my books! Presumably it will be easier to find a buyer in London, so that's good news."

Jakob nodded his sceptical assent, "Perhaps. Ja, perhaps".

The shrouded city

With the Norfolk coast in sight the *Stanislav* turned south and immediately surged forward as it was gripped by a strong current running parallel to the shoreline which pulled it around the bulging coast toward London. The wind however was stiff and against them, so they had to tack back and forth to make some headway, and the battering of the hull through the cross-waves was hard on the bodies of even the most seasoned sailors.

They passed Yarmouth, on the tip of the bulging shore, and then spied a smudge on the coast that must have been Ipswich, but which was mostly obscured by mist. The locations of both trading ports were familiar to the crew from previous trips. After a while the current lessened and the wind increased, slowing them down so much that some of the sailors were openly questioning whether they would make it to London during the daylight.

A thankful murmur rapidly spread through the crew when they finally entered the estuary proper, although the current died away entirely, leaving them to tack back and forth into the wind with very little progress to show for it. After a half hour, however, the wind shifted and they starting making a stately speed up the river. Soon Jacques noticed that the landscape was slipping by more quickly than previously, and faster than he would have expected. He realised the tide had turned, quite literally, and they were riding the flood tide up river and must be making almost 5 knots regardless of the wind.

They passed a couple of tributaries on each side before the river swung south and then west again. Closely eyeing the dangerous mud flats as they streamed past at uncommon speed, they saw a fortress on the north bank, which the boatswain said was called Tilbury Fort. Its two tiers of variously sized cannon ominously covered the narrowing river for over half a mile, and reminded Jacques of the defences deployed at the Tour Royale in Toulon. He wondered about the accuracy of the gunnery and whether they'd be able to hit a ship sailing at this speed, and how bad the damage would be if they were hit. He had once seen the Tour Royale fire upon a galley that was attempting to escape when the slaves had revolted, and after merely being splashed by the first few range-finding shots, two cannonballs had hit the galley nearly simultaneously, tearing great holes through the hull. The galley had sunk to the echoes of the guns and the screams of the still chained slaves. With a shiver he chided himself, remembering he was a merchant seaman now and was unlikely to be fired upon in anger.

As he crossed the deck away from the sight of the guns an eerie moaning sound caught his attention and he swivelled to look toward its source. It came from a small disused wharf and a collection of tumbledown warehouses on the south bank. Georg saw him eyeing the village and said it was called Gravesend, and that it was home to the souls of drowned English sailors. Jacques shivered involuntarily and turned away from the laughing Georg and instead went below decks to talk with Jakob. Jakob explained that many old wharves like Gravesend were no longer in use and all unloading was done further upriver. The moaning he had heard was just the wind whistling through the abandoned buildings. Probably.

He idled away half an hour chatting to Jakob about what they would find at the Steelyard, before he heard the urgent clang of the ship's bell and running feet on the deck. Jacques left Jakob and quickly went topside.

On deck he was surrounded by a swirling clammy fog. One minute he could see both riverbanks, and the next he could not even see the sides of the ship. During one of the clearer moments Georg told him to climb to the crow's nest which might be above the fog-bank, and if it was then he should shout down directions to keep the ship mid-channel. Miguel followed him up, stopping at the cross-bar of the mainsail so he would be able to relay messages down to the deck. The precautions seemed excessive until the fog swirled around the ship again, obscuring vision and muffling even shouted voices. From Jacques' elevated position he marvelled at the view he now had over the silky fog-bank, and dutifully shouted down directions to Miguel, who repeated them to Georg. Working together they kept the Stanislav in the middle of the river heading relentlessly toward the shrouded city.

Floating above the fog-bank Jacques felt strangely detached from earthly considerations, more like an eagle soaring over the clouds, hearing no distinct sounds except the wind in the sails and the gulls calling to each other as they wheeled around him. At his occasional shouted instruction the river took them in a great curving loop, first heading south, then west, and then north again. On the southern shore the ornate superstructure of a magical palace jutted through the thinning fog, one minute visible, the next hidden. But mostly it was just the tops of trees for miles on both sides.

They were seemingly alone, cruising serenely on the tide, but as the river straightened out into a westerly flow both banks were gradually outlined by the masts of stationary ships, perhaps at moorings, perhaps in repair facilities. Jacques advised caution and the crew took in sail to slow the ship. Despite their slower speed other ships would appear suddenly out of the fog-bank and swift action was sometimes required to avoid collisions.

Jacques thought it would have been much wiser to hire a pilot, just this once, to guarantee safe navigation up the river, even though Hanseatic ships weren't obligated to do so like other ships were.

Maybe I should suggest it to Georg or the Captain? he wondered. But remembering the Captain's parsimony he laughed out loud at the thought and concentrated on his task.

As the minutes passed the fog gradually dissipated, and Jacques saw church steeples materialise to both his left and right, first their mounted crosses and then their spires, followed by indistinct rooftops of surrounding buildings. Suddenly an immense white fortress loomed out of the thinning fog on the north bank, with rings of tall stone walls and coloured flags hanging limply. He bent down to shout this significant sighting to Miguel, and as he stood again he looked around in confusion, first left, then right, then straight ahead. Alarmingly there were houses emerging from the fog on all three sides! He shouted down to Miguel that they should immediately stop because the river had ended, and heard laughter in return. However he felt the ship slow to a stop and heard the splash of the anchor.

As the last of the fog was shredded by the breeze he tried to understand how a major river could end so suddenly and houses emerge on three sides. The taller houses were directly ahead so initially he looked left and right, but could see buildings stretching away into the distance in both those directions. He peered at the tallest houses in front of him and slowly tens of buildings were revealed to be on top of a great stone bridge that spanned the river surmounting twenty or more arches. Peering through the arches he could see dozens of smaller river craft navigating the waters beyond the bridge, some with small sails, though many were rowing boats. With a last look around at the wonder of the place he shook his head in awe and clambered down the rigging to join his comrades securing the ship.

The Steelyard

While Jacques and the crew stowed the sails and tidied the deck, he kept gazing at the town and the impressive bridge. He noticed a small boat being rowed out in their direction, and when he was certain it was coming to them he shouted out in Polish "Row boat approaching", and ran to lower a rope ladder over the side.

An overweight customs official climbed awkwardly aboard, and as he stood panting on the deck he glanced around him with a distasteful expression on his face. Within moments a slender, ferret-like assistant joined him. Georg came over and took them to the Captain's cabin where they received a small bag of coins. The assistant quickly flipped open a little writing table that hung from a cord around his neck, checked the coins, and scribbled in a ledger that lay on the table.

Jacques later learned that this payment was a berthing fee.

He saw Jakob inviting the official into his cabin and knew he would be describing the cargo and showing his League papers so there would be no duties incurred either. Moments later the assistant emerged with Georg and was taken below to confirm that the cargo matched the descriptions given by Jakob.

It was all over in minutes, and the odd looking pair quickly climbed over the side and were back in their boat rowing toward an impressive looking Customs House on the north bank.

The Captain called for Georg and after a hurried conference returned to his cabin whilst Georg pulled a coloured rag out of a locker and waved to the shoreline. Some ten minutes later he and Miguel nimbly went over the side rail and into a small sail boat that had pulled up alongside. The boat angled sharply away from the Stanislav, raised its sail again and whisked them away toward one of the arches under the bridge.

As he coiled a thick rope around a stanchion, Jacques kept peering in their direction to check on their progress and saw them turn toward the bridge. Despite the breeze filling the sail as it turned toward one of the central arches the small boat seemed to decelerate and took several minutes before it finally emerged on the far side of the bridge. As it headed toward the north bank Jacques lost sight of it amongst the other river traffic.

Enough time passed for the crew to have finished securing the ship before two other small sailing ferries shot from under the bridge and converged on the Stanislav, with Miguel in the lead boat. The Captain directed the crew and soon the ship's small crane was swinging their cargo of bales of fur and crates of honey over the side to the waiting boats.

After a dozen trips by the small ferries the unloading was complete, and the men drew straws to determine who would stay behind on the ship and who would visit the Steelyard and London town. Luckily Jacques accompanied Jakob in one of the last boats, his precious books wrapped in waterproof skins and tucked firmly under his arm. As their boat approached an arch in the bridge Jacques saw white water foaming through and realised the upriver water level was higher and the bridge pilings formed a kind of weir, with the river water surging around them making passage very difficult. Jakob explained how the bridge piers constricted the flow of the river and caused the height differential they had just navigated. Apparently at the wrong time of the year the rapids were dangerous, being the same height as a man, though that didn't always stop the foolish from trying to navigate them - often with deadly consequences.

Shortly thereafter they bumped up against a set of wooden stairs alongside a tidy wharf where their cargo was still being stacked by an industrious trio of warehousemen. Wading through the foot or so of water on the stairs, through wooden gates with carved Hanse eagles surmounting the gateposts, this last group from the Stanislav finally entered the Steelyard.

Jakob was immediately greeted by a large man in fine furs and crimson shirt with enormous puffed sleeves, who gave him a great bear hug and loudly called him brother, then led him away. Meanwhile, Georg led Jacques and the rest of the crew to a set of small apartments where they were told to settle in and then join Jakob and the Captain for a celebration feast in the communal dining hall later that evening. Each apartment held four crew members, yet felt considerably more luxurious than the hammocks that swung in the bowels of the Stanislav.

After securing his few belongings Jacques set off to explore the Steelyard. It was evidently a large self-contained community with all they needed for everyday living. The wharf and crane they had already seen beside the river of course, with the caretaker's private quarters beside them. North of these were a variety of apartments and quarters for visiting merchants and seamen of various social ranks. Jacques thought there was enough lodging space for at least 200 people, but the Steelyard was eerily quiet and he had only met a couple of dozen who were not from the Stanislav. Beyond the quarters was the dining hall and then finally a drinking hall, from the windows of which you could see down into the street of the city. There was even a small church. A couple of areas of the complex were guarded and Jacques was told they were for senior Hanse merchants only, but otherwise he had been unhindered in his access to the community. After weeks at sea he was keen to regain his land legs and spent some time walking through the gardens that graced the western edge of the Steelyard. With trees and shrubs and even a few early spring flowers it was a calming oasis where he paused to reflect quietly on his journeys of the last couple of years.

The meal that evening was a raucous affair, with sailors and merchants alike eating and drinking together, and to excess. As the meal wound down most of the crew moved into the drinking hall, where Jacques realised some of the local London merchants had been allowed in as well, although the Steelyard staff were careful not to allow them further into the complex. The locals and the Hanse merchants talked business but no contracts were signed nor money exchanged, which was probably a good thing as many were fairly unsteady on their feet. At one point later that evening there was an indignant outburst from one group of Hanse men who shouted angrily at a couple of the locals, something about a petition to the King by London merchants. Jacques was intrigued for a while, until his attention was drawn to a group of sailors who were going out into the town, to drink and gamble and find other entertainments. Some of the permanent staff gave them strict instructions to be back before midnight when the street doors would be locked. Jacques, who was exhausted, decided not to accompany them. Instead he was invited to join Jakob at a table in the corner, where he was introduced to a local bookseller. The man wasn't personally interested in Jacques' books but thought he knew someone who might be, and gave directions to his store which he encouraged Jacques to visit later that week.

No dice

After breakfast the next morning, Jakob and Georg assembled the Stanislav crewmen in the yard outside the warehouse.

Jakob called to the men, "I need three volunteers to work in the warehouse. I warn you it will be hot and dusty work. We'll be counting and sorting the goods stored there. Look lively now…"

Jacques volunteered straight away but it took a few moments before anyone else stirred. Reluctantly Marek and Piotr stepped forward.

Jakob smiled, and continued in a conversational tone, "I'm sorry but it will probably take us a few days," there was a titter of condescending laughter from the remaining crew, "so the warehouse caretaker has promised to give you beer and some of his wife's special kielbasa every afternoon until we are finished. Follow me now and I'll take you to the caretaker."

Jacques knew Jakob pretty well, and threw a penetrating glance at the merchant as they walked off to the warehouse. He mused to himself, *You have a mischievous glint in your eye, Jakob. What are you up to?*

Behind them he heard Georg call out, "The rest of you good-for-nothings, you're with me. We're going back to the Stanislav to careen the hull," there was a loud outpouring of groans and quite a few salty oaths. Jacques laughed to himself understanding why Jakob had been amused, meanwhile Piotr muttered to Marek, "Thank goodness we volunteered for warehouse duty. Careening is disgusting filthy work. Hauling the ship over onto its side is not so hard, but scraping the barnacles off the hull is slimy and smelly. They will be doing that for days."

The three sailors listened carefully to the old caretaker while he explained the work. Then Jacques asked, "Don't you have storemen here to keep the warehouse organised?"

"You must be Jacques? Jakob said you were a big inquisitive fellow and he was sure you would volunteer.

"Ja, I normally have two or three dozen storemen to organise and count the stock. We store it here for the merchants while they find customers and settle contracts, sometimes that might take them several months. There is English wool and cloth waiting to be exported, and a mixture of timber, furs, resin, flax, honey, wheat, and rye being imported from a variety of kontors. So we are constantly juggling goods in and out.

"But almost all my normal staff left this winter and returned to Gdansk."

Piotr was interested as well, "But why did they leave?"

"Over the last year there has been growing bitterness against foreigners. Not from most people, they are fine. But from organised groups of apprentices. Some evenings they are whipped up into angry mobs. A man was killed last month and another merchant's house was ransacked. They say we are stealing their jobs. It is all nonsense of course, they are just angry young men being manipulated by others for political motives."

Nodding sadly as he stroked his beard he continued, "But it can be scary sometimes, so many of my staff have left the Steelyard and travelled back to the security of their homes and families on the Baltic coast."

As a reward for their warehouse work, every evening they were permitted to leave the Steelyard after their supper and sample the delights of the nearby alehouses, taverns, and gambling dens. Initially Jacques had gone with Piotr and Marek, but quickly tired of the swaggering superiority they displayed when drinking together. So after a few days he had struck out on his own, trying a couple of different places each evening. A few days later he was wandering aimlessly when he spotted some friendly looking Portuguese sailors heading north from the riverside. He joined them as they walked past warehouses and churches, up Dowe Gate Hill, and into a narrow lane on the left. Here the upper stories of the buildings hung ever further over the lane, blocking the fading daylight and making the cobbled street seem very gloomy. About half way down the lane a blaze of light signalled an alehouse, and a signboard hanging from an upper floor announced it as *The Bishop's Skirts*. He liked the name and said he was going in and with a wave he parted company from the others.

It was a jolly place with a bright fire driving out the damp river air, and a genial mix of patrons. To ingratiate himself with his new companions he said his name was Jack, thinking that it might make him seem less foreign, and bought a couple of rounds of ale.

After that night he returned to the *Skirts* as often as he could, and the friendly little alehouse quickly became his favourite.

He encouraged his new drinking friends to talk about all sorts of things so that he could join in and gradually learn to mimic how they spoke. He was self-aware enough to recognise that yet again he was trying to acquire a *family,* to replace the one he had lost.

He learned that on Saturday nights they often played dice games, which got him excited because onboard the Stanislav he had managed to win quite often when gambling at dice. He realised however that the English played by different rules, and not wanting to lose his money through ignorance he decided to study the game before indulging himself. There would be no dice for him tonight.

On Saturday it was already dusk when he turned into the tavern and found a seat. He paid the barmaid a groat for a tankard of Dragon's Milk ale which had the creamy taste he preferred over the more sour Dagger ale, and settled in to watch the action. Halfway through the evening a well dressed Italian was steadily losing to a trio of Londoners. All four seemed new to the *Skirts*. The game was called *St Pauls*, and players bet on how close to a total of 31 they could get when rolling the dice successive times. The Italian had started out well but suddenly started losing badly, all his opponents scoring 29, 30 or 31 on consecutive turns.

Two tankards of ale suggested to Jack a pressing need to relieve himself, so he excused himself and dashed through light rain to the privy behind the alehouse yard. No longer desperate, he paused before making the return trip to see if the steady London drizzle was going to ease off. It was then that he heard shouted accusations and oaths coming from the inn. A moment later the three Londoners dragged the Italian out into the wet yard and started beating him, until he collapsed onto the ground and rolled into a ball trying to protect his head, which seemed to be already bleeding profusely. A few more kicks then one of them reached down and snatched away the purse from the man's belt, whilst a second reached inside his own coat. Seeing the flash of a blade in the moonlight Jack knew it was time to act or see the Italian gutted like a fish on the cobbles.

Instinctively he leapt from the shadows toward the attackers, arms stretched wide to increase his apparent size. He had no particular fighting skills, after all he was a sailor not a soldier, but he was big and strong and had the element of surprise. He knocked the nearest man off balance who then caromed into another, sending them both crashing to the cobbles in a tangle of arms and legs. The third was startled and belatedly drew back the fist that held the knife, ready to strike the shadowy adversary, but Jack's flying elbow caught him squarely, and luckily, in the face, and he was unconscious before he hit the ground.

Jack kicked at the knife and it span away into the darkness, then he reached down and scooped up the Italian. He half carried and half dragged the deadweight into the lane, and quickly zig-zagged southwards between the cottages and workshops. A rising halloo behind them suggested they were going to be followed by more than just the downed attackers, but the rain soon intensified and masked all sounds.

Soon they were in the warehouse district near the river, passing tall buildings and cranes that rose half-seen in the scattered moonlight. Jack quickly recognised it as an area called Three Cranes Walk, and knew from his explorations that it was immediately west of the Steelyard complex. He paused in the deeper shadows of a warehouse doorway to give the Italian time to catch his breath.

"Grazie, grazie," panted the older man, leaning over with hands on his knees, and sucking in lungfuls of cold air. "My name is …" more deep breaths, "My name is Cardano, Gerolamo Cardano. I am in your debt my young friend."

Jack could just pick out a growing number of muffled shouts ringing back and forth from the direction they had just come.

"You are not in debt Signore, you are in trouble, and now so am I. We need to get out of here quickly."

The attackers must have called on friends who were eager for some Saturday night fun hunting down a foreigner. Jack remembered the caretaker's words, and realised it wouldn't be hard to find a dozen or more xenophobic apprentices in any tavern with tensions running so high in the City. He looked around them, desperately trying to penetrate the gloom and the pouring rain, thinking hard. *Is that the wall of the Steelyard complex? It could be, yes. Too high to climb and no doors on this side. The apprentices are probably watching the main entrance already. How can we get inside safely without being seen?*

Movement on the river caught his eye. Leaving Cardano in the doorway, Jack ran to the quay and attracted the attention of a passing wherryman. Giving the man two pennies he told him to row directly across the river and to deliver two sacks to the other side. He quickly placed two sacks of wool from the wharf into the back of the wherry and waved the man off.

Returning to the Italian he steered him toward a set of external stairs, indicating that they should climb up the side of the warehouse. Cardano resisted even as he took the first couple of steps, "Up here? Are you sure?"

Jack pushed him up another couple of steps, all the while desperately trying to quieten the man's questions, "Shh, shh. Signore! The danger. Climb faster and stop talking," he hissed.

Cardano finally took the hint and they steadily climbed higher. As they neared the roofline a group of searchers came down Cousin Lane, directly between the warehouse and the wall of the Steelyard.

Jack and Cardano froze, instinctively knowing that if the searchers looked up they were doomed.

Then one apprentice leapt toward the dock and pointed out at the wherry, already half way across the Thames.

He has taken the bait, thought Jack excitedly.

By the light of the quarter moon the river sparkled silver where the oar blades rhythmically rose and fell, giving away the location of the wherry, and there in the back of the boat were surely the two huddled figures they sought. The men crowded on the quayside roared their displeasure and began shouting somewhat incoherent instructions to the wherryman trying to get him to return to shore.

Jack and Cardano took their opportunity to creep up the final stairs and onto the roof, out of sight.

Jack crept around the flat roof urgently looking for an escape route. With a sinking feeling he realised there was no way down except the stairs they had just taken. Gritting his teeth he glanced back toward Cardano realising he'd have to admit to his error. Just then the Italian leaned on one of cranes that were mounted on the roof and it started rotating under his weight, almost causing him to loose his balance and fall over.

It gave Jack an idea.

He unhooked a tether from a crane arm, and tested the jib's arc of rotation, then backing up with the jib he grabbed Cardano and told him to hold on tight. Without giving the man time to object he ran a few steps toward the edge of the rooftop and with a wild leap he launched them both across the lane. The jib swung them silently over the heads of the clustered mob below, then over the Steelyard wall. The pleasant garden he had so recently been resting in flashed by in a shadowy blur.

Jack had judged the strength of the swing just right and as their motion slowed he nimbly hooked his leg over the railing of the Steelyard tower and hopped onto its small balcony, pulling Cardano with him. He quickly swung the crane jib back the other way in a gentle arc. Searching around in minimal moonlight he finally found a small door, which opened onto a totally dark stairwell that plunged down inside the tower. They stumbled their way to the bottom of the stairs, where Jack quieted Cardano once more with a universal "Shh".

He knew that the tower was in the restricted section of the Steelyard complex, where sailors didn't have permission to be. He listened at the door and heard what he thought were servants clearing away the remains of a meal. Should they wait, or was there a way to get safely past them?

He turned to Cardano, and said "Your coat, quickly give it to me" and pulling it on to disguise his sailor's jerkin he then threw his arm over the Italian's shoulders and loudly burst through the door and entered the Hall like he had every right to be there, much to the surprise of the men still clearing the tables. With a nonchalance that he didn't feel, he waved drunkenly toward the ceiling and said in Polish, "And so as I said before dinner, Copernicus' theory can only be validated through careful study of the proper motions of the Planetae, seen from the tower on a clear night. Ah, here we are, let's get some more ale. You there, which way to the wein-haus?"

The servants just shook their heads at the mad antics of the Hanse merchants and returned to their work, but one grunted and jerked his head toward a door across the room, before he too carried on wiping down the tables and collecting empty jugs.

Jack weaved his way between tables to the opposite door, continuing to exclaim drunken nonsense from his recollection of *De Revolutionibus*. Upon exiting the room he quickly recognised the corridor from his earlier explorations, and as soon as the door closed behind them he marched Cardano through the Steelyard's maze of buildings until they reached the accommodation section on the far side. He checked one of the apartments and finding it empty he helped Cardano inside and lowered him to a chair.

They both burst into nervous chatter, amazed at their lucky escape. As Cardano took his coat back he asked, "Why did you take us to the roof instead of just getting in the boat?"

Jack paused and realised he hadn't even thought of that far simpler plan, "Um, yes. That might have worked too. But here I have friends and um, well I'll go and find one of them now."

He hurried out to find Jakob, who with his greater authority and wisdom he hoped to make a plan.

Up river

Jakob and Jacques returned to the apartment to find Cardano quite calmly cleaning the blood from his face with a cloth and a pitcher of water he had found in the room.

Standing, he bowed and in flawless Polish thanked them both for saving his life and for giving him shelter. Switching to English he went on to explain, "I am a physician and mathematician, perhaps you have heard of me, visiting these damp and miserable shores from fair Padua. I was playing dice in that tavern, and doing rather well I might add, when I noticed the other players were starting to get winning dice rolls that were improbable and indicated to me that the dice were weighted. When I accused them of cheating they acted in concert to drag me into the yard and started beating me. If young Jack had not intervened I fear I might not have survived their attentions."

"Wait a moment please. Who is this *Jack* who helped you?" asked Jakob, clearly confused.

"Ah, that is the name I have been using when out in the city amongst the English," replied Jacques, a little embarrassed.

Jakob waved Cardano to a chair, "Signore. I am so sorry for your troubles, really I am. Normally we would offer a fellow foreigner all the hospitality and shelter you need, for as long as you need it." He hemmed and hawed for a moment which Jack thought quite uncharacteristic, "Look. There is no polite way to ask this. There is an unruly crowd in the street outside our gates, they are brandishing torches and generally complaining that the Steelyard is harbouring fugitives from justice. Do you know anything of this accusation?"

Cardano looked confused, "They cannot mean me, surely? I only arrived in the city yesterday. I have been requested to visit the notable mathematician Dr John Dee to discuss Euclid and also to consult on his new paradoxal compass that he has written to me about. I hope to use information on his compass in a book I am writing. And last week I was in Scotland, an even wetter country I might add, although it has some redeemingly pleasant moorland. Anyway, I was consulting on the health of the Archbishop of St Andrews, John Hamilton. As you may know he cannot speak, in fact he has not said a word for several years, and indeed can hardly breathe. I have prescribed a cure, which my servant has stayed to administer for the next couple of months, and I am very hopeful he will make a full recovery."

Jakob, removed his cap and scratched at his thinning hair, before hesitantly asking, "The gamblers in the tavern…did you hear any names? Maybe they are not simple ale-hogs but men of some influence?"

Cardano thought for a moment, "During the game they used the names John, Richard, and the third one, mm, ah yes, he had a full black beard, squared off at the bottom, you know, like a spade, he was called Nathaniel I think. Does that help?"

Jakob shook his head, "Not to me, no. Jacques, why don't you go and check with the caretaker? He lives in London full time and might know the names of common troublemakers."

A few minutes later Jack returned with a troubled look, "There is a man. Tall and with a square black beard. Nathaniel Panshawe. He is a known instigator of violent mobs. Apparently last year when a group of Thames Porters tried to create a fifth Brotherhood, it was Nathaniel who led the gangs that broke their resolve. There were violent clashes between dozens of men, with several found floating in the river in the following days. No one ever found out whether he had been hired by the four Brotherhoods or by the merchants, or even just led the mob for devilment. It seems possible that you have inadvertently antagonised the one man on the riverside who can whip up a mob of men willing to take on anything and anyone in their path. The caretaker is worried that Nathaniel will be able to influence the port authorities sufficiently to force an inspection of the Steelyard, even though we are normally free of their jurisdiction. And then if you are found here, that will be bad for us all. He will join us shortly."

Cardano blanched and tried to explain that he had not done anything, merely called out their cheating, and that they had already stolen all his money, so why persist in tracking him down?

Just then the caretaker entered the room, followed by two of the merchants who were semi-permanently stationed at the Steelyard. They took Jakob to one side with worried looks and gestures.

After a hurried consultation Jakob explained that Cardano would have to leave. Tonight. The mob at the gates had doubled in size, and more were joining them by the minute. Flaming torches and a few weapons had been seen. An informer had managed to sneak into the Steelyard by boat and said that the mob's grievance was now mostly a complaint about the Steelyard's special trading privileges, although there was a strong undercurrent of general xenophobia and from some of the crowd there were still shouts of "hang the papist".

Jack looked at the terrified Cardano and at the resolute merchants and caretaker, and stood up hesitantly. "This is partly my fault, I brought Cardano here, thinking it was to safety but not realising the trouble on our heels. If you will all allow it, I will take him away, perhaps further up river, and leave the crowd at the doors with nothing."

Jakob glowed, his pride in his mentee's words evident to all. Another whispered conference sealed the decision, and the two were hastily led to the loading dock. No lights were used, in case anyone was watching. A skiff was already moored to the stairs and as Cardano was helped into the back Jakob pulled Jack aside. "Here are your books, and a purse of ready money. If you will allow it, I will keep investing your trading capital until we meet again. Leave messages for me at any Kontor. And Jacques…" he choked off whatever he had been going to say, and turned his head away, though not before Jack had seen a tear glistening in his eye. Then a brief but somewhat embarrassing bear hug, and Jakob turned and was swallowed by the night.

"Quickly," unseen hands hustled Jack into the business end of the skiff and tossed the painter in a coil at his feet. As they were pushed away from the stairs Jack marvelled at the speed of operation. Only a couple of minutes had passed since the decision had been made in the apartment.

Cardano looked around wildly, and with rising panic evident in his voice he asked in a low voice "Do you know how to row?" Jack almost laughed out loud, but stifled it, and as an answer started pulling steadily toward the middle of the flow, glad to find the tide helping them travel quickly up river.

Chapter 10 - Exhortation

March 1552
Rome, Italy

Villa Giulia

The shimmering heat haze over Rome heralded yet another hot March day.

The tall churchman stooped as he exited a small stone capella in the garden of a grand house. Perspiration immediately started beading on his forehead, despite the shade offered by the flowering trees of the garden.

Cardinal Reginald Pole had spent the last hour at prayer in the cool privacy of the garden chapel, and blinked rapidly as his eyes adjusted to the bright midmorning sun. He breathed in the fragrant aroma of the garden and gave a thankful blessing to God.

A glance toward the house revealed Alberto, his private secretary, pacing back and forth with the day's letters and dispatches under his arm. Pole's pulse quickened as he allowed himself to imagine that he might finally receive his long overdue invitation for an audience with Pope Julius. With an effort of will he quelled his building anticipation and forced himself to walk slowly along the winding garden path past a statue of Athena, that doubled as a sundial, and continued around an ornamental fishpond. He automatically adopted a pious attitude, clasping his prayerbook in front of him with rosary beads entwined around it and his head bowed deeply enough for his bushy beard to rest on his chest. To a casual observer he would have appeared calm, but in reality his mind was a seething cauldron of concerns and injustices. He tried to think of other matters, or to clear his mind entirely in the manner of the eastern mystics he had read about, but it was no use. The harder he tried to divert his mind from his current humiliation and past failures the more his thoughts turned back to them.

He paused as he entered the welcoming shade of the loggia and ground his teeth in quiet but intense frustration. Despite being a senior cardinal of the Catholic church, which meant he was arguably one of the hundred most important men in Europe, he believed that his entire life had been a series of missed opportunities, where he had been ignored or misjudged or passed over, whilst less able men had achieved advancement. He could hardly tolerate the injustice of it any longer. He felt like a keg of black powder, ready to explode at any moment.

He thought back to his recent journey from the ecumenical council in Trento, a small walled city in the Alps, where he was the one of the three Papal Legates representing the new Pontiff during the discussions on the Counter-Reformation. The trip back from Trento had been an arduous eight days, through freezing mountain passes, then gradually descending into more temperate countryside, until they reached the broad sunlit meadows of Umbria and finally, Rome. He had sent Alberto ahead to rent appropriate accommodation, resulting in this house in the expensive Borgo district, between the Tiber and the Vatican, conveniently located so that Pole could easily attend on the Pope as soon as he was invited.

Then nothing. For eight long humiliating days. No summons, nor even an acknowledgment from Pope Julius. His temper, always simmering close to the surface, had boiled over, and he had sent Alberto on multiple errands, often during the hottest parts of the day, gathering the opinions of the few other cardinals who were still in the city, and relaying messages to and from the ambassadors of Spain, France, the German Principalities, and the Holy Roman Emperor, in a self-important frenzy.

With his eyes closed he clenched his hand so tightly on the rosaries that the beads dug painfully into his palm. He knew his mind was following a familiar pattern and descending into near despair, but he couldn't stop it, indeed he almost relished it, as though greeting a faithful friend, always waiting there to embrace him.

Two short years ago he had been close, so very close, to achieving success and being elected Pope himself after the death of Paul III. He had worked so hard for it, striking deals, making promises and agreements, even providing a little financial encouragement where necessary. He had played the three main factions off against each other, sliding through as a compromise candidate to all. Well almost all. But then it had slipped away from him.

He had started with the tepid support of Charles V, the Holy Roman Emperor, and thus all the cardinals in his faction. Yes, he got this support mainly because he wasn't French, that is true, but every vote counted no matter the reason. Perceptively, he had promised the Farnese faction that he would support their family claim to the Duchy of Parma, however dubious, so their allied cardinals voted for him too.

A few judiciously placed bribes had taken him from there to within two votes of the required two thirds majority. Just two votes short!

The French cardinals, who had initially been absent from the conclave, now started trickling in, led by Charles of Guise, the Cardinal of Lorraine. As their numbers increased and Guise's bribes outmatched his own, Pole saw his support ebb away, until another compromise candidate, Giovanni Del Monte had emerged triumphant, choosing the name Pope Julius III.

He had tried to accept it as God's will, but whilst he professed a belief in justification by faith over works he didn't believe in predestination. Rather, in his heart, he blamed a living person. The same person he blamed for all his problems.

King Henry VIII of England.

Yes, Henry is already dead, he thought testily. *But he deserves to burn in Hell for all eternity.*

Angrily he kicked out at a potted plant. The pot cracked and spilled dark soil onto the path.

He squeezed his eyes shut and every fibre of his being shook with hatred at the memory of the fat, lecherous, self indulgent, monster. *Yes monster!*

Henry was actually his distant cousin, so he could easily bring the family tree to mind, particularly the key personages.

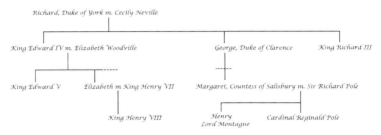

They shared the same great-grandparents, Richard, Duke of York and Cecily Neville, but to Pole that is where the similarities ended.

He had been thrust into the clergy against his will, because his mother could not provide for all her children. Why could she not provide for them? Because of the miserly King Henry that is why.

Then Henry had the audacity to ask for his assistance, seemingly oblivious to his role as Pole's tormenter. He wanted help persuading continental theologians of the justness of his request for an annulment from Queen Catherine of Aragon. Pole had tried, but his heart wasn't in it, and even when Henry tried to bribe him with a bishopric, he had disagreed and instead had fled the country until the pressure relented.

He even tried to warn Henry of the dangers of pursuing a marriage with the Boleyn whore, but his suggestions were angrily rebuffed.

There had been a blaze of hope for him when the Spanish ambassador, Eustace Chapuys, had promoted Pole's own dynastic claim to the English throne, and suggested a marriage with Henry's daughter Mary to seal the deal, but it had come to nothing.

Then it had all spiralled out of control.

Thomas Cromwell had written, on behalf of the King, requesting Pole's support of the King's upcoming marriage and of his claim to Supremacy of the Church in England. Pole's answer, and he smiled maliciously at the memory, had been a theological treatise that he had published, called *Pro ecclesiasticae unitatis defensione.* In the treatise he had taken a delight in denouncing Henry's marriage requests and his attempted Supremacy of the Church, and in fact had urged foreign princes to depose Henry.

His smile faded as he recalled his own mother's angry letter to him denouncing his folly. He knew Henry would have pressured her to write thus, and it only fuelled his hatred of Henry all the more.

This *folly* had however brought him promotion to Cardinal, something he had not been sure he really wanted, but it meant more prestige so he had accepted. Then it brought an appointment to Papal Legate for England. This he liked, because he felt it really rubbed Henry's nose in it.

The Pope then ordered him to several tasks that culminated in trying to organise an embargo of England with the assistance of the Holy Roman Emperor. Tasks that he gleefully executed.

Maddened by Pole's treachery, Henry had arrested all of Pole's family, executing most of them. He had even sent assassins to kill Pole himself, but they had fortunately failed and Pole had built a capella to give thanks at his then residence in the Appio Latino quarter of Rome.

Henry, the vindictive egomaniac, had then imprisoned Pole's blessed mother, Lady Margaret Pole, Countess of Salisbury, in the Tower of London. Finally he had ordered her execution.

Worse even than that, was the report from Chapuys who claimed she had been butchered, the axeman taking multiple wild swings before finally severing her head. *And why had Henry done this to a gentle and noble woman? Revenge, that was why! What kind of monster was he? It was intolerable!*

Henry had of course cut off all Pole's English benefices so he was exiled from England and had no financial support, unlike his papal adversaries. His meagre savings and the loans he could raise had been insufficient to bribe enough cardinals during conclave, and now he faced ruin.

Even though Henry was dead and buried, his bastard child Edward was reigning as King, the son of Henry's third supposed wife. *How many wives does a man need for heaven's sake?*

Edward was holding fast to the Reformed religion that Henry had allowed to flourish. Indeed the child seemed wholly committed to the Reformation, even though Catholic spies all reported a general level of unrest in the population, especially outside London, and a desire to return to the true faith.

Who better to lead them on that journey back into the fold? Who better to return them to the grace of God? Who better to bring them back from being heathen outcasts with damned souls? Who better than me, Reginald Pole? I could have been king myself if fate had not intervened to rob me. Please God, grant me one small opportunity ... and appropriate financial backing of course, and I will do your works to my dying day.

Breathing deeply he fought to bring his raging mind under control, then forced his feet to move again, hoping that action would quell his turmoil.

Even while standing under the loggia yet more sweat had sprung out under Pole's zucchetto, and as he entered his office he closed the door behind him, ripped off the skullcap, and wiped his head with a small cloth. He barely had time to replace the cap and to compose himself behind his desk before an urgent knock on the door announced

Alberto.

His secretary bustled into the room with his armful of correspondence, and there, at the top of pile, in pride of place, bearing the papal seal, was a slim letter from the Curia. Finally!

He snatched it from the pile and taking up a stiletto he broke the seal and hastily opened the letter.

It was a summons to attend on the Pope immediately.

At Villa Giulia.

Pole muttered an unchurchman-like oath under his breath. Villa Giulia was the Pope's palatial new house that was still only partially constructed. It was in the Vigna Vecchia area of Rome, on the slopes of Monte Parioli, on the opposite side of the River Tiber and on the north edge of the city. It would take at least an hour to reach and would be torture in this heat. He would have far preferred to visit the Pope in the nearby Vatican.

Telling Alberto to arrange a closed carriage for the trip, Pole left the room to prepare for a visit to His Holiness.

When he reappeared, Pole was dressed in his best cassock and pellegrina, a dark red coloured ensemble that he believed lent him an air of deep piety. Giving final orders to various servants he exited the house, and with a frown he walked toward the waiting carriage. As he climbed in he wondered why Alberto was looking more shifty than usual, and especially wondered why he seemed to be fingering something under his tunic.

As he climbed toward the cushioned seat in the shade of the carriage Pole noticed a dark shape sitting in the opposite corner, and, fearing an attack of some sort, he loosed the blind with a snap and let bright sunshine fill the interior.

The very rich, very self-assured, Frenchman, Charles of Guise, Duke of Chevreuse, Cardinal of Lorraine, apologised if his presence had startled his fellow Cardinal, without managing to sound like he meant it.

Pole quickly recovered from his shock and replied with a formal greeting of his own, as though they were still close colleagues and not political rivals.

His thoughts were mentally lashing Alberto.

That greedy churl Alberto must have accepted a bribe to allow Guise the opportunity to ambush me like this. He'd probably been feeling the weight of his purse beneath his tunic - no doubt bulging with French gold. I will reprimand him on my return - and maybe confiscate the gold!

Meanwhile, Guise had started talking in an unctuous tone.

"My dear Pole, our interests are converging. Let me assure you that my family's assistance would be available to you, if you should need it, in the months ahead."

He inclined his head to acknowledge the offer, while thinking furiously. *What is the duplicitous French bastard talking about, and what does he know that I don't.*

Instead of revealing his ignorance he merely waited for the Frenchman to continue.

The carriage pulled away from the house with the smooth motion only possible with the best teams of horses and the most modern carriage. Pole realised it was Guise's own carriage and team, which he would no doubt have noticed before he entered if he hadn't been so caught up in his thoughts. Cursing again at his secretary's greed, he reset the blind to keep out the heat, aware that the air temperature in the carriage had risen by at least ten degrees even if the political temperature had plummeted.

The slight breeze caused by the movement of the carriage through the torpid air was welcome to both men, swaddled as they were in their clerical robes, and Guise used their mutual discomfort to make small talk at first, and then choosing his words carefully, he starting discussing the political situation in England, Scotland and France.

"You know of course my dear sister Mary of Guise, the widow of the late James V of Scotland," a stiff nod from Pole, "There is some chance she will be persuaded to take over the Regency of Scotland from the Earl of Arran, and preserve the country for her daughter Mary. My sister will ally Scotland firmly with France, and of course she follows the true faith, and so would prefer to see England adhere to Catholicism as well," and here he paused significantly, "Under the current king or another... or even under a princess."

"If anything, um, untoward were to happen, say," and here Guise peered at Pole significantly, "to the sickly King Edward, then his sister Mary Tudor will inherit the crown by the terms of her late father's will, and she will need to gather true and powerful men around her to help bring England back to the Mother Church. In such a circumstance we would use all our influence to help you, my dear Cardinal Pole, to gain leadership of the Church in England, so you can provide help to the Princess when she needs it the most. No doubt she would be very grateful also."

Pole, merely nodded, but his mind was racing.

Did I hear him right? His family will help me to become the Archbishop of Canterbury, Primate of all England?

I suppose my return to Canterbury would remove me from Rome, leaving Guise as the most influential cardinal over this weak buffoon of a pope.

Dynastically, it would help ensure England didn't align too closely with Spain… which would otherwise be all too natural with Mary Tudor being cousin to Charles V, King of Spain, the Holy Roman Emperor. And Charles is of course currently battling Henry II of France in the Italian wars.

And I do have a good relationship with Charles…

Guise interrupted Pole's deliberations, "Of course your expenses whilst preparing for such a great undertaking are likely to be considerable, and as your friend the House of Guise would insist on being allowed to help fund such Godly work."

Pole didn't appreciate being ambushed in the carriage in this way, but being in debt to the moneylenders who had funded his attempt at the papacy was no fun either, and taking French money was always a double joy, first to have it and second to deprive them of it.

"Of course you will need to exercise canon law to deal severely with the heretics that have led the Reformation, men like Cranmer," and with a sneer his personal disdain for Pole shone through as he added, "I wonder if you would have the stomach for that?"

The carriage turned sharply right, swaying Pole against the padded side. He lowered the window blind to check where they were, just in time to see the towering bulk of the Castle Sant'Angelo pass to their rear as they clattered over cobbles onto the Ponte Sant'Angelo.

A consummate politician, Pole turned his mind away from Guise's insult by changing the subject. He gestured through the window, "Amazing to think that this bridge is fourteen hundred years old, is it not? And look there, the new statue of Saint Paul, by Paulo Romano. Whenever I see it I am reminded of the conversion of Saul of Tarsus, and thus Paul's idea that salvation is based on faith and not good works nor works of the law. Canon law or otherwise. I know some think that heretical…" He smiled sweetly to Guise, whilst he imagined taking the statue's broken sword and plunging it through the Frenchman's body. Several times. His hand twitched in response as though itching to perform the actual deed.

His mind screamed, *Then we would see who has the stomach for action!*

As the carriage slowed to a halt outside an elegant mansion Guise said, "I will leave you now. Please keep my carriage at your disposal for the rest of the day. Whatever happens with Pope Julius, remember my offer." And then he was gone and the carriage continued its journey north out of town.

An hour later Pole had finally managed to calm down, as the carriage slowed and described a wide semi-circle, then halted in the shade of a spreading umbrella pine tree. Servants immediately opened the carriage door and helped Pole down.

He was facing a two storey house with a pleasing symmetry, two tall windows on each side of the central stone entrance. Pole had heard that a large fortune was being spent on the villa but he couldn't understand how that could be, it didn't seem much larger or grander than the house he was renting in Borgo. *Perhaps a hundred feet wide. Not so big.*

He entered the building and was guided to a reception room on the right. While he waited he looked around the room and marvelled at the beautiful decoration on the walls and ceiling, with rich geometric patterns and nymphs cavorting amongst painted clouds. *Expensive yes, but a fortune, surely not.*

A cleric entered through a door at the rear of the room, passing a guardsman who was wearing a colourful red and yellow striped uniform. The cleric bowed hastily to the English cardinal, and invited Pole to follow him to meet the Pope.

Pole followed the man as he retraced his steps, out and into a magnificent, semi-circular loggia surrounding a huge courtyard.

Pole stopped in awe. The loggia was tunnel vaulted and supported by twenty-five foot tall marble columns. The vaulted ceiling and the walls were covered in more exquisite patterns and paintings in vivid colours, like the room he'd just left. Directly in front of Pole was the main archway from the loggia to the courtyard, decorated with paintings of two naked men drawing apart a curtain. He blushed deep red to match his cassock and when he tore his eyes away he saw the cleric watching him with a faint knowing smile, and a very Italian shrug. Beyond the cleric the courtyard loomed hugely. It was being criss-crossed by at least a dozen people, some servants, some gentlemen, some churchmen. Those furthest away at the other end of the courtyard looked tiny, because of the distance, and a dawning realisation settled on Pole that the building was actually very very large, and perhaps did require the enormous fortune being spent on it.

The cleric gestured to the Englishman and led the way around one curve of the loggia. Part way around they had to step out into the heat of the courtyard to avoid a set of scaffold and the artists working from it to paint the ceiling. One of the artists called down to a bearded man who seemed to be directing the work, who Pole recognised as the famed Giorgio Vasari, the artist and architect. Clearly intent on giving the Englishman a grand tour, the cleric led the way across the remaining courtyard, through the simmering heat, to the far building where they ascended an exterior staircase to the next floor before entering into the shaded interior.

They continued directly through this building, passing an intersection with a corridor on both sides. Down the right-hand corridor movement caught Pole's eye. He glimpsed a man partially wrapped in a bedsheet slip out of one room and scuttle in the direction of another. Shocked, Pole hesitated, as did the other figure, who after a moment's pause purposely let the sheet fall and then sauntered casually to the other room and disappeared from sight. His mind reeling, Pole stumbled forward to catch up with his guide.

The tour continued for many minutes as the cleric clearly enjoyed what he thought was Pole's continued appreciation of the beauty of the building, until they finally emerged onto a balcony where three marbled arches looked out over a central sunken pleasure garden, and across to another three story building. Down below a central fountain tinkled in a sunken grotto, surrounded by dozens of prelates leisurely enjoying alfresco dining and drinking. This was clearly where the party was. The cleric smiled and with a sweep of his arm said "Welcome to the Nymphaeum of the Villa Giulia".

Two sets of marble stairs curved down to the main level. Choosing the right-hand set the cleric led the way down past statues of nymphs and Roman Gods in niches, until finally Pole was thrust amidst the crowd of cardinals and curia officials drinking, dining, and chatting, in the cool centre of the nymphaeum. As he moved through the throng he was greeted by normally staid colleagues who were clearly having a good time and assumed he was there to have one too. Around the dining area Pole glimpsed the shadowy figures of both men and women flitting down passageways to grottos and private rooms. Too stunned to do or say anything he let himself be steered through the crowd towards the far side, where Pope Julius III reclined.

As they progressed through the diners a young figure in cardinal's red darted through the crowd and then abruptly slowed down and covered the final few feet to the Pope with a languid ease, where they greeted each other with a familiar embrace, and shockingly, a kiss on the mouth.

The cleric brought Pole forward the last few yards and announced him, whereupon Pope Julius rose to greet him. Julius turned and gesturing to the other newly arrived cardinal, who was introduced as Innocenzo Ciocchi del Monte, Secretary Intimus to the Pope. The Secretary Intimus turned toward Pole, who's jaw fell when he recognised the face of the man with the bedsheet. Just how *intimus* were the Pope and the Secretary? And indeed who else had the secretary so recently been intimus with?

Innocenzo leaned close, whispering a few words to the Pope, then turned and throwing a dazzling smile at Pole, walked away, quickly blending into the crowd.

Venetian Ducats

"Walk with me", and with that simple command Pope Julius led Cardinal Pole away from the crowd and into a guarded passageway. A few turns later the corridor terminated at a double door, that opened for them as they approached. Beyond was a large, beautifully decorated room with a walnut desk and comfortable chairs. Clearly this was the Pope's private study.

He gestured to one of the chairs, which Pole gratefully sank into. Meanwhile Julius continued to stroll around the room, admiring the art and stroking the graceful limbs of the statues in a tantalising way, all the time discoursing on the piety of the artists and the brilliance of their work to the greater glory of God.

Finally he returned to the desk and quickly wrote a brief note, which he sanded and then sealed with hot wax.

Bringing the one-way conversation to what seemed like the point, Julius lamented the lost souls of the English people, and especially the sadly misguided King Edward.

After a few minutes he became more specific, "Edward is the cancer at the heart of this pestilential reformation in England. If he were not there and, say, Mary were to replace him, then true religion could return and flourish, and all would be well. See that it happens, for the good of the souls of your countrymen, and for yourself, if not for the Church."

Placing the sealed letter in Pole's hand, he continued, "Do not fail me in this brother cardinal. When you succeed, your countrymen will be returned to God's grace, and you will have power in abundance. See Cardinal Ricci on your way out, he will furnish you with the wherewithal to achieve God's will in this matter."

Julius nodded to a previously unseen attendant, then shuffled some other papers on his desk whilst the attendant approached and gestured for Pole to follow him.

Pole was led out of the room and back to the main section of the villa, where an immaculately attired Cardinal Ricci took the letter from Pole, and nodding to himself left the room, then returned mere moments later followed by two servants with a small but heavy chest that they carried out to Pole's waiting carriage.

Somewhat dazed, Pole remounted the steps to the carriage and was whisked away, on the journey back to his palazzo. With some trepidation and mounting greed, Pole reached down to the chest. He twisted the key and flipped up the lid to reveal a glittering mass of golden coins. He dug his hand in as deep as he could and lifted some of the coins from the chest, his eyes growing bigger as he saw a mixture of Venetian Ducats, French Ecu, Florentine Florins and even some Gulden from the German states. He spent many happy minutes digging into the pile and comparing size and weight of the coins. It was a long time since he had seen anything so splendid. Fortunately the return trip was no faster than the outward trip, and thus gave Pole time to come to terms with his new wealth and with everything else he had seen and heard.

That evening it required two hours of contemplative prayer in the private sanctuary of his cappella for Pole to formulate the method for safely striking back at the upstart Tudors, avenging his family, and starting back on the path to his ascendancy.

Keeping him safe he would have the alliance of the Guise family, and the blessing of the Holy Father. Oh, and a large box of papal gold, and promises of French gold when he wanted it. He was so pleased with the day's outcome that he didn't even discipline Alberto. Although he did confiscate his bag of coins.

Part II

"Thoughts black, hands apt, drugs fit, and time agreeing;
  Confederate season, else no creature seeing;
  Thou mixture rank, of midnight weeds collected,
  With Hecate's ban thrice blasted, thrice infected,
  Thy natural magic and dire property
  On wholesome life usurp immediately."
                    - William Shakespeare. Hamlet.

Chapter 11 - Complementation

Friday the 1st of April 1552
Richmond, West of London

Kat Arden

Jack threw down the hand of cards he held and exclaimed, "How could you know that I held the Pope of Diamonds?"

Gerolamo sighed, and started to explain his theory again, "I didn't *know* Jack, it was just extremely likely given the total number of cards and the cards we have already seen played. Think of it this way…"

But Jack had had enough, and snorting his disgust he said, "I cannot listen to your over-long explanation again, not on an empty belly. I'll go out and get us some food and drink for our supper." With that he rose from the table and reached for his cloak and money bag.

Gerolamo gathered the discarded cards and quickly shuffled them, fanned them out, split the pack and shuffled again, before squaring up the pack and placing it in a neat pile on the table. Then with exasperation evident in his voice he said, "This last month of secretive travelling from one village to another has been very trying. And, I know, I know, I have not always seemed appreciative. But I really do thank you for accompanying me. We both know that I would not have survived on my own. I just hope we gain some definite information about Dr Dee's location soon. This impoverished existence is almost more than I can endure. If I had been able to stay in London a few more days I am sure I could have contacted several scholars and learned exactly where Dee resides and then we could have gone straight there. Alas, that dratted mob outside the Steelyard put a stop to that. I curse my weakness for gambling, I truly do, but watching the run of cards does permit me the occasion to perfect my mathematics of probability don't you think?"

Jack had lingered at the door to see if Cardano had anything useful to say, but now let it bang shut as an unspoken comment on the Italian's whining.

As he headed down the stairs he lifted his hood in anticipation of the cold dank air that seemed to swirl through this little town every evening.

He stepped out into the street and shivered. For a brief moment he tried to recall the warmth of the golden sunshine he had enjoyed in his youth, but the miserable dampness oppressed him, and with a little shake to throw off the partial memories he turned down Water Lane toward the square where the vendors gathered to sell their wares. Richmond Palace was only five minutes walk to the north, but looking at the poverty of the people thronging in the street it could have been five hundred miles. He passed the butcher's stall with skinned rabbits and wild game hanging from hooks, and he regretted that he had no fire nor implements to cook such meat even if he had the funds to buy them, which he didn't.

His bag of coins was considerably diminished after a month of slow travel by foot since abandoning their dinghy near Lambeth. He was unused to paying for food and accommodation and was alarmed at their rate of expenditure, and the accompanying reduction in funds.

He drifted unconsciously towards the smell of roasted chestnuts offered by a hunchbacked old crone in a shawl, and bought a dozen for a farthing. As he popped one into his mouth, savouring its warmth and taste, he caught sight of an attractive young woman across the square haggling with a tinker and his pulse quickened involuntarily. A huddle of chatting goodwives drifted in front of him, and though he craned his neck to better see the girl, when the small crowd moved on she was gone. He looked all around in some alarm at having lost sight of her, but to no avail, and shrugging, he permitted himself a little smile of self pity.

A shouted cry caught his attention, "*Pasties*...Get a mouth watering pasty here. Fresh today."

As if under a witch's spell his mouth watered immediately. He knew of this kind of pie, it was baked without a dish, folded over on itself. He had encountered it on his trips to Great Yarmouth on the *Stanislav*. He remembered that the townsfolk there proudly claimed to have an ancient King's Charter for making the pasty. The pie filling could be anything from turnip or other vegetables, to venison, or even herrings. Another great benefit of the pasty was its unique "D" shape, it could be easily carried and would stay warm for several hours making a wholesome meal that would be very welcome right now.

He quickened his pace and bought the last two that were available, one venison and one pork, then retraced his steps back to the accommodation he and Cardano were sharing.

Jack climbed the steps to their top floor room and called out as he entered, "Gerolamo I bring us wonderful pies to eat. You must try this pasty, a rare delicacy in this God forsaken land…"

He stopped abruptly, eyes trying to focus on the blade that had appeared suddenly against his throat, hovering motionless, yet with deadly potential.

Slowly, he let his gaze travel along the length of the steel blade, over the gloved hand and the leather vambrace, to the white linen shirt. He couldn't see further without turning his head - and that didn't seem like a good idea. Still, he wasn't too worried. Years as a slave and then the junior in a crew of sailors had taught him that fear didn't serve you well, and anyway, if the wielder of the knife had meant to harm him he would be dead by now.

He extended his arms toward the table and slowly, ever so slowly, lowered the food onto it, the knife tracking his every movement. Ahead and to his left he saw Gerolamo all trussed up on the trestle bed like a poached deer, with a gag in his mouth, his eyes bulging out as he silently watched the little drama play out in front of him.

"Well, what do you want? My food? My purse?" and casually Jack tossed his depleted purse onto the table beside the food. He sensed the person circle further behind him, but he still did not dare turn his head, the knife was too close. Something here wasn't quite right though. The angle of the knife implied his attacker was shorter than he was, and the smell….there was no smell! He was used to people smelling of something, their profession perhaps, or of the sea at best, but this person had no smell at all. Before he had time to draw any conclusions the knife was withdrawn and a booted foot kicked him violently forward so he barely missed the table and fell headfirst beside Gerolamo. Twisting agilely he was about to spring to his feet when he saw the blade again, directly in front of his face.

His eyes lifted from the knife to the attacker and he let out a small exclamation as he recognised the girl from the square. She might be a girl, but she had bested him in this fight and had a naked blade threatening his face, so he sat down and tried to appear non-threatening. In fact he smiled. It wasn't a calculated ploy, he just couldn't help it. The girl was beautiful. Dark, smokey, almond shaped eyes in a clear pale face, with dark hair pulled into a braided ponytail, and ruby red lips. A full length cloak hung from her shoulders, and he saw she wore men's hose tucked into good quality knee length leather boots.

The vicious point of the knife touched the tip of his nose, "You've got nothing to smile about. Now tell me. Who are you, and why are you searching for John Dee?" Then before he could answer, "Quickly now" she urged, gesturing with the knife.

Jack saw no reason to lie, "My trussed up companion here is Dottore Gerolamo Cardano, a renowned mathematician and physician from Padua," but with his discomfort and embarrassment needling him, and thinking he might sound clever, he sarcastically added, "Perhaps you've read some of his work, *Ars Magna*, or *De Subtilitate*?". The knife, which had started to retreat, leapt towards him again. The girl's irritation was evident and, he realised, justified, "I advise you to be more careful with your choice of comments, else I may be less careful with my knife."

Jack gulped, and wondered why he'd chosen to provoke the girl so unwisely. He started again. "My name is Jack. I'm helping Dottore Cardano find Dr Dee so they can consult on some mathematical theories. We don't want any trouble, and we haven't hurt anyone. Now perhaps you can explain who you are, why the Dottore is tied up, and why you're threatening me with that blade?"

The girl looked at him carefully, looking for signs of evasion or deceit. Seeing none she relaxed a little and gesturing that Jack should stay where he was she carefully sheathed the knife and sat down. "Untie your friend, I want to ask him a question." Jack did so, and Gerolamo coughed as he spat out some of the rough fibres of the gag and massaged his abraded wrists.

Looking at Gerolamo she asked in a sing-song cadence that Jack recognised as Italian, "*Quanti figli hai e quali sono i loro nomi?*"

Startled, Gerolamo replied in the same language, "*Ho tre bambini. Giovanni, Chiara, e Aldo. Ma, mia moglie, dolce Lucia, è morta adesso. Hanno bisogno del loro padre. Per favore non uccidermi.*"

Nodding in confirmation of the information, she replied "I'm not going to kill you, Dottore. But if your three children need you so badly now that your wife is dead, why are you dawdling around the English countryside with this flat-footed oaf?" This last comment came with a nod toward Jack, who bridled at the name, whilst simultaneously checking out his feet.

Gerolamo quickly explained that Jack had saved him from a street gang, and was helping him search for Dee, who had requested a consultation with him, before he returned home to Padua.

She walked over to the window and looked out at the street which was almost empty of people, then she paced around their tiny garret, inspecting their few possessions, mainly books, as she introduced herself.

"My name is Katherine Arden. You can call me Kat. I work for Doctor Dee. He sent me to find you when you disappeared from London."

Gesturing to the table, "You should eat your food while it is still warm. Then you will be coming with me Dottore. Tonight. You too flat-foot, if you want to. Dr Dee is currently lodging in Kingston, a town not far from here."

At this Jack exclaimed to Gerolamo "I told you he might be in Kingston..."

The girl's withering glance, cut him short.

Kat continued, "We will have to be stealthy, the agents of Spain are following all leads to find him, and you have given them plenty. I traced your flight from London to here, and frankly was pretty alarmed at your fumbling attempts to locate Dee. In the last two days alone amongst the dozen or so people you have spoken to you have asked for Dee's whereabouts from a Spanish intelligencer and a known Catholic sympathiser, though I'm sure you didn't recognise either of them. And both of them will have reported back to their handlers by now. So not very discreet enquiries, gentlemen! All you are managing to do is help lead the King's enemies to Dee."

After their scant meal the light from the grimy window was fading fast, and so, after checking that Kat approved, Jack lit the stub of a candle and they continued talking for another hour or so. The candle flickered in the draughts that came from all directions, and a sooty trail rose up from its wick, winding around itself as the flame danced. Jack explained his recent past on the Hanse trading ship, and Gerolamo described some of his work, although that quickly went over the heads of both of the youngsters. Kat checked the window several times, though what she could see in the darkening street she didn't say.

Kat said they would have to travel at night to ensure they didn't lead the Spanish or the Catholics to Dr Dee, but not to worry because there would be a quarter moon tonight, enough light to travel safely. Jack packed up their books, and pocketed the last of the horse chestnuts.

Before they left Kat smeared dirt on Jack's face, saying it would help keep him hidden in the darkness. She turned away toward the window again, but not before he had seen her smiling to herself. He wondered why that might be.

Kat casually checked the street one more time, then froze. She had seen the man she thought of as The Goat, because he was hairy but nimble, although she had heard someone call him Tomás. Almost in a panic she span round and whispered harshly, "Grab your packs gentlemen, we have to go. Now. No questions, just follow me, and don't waste time looking back!"

She pushed the table up against the door, then gestured for the men to follow her, not waiting to see if they did. She ran to the back of the room, and used her knife to pry open a small door in the panelling that neither of them had seen, even though they had roomed there for a week. Waving them out onto a shallow rooftop she closed the door carefully behind her, then led the way across and down sloping roofs until they emerged at ground level. As they scurried after her they heard a crash of splintering wood, like a door being forced by a heavy shoulder, followed by muffled shouts, but they didn't stop and they didn't look back.

At a trot they followed Kat though a field of vegetables and then straight out onto heathland. They threaded their way quietly between several small cottages, not getting closer than a couple of hundred yards to any of them. Just as Kat had predicted there was a quarter moon and just enough light to avoid obstacles. Jack risked a few glances back but as he hadn't heard the pursuers since they left the house he gradually relaxed and started to enjoy the moonlit escapade.

They continued roughly south for thirty minutes, tracking parallel to a dirt road on their right and the river beyond that. The heath gave way to occasional scrubby trees, then sparse woodland. As they entered the woods Kat told them they had to veer further away from the road and that meant they would be going uphill. When Gerolamo asked why, she said bandits often lay in wait at dusk nearer the road, hoping for easy pickings from unwary travellers.

Their progress slowed dramatically when they entered deeper woodland, as the moon was often obscured and they constantly stumbled through brush and gorse. Gerolamo tripped over a fallen branch and crashed headlong into a briar patch, scratching his face.

Another hour and they scrambled to the top of a small hill that was clear of trees. Kat paused and looked to the east, through a gap in the foliage. Jack could see nothing in the darkness but Kat pointed confidently, "You can see St Paul's cathedral during the day, over there. Its high steeple spearing the sky. I have heard it said that it was here that the late King Henry had awaited a rocket fired from the Tower of London as a signal of Anne Boleyn's execution, before focussing his attention on his new love interest, Jane Seymour."

The way Kat said it made Jack shiver involuntarily. She poured such scorn into the description of the King and his actions that he feared she would be instantly arrested if she were overheard.

Turning to Gerolamo he saw the man examining the irregular shape of the boulders on the top of the hill. Kat walked over and explained casually, "And these are the markers of an ancient burial site. Despite being called *King Henry's Mound*, the locals say the mound is far older. They say there are wights that walk the forest around the time of the full moon."

Both Jack and Gerolamo glanced involuntary at the moon and tried to determine whether it was close enough to full to be worried, and then decided that worrying was the safe choice and quickly moved off in their original direction of travel leaving Kat, with hands on hips, shaking her head.

Kingston

Kat led them out of the woods as dawn was breaking, through Kingston Gate and past the night-watchman who called out a greeting to her when he recognised her, down Hogs Lane, and into the prosperous looking village of Kingston-upon-Thames.

Kat explained that the village was built around five roads that radiated from a single point on the riverbank. That point was the eastern end of a long, narrow, wooden bridge that crossed the river. The nearest point of interest on the other side was another of the King's palaces and his deer park, but the roads also radiated from there to the west of the country.

"This is the only crossing point over the river between here and

London bridge. Many travellers come through the village and that means it is always busy with traders trying to sell their wares to new customers. It's an ideal spot to hide in plain sight."

Jack knew that when he had left the *Stanislav* it had been moored immediately downriver of London bridge. He thought on what Kat had said, *if I took a boat from Kingston I'd be able to get almost all the way to the Stanislav, perhaps shoot the rapids under London bridge and I'd be back alongside her.*

Even as he thought this he wondered if the *Stanislav* would still be moored there. It had been many weeks since they arrived and usually the Hanse merchants would only stay in port long enough to off-load their cargo and load up the replacement. He suddenly felt isolated and very alone in a strange country.

Kat led them into a side road and then through a nondescript door into a large warehouse. The ground floor was a jumble of crates containing tools, sacks of grain, coils of rope, and piles of timber. Gerolamo sneezed as he followed Kat's winding path through the dusty stores, then ducked after her behind a leaning panel that obscured a set of stairs, and so up to the first floor. Jack trailed behind carrying all their books since the older man had tired of his share of the burden during the night, and as he paused near the bottom of the stairs he saw several horses quietly eating their hay in a stable attached to the far wall of the warehouse.

On the first floor they found much more order and cleanliness, with a series of tables laden with brass instruments on some, parchments on others, and finally, at the far end of the room, a large complex wooden frame.

Two almost identical young boys, who couldn't have been much older than twelve, looked up from their work and seeing Kat they both shouted in joy and ran over to embrace her. Blushing bright red, she made half-hearted attempts to push them away. The third occupant was a pale, severe young man, his face covered in smallpox marks, seemingly making adjustments to an armillary sphere, peering owl-like through a wooden prince-nez fixed tight to the bridge of his nose. Removing the lenses he stared at the new arrivals and coughed in a vain attempt to attract their attention. Failing, he walked over and standing a few feet off he pulled himself up to his full, but not very great, height and gestured dismissively at Gerolamo then Jack, "Welcome back Katherine. This must be the Italian mathematician that

Doctor Dee sent you to find, but who is this dull looking fellow with the dirty face?"

Seeing Jack bristle at the jibe, Kat stepped forward quickly and introduced both Jack and Gerolamo, then bowing toward the young man she said "And this is Roger Cook, Doctor Dee's principal assistant." Roger fairly preened at the phrase and seemed to stand a little taller yet. Then Kat asked Roger, "Where is the Doctor?"

"He just left for the palace, and he won't be back until nightfall. He was asking after you yesterday, and seemed worried you had yet to return."

Kat grunted and turned to her companions, "Come with me, I'll find you somewhere to rest and get clean." She led them up another flight of stairs to a series of small rooms that served as sleeping quarters for the Doctor's various assistants.

"Here's the lads' room Dottore, we prepared an area of it and a mattress for you. Jack, you will have to share this room as well, I'll have one of the boys bring in another mattress. I'm sorry about the limited space, but Roger won't let anyone share *his* room, and you can hardly share with me can you?" at this last comment she looked sideways at Jack. He blushed to his roots and tried to stammer out an answer, but before he did she turned and walked away. He noticed that her hips swayed as she walked, and she seemed more feminine than she had whilst they were travelling.

Gerolamo ignored the exchange between the two youngsters, and pushed his way into the room, exhausted after their moonlit trek. He collapsed onto the mattress and lay there groaning and massaging his feet, while Jack dumped their belongings, and then left to explore the rest of the building.

Jack walked along the same corridor that Kat had gone down and sped up past what he assumed was the door to her room. Beyond there he found a large unused area, with more supplies scattered about in piles. He went to the far side of the space and easing open some shutters he looked out west. He saw the narrow wooden bridge crossing the river, and beyond that an extensive hunting park to the north and a huge geometrically designed garden to the south. It contained avenues of mature trees and walking paths winding near gentle streams. From Kat's descriptions he guessed that beyond these would be Hampton Court Palace, currently occupied by King Edward and his court.

Jack returned to the room, washed the dirt from his face, and decided to head downstairs to learn what he could.

Roger pointedly ignored him, but the twins introduced themselves as Edward and Henry, but said he could call them Ed and Hal. They excitedly showed him around. Jack said he was especially intrigued by the large wooden frame, and the boys beamed, and each took one of his hands and almost ran over to the frame. They said that it was a printing press, which intrigued Jack, because he had never seen one before despite his interest in books. They explained how they were responsible for arranging tiny blocks made of lead, into many rows in a flat square wooden frame. Each block had a letter of the alphabet visible on it, although the letter was written backwards. As he watched, the boys quickly placed more blocks into the frame, until it was full. Then after carefully double-checking their work, they took a stick with a leather ball on the end and soaked the ball in a bucket of goopy black ink, then wiped the ball over the letters until they were all evenly covered. Then they carefully laid a damp piece of paper over the whole tray of letters, and pinned it into place, before turning a handle that they called the *devil's tail,* which pressed the paper down onto the letters. When the pressing was complete they removed the paper to show a whole page of writing. Jack was amazed. He had seen printed pamphlets and books before of course, both in London and in Gdansk, but he had never seen how they were produced. Carefully hanging the page on a line so it could dry, Ed said "on a busy day we print hundreds of such pages. Doctor Dee writes a different page of astrological predictions every week, then we lay out the letter blocks so they carefully reproduce the predictions onto a page of printed text. Then we produce hundreds for distribution and sale in London to folks wanting guidance for the coming weeks."

Jack laughed and said he wasn't so gullible as to believe such a story, but the serious faces of the boys gave him pause to reconsider.

The rest of the day passed in mundane matters, resting, washing, and swapping stories. A local woman came in the afternoon and set out cold meats and fruit on one of the tables, then left again without saying a word to anyone. They all gathered in anticipation of the meal, but by unspoken agreement no one touched the food, and any conversation was dull and stilted.

Then, before anyone realised it, John Dee was standing before them.

A frisson of excitement ran through the group. Dee's team was suddenly eager and alert, Jack felt energised too, and even the older Cardano sprang to his feet.

Doctor John Dee was a gaunt young man, with a thin face sporting a fashionable goatee beard and very dark, almost black, intense eyes, that seemed to penetrate to your soul when he turned his powerful gaze on you.

Looking at the assembly his face lit up with a smile that revealed his joy. He strode to Gerolamo Cardano and gripped his hand with visible intensity, then laughing he gave the older man a brotherly hug and welcomed him to his home in fluent Latin. Cardano was initially surprised at the over-familiarity then delighted at his welcome. Dee paused briefly to say a few words of thanks to Kat that left her looking very pleased, then the two mathematicians linked arms and walked around the room in animated conversation for the next half hour, and it would have been longer except that Kat dared interrupt them and suggest the guests might be hungry, not to mention the rest of the team.

As they sat for their meal Dee explained to the group, "Dottore Cardano has graciously agreed to stay with us in Kingston for a few months and assist on a couple of projects." The chatter over the meal was full of excitement at what projects they might be able to advance, as they had started several but their priorities hadn't been clear, so none were getting completed. Meanwhile Dee and Cardano tried to talk of algebra and equations, but were frequently interrupted by questions from Roger, Kat and the twins.

Jack looked on, and was pleased for Gerolamo, the man he now thought of as a friend, despite him being twice his own age. At the same time he realised he felt excluded from the chattering group. Adrift, without purpose. He played with his food as he realised he had no one, and had nowhere to go. For nearly two years he had had the companionship of the crew of the Stanislav and the friendship of Jakob, then on the flight from the Steelyard, which had been all consuming, it had been him and Gerolamo against the world. Now? Well now he didn't know what he would do.

Kat kicked Dee's foot under the table and nodded towards Jack.

In a loud voice that cut across the rest of the conversations, Dee asked Cardano how he had managed to evade capture in London and find his way to Richmond. As Gerolamo explained the events it was clear that Jack was the hero of the story, and that gave Dee the opening he was looking for.

"Jack, it seems I owe you my thanks for saving Dottore Cardano and helping Kat bring him safely to visit me. Perhaps you would agree to stay on with us here and help with my mapping work, and perhaps other matters? I am developing a paradoxal compass for navigation in northern seas, and I could use some practical help. Also, we have much equipment under construction, which is somewhat labour intensive, you might be a great help with that too. What say you?"

Jack was startled out of his self-absorbed reverie by this statement and looked up from his food to see everyone looking at him expectantly. His gaze swept the attentive faces and paused at Kat's, whose normally mocking eyes were suddenly inscrutable to his gaze. Tearing his eyes away he turned to John Dee and smiled, "I can think of nothing I would like to do more than to stay and help".

Afterwards, Jack couldn't have said why he had agreed to Dee's offer quite so readily, but he was happy he had, and soon started integrating into the life of the group.

Paradoxal compass

After breakfast on Monday, Dee called Kat and Cardano to join him. Jack overheard the tail end of the conversation.

"Your invitation has arrived Dottore. An invitation to see the King at Hampton Court tomorrow, just across the river to the west of here. Kat will guide you there."

"But surely you'll be coming too?"

"No. This is your moment in the sun my friend, you have waited long enough. I would be a distraction."

Jack guessed that invitations to court were extremely valuable, and so recognised the generosity of Dee's withdrawal. His appraisal of the man inched up a little further.

Leaving Kat and Cardano conferring in hushed tones, Dee strode over to Jack rubbing his hands together in anticipation.

"Now Jack, let's find out where your skills lie shall we? Hmm?"

"Mayhap you could start by helping the twins with the press that you showed so much interest in? They say it needs some maintenance but they are not able to disassemble it without adult help. Such manual labour is not my metier, so while you do it I will calculate some astrological charts and then write out the next set of almanacs for them to print tomorrow."

"I'd be happy to help anywhere I can," said Jack, and he went off to find Ed and Hal. He spent the day greasing the machine's many parts and learning how to disassemble and reassemble it.

By supper-time Dee had reappeared and handed the freshly composed tracts to the twins. He asked whether Jack had made any progress, and so Jack printed a page to demonstrate his mastery of the techniques involved. Dee approved of the much quieter operation and of the sharper print quality. The twins seemed as pleased as Dee, and beamed approval of their own tutoring skills.

The next day Kat and Cardano set off before breakfast to cheers from the rest of the group.

"The twins have an efficient routine for print days. So rather than disturbing them, Jack, would you join Roger and me at the instrument bench?"

Roger made a great show of demonstrating the instruments and boasted of his deep knowledge in their operation whilst Dee, a study in tolerance, looked on silently with a neutral expression.

Annoyed at what he felt was Roger's condescension, Jack pre-empted the demonstration of the astrolabe by grabbing it, holding it up, and sighting on a high window while describing its use. He described why and how it was superior to the more traditional cross-staff for finding a ship's latitude especially in a rough sea. As he spoke he remembered his days on the Stanislav learning with Jakob, and said excitedly "the astrolabe combined with astronomical tables, or ephemerides, allows better navigation over large distances and is the secret to crossing the great oceans. Erm, not that I have done that you understand, crossed the great oceans I mean."

Roger was visibly angry at the interruption and at the clearly more practical knowledge shown by Jack, but before he could say anything Dee excitedly exclaimed "Ah Jack, you must read the book *Tratado da Sphera* by my friend Pedro Nunes, the great Portuguese mathematician and navigator. I am confident you will be able to assist with the creation of a new map that his ideas are shaping for Gerardus Mercator and myself. Come and see me in my library this evening and I will find it for you to study. But for now, let us all proceed to work on the repair of this Islamic armillary sphere which Roger started on yesterday. It was damaged during transportation and will take much skill to return to its former state as it is a very advanced and delicate device."

Roger grudgingly cleared the table top and positioned the sphere in the middle, whereupon all three of them began to inspect it carefully before beginning to work on it together.

After supper that evening Jack was admitted to Dee's library to see Nunes' book, and marvelled at what looked to be a hundred other books and manuscripts. He remembered his own trading books and asked Dee if he knew anyone who would want to buy them, "Why, this is providential indeed. I have been searching for an original copy of *De revolutionibus* for a while as I only have a poor translation currently. If you would allow me to buy it from you I would be most grateful. Additionally you would still be able to read it for yourself here in the library." And so the deal was done, and Jack added a small bag of silver coins to his few other possessions in the room he shared with Cardano, Ed and Hal.

It was well after dark when Kat and Cardano returned. They were weary and hungry, because, as they explained, they had had no rest nor food since noon.

Cardano had a successful but short audience with the young King, who had been somewhat ill and who had quickly retired back to his private quarters. Following that he had been in great demand for discussions by a variety of great men of the court. One of these men was Sir John Cheke the King's tutor in Greek, who had requested that Cardano cast his horoscope, which Cardano had readily agreed to do. Cardano excitedly shared stories of the magnificence of the court and the sense of power of the noblemen, and Kat gushed at the vibrant colours of the ladies' dresses and the gemstones that adorned them, which made Jack smile as even after their short acquaintance he knew that Kat's normal idea of dressing smartly seemed to involve buckling on a well made sword.

Jack was, however, puzzled and asked Dee, "I know Gerolamo is your guest, but are you not upset that he has been asked to cast Sir John's horoscope, and not you? Will you not miss the income?"

Cardano and Kat paused their conversation to hear the answer.

"Aha Jack. A merchant's mind spins in your head I see, your time spent with the Hanse has not been wasted. But to answer you, by themselves horoscopes are a useful, although minimal, source of income. Their greater value, as I think you guess, are the connections that they enable the astrologer to establish, and even better the introductions to powerful patrons. But horoscopes also require prodigious amounts of time to calculate. Time that I can ill afford at the moment. So I am happy for Dottore Cardano to get the commission - better he than one of my other rivals, eh?"

Jack saw Gerolamo relax, presumably glad not to have offended his host.

The next day Dee announced over breakfast that he and Cardano were going to work on the mathematics for the Paradoxal Compass all day, and again invited Jack to join him. Roger's head snapped up and he looked daggers at Jack. Jack noticed the poisonous look, and also noticed that Kat was frowning a little, but none of them said anything.

The work was complex and not at all familiar to Jack, and he ended the day with an aching head and was more than a little embarrassed at his mathematical inadequacies. Dee, however, threw an arm over his shoulders in a comradely way and exclaimed, "You did well Jack, those equations are pretty advanced and normally require many years of study before they are even understandable, but you seemed to have an intuitive idea of what they meant. You are going to be an invaluable aid to our work." As Dee went to prepare himself for the evening meal Jack saw Roger glowering balefully, and wondered what was wrong with the ill-tempered young man.

A bell tinkled from somewhere below in the warehouse, and Kat slipped away from the communal dining table for a few moments. When she returned she handed a note to Dee, bending and whispering "From one of Cecil's men" just loud enough for Jack to hear. Dee opened it and scanned the text, an eyebrow raised and a triumphant smile, then he tossed the note on the fire, and continued with his meal.

At the end of the meal Dee announced to the group "On the morrow I will go to visit Master Secretary Cecil at his house in London. Jack, I need you and Kat to come with me. Kat, can you secure a passage on the morning ferry for us? We will need to be there no later than noon."

Next morning Kat and Jack met on the ground floor of the warehouse, which was a bustle of activity despite the early time. The twins' leaflets were being shipped out by horse and cart to London, and two different deliveries of books and instruments were arriving at the same time.

In a shadowy corner of the warehouse a stooped old man in a deeply hooded cloak was searching through the contents of a crate, and even as they watched he took a manuscript from the crate and slipped it inside his tunic. Kat ran over in an instant and span him around by his shoulder while shouting for Jack's assistance. An almost gleeful sounding cackle emanated from the hooded figure. Kat held a knife to the old man's neck and glanced toward Jack who was leaning against a post, not in the least concerned, and certainly not coming to help.

"Well?" she hissed, "You saw what he did, are you going to help me?"

Jack sauntered over, much to her irritation, and threw back the beggars hood, to reveal a smiling John Dee. Kat released his shoulder in shock and took a pace backward. Dee stood upright, then made a small bow to both of them.

"H...how did you know?" she asked Jack.

"The hands," Jack pulled the wide sleeve up Dee's arm, "they are the hands of a young man. And the boots are too well made for a beggar. Besides I recognised the buckle on them to be the same as the buckle on Dee's boots when he returned from court last week."

Jack spotted an admiring look on Kat's face, or imagined he did anyway.

"Well spotted young Jack, and do not feel badly Kat, for I am in disguise. I am pleased it is good enough to fool even you who know me so well. Come let's to the boat!"

Kat and Jack led the way to the waiting ferry, with the disguised Dr John Dee following them, successfully looking more like a vagrant than an occasional advisor and tutor to the King's court.

At Cecil House, on the Strand, the trio were shown through several richly decorated rooms, before waiting in a well-appointed, but cold, ante-chamber. Dee had removed his disguise and wandered the room looking at the paintings and wall hangings, spending all of his time on the family portraits and ignoring the landscapes and religious pieces.

Finally Dee was called forward into Cecil's study, where he stayed for a couple of hours. When he emerged he looked sombre. Taking his cloak back he swirled through the corridors of the grand house and Jack had to run forward to remind him to adopt his shrunken hunchback pose again before they exited the house. Then back to the river for the journey home, and from Dee only the mysterious "I can speak nothing of this matter until we are safely on the water."

On the returning ferry, huddled together at the back, Dee brought them into his confidence with a quick reprise in a mumbling voice, as though talking to himself as much as to them. "The King has been unwell these many weeks. There are rumours starting amongst the courtiers and servants. Cecil wants me to visit the King, mainly to calm the panicky doctors themselves rather than to demonstrate any medical skill. Then he wants a decumbiture chart that he can discreetly be indiscreet with, preferably saying that the King will make a full recovery of course."

Kat nodded during the monologue, but Jack didn't follow and exclaimed nervously "A *what* chart?"

Dee looked up sharply, then his demeanour softened as his eyes focussed on Jack's alarmed face. A brief touch to Jack's arm, and a soft smile, "I'm sorry, Jack, forgive me. Your presence within our little team seems so natural to me already that I keep forgetting you are new to my work. A decumbiture chart is an astrological forecast specific to one person, cast for the time they took to their bed with their malady, designed to speak about their future health....or lack of it." Jack's confusion was placated by Dee's soothing words and mannerisms.

"Such a forecast for a king is not to be undertaken lightly, but how can I refuse? If I forecast the King's death it is treason regardless of the actual outcome of the malady, on the other hand if I forecast a recovery and no such recovery occurs then the court's displeasure will be made clear to me, probably by the actions of the good Sir John Gage, Constable of the Tower of London, possibly with pincers and hot irons. Not my preferred evening entertainment!"

"But how can they hold you responsible if he doesn't recover?"

"Ah. How naïve. They look to place the blame somewhere Jack, that is simple human nature. And for the most part even the great men of the land are quite simple...in fact *especially* the great men of the land!"

"Then don't do it - its a no-win situation."

"Ah but Jack, there is a possible win. And to rise up in the world we sometimes have to take risks. After all, the forecast does have the validity of my craft behind it, I don't just make this stuff up! So if the chart says he will recover, then....he should in fact recover, and all will be well. If the chart says otherwise then....well I can always burn my work and say I have been too busy or too ill to cast it, and hope for the best.

"And if it plays out well there will be no shortage of more clients knocking on my door for their own forecasts, and eventually more patrons. I need a few more well-heeled patrons, as Kat here tells me all the time, I tend to spend more on books and instruments than I make from clients.

"Which actually was the one piece of good news that Cecil gave me. I have been awarded a gift of an annual royal pension in the amount of a hundred crowns for two books I wrote last year and provided to my friend John Cheke for the King. If I am lucky I might even receive it!" At that last comment he laughed, explaining "Tudor gifts can be generous but they often fail to materialise as cold hard cash in your purse."

The fate of her mother

As Dee retreated into deep thought, mumbling occasionally to himself, Kat warily watched the other passengers, alert to any interest in them, or to any movement in their direction.

She saw Jack stretch and then agilely go forward and start mixing with the crew. They must have been talking about the boat and how to handle it in the river because they were pointing at the different ropes and pulleys. Jack was clearly in his element, smiling and even laughing with the crewmen.

She took pleasure from his obvious joy. If ever she had doubted his story about being a sailor for the Hanse then she believed it now.

She watched closely as one of the crewmen untied a rope and gave it to Jack, who hauled on it to adjust the position of the small sail, the muscles in his back springing into sharp relief beneath his shirt. He tied off the rope and slapped the other man jovially on the back, his face beaming. He started to return to his seat so she quickly looked away, struggling to stop the colour she felt rising in her neck and face. She chided herself for letting her attention be diverted from the task at hand, and told herself she was just concerned that Jack might have being giving away information, however unwittingly. Deeper down she was aware of a curiosity in her new companion that she was unable or perhaps unwilling to suppress.

Forcing herself to ignore Jack, she stared at the waves from the bow, and the diving of the small gulls, and gradually her gaze lost focus as she thought of her situation and social position. Her mind went back to her struggles to survive and to achieve independence after escaping the fate of her mother and the anger of the mob, and the debt she owed to Dee.

As the ferry bumped against the pilings she was shaken from her reverie, and realised with relief that they had arrived back at Kingston.

Chapter 12 - Criminalisation

Saturday the 9th of April 1552
Kingston, West of London

The King's Tun

The hooded figure strode through the gloom of early evening. His boots sounding loud on the oaken planks of the bridge as he crossed the river, past the marketplace with its stone cross, all quiet at this late hour, and along Horse Fair road. He kept to the shadows as he passed the entrance to the lively ale house, *The King's Tun*. If any sots had glanced his way they certainly wouldn't have seen any resemblance to the shuffling old beggar that had crossed the bridge in the other direction, from Kingston toward Hampton Court, that same morning.

He strode past the *Tun*, turned right into an alley where he was swallowed by deep shadows and disappeared.

When John Dee reached the first floor of the warehouse he threw back his hood and was greeted with shouts of welcome from the group, who were preparing for the evening meal. Pottage again.

After eating, as though by some unspoken command, Cardano absented himself and everyone else stayed. This was family business.

"First the good news. At Hampton Court Palace in a small parlour he has somehow acquired for his own use, I had a privy meeting with our new patron, the Earl of Pembroke, Sir William Herbert. As we know, and indeed as I foretold, his wife Anne passed into God's grace just six weeks ago, may she rest in peace. He is naturally very concerned for his family's future and wants me to provide suitable assurances. He has provided his daughter Anne's birthdate, and also his newly betrothed's birthdate, who is also called Anne. Indeed I suspect the man goes to some lengths to ensure all the females in his life have the same name for the avoidance of error."

There were smirks around the table, especially from Kat.

"He wants to marry Anne Talbot in May, and of course needs confirmation that he is doing the right thing by his purse before the date. So we have our work cut out for us. The man seems totally avaricious and unscrupulous, nonetheless, the extra income from his patronage is welcome.

"A little later I was escorted to the King for a brief audience. His majesty is a remarkable young man, who though clearly not feeling well, thanked me for my efforts as I gave him the decumbiture chart we prepared, and he passed it to William Cecil immediately."

As Dee's gaze swept around the table, Jack's eyes followed, and he noticed that everyone was rapt with attention. They waited for Dee to continue.

"Of course it predicts that the King will return to full health. Indeed after seeing him myself, I would say he is already recovering, probably from a bout of smallpox. In a few more days he should be feeling significantly better," he shrugged.

Jack saw the group grow uneasy, waiting pensively on Dee's next words.

"But strangely, that is not my main worry. And so to the bad news. During the afternoon I was able to circulate quite freely around the lesser areas of the palace and noticed that there is a strange tension in the air. A feeling of suspicion even. I liked it not.

"To cap it all, just before I made my journey back, I had an audience with two Principal Gentlemen of the Privy chamber, Barnaby Fitzpatrick and Henry Sidney. They are both worried about loyalty within the ranks of the King's servants. Nothing definite, but they are very concerned. They have a feeling that something isn't quite right."

"Why not just replace all the servants if there is any doubt as to their loyalty?"

"Yes, that is an obvious solution, Jack. In fact, I suggested it myself. But they fear it could be interpreted as a sign of weakness. Plus the task of recruiting a hundred new staff would only encourage malcontents and schemers to apply, sensing an easy opportunity to sneak into the King's service and potentially do harm. No, the Gentlemen think, *better the devil they know*."

"What does it matter to us anyway?" asked Roger dismissively.

"If harm befalls the King, then my decumbiture chart would be shown to be in error and I would lose face, to say nothing of my head!"

"What can we do to help?" asked Kat, glaring at Roger.

Dee turned toward her and smiled, "Well, thank you for asking Kat. I have pondered this since learning of their disquiet. As I returned to Kingston I noticed quite a number of palace servants going in the opposite direction, that is, back to the Palace. It got me to thinking…the only realistic opportunity for someone of ill-intentions to bribe a servant is when they visit Kingston. Without bribery and conspiracy it would surely take a complete zealot to act alone, and I think such a person would be soon uncovered by the palace guards. So we should watch the servants coming to Kingston and look for strange behaviour. Unfortunately I cannot do the watching myself, it is too risky, I would be recognised for sure. But you five could take it in turns and watch them as they come into town and go about their own or the palace business."

"And how long would we be expected to do this?" asked Roger in a surly tone, "Tis not an agreed part of our employment."

Jack saw Dee's black eyes turn flinty, but Kat saved the day, "I will create a schedule. We can go in pairs, one day on, and one day off, Jack and me, then the twins. Roger doesn't need to be disturbed from his lab work. We could sell pamphlets at the town's cross while watching for the incoming servants and then follow anyone looking suspicious."

Dee nodded.

Jack thought it would be better if each twin had an adult with them, but Kat's plan meant he could spend a little more time with her, so he kept quiet.

Despite having avoided the extra duty Roger looked angered. Jack thought there was no pleasing the malcontent young man.

Over the next week or so the two pairs developed reliable tactics. One of them sold leaflets for a penny each, and the other would follow anyone that looked like a palace servant. Then they would switch places.

Kat showed her experience and cunning by creating simple disguises for each of them. Each day they trailed a half dozen or so people, and they were starting to understand what constituted normal behaviour for servants in the town, and were becoming quite adept at following people without attracting attention.

Wednesday was market day, and they expected the town to be at its busiest. They agreed that all four of them should go out to ensure they could trail multiple servants at the same time if necessary.

Around midday Kat signalled to Jack that he should follow a well dressed older man who had a pronounced limp.

Jack picked up the small bundle of firewood that constituted his disguise for the day, and settling it under one arm he set off after his quarry, carefully keeping a few yards distant.

He seems nervous, thought Jack, as the man stopped at a stall selling pottery, but instead of looking at the pots and bowls he actually spent more time peering suspiciously into the crowds surrounding him. At one point he looked directly at Jack, but his eyes flicked down and presumably saw the firewood under Jack's arm, because his gaze continued on to inspect others. *Thank you for the disguise, Kat.*

Jack maintained his place in the drifting crowd as it passed the man. He risked a quick glance back over his shoulder and saw the servant had yet to move away from the pottery. Another minute and Jack was almost twenty yards past his target, and felt in danger of losing touch with him if he didn't do something drastic. Luckily he spied an old woman sat on a log, squeezed between two established stalls, selling firewood. So he stopped and bartered with her. The transaction lasted just long enough, and as he sold his firewood to her for a groat, he risked a glance around him and saw his quarry duck into the doorway of the *The King's Tun*.

Jack sauntered over and paused at the door of the tavern, letting his eyes adjust to the dim light of the interior. He glimpsed the man hobbling over to a bench near the rear of the room, where a younger man was already seated with a beaker of ale. Jack's heart leapt. Surely this was no chance meeting.

A serving girl poured ale from a jug while the older man looked around nervously. Jack joined a large group nearby, and roared with laughter at an unheard joke. He cast furtive glances over to the seated pair, and saw their heads together having a hasty conversation. *Is that a money bag changing hands? And what was that? Was it a small bottle?*

After a few more minutes they seemed to be concluding their transaction, so Jack hurriedly left the inn before they did, rushing back to Kat to explain what he had seen. They called over the twins, sending Hal to fetch Dr Dee and left Ed to gather the unsold pamphlets and take them back to the warehouse. Their plan was simple, Kat would await the limping man's return and follow him, whilst Jack would return to the *Tun*, and either detain or trail the younger man, whichever seemed most prudent, until Dee could arrive.

Jack returned and paid for a small ale, then sat near the young man.

He nursed his drink as he watched and waited, worrying that Dee would come too late. The man started collecting his belongings, then, at the last possible moment, a hooded figure slipped through the crowded room and settled beside the young man. Jack quickly slid onto the other end of the bench, penning the man between them.

"Perhaps we should have a friendly drink while you tell me all about it? Young master John Hawkins," said Dee. Startled, the other man started to rise, but Jack's arm was thrown over his shoulder and pinned him to his seat. Like a cornered coney he looked wild-eyed left and right, then slumped in place, with his head in his hands.

Wild heather

A brief ten minutes later Jack left the *Tun* at a trot, and went straight to a seller of herbal remedies he had previously spotted in the market place, and made a quick purchase.

Jogging back to the market cross, he looked around desperately for Kat, and started to panic when he couldn't spot her. A tugging at his sleeve drew his attention to Ed, who confidently led him across the bridge and down one of the paths, where he pointed out Kat's receding figure. She was discretely following the limping man who was well on his way back to Hampton Court already.

Jack ran to her and pulled her aside for a hasty conference. As he leaned close to whisper he breathed in the scent of her hair and the words caught in his throat. Swallowing, he forced himself to relay Dee's plan, and slipped a vial from the herbalist into her hand. Perhaps holding her hand for a moment longer than necessary he whispered, "Be careful, we don't know if he's dangerous".

Did she really snort as she turned away? Girls!

Taking a shortcut through the topiary the pair emerged on the path ahead of the man. Jack loitered behind a bush and watched as Kat confidently walked back along the path toward the man, her long skirt swirling rhythmically around her, calling out in a sing song voice, "Heather? Lucky heather, good sir? A groat for a sprig?" The man tried to gruffly push past her, but she closed the remaining distance with a quick stride, "Looks like you need the luck sir, take the heather for free, and may God smile on thee" as she leaned in to give him the heather Jack watched in wonder as her hands skimmed over his tunic in a blur of movement. Stepping back she brandished another piece of heather and turned toward an approaching duo of young ladies and cried out once more "Heather? Lucky heather?"

The limping man looked at the sprig of heather pressed into his hand, and angrily threw it to the side and continued on his way at a fast limp.

As the ladies stepped around Kat to avoid her, Jack went to join her and after receiving a nod of confirmation they exchanged smiles and quickly walked back to Kingston in high spirits.

John Hawkins

Dee sat hunched in a deep chair near the fire in a rented room at the back of the inn. The landlady, pleased at the unexpected rental, had readily brought in a platter of cold meats with bread and cheese, and in the centre of the table stood a large jug of home-made ale, with a half dozen beakers clustered around it.

Kat and Jack burst in excitedly, and spotting Dee they rushed over to him, words tripping over themselves as they hurriedly related their accomplishment.

"You should have seen Kat, she was amazing…"

"He was such a grumpy old man, it was a pleasure to thwart his plan…"

"One minute singing out 'Lucky heather' the next swapping the vial in a blur of movement…"

"…And what should I do with it…" she held up the vial and started to take out the stopper.

Dee leapt up and closed his hand over the vial and her hand, "Stop, don't even smell it. It is the fastest kind of poison, even a sniff will make you ill." He took the vial and threw it into the blazing fire where with a pop and a flash the glass cracked and the liquid vaporised and exited through the chimney.

"There is no evidence now."

"So how will the poisoner be punished? And where is he anyway, the cur, wanting to kill in so evil a manner?"

With a deep sigh that was almost a groan, John Hawkins stood and walked towards them from the unlit end of the room, and sat in the chair opposite Dee.

Kat and Jack reacted the same, stepping in front of Dee to protect him from the attack that….didn't come. They watched Hawkins warily for a moment then turned to Dee with upraised eyebrows.

Waving them to a nearby bench Dee gestured to Hawkins, and said "From the beginning."

John hung his head and drew in a shuddering breath, then looked up, tossing back his shoulder length wavy black hair.

"First you should know, I 'ave killed a man afore."

Jack was shocked and glanced at Kat then Dee, but neither of them registered any emotion.

"It was not on purpose, it was in a fair fight, and he had started it as well. In a tavern back at home, in Plymouth. He had said me father was a pirate and I told him to take it back or step outside and let me defend his honour. And outside we went. He pulled a knife but he was not very skilled and in his rage he missed me and fell over a low wall and stabbed hisself in the neck like the eejiot he was. He were dead afore we could stop the bleeding.

"So I was pulled up afore the Justice then locked in the town jail awaiting sentencing. They would ha' hung me by the neck too, cuz the coroner said I was the aggressor. But a Lord was passing through and stepped in, and after hearin' the story he had them release me. He said he had the ability to give a King's Pardon. They didn't want to do it, but he forced them, and finally they let me go."

"And who was that Lord, hmm? It is important for your story, John."

"This was five year ago, I was only fifteen. The noble was Thomas Wriothesley, 1st Earl of Southampton.

"I left Plymouth afore they changed their minds, and thought the incident forgotten. Until,"

"Until what?" asked Jack, rapt with attention at the other man's story.

"Until two weeks ago.

"I was approached in the boarding house in Honey Lane where I had been staying for a couple of months. Two rough men took me to see a man who called hisself Gregory Ballard, said he was a Yeoman Warder at the Tower, and I was to come with him. Not to be locked up, but to visit a prisoner."

He paused in his tale, and Dee had to prompt him to continue "And who was this prisoner? John?"

"I recognised him not, but he said he was a Bishop of the true faith, and his name was Gardiner."

Kat inhaled noisily, "Bishop Stephen Gardiner? He has been in the Tower these last three or four years."

John nodded. "The same. He said I must procure some poison, and meet a man from Hampton Court Palace in this here inn. Or else."

"Or else what? What could induce you to do such a thing? You must know it is for use against the King. That's treason! You'd be caught, hanged, fed your own entrails and nailed to five different city gates by five spikes before sundown." Jack shook his head at the stupidity. He had risked similar treatment himself in Toulon, but at least he was trying to escape, not to kill someone, and certainly not a king. He found he was sweating uncomfortably at the idea of the outrage, and edged closer to the fire to gain warmth.

"Gardiner said he knew my story, from Wriothesely who had told him before he had died a couple of years ago, and demanded payment of the debt, or he would make sure the King's Pardon was revoked and I'd for sure be sent back to Plymouth to hang by my neck till I was dead." Having spoken his story aloud he shuddered and seemed to shrink in on himself.

He looked at each of them with such a pleading in his eyes, "It was a choice between certain death, and possible death....what could I do?"

Dee gestured to Jack, who passed around beakers of ale. Then after supping they continued into the food, not realising how late the hour had grown as they had listened entranced to Hawkins' tale of enforced treachery.

Dee reached out and touched Hawkins' shoulder momentarily, and he straightened as though energised. Dee looked to his companions and said "John didn't want to do it of course, and he knew full well the King was the target. But he was in a bind. What choices did he have? Luckily we were in the right place at the right time to foil this madness, and now the Chamberlain is carrying a vial of skerrit water to the King's dinner. It has a sweet and yet peppery taste and might even do the lad's stomach some good.

"Tomorrow I will alert Cecil to the plot, and we will try to catch the Chamberlain in the act. I will also suggest doubling the intelligencers around Gardiner, but the old man is wily and unlikely to put himself in our hands."

"And what of Master Hawkins here?" asked Kat, running her eyes up and down him in a way that alarmed Jack.

"John will be leaving town for a while, after reporting to Yeoman Ballard that the deed was done of course. I foresee travel, oceans, and possible riches in his future."

Chapter 13 - Gratification

Thursday the 28th of April 1552
Hampton Court Palace

Reward enough

A rather intimidating array of Yeoman Guards, the King's elite bodyguard, had escorted Dee, Jack, Kat and the twins, from Kingston to the Palace. After a short wait in a gilded ante-chamber they were shown through to the young King's presence chamber, where Sir William Cecil was to conduct the ceremony. Many nobles and foreign ambassadors were present, including the Imperial Ambassador from Spain.

Dee's whole team were heroes of the hour, and were roundly praised, by Cecil, the courtiers and the King himself. Dee, as the leader was asked to name his own reward.

"Your Grace is too kind. It is reward enough to be able to dash the schemes of those who would do you harm…"

"As you wish…" replied the King, mischievously ready to move on to his next appointment.

Cecil harrumphed, "But still his Grace would bestow some gift, so quickly name it Doctor."

Dee needed no further urging, and casting modesty aside he injected, "Well, there is an old Abbey whose library is said to contain many ancient texts and important books. St Augustine's in Kent. I would peruse its collection and see if anything might be salvaged from the monks and put to use in your Grace's Kingdom by myself, your most faithful servant, Johannes Dee." He swept into a low bow, and risked a glance up to the King.

The boy was clearly intrigued, Dee knew he loved learning from the tutoring he provided in mathematics.

"It is so granted. But Doctor Dee, if you find anything *really* good - you *will* bring it to me first won't you?"

"Your Grace..." bowed Dee again.

As the team exited the chamber Cecil came over and in hushed tones relayed the news that the guilty Chamberlain had died suddenly during torture before he had been able to name any accomplices. "Can you determine who the instigator was by using any of your black arts?"

"They are not black arts! They are proven scientific methods. And anyway they cannot be used in that manner."

"Ah, too bad. And 'tis a pity the procurer of the poison couldn't be apprehended, but you say he has escaped overseas," Cecil looked sideways at Dee.

"Yes. Well. We don't need the middleman. We know that Bishop Gardiner suborned him, using a Yeoman Warder as his go-between. We suspect that Gardiner was directed from Rome, probably not the Pope directly, but rather I suspect Cardinal Reginald Pole, who we know harbours a hatred of the Tudors. But it all emanates from the Pope and his accursed minions. Even the Spanish Emperor would not stoop to poisoning another monarch."

Cecil nodded sagely.

Dee changed the subject, "I had hoped to talk to Sir John Cheke about his plan to add more manuscripts to the King's library. Is he at court today?"

"He is at his home, recovering from a bout of sweating sickness. We were all really worried that he might not pull through. Except for the King, he was always positive. He was heard to say *'No, Cheke will not die this time, for this morning I begged his life in my prayer and obtained it.'*"

Dee merely lifted an eyebrow.

A servant approached and told Cecil he had a visitor, and as he turned to go he told Dee to stay cautious and alert, "Your growing notoriety might make you a target too".

"Who is doing the forecasting now, my Lord?" said Dee bowing low.

With a brief laugh Cecil left them.

A palace scribe handed Dee a scroll with the King's seal, and they were escorted away. Once clear of the palace Dee turned to his colleagues and rubbed his hands in glee.

"Excellent, excellent. I have long wanted permission to see the library of the famed St Augustine's Abbey.

"You know the original temple and grounds were donated 900 years ago by the Anglo-Saxon King Æthelberht to please his christian wife Queen Bertha, so that the missionary Augustine could found an Abbey. It is widely believed that rare gnostic knowledge as well as early English learning flourished, and that the Abbey acquired an extensive library of perhaps 2000 books. And we all know I love a good book. It will be a longish trip, so let's get back and start planning."

Chapter 14 - Precipitation

Tuesday the 10th of May 1552
London

An escape route

Tomás pushed his way through the crowds gathered at Eleanor's Cross listening to a reformist preacher. He gritted his teeth and tried to close his ears to the blasphemy. Regardless, the words flowed into his mind unbidden. The man was ranting hysterically against the Pope, and claimed that papist intelligencers and assassins were everywhere in London and the wider kingdom, and should be rooted out and burned at the stake.

He had cleared the edge of the crowd and was picking up speed heading east down the Strand, when he realised he was still violently shaking his head in an effort to empty it of the man's hateful words.

It took an effort of will not to glance toward Cecil house as he walked past it, though he knew every vantage point from which to do so because he regularly spied on the personages coming and going to the English statesman's residence. Instead he continued resolutely in the direction of St Paul's cathedral which loomed in the distance, towering over everything else in the city.

After passing the still incomplete Somerset House on his right, which the recently executed Duke of Somerset, Edward Seymour, no longer needed, he paused and watched the crow-like lawyers in their black gowns swirl around the Temple Church and the Inns of Court, then he turned and almost jogged to the rented house in Bell Yard.

He knew there was no handle, because he had removed it, and so he rapped on the door and waited. Minutes passed until a small cover was slid aside, and in the gloom beyond he could just see Cristóbal's eyes staring back at him. As the door closed behind him they embraced like brothers and he asked with just one word, "Renard?"

Directed to the back room that overlooked their small orchard with its half dozen chickens, he found Renard working on correspondence.

He faced Renard, took a breath to fortify himself and reported, "The King has recovered. Now the courtiers are busy trying to pin the blame for his illness on attempted poisoning by persons as yet unknown."

"And who do they suspect of this crime?"

"Your Excellence, the clever money is on agents of Cardinal Pole, but some whisper that it may have been agents of the Lady Mary. Not many dare say such a thing within the King's hearing, as he will countenance no ill word against the sister whom he loves. But still, the rumour is there." He rushed to add, "No one has any proof of anything, it is all speculation. The poisoner's heart failed when he saw the torture instruments, and he died, they had not even started using them."

Renard paled, "This is bad. Very bad. These English nobles are too hot-headed for my liking, and their child-King is too easily led, especially by Northumberland, who loves us not. We must offer the Lady Mary an escape route out of this country before her movements are curtailed, or worse. I will request a ship for the full moon on 6th of June, and in case we cannot persuade her that quickly, a second ship on the next full moon which is, let me see here, the 6th of July. We dare not take longer else she may be moved against, and if she is, our master will not take it kindly."

He quickly wrote a letter and sealed it, handing it to Cristóbal. "Take this to our agent at Billingsgate, for hand delivery on the next reliable ship bound for an Imperial port. I will away to Mary to convince her of the importance of this plan."

"She will not go, you know this. We tried it two years since and she did not go then either."

"Still I must try. Tomás prepare my horse."

Breaking his oath

Gregory opened the heavy door and waited respectfully to be admitted to the room. Stephen Gardiner was standing still, peering through a window made of many small panes of glass. One of Gregory's cousins was a glassblower, so he knew that each pane started as a bulb of blown glass and was then flattened into a small sheet, and that was why each one had a circular impression in it. It was also why they were so expensive. Looking over the Bishop's shoulder he marvelled that he could see clear across the City, toward a somewhat distorted St Paul's cathedral in the distance.

After a moment Gardiner turned and acknowledged his gaoler, "What is it Ballard? I'm busy."

"Your Grace," he walked over to the Bishop and extended a sealed letter of stiff parchment, then took a respectful pace backwards.

While the Bishop read the letter Gregory surreptitiously looked around. In addition to the glass window, the richly appointed room contained tapestries with hunting scenes, a couple of stout wooden chests, and several pieces of heavy wooden furniture including an ornate desk that was covered in important looking papers, scrolls, and even a couple of books. In the far wall was an arched doorway, the door slightly ajar, revealed another room in which he could see a curtained four-poster bed.

He tried to suppress his ever-present bitterness, but dark thoughts came unbidden and twisted his features into a barely suppressed snarl. *And after thirty years service to the King, I myself have a small two room apartment in one of the residential blocks in the Tower courtyard, with a small smokey fireplace and a bed that I made for myself after some nagging from my beloved Margery, and that is topped by a straw mattress. And my window opening has an oiled cloth stretched over it that keeps out most of the bad weather but also most of the light. Luckily we can't see through the oiled cloth, because if we could all we would see is the dung heap from the twenty horses kept for use by the Tower Warden and messengers.*

With a little effort he brought his attention back to the Bishop and coloured deeply as he realised the Bishop had already written out his reply and was holding it out for Ballard to take, and was watching him shrewdly.

"You have your freedom Ballard. At any moment of your choosing you can take that wretched woman you call a wife and go to the market to choose your own food. You can go to church on Sunday and worship largely as you wish. You can go to Southwark to watch the bear baiting or choose to watch a mystery play.

"I can do none of those things because I am held here, a prisoner these last four years, awaiting the King's pleasure. So do not envy me, and do not be bitter. Rejoice in your own simple life, and give thanks to God."

Gregory, humbled, immediately knelt and recited a prayer of contrition.

Gardiner placed a hand lightly on his head and uttered a short benediction, "Rise now. I have new secret work for thee. Take this, my reply to Sir Thomas Cheyne. Put it directly into his own hand yourself, do not trust any other. He is in London, visiting his sister this week, at the address I have written here on the letter. And Ballard. Go quietly, and go in the night, and use the servants entrance to their house. Do not be seen and for goodness sake speak to no one about this. When you return I will have another of these coins for you." He pressed a coin into Gregory hand.

Gregory held the coin, gazing raptly at its dull sheen, while the Bishop turned and stared out of the window again.

The gold sovereign represented about two months wages. He realised that by taking it he would be breaking his oath to the King, and his fellowship with the rest of the Warders. He was stepping further into the dark and there could be no return.

With a curl of his lip he slipped the coin into a tiny pouch that Margery had sewn inside his tunic. *They can all go to Hell, I'm taking the money.*

Flee the country

"An awkward assignment no doubt. So how did you handle it?" asked Cecil, as he poured William Herbert a glass of claret.

"After reading Dee's prediction I had some good men placed as watchers around Lady Mary's house in Hunsdon and sure enough the very next day a rider approached and stayed for several hours."

"That is hardly proof of anything, she is allowed visitors after all."

"Yes but my spy in her household reported the details of their conversation. The visitor tried to convince her to flee the country, or at least to be ready to do so at a day or two's notice. Apparently there will be a ship waiting offshore on both of the next two full moons. The visitor told her she was suspected of being behind the poisoning of Edward. She said it was absurd, and no one would believe it, and indeed rather than flee she threatened to go to Edward and tell him so. He dissuaded her from that action and she quietened. He seems able to exert more influence over her than anyone else, but even he couldn't convince her to leave the country."

"Indeed. And have you determined the identity of this mysterious person?"

"Not yet, but we will. They spoke in French, but then Mary cannot speak Spanish so that proves nothing. He wore the latest French styles which is odd, because he acted in Spain's interest. Perhaps he is Burgundian."

"Anything more?"

"Yes. My man called upon Mary just a couple of hours later. He warned her of increased Spanish intelligencers in the area and suggested she be on her guard. Not very subtle, and I wonder how he managed to keep his face straight as he told her, but no doubt she now knows that we know and will be even less likely to dash for the coast. And to make sure of it I have doubled the watchers."

"Good, good. So Dee proves his worth yet again. The man and his craft are a marvel.

By the way, did he mention anything else in his last letter?"

"Actually he did. He suggested I prepare a gift to give to the King when he visits my house during the upcoming royal progress. I didn't even know a progress had been planned!"

"Ah, yes. I was going to mention that. Sorry. Late August, you can expect the court to stay a week with you at Wilton House. Of course they will need to be sumptuously fed, and er, there may be a lot of them."

"Well a good thing Dee already warned me. The servants are preparing the house so it will be well aired and clean in good time, and I have some craftsmen preparing a camp bed as a gift. I am having it decorated with pearls and precious stones. It should make his Majesty more comfortable on the remaining nights of his royal progress, and cement me firmly in his good graces."

"You are already one of his favourites have no fear, but such a rich gift can do no harm."

Chapter 15 - Orchestration

Monday the 16th of May 1552
London

Less than fully competent

Renard faced his lieutenants, Tomás and Cristóbal, "You say it was delivery of a letter to William Herbert that alerted him to my plan to offer the Princess Mary passage to the continent? And now Herbert has confronted her to display his knowledge of our actions, which makes us look less than fully competent. Who leaked the information? Who sent the letter?"

"Sire, there are bundles of letters every day to Cecil House. We cannot trace the sender of the letter. Nonetheless, we know the author anyway, because we have an informant in the household who overheard Cecil and Herbert discussing the matter."

"And when were you thinking of revealing this important information to me?"

Spluttering under his leader's glare, Tomás replied quickly "Sire, the author of the letter is Doctor John Dee. He is a magician of the dark arts who works for Herbert. He does not need an informant in our organisation - no one leaked any information. We do not have a traitor here."

"Ah, Dee. The arch conjuror. Again he interferes in our work. So he is working directly with Cecil and Herbert now is he? That can do no good for us. He must be eliminated before he divines any more of our plans, and perhaps even identifies us. Our mission is too important to risk. Double the amount of gold we are offering for his location. Someone must know where he is, and will give him up. Find him. Then kill him."

Do not fail me

"Come in, man, come in", commanded a bluff Sir Thomas Cheyne, as a servant led in a timid Gregory Ballard.

Taking the proffered letter, he blanched when he looked at it, instantly recognising the sharp, biting angles of the letter M and the curl on the A, as the writing of Bishop Stephen Gardiner.

Muttering to himself as he broke the seal and unfolded the letter he stepped closer to the window to get more light.

"… the plan was not successful…foiled by the tame magician…Dee cannot be allowed to live….see to it by the feast day of St Barnabas….do not fail me in this.

"God's teeth! The man is a Bishop yet orders death as though it were a new coat. He pushes to the limit and then beyond."

He crumpled the letter in his fist and paced the room. Realising the courier was still in the room he tried to compose himself, squaring his shoulders and settling at his desk.

What would he do?

What *could* he do?

Yes, he was religiously conservative and would prefer a return to the old religion, but he was no murderer. Not normally anyway. He was getting sucked into this plotting further than he wanted.

He pulled a sheet of paper to him and prepared his quill. But what to say? He was in too deep and could see no way out.

He shook off his indecision and began writing.

Chapter 16 - Assassination

Friday the 27th of May 1552
Kingston, West of London

Footsteps behind them

The tension amongst Dee's team was thick enough to slice, as Jack read the itinerary for the trip to St Augustine's Abbey one more time.

The trip was planned to take four days by horse and cart, from Kingston to St Augustine's Abbey, and four days for the return.

They would stop at pre-arranged lodgings; first in Sevenoaks, then Maidstone, Ashford, and finally on to Canterbury where the Abbey was. They would stay for two nights in Ashford because the biannual fair would be in progress and Dee said it would be a chance for him to meet other scholars.

On the return journey they would stop in Faversham, Rochester, Greenwich and finally back to Kingston.

Jack had overheard Kat as she almost pleaded with Dee to change the itinerary, but rushing from task to task he had brushed off her request. Since then she had been distant and moody.

Dee had told the twins that they had to stay in Kingston to continue to print and distribute pamphlets. This had disappointed them, as they would miss the Ashford fair and miss the searching at the Abbey as well. They continued their printing work but did so with poor grace, banging down boxes of pamphlets and slamming the printer instead of taking proper care.

Meanwhile Roger, no great surprise, had refused to accompany them at all, and was now avoiding the rest of the team by staying in his room.

Jack shook his head as he tried but failed to understand how otherwise rational people could allow themselves to become so upset.

Together with Gerolamo, Jack carried supplies to an open space in the ground floor warehouse, ready for loading onto a wagon. As they carried a heavy box between them Kat stepped into their path and when they bumped into her she angrily shouted that they should watch where they were going. Jack glanced at Gerolamo and rolled his eyes, the older man merely chuckled silently to himself.

Later, Jack was taking a break from the preparations when Dee approached him and suggested that they should go and hire the wagon. Readily agreeing Jack called out to Cardano and said they'd be back before it got fully dark. The older man was sat on a crate mopping sweat from his brow and merely waved them off.

The proprietor of the *The King's Tun*, Walter Harcourt, was known to loan out his wagon at a fair price, and so they walked through the back alleys of Kingston towards the inn.

Normally these narrow streets between high walled warehouses ensured a degree of privacy which they sought, but tonight Jack was sure he heard footsteps behind them, although in the gathering gloom he could see no one.

Just as the alley angled slightly left two men stepped out of the shadows and blocked their path in a clearly intimidating manner. Jack looked over his shoulder, and urgently whispered to Dee, "Two more behind us."

The weaselly man ahead of Dee spoke with a sing-song accent that Jack couldn't place, "You didn't predict this with yer black art conjuring did ye Master Dee?" and as he said it he pulled a cruel looking blade from beneath his cape. His bigger companion hefted a crude cudgel and smashed it against the wall with a muscular back-handed swing. He flashed a mostly toothless grin that told of the enjoyment he expected over the next few minutes. Jack risked a quick glance behind and saw the flash of steel as both men drew vicious looking blades.

"Gentle fellows, whatever do you want, some gold perhaps?" asked Dee, sweeping his palm that seemed to glow with yellow light across his body in a horizontal gesture.

The men paused, the light from Dee's hand reflecting in their eyes as they tracked his movement.

Jack wasn't waiting.

He hurled himself forward, and his forearm smashed into the throat of the cudgel wielding brute with a satisfying crunch. The man fell to his knees his mouth a black 'O' as he tried to draw in a breath but merely whistled instead. The weasel was fast, drawing back his sword arm ready to swing his blade in a move that would surely decapitate Jack. But fast wasn't fast enough as Jack's momentum carried him forward crashing into the weasel. His fist held a knife that pricked the weasel's chest, and as they fell to the ground together the blade dug deeper still - up to the hilt. The surprise on his face was brief before his eyes rolled up in his head and he lay still.

Meanwhile Dee had spun around and gestured to the floor in front of the men behind them. As they stepped forward they were engulfed in a sheet of bright yellow flame that clung to their hose and jerkins. They dropped their weapons and frantically tried to pat their bodies to stop the flames but their hands started burning as well. They turned as one and ran toward the river only a few hundred yards away.

As Dee helped Jack to his feet they heard two muffled splashes.

They continued their walk toward the *Tun,* the splashes and whistling gradually fading.

Dee said nothing about the attack, so Jack decided two could play it cool, and merely resumed their conversation, "Will Master Harcourt's wagon be big enough to seat all four of us and our supplies, or will some of us have to ride? I ask because, ahem, I don't know *how* to ride. You know, life at sea, and all that."

Dee raised an eyebrow, "Kat and I will ride. You can drive the wagon most of the time and practise riding a little each day. Oft times the man who can't ride is the man left behind! We start our journey the day after tomorrow, make sure we are ready. Tomorrow I have … *an appointment.*"

Chapter 17 - Mystification

Saturday the 28th of May 1552
Hampton Court Palace

An evangelical realm of Christ

Dee crossed the bridge over the moat of Hampton Court Palace, walking confidently toward the Great West Gatehouse whose red-brick towers loomed three storeys above him. Unconsciously he stretched to his full height as he passed under the oriel window and through the arched gatehouse itself.

Stretched before him were serried ranks of pikemen in red tunics, forming a ceremonial guard across West Court toward Anne Boleyn's Gatehouse. Even before he was close enough to see the details he knew the face of the gatehouse held the great astronomical clock, with its zodiacal wheel and mute symbols of heaven on earth. *If I had designed it for them, it would have more details on it*, he thought.

In the gatehouse he was guided to his left, up a wide set of stairs, and into the cloaking room behind the screen of the Great Hall. He was approached in silence by two gentlemen ushers who placed a full length hooded white cape on his shoulders. He waited as they fastened it with a golden chain, and drew the deep hood over his head. Stepping aside they gestured for him to enter the Great Hall. He stepped through the screen into the hall and paused to admire the surroundings.

The glorious hammer-beam ceiling shone a golden brown as light flooded through the dozen huge stained glass windows. Over twenty similarly dressed people lined the hall, hoods raised, faces hidden. At the far end on a raised dais sat King Edward, with Cecil at his right hand, and Thomas Cranmer the Archbishop of Canterbury, on his left flank. Dee approached, and knelt before the King. Cecil stepped forward and proposed Dee's admission into the fraternity listing his recent accomplishments and services to the cause. Then Edward spoke.

"The Brotherhood of the Red Rose is an Order of worthy disciples dedicated to supporting and defending our Evangelical Realm of Christ. We use scripture as our sword and shield against idolatry, greed and heresy.

"By taking the oath here today you promise, in the presence of your new brethren, to submit to our collective wisdom, to work tirelessly for the good of this Realm, and to preserve our secrecy, never naming your Brothers and Sisters of the Red Rose, unto death."

"I so swear," said Dee in a confident voice.

Two dozen voices responded in concert with a resounding, "Amen."

"Arise Brother Dee, of the Order of the Red Rose. May Christ guide your spirit, as he will surely save your soul.

"Go with Brother Cecil, who will induct you into our secret ways."

Chapter 18 - Benediction

Early Summer 1552
The Journey to St Augustine's Abbey, Kent

A dancing bear

On the third day of their journey, it was Jack's turn to drive the wagon, as they journeyed toward Ashford. They passed alternately through lush meadows, tiny hamlets, and dense woodland. "Ideal ambush territory", Jack muttered, and found himself anxiously peering into the gloom of the foliage.

He chided himself for the caution, but every time he saw a rider on the track ahead of them, or any movement within the woods, his pulse would spike.

At one point he threw the reins to Kat and jumped down from the wagon and sprinted a couple of hundred yards back the way they had come, thinking to catch better sight of the persons he was sure were trailing them, but he found no one.

Kat tired of his paranoia and climbed down from the wagon's bench seat, untied her horse from the tailgate and rode fifty or so yards ahead to catch up with Dee who was riding a sedate, grey palfrey. Agitated as he was, Jack still noticed that as Kat and Dee rode alongside each other, the tension of the last few days was still evident, and they were not talking.

The closer they got to Ashford the busier the road got, until it seemed to Jack that everyone in the County of Kent must be going to the fair.

Cardano clambered into the back of the wagon, muttering something about the extremely low probability of attack on the King's highway, and the annoying habits of the youth.

Jack realised he was not only driving the wagon, but also driving his friends to distraction. Nonetheless, he couldn't shake the constant feeling that they were in danger.

The light was failing as the little group passed a squat stone watermill and finally entered the village of Charte Magna. They halted outside the *Hog's Head*, their lodgings for the night, and two stable-lads immediately rushed out to care for their horses. Inside, beside a warming fire the group's spirits lifted as they discussed the excitement that would be offered by the fair. Even Kat seemed cheerful.

The next morning they walked a couple of miles into Ashford. Dee admonished them not to attract any attention, and then they split up to explore the fair each according to their own interests.

Jack had never been to a fair before, and spent several happy hours sampling edible treats until he had but very little ready money left. He admired the livestock in a competition, belly laughed at puppet shows, watched fire-eaters, and even saw a dancing bear. At one point a parcel of live rabbits were turned loose into the crowd and a gaggle of whooping young girls and boys raced around trying to catch them.

He sauntered over to a noisy crowd and watched a couple of wrestling bouts, and rashly placed a few penny bets on the outcomes, luckily winning more than he lost. He was sorely tempted to join in himself as he was sure he could overcome the lumbering men who seemed the strongest contenders, and the prize purse sounded attractive. However, his good sense overcame his arrogance and he decided that wrestling at the County fair probably wasn't a good way to keep a low profile.

As he turned toward other attractions he caught sight of Dee beyond the crowd who were watching the wrestlers. He was huddled close to a tall, young man and was talking quite animatedly. Jack tried to walk in their direction, part curious and part protective, but for every step toward them he found himself taking two steps sideways to avoid other revellers. As the wrestling bout ended to mixed cheering and jeering, the crowd dissipated and Jack thought he might make swifter progress, but instead he found himself surrounded and unable to move at all. He jumped up and down on the spot a few times, gaining just enough extra height to glimpse Dee with his arm over the other man's shoulders as they turned away deep in conversation and disappeared from his sight. With his last jump in the air he caught a clear look at the other man. It was John Hawkins. The attempted poisoner.

"Jack. Jack." He heard his name shouted from behind him. He turned to see Cardano waving from just outside a brightly coloured cloth tent. He was smiling broadly and gesturing for Jack to join him. So he pushed his way across the green until he reached Gerolamo's side.

"I have applied my probability mathematics with splendid results this day", he hefted a bulging coin bag, "Let's go and celebrate. Dinner is my treat!"

Jack, ever hungry, smiled in return and walked with his friend. Casting a final glance to where Dee had been he noticed a young urchin following a few paces behind them.

"Begone lad, get to your home," he tried to wave the lad away.

"Nay, Jack, leave him be, young Matthew here is with me."

In response to a mute appeal Cardano explained that the lad was part of his winnings. Apparently the boy's parents had sold him to pay off a debt, and he had been passed from owner to owner for several weeks until finally being used as a wager in the card game against Cardano, who now had possession.

Stunned, Jack said no more, but privately wondered how this man he considered a friend could accept the concept of someone else being his possession, and what on earth Cardano would do with the lad anyway.

That evening when they reconvened in the *Hog's Head* Dee was blunt, "The boy should be returned to his parents, with a bequest from your own purse to provide for him if you like. Failing that, he is entirely your problem. Make sure he is not a liability and keep him out of my way."

Fyndon's Gate

They gathered outside early the next morning. Jack shivered as a chill mist swirled around them and gladly hustled round to the inn's stables to get the wagon ready when Dee asked him to.

The day warmed up quickly though, burning off the mist and soon it was hot enough for Jack to slip off his cloak and use it to soften the hard wagon bench seat. Dee led them through the village of Wye, where they forded the river, so they could approach Canterbury somewhat from the south. It was a good choice, and they had an easy ride without needing to cross the winding river again all morning.

After a few hours they could see an imposing square stone keep with a town wall behind it. Dee said it was Canterbury Castle, being used as a gaol now. Beyond it the magnificent Canterbury Cathedral towered over everything else behind the town wall.

The group skirted south of the town walls, and finally halted outside the imposing gatehouse of St Augustine's Abbey.

Jack admired the fine looking structure. Two tall octagonal towers rose at least forty feet high, well above the main gatehouse building. A pointed arch between the towers contained a massive oaken door, and above the arch a row of fine windows was topped by crenellations. Either side of the gatehouse a high stone wall kept the sanctuary private, although a motley jumble of dilapidated buildings pressed up beside it.

Dee's loud voice pulled him from his reverie, "It is over two hundred years old, and will likely still be here later in the day if you want to gawp at it, but perhaps now we can go inside?"

The doors were open so in they went.

Dee pulled up his horse quickly, and Jack immediately understood why. The former abbey was a hive of activity, but not in a good way. Workmen hurried to and fro carrying tools and materials, or leading oxen with carts piled high. Over a general hubbub could be heard the steady chink of masons' hammers. But the men weren't building something, they were tearing it down.

A stout foreman waved over at them and waddled over self importantly, demanding to know their business. Dee dismounted and showed their papers with the King's seal, and grudgingly they were allowed access to the site.

"You're a bit late for the scriptorium though," and with a nasty cackle he lumbered away.

"Are you sure it will still be here later in the day?" teased Jack.

He immediately felt bad about the quip as he saw Dee looking about in despair.

Only partial walls of the great abbey church remained, and they seemed to shrink further while they watched, as workmen hauled away cartload after cartload of stone.

Dee shouted to a passing labourer "Was that building the scriptorium?" as he gestured to part of the ruin.

"I don't know what it was, but you're welcome to look over what is left."

Dee called to them, "Jack, Dottore, and you too Kat. Quickly, we must salvage what we can." And with that he strode over to the nearest partial building and began darting between piles of debris.

The others fanned out to check the buildings nearest to them, so Jack wandered toward the south side of the site where he could see a serious bonfire burning. He ventured as close to the fire as he could and used a long stick to poke through the ashes. Pushing aside some smouldering rags he realised that underneath were the remains of several books. He inched closer to try to scoop them out, but the heat drove him away. Agitated, he looked around and saw a labourer walking back toward the main site. Jack ran up to the man and asked if he had burnt the books from the scriptorium, "Aye, I did that. And that was the last of them." Disappointed, Jack was turning to go when the man called to him, "but many more were kept in the royal apartments." When Jack looked confused, he pointed toward the gate where they had entered, "Up there in Fyndon's Gate, where the nobility sleep during their visits."

Shouting his thanks Jack turned and jogged all the way back to Dee. As he explained what he'd discovered Dee was alternately downcast then ecstatic.

Calling the others he rushed to the gatehouse, waving his royal warrant as he passed the guard. He plunged up a winding stairs with Jack and the others close on his heels. On the second floor he opened a door into a reading room lined with shelves of books and scrolls. With a joyous shout Dee embraced Jack and immediately started scouring the books.

"Shout out the titles of anything interesting," Dee told the others, even as he started pulling out one book after another and examining their contents.

"*Miracles of Our Lady*", shouted Jack. "No, we don't want that moralistic nonsense," said Dee.

"Horace's *Opera*" said Kat. "Certe non," said Cardano, and after a couple of seconds silence he translated, "Certainly not."

"*Recuyell of the Historyes of Troye*, no.", said Dee himself.

"*La légende dorée* ?", asked Jack. "No".

"I have Euclid's *Elements*" said Cardano. "Well that's something anyway," replied Dee, "put it to one side."

"*De natura rerum*, by St. Bede the Venerable," sang out Jack, starting to enjoy himself. "Yes, yes. Keep that one Jack," said Dee.

"*The Chronicles* by Jean Froissart," said Kat. "Well the King might enjoy that, so keep it out," replied Dee.

"*Speculum Humanae Salvationis*", said Cardano. "No".

"*The Canterbury Tales*?" asked Kat. "Appropriate, but no," replied

Dee.

And so it went for a couple of hours.

Most of the books were Bibles, psalters, prayer books, and Book of Hours, which made sense for an ordinary Abbey library.

"Where are the gnostic papers and scrolls? Where is the early learning? Surely there is more somewhere?" Dee was getting frustrated.

Another hour was spent going over all the books again, in case they had missed anything. Finally they had to admit they had everything of interest.

Dee sat cross-legged on the floor with *De natura rerum* open on his lap, and the other half dozen books in a couple of forlorn piles beside him.

When Kat returned from the wagon with some flagons of ale for refreshment she said, "One of the labourers told me that before Abbott John Essex surrendered the abbey to the King there had been suspicious activity for several nights."

"Suspicious activity in the night is one of the reasons the monasteries were dissolved!" quipped Dee.

"No, seriously. He said several monks had pushed covered handcarts out of the abbey precincts under cover of darkness. No one knows what they carried or where they vanished to."

"Interesting," said Dee, "Did he say where the good Abbot is now?"

"He was given a pension and a small manor nearby."

"Good work Kat. Let us take these books to our wagon and repair to the White Hart in Canterbury, our hostelry for the night. Tomorrow we start early and pay a respectful visit to the good Abbott."

St Martin's

Jack drove the wagon again in the morning as they followed directions to Sharling Manor, in the village of Petit Sharling. Within an hour they arrived at the manor house and dismounted.

Jack was impressed. The honey coloured stone house was unusual for the region and although the frontage was asymmetrical it was pleasing to the eye. The well manicured lawns and tidy entranceway added to the feeling of welcome.

A stout but kindly looking woman emerged from the side door, wiping flour from her red, worn hands as she approached them. After exchanging introductions Dee asked for John Essex.

"You have just missed him gentlemen," replied the woman.

"Where has he gone, we only need a few minutes of his time?" asked Dee.

"To his maker. He died last week. I am just now making the pies for the funerary feast later this afternoon. You'd be welcome to stay I'm sure."

Dee growled and turning away he pounded his fist into his palm in evident frustration.

"Does he have a large library in the house?" asked Jack.

"Nay, he was done with all that business when he finished at the Abbey. He just had a bible and a prayer book. He studied them all day, every day. A godly man he was, very pious and no mistake."

"Where will he be buried?" asked Kat, Jack sensed she was as keen as he was to get some good news out of this trip.

"We had hoped he would be buried here at our All Saints church, but his will stated he should be interred in a crypt he had got ready, in St Martin's church, near his old abbey. Very particular about that he was." She nodded firmly, clearly impressed with the ex-abbot's pre-planning.

Jack raised an eyebrow in Dee's direction, who nodded in return. "Thank you for your kindness goodwife. If we can just water the horses, then we will be on our way."

They journeyed the five miles or so back to Canterbury. *The trip seems faster this time. No doubt a trick of the mind when the terrain is familiar,* thought Jack.

The midday sun was beating down on them when they arrived back near the abbey and asked after St Martin's church. They were directed through a small orchard at the rear of the abbey site, into a lush meadow.

There stood the old church, made of mortared brick and flint. A crook-backed priest was leaving the church, leaning heavily on his staff.

"Give you good evening Father. Is this St Martin's parish church?" asked Dee.

"Good evening to you. Yes, this is St Martin's," he continued proudly, "This is the oldest church in England. In fact some say it is a thousand years old."

Jack was sceptical, "A thousand years? I can't even imagine how long that is. And the building looks in good repair, the mortar seems sound. Are you sure?"

"It is indeed. In fact the tomb inscriptions to be found inside will confirm it if you care to enter and read them."

"Maybe I shall," replied Jack.

"Then do it today, and give thanks to the Lord, for tomorrow the church will be full of mourners for the late John Essex who will be interred in the afternoon. But now you must forgive me leaving, I have to give last rites to a parishioner who is slowly passing into God's grace." He shuffled away, looking not so far from grace himself.

They went inside and quickly found the abbot's tomb, because it was in the middle of the aisle, maybe six yards from the doorway. It was ready for the interment tomorrow, with the engraved stone cover partially askew. The engraving depicted a monkish man with hands pressed together in adoration. While Dee studied the tomb Jack went exploring. Near the entryway he found a stone tablet affixed to the wall, with faded writing chiselled on the upper part, and more recent engraving below. Intrigued, he traced out the faded lettering with his fingers to help read the archaic script.

HERE LYETH BERTHE †
WIFE OF ÆTHELBERHT
DTR OF CHARIBERT THE FRANK
YR OF OUR LORD DCIX

As he slowly discerned the letters and pieced together the inscription, he became aware of Matthew, squatting in the aisle, watching him with his wide eyes shining luminous in his urchin's face. He was tracing the letters on the ground at the same time as Jack traced them. Something odd happened though. After tracing out 'Berthe' Matthew drew the cross but didn't trace any more letters after that.

Jack knelt down and gently asked him why he had stopped. Slowly, and it seemed to Jack, a little fearfully, Matthew reached out for Jack's finger and pressing it to the slab on the floor he traced out a cross. Jack was confused for a moment, and then realisation dawned. On the floor was an almost invisibly faint symbol:

"'Here lies Queen Bertha.' Here. Literally here, at the sign of the cross. She is buried underneath this slab!" said Jack. He ruffled Matthew's hair and smiled at the lad. He placed his hands flat on the floor and closed his eyes, willing his perception to sense anything beneath his palms. He thought of the nearly one thousand years of devotional worshippers whose feet had worn away the cross as they entered the church. A church that was the initial home of the religion that Bertha had made possible for Augustine to introduce to the country. He shook his head, still not quite believing the enormity of time that it represented. He tried to reconcile such beliefs with his own experiences, but couldn't manage it. He shook his head to clear his thoughts, and opening his eyes he smiled again at Matthew. Then he stood and faced the tablet once more.

The second inscription was quite fresh and easy to read, but made little sense.

KNOWLEDGE EXISTS BETWEEN PIETY AND SAINTLINESS

"Very profound," muttered Jack, as he turned to check on his colleagues. They were gathered by Dee, and it sounded like they were planning their next move. Joining them he heard Dee decide, "It has been a trying day. We should go to our lodgings, and plan our next move over a small ale. Or two."

In the common room of the White Hart they eagerly took beakers of ale from the serving maid and sought to drown the disappointments of the day. Dee slumped forward as he tried to summarise the search thus far. "So what have we got so far?" He ticked off fingers as he recounted their results, "First, we found the remaining books at the abbey, and have taken the best of them. Second, we suspect the Abbot spirited away anything truly valuable months before the surrender of the abbey to the King. Third, he died last week, the wretch, and now he can't tell us where he hid all the abbey's learning. Fourth," he paused, "There is no fourth."

Jack suddenly went very still, his mind racing with fragments of images that he struggled to comprehend. Sweat broke out on his forehead. He felt they were missing something. *He* was missing something. One part of his mind saw that Kat was staring at him slack mouthed, but he couldn't stop his mind swirling.

Monks pushing handcarts laden down with books under cover of darkness.
Matthew tracing a cross on the flagstone….Queen Bertha's resting place.
Bertha was venerated as a Saint in Canterbury.
Abbot John Smith piously bent over the bible.
The Abbot's tomb is a gaping hole in the floor of St Martin's.
Knowledge exists between saintliness and piety.

"Matthew. Where is Matthew? Has anyone seen Matthew?" asked Jack.

The others looked around them, realising they had not even thought about the lad, Cardano blushed at the oversight and blustered that "I'm sure he's here somewhere".

Jack jumped to his feet, "We have to go back. Come on, quickly." He rushed from the inn and as the others emerged into the gloom he was already leading their horses and wagon out of the stables. Urging them to their mounts he jumped on the wagon and whipped the horses to a trot, back in the direction of St Martin's church.

Surveillance

Cristóbal grunted as the serving girl left a jug of wine and a basket of bread at his table. From his corner in the White Hart he could just see through the modest crowd of patrons, past the corner of the bar, to the table where Dee's group sat.

It had been a tiring day following Dee's team back and forth, always staying out of sight yet not losing track of them. He relished the chance to relax and let his guard down a little. The two local men he had hired were joking noisily with the serving wench, which helped them blend in, but he wished they would stop so he could more easily see across the room. He daren't risk rebuking them for fear of his thick accent raising suspicions.

Casually he reached forward to pour himself more wine, the light from the nearby fire illuminating him just long enough for the serving girl to see his disfigurement and visibly shiver. Cursing silently he leaned back into the shadows and cupped his beaker of warmed wine.

Finally the girl left them and he cast a glance across the room. Where was Dee? Their table was empty, "Mierda!"

He sprang up, spilling the wine, and sprinted out of the common room, just in time to see horses disappearing into the gloom.

Scientia Pati

They crowded around Jack as he pushed open the door to St Martin's, and then paused. They all heard it at the same time, a quiet, muffled sobbing, coming from somewhere inside. "Get some candles," whispered Jack as he carefully crept forward. Moments later Dee was beside him shielding a flickering candle that cast a weak light through the nave.

"Matthew?" called Jack quietly. There was no reply but the sobbing seemed to relent. A tiny voice echoed "Jack? I'm down here."

Rushing forward they peered down into the abbot's final resting place, and saw Matthew staring up at them, his tear-streaked face grimy with stone dust and dirt.

Dropping to a prone position on the stone floor Jack reached down his strong arms and gripping Matthew's hands easily hauled out the thin child. Cardano wrapped him in a cloak and Kat passed him a water bottle that he greedily drank from.

Dee and Kat started quizzing the child at the same time, but before he could reply a screech of stone on stone cut through the babble. They all turned to watch as Jack hauled the engraved tomb lid further out of the way, and to their amazement he then jumped down into the crypt.

Holding a candle close to the end wall of the crypt he peered closely at the smooth stone. He brushed away dust with the flat of his hand and there he spotted a faint carving.

SCIENTIA PATI

He read the letters out loud and Dee translated the Latin, "*Knowledge endures. A strange epitaph for an Abbot.*"

Boom. Boom.

Jack threw his shoulder at the wall of the crypt again and again, and the dull booming echoed throughout the church, "It is hollow," he called up. He ran his hands over the rest of the wall, and after a few moments he called up, "There is a small hole here, like a keyhole, bigger than my thumb but too small to grip. Look around and see if there is anything up there that looks like a large key or at least could poke though this hole."

While Jack continued to feel all over the wall he heard his colleagues above searching the church.

"There is nothing up here, it is quite an austere interior," said Cardano.

"Except, perhaps this," and Dee sprang onto a bench and peered closely at the bronze cross hung on the wall by the alter. He struggled for a few moments then simply unhooked it and jumped down. He rushed over to Jack.

"Perfect!" said Jack as he examined the end of the cross, seeing a hook shape on the bottom. He inserted it into the hole, "It's an exact fit. The abbot must have had it made specially."

Carefully he rotated the cross in the hole, so the hook snagged behind the edge and then carefully he started to pull. He strained for a few moments, but he was used to pulling an oar and this would be no match for his strength.

With a pop, the shape of a shallow door appeared and after another slow pull it swung open with a sigh as sealed air escaped, puffing dust toward Jack. "I have opened a door," he yelled.

"So we see," said Dee's voice very close to his ear, making him jump a little, so intent had he been on the door that he hadn't noticed Dee climb into the tomb with him. He extracted the *key* as he now thought of it and set it aside, instead gripping the door with both hands and heaving it fully open. Dee passed him another candle as his had blown out when the door opened, "Careful now Jack".

Ducking through the door he saw a wondrous sight. Books and scrolls of all types and sizes were stacked on an array of shelves, and sitting by itself facing him was an ancient and ornate jewel box. He reached for the box and was surprised how heavy it was, perhaps being made of a very hard type of wood. He opened the lid and inside was, "Nothing!"

"Never mind jewellery. Look at these book titles," said Dee, "*Surath Ha-Ares*, ah that translates as…, wait a moment, *The Form of the Earth*. This is much better. It is a scientific treatise on astronomy and cosmography, by Abraham Bar Hiyya Ha-Nasi. Written in Hebrew. And *Geography* by Ptolemy, and look over here *De Re Aedificatoria*, and here *Divina proportione*, and look at this, *De dissectione partium corporis humani libri tres."*

Dee was vibrating with excitement, "Well done Jack, well done! This is what we came for. The scientific library of St Augustine's abbey!"

They formed a human chain, with Dee passing books to Jack, who reached up and placed them in the aisle, then Kat and Matthew would take them to Cardano, who then placed them in the bed of the wagon, under a tarp to keep them out of the light rain that was now falling.

It took nearly an hour, but finally they had emptied the vault of everything except the jewel case. Later Dee would say he only opened it out of curiosity, but whatever the reason he saw an inscription on a slip of parchment in the lid, and read it out to Jack.

ONLIE THE PURE OF HEART WILL FIND IT
ONLIE THE IMPURE OF BODY NEED IT
◎ THE BLOODSTONE OF BOIORIX ◎
IN THE HOUSE OF JUSTUS
FOUR GREEN MEN WILL TAKE YER
TO THE SHRINE OF THE SCOTTISH BAKER

They stared at each other for a few minutes, then frantically searched all the corners, nooks, and crannies of the vault but found nothing except spiders. Jack opened the jewel case again and used his thumb to measure the size of the indentation in the cloth interior, big enough for a hen's egg at least. He blew a long low whistle, "Phew. That was one big jewel. Surely it is the *Bloodstone* that is mentioned in this message. Somebody must have borrowed it and forgotten to return it."

Dee closed the box and with it under his arm was assisted up into the nave, "Close it up Jack, it is time we were gone."

They returned the cross to the nail where it had been hanging, pushed the tomb lid back into place, and left St Martin's like thieves in the night, which Jack acknowledged to himself, they were.

Dripping wet in nearby foliage, Cristóbal kept watch, fascinated. They had clearly loaded many items into their wagon, but were most excited about something that Dee held under his cloak. Returning to the horses and hired men he wondered if he should try to steal the item, or stay on plan and just keep waiting for his chance to silence Dee forever.

Chapter 19 - Overstimulation

Saturday the 4th of June 1552
Returning via Faversham, Kent

Dee was furious

Dee had to pay the landlady extra for a late breakfast for the team, as everyone had slept in after their midnight exertions, but with a rich haul of books safely on the wagon in the inn's yard he seemed content, happy even.

He explained that they would begin the return journey immediately but, as per the itinerary they would travel back through Faversham, then Rochester and Greenwich. When pressed on the reasons he merely said he had business in all those towns. The others were hungry and didn't really care what route they took. Except Kat. She quickly finished her food and then making some excuse she stepped away from the table, disappearing in the direction of the room she had used the night before.

An hour later the group was ready to leave, except Kat was still missing. So was her horse. Dee was furious, he seemed to take her desertion very personally. Jack didn't know what to think, her sudden absence made no sense. Nothing else was missing, the books were still under cover in the wagon, the gear was stowed. Just Kat and her horse were gone, as if they had never been. They quizzed everybody they could find, and a stable-lad finally remembered seeing her leaving alone earlier that morning.

Reluctantly they set off north.

After several hours travelling they crested a rolling hill and paused to look down toward the small town of Faversham, nestling on the banks of a small river that wound further north toward the Swale estuary and beyond that the North Sea. A faint waft of hops was carried on the breeze toward them. Dee explained that there were two breweries in the town, making good use of the local hops harvest. Jack looked at the town with indifference. He was worried about Kat's absence and with a start he realised how much he missed her. The shy smiles, the sway of her hips, her bravery and cleverness.

Dee said they would find their next lodging house, *The Phoenix,* beside the brewery that lay just beyond the church, St Mary of Charity.

They continued down the gentle hill and into the town.

As soon as the landlord, John Ward, heard Dee's name he rushed over and handed him a sealed message, saying it had arrived by royal messenger that same morning.

Dee suggested they have a light meal before reading the letter, and when Jack asked why, Dee said the message was in code and would take a couple of hours to decipher.

While they ate their meal the landlord's daughter flirted outrageously with Jack, who remained civil but didn't banter in return. His mind was still churning over the possible reasons for Kat's absence, and he only picked at his food, pushing it around the plate uninterestedly. Without Kat, he realised, the world was less interesting, the food was tasteless, and showing attention to other women, however comely, seemed like apostasy.

Dee spent half the afternoon deciphering the coded message, while Jack looked on, anything to take his mind off Kat. Finally, Dee finished and read the plain text message to himself. Then he jumped up and taking Jack with him he called to the others and read the message out loud.

"It is from William Cecil;

My Goodly Friende Doctor Dee

I commend me very humbly unto you. I know not where to start with oure grate calamitie for his Majestie is once again taken ill so grevous with nightly paynes and broken helth. He seeks indeed, we all seek your counsel in this tyme of his greatest neede We stande redy to receave any offer of succer to preserve his lyffe. We have sondry offers to ease hym of the torment of the head, which the offerers beleave will assist, from the quicksilver to the tyncture of Gold. And yet I feare for his Majestie and would sooth receave your owne advise not wythstanding the chance of offendynge the worthie phisiks who hav done their best alreadie. Prithee keepe this intelligence a secret unto yourselffe. Yow se that my hand now parrets my hart withowt excuse.

Your assured

Brother under the Rose

William Cecyll

"Why does he call you his *Brother under the Rose*?" asked Jack.

"That is all you ask? He writes that the King is dying and you question his manner of signing off?"

Jack blushed and stammered back, "It was strange is all. So, the King is ill, well of course that is serious. We should travel back with all haste if they think you can assist him."

"That is more meet. However, we have only just arrived here in Faversham and I have a few hours of business to attend to. Surely one day's delay will not do any harm to anyone? Jack, you come with me."

He grabbed a cloak and cap and strode briskly from the room, with Jack hurrying after him.

Chapter 20 - Ebullition

Saturday Afternoon the 4th of June 1552
Faversham, Kent

Inspecting the accounts

Dee guided Jack through the small town and a further mile beyond the western edge, to a fenced compound near the river. A gruff watchman emerged from a hut by the gate. He recognised Dee and bowed toward him, Dee flapped a hand in a slightly embarrassed way in return.

They threaded their way through a seemingly haphazard collection of sheds, passing two men who were struggling with a large barrel of water, toward the epicentre of the compound, a small wooden house. Beyond the house to the left Jack could see an extensive although slightly strange farm, where several labourers were toiling in the fields between dozens of long raised mounds of earth. There were no plants growing on the mounds, and yet the men seemed to be watering them anyway, which seemed pretty odd. To the right he could see a small stone built hut with a waterwheel dipping lazily into the stream.

A stiff north-easterly breeze chilled Jack, who had no cloak, so he was pleased when they finally reached the house.

Dee was greeted courteously by an elderly man with ink stained fingers, who then turned to Jack, "Greetings, young sir. I'm the overseer of this manufactory. My name's Inkbold, Tobias Inkbold." Jack thought the name particularly appropriate, but didn't comment.

Inkbold led them through to an accounting room. Ledgers were stacked about, and a particularly large one was open on the main desk in the centre of the room. Dee immediately sat at the desk and started inspecting the accounts, alternately asking questions or grunting in acknowledgment to answers provided by Inkbold.

Jack was left to entertain himself, so he inspected a variety of curiosities arrayed around the room. He picked up one, a fist-sized clay pot with a string emerging from the inside, and was hefting it in his hand when suddenly Dee appeared beside him and deftly retrieved the pot and placed it back on the shelf, "Careful with that Jack."

Turning to Tobias he asked, "Do we have anyone who can show Jack around the facility?"

Inkbold rang a small bell and a burly workman in a leather apron soon presented himself, "Stephen Greenwood, at your service."

Dee explained what he wanted and Stephen readily agreed, but looking at Jack's thin jerkin he suggested a hat and cape should be worn, "The wind is picking up now and will soon bring in a squall of heavy rain from the North Sea if I had to guess, and I'm usually right now ain't I, Master Inkbold?" Inkbold nodded his agreement.

Jack didn't mind the cold or rain, he had been a sailor after all, but a little comfort was pleasant when it could be had, so he gladly accepted when Dee volunteered his own cap and cloak with the comment "Use mine, but try to keep them clean if you can, eh Jack?"

Setting the ambush

Cristóbal had carefully followed his quarry from the inn and all through the town. As he watched them pass through the gate and into the relatively open farm he realised with a rush of excitement that Dee was finally isolated and his opportunity to attack had arrived. He saw them disappear into a small house.

He rushed back to the town and collected his men. They gathered up crossbows and newly sharpened swords, concealing them in sacks so they could carry them through the town without raising any alarm.

He smiled grimly at the odds. Six of them against Dee and his young assistant. His hand unconsciously went to his neck and chin and stroked the still painful puckered skin where he had been burned by Dee during the last attempted attack in the alley in Kingston. He would not fail this time. He could not.

He swaggered confidently toward the gate, like a gentleman with every right to be there, and slow enough not to cause alarm. The gatekeeper stepped out of his hut as expected and raised a hand in the universal signal to stop. Moments later he dropped wordlessly to the ground, felled by a single blow from a cudgel, wielded by a giant of a man who had risen silently from the reeds behind him. The body was immediately dragged out of sight into a ditch. Cristóbal nodded at

Pádraig, the Irishman with no love for the English who he had recently recruited.

The other four hurried over, distributing weapons, and looking questioningly toward their paymaster.

He loved the feeling of command, and waited for a few beats before setting the ambush as he silently revelled in their attention.

He gestured that two men should stay hidden by the gate and the other two should set up behind a nearby pile of firewood.

He took Pádraig and entered deeper into the compound.

How long will I have to wait for my revenge?

He didn't know the terrain nor how many workmen there might be, so he felt the safest plan was to wait for Dee to return and catch him in a crossfire of arrows, finishing him with blades if necessary. In fact, now that he thought of it, he savoured the idea of running a blade through Dee. Perhaps he could keep Dee alive long enough to stab him slowly several times. It would be sweet revenge after the burning he had received from the magician.

He dodged out of sight behind some water butts as a labourer wheeled a handcart of dirt towards one of the sheds oblivious to their presence.

Dark clouds were scudding in from the north, and he hoped Dee would not stay in the house too long else the rain might interfere with his plans.

He saw movement in the front room of the house and his pulse quickened. A labourer wearing an apron exited the house and pointed in the opposite direction, deeper into the compound, he was followed by Dee, his cap and cloak clearly visible despite the gathering gloom.

Cristóbal grinned and rubbed his hands together, he turned and muttered, "Pádraig. Be ready with the crossbow."

Are you the astrologer?

In Faversham, the captain re-read his orders to make sure there would be no mistakes and called his men close, "We are to take the astrologer and the boy that accompanies him, and any items that seem important. If the astrologer resists, kill him, otherwise do your work quietly and respectfully. We want no property damage and no civilian rioting. If anyone asks, we are acting on the orders of the Privy Council."

The troop of men entered the Phoenix inn quickly. The captain told the innkeeper to stand aside and there would be no trouble. Using the directions to the visitor's room the troop of men rushed the stairs.

The soldiers burst into the room and saw Cardano playing cards with Matthew. Two men grabbed him by the arms as he tried to stand, and the captain confronted him, "Are you the astrologer?" Nodding his assent Cardano was dragged away down the stairs to a waiting wagon, together with Matthew who was taken by another soldier. Two others searched the room and quickly found the jewel box which they gave up to their captain. "This must be what all the fuss is about," he muttered to himself in satisfaction. With the box under his arm, he and the remaining men left the inn.

Bound and gagged, Cardano lay in the bed of the wagon, bouncing and jolting with every rut and rock in the road. The only thing he could see was Matthew, wide-eyed and frightened. The sky quickly became darker as rain clouds raced in from the sea. As the rain started the wagon briefly halted while the driver threw an old tarpaulin over the captives, which all in all Cardano thought was fairly compassionate and gave him some hope.

De La Pirotechnia

As Jack exited the house with Stephen he realised that the wind had already strengthened considerably. Stephen pointed toward the men labouring amongst the mounds and led the way.

"We are farming saltpetre here, do you see?" he shouted to Jack, gesturing to the long mounds as they passed them.

"No I don't see. I know what saltpetre *is*, it is one of three ingredients used in the making of black powder. And I know that Hanseatic ships import saltpetre in large quantity to England, I have done so myself. But I don't understand why you'd need to farm it, nor do I understand what that even *means*. Does it grow?"

"Aye, it does grow. In a sense. It is a special technique that yon Doctor Dee introduced after reading it in a book called *De La Pirotechnia*. We have a copy in Inkbold's office, although I can't read it. It was written by some expert in metal from the Republic of Siena," he leaned a bit closer and said conspiratorially, "That's near Rome where the Pope is from you know."

They were passing the labourers and Jack gagged as a sharp rank smell assaulted his senses. "What on earth is that awful smell?"

"Ah, yes. That's why we are down-wind of the town isn't it lads?" the labourers laughed and continued their work.

"You see, in these clay lined mounds we have alternating layers of decayed animal dung and then limestone and wood ash, then more dung, then ash, and so on. We have to keep it damp with urine, that's what they are pouring onto it, and why it smells especially bad at the moment. Then after about a year when its good and ripe, our saltpetre man, that'll be Jakob my brother, he digs out the black soil and we wash it through with clean rainwater that we have collected and then concentrate it in our boiler shed by ebullition, until all the water is gone and what we are left with is pure saltpetre crystals. Do ye see? The crystals form in the mound as the wet dung and the ash merge together over time.

"Master Inkbold manages the whole thing he does. He's a good man. He does all the hiring and we're glad of the work, aren't we lads?

"And Doctor Dee is the owner and mastermind of the whole thing, but we only see him a couple of times a year. He told us when we started five years ago that saltpetre is rare in England which is why it is imported, but in times of war the imports might be stopped and our supply here would therefore become very valuable. He even promised us a share of the profits when that happens."

"And do you sell the saltpetre?" asked Jack.

"Aye, some of it. But we also make black powder ourselves. I'll show you that part of the operation next," replied Stephen, guiding Jack out of the mounds, back past the house, and toward the various sheds that Jack had seen when he arrived. Jack noticed a light in the window of the house, and realised the approaching storm was darkening the day earlier than normal.

They entered the first shed, where a fire under a metal vat filled with liquid was clearly where the saltpetre was being concentrated. Another worker was shovelling ashes from an old fire into a handcart, "Those ashes will be added to a new mound, nothing gets wasted here you see."

They looked into a second well built shed and saw a pile of dull yellow rocks and powder, "Sulfur" said Stephen. "That comes here by ship, delivered to our jetty. Stinky stuff, but it helps the black powder catch fire, so we need it in the mix."

"And finally our charcoal shed," Stephen indicated a large shed, "The charcoal is made at another facility beyond Canterbury. We don't want all that wood burning going on here see, too dangerous," he tapped the side of his nose with a dirty finger, "*Safety first*, that is our watchword here, young sir."

They then headed over to a widely spaced row of four smaller sheds. "These are our storage sheds for finished powder. This first one is for cannon powder, it has bigger grains of black powder." He gestured at the next shed, "This next one is blasting powder. It is finer, so it burns much faster especially if contained."

They continued down the line past demi-cannon powder, and finally to the fine powder shed.

"Is the mixture different for the different powders?" asked Jack.

"Aye, a little bit different. But mostly it is the shape and size of the powder particles. Here, we'll give ye a small demonstration."

He called over one of the young labourers, whispered some instructions, and the lad nodded gleefully and ran off to gather materials.

"Let's set up in an open space away from the sheds," said Stephen.

"It is getting dark quickly with all this cloud," noted Jack.

"Aye, it can get gloomy fast in these parts. Ah, here comes Peter now."

Jack watched as Peter placed a brass dish on the ground and poured a handful of powder from a small barrel he carried. "This is cannon powder" said the lad, as he placed the barrel on the ground a few yards distant from the dish.

They stepped back a few paces and Peter used a long glowing stick to touch a spark to the pile of powder.

With a whoosh, the powder burned brightly for about ten seconds, the bright image searing into Jack's eyes in the gathering gloom.

While Peter went to fetch a second sample Stephen explained how a few years ago they had started out grinding each of the ingredients in isolation, and then mixing the ingredients together to obtain a resultant black powder. But they had struggled to get a consistent burn in the resulting powder, especially if they transported the barrels to a customer and then had to demonstrate it. "Doctor Dee has done many experiments to get it right and recently showed us how to mix the ingredients first, dampening it a little, and then do the grinding of the mixture.

"That way the process is safer because the powder is damp. And importantly all the ingredients are ground to the same size at the same time, and that constant size helps the consistency of burning. For finer powder we just grind for longer. We used to use some donkeys tethered to a wheel, driving a machine with hammers which would pound the powder all day long without tiring. And the donkey droppings are good for the mounds too - we never waste anything here you know!

"But now the Doctor has built us a mill on the river, and using the power of the moving water we turn great grinding stones that fine the powder consistently all day long."

Peter trotted back with another small barrel, and repeated the preparations. This time he cautioned them to move further back while he sat on the barrel and with fully extended arm and long stick he touched the spark to the small pile of powder he had placed in the dish. With a violent surge the powder flashed in an instantaneous burst of flame, the white light piercing Jack's eyes and leaving an after-image as he blinked to regain his sight.

Immediately afterwards he heard the whistle of a crossbow bolt, so familiar to him from his days on the war galley.

Chapter 21 - Intensification

Saturday the 4th of June 1552
Borgo District, Rome

I have prayed for his soul

Alberto hoisted his robes and raced up the Via Plauto, drawing disapproving tutting from a clutch of clerics who were passing in the other direction, toward the Vatican. As he reached the entrance of the alley that led to the rear of their palazzo, he paused to catch his breath. His chest heaved from the unaccustomed exercise and he grimaced with loathing at the gently rising cobbled surface that lay before him, shimmering in the midday heat. He sucked in a lungful of air, and continued his scuttling run under clotheslines strung overhead that were filled with the day's washing, and as cold drips of water fell from them and plunged down his neck he cursed the women who had hung them out. With leg muscles burning, he turned a sharp corner and brushed past a large jasmine plant climbing the wall, a couple of stems broke off and exuded a milky sap onto his shoulder, but he didn't notice. Any other day he might have delighted in its small white star shaped flowers and deep sweet fragrance. Today, however, he raced past and headed toward a stone archway in a nondescript wall. Hoisting his keyring from within the folds of his robes he fumbled for a moment before inserting the correct iron key and heard the satisfying clunk as it disengaged the lock. He slipped through and locked the door behind him.

Leaning back against the door he took a moment to compose himself, wiping sweat from his forehead with his sleeve and allowing his breathing to return to something like normal. His master didn't appreciate panic, even when it was warranted.

Upon hearing Alberto's hesitantly delivered message, Pole collected all the correspondence he had from his agents in England, the most important of which was from Bishop Stephen Gardiner, whose letters had to be smuggled out of his apartment in the Tower of London. All went into a satchel that Alberto carried as the pair prepared to respond to the urgent summons from the Pope.

Rather than meeting at the Vatican Palace, which was handily near the Borgo, their instructions were to attend on the Pope in Villa Belvedere. The villa was north of the Palace on a hill with grand views over St Peter's Basilica, and over Rome to the east. Pole knew that the sloping parkland between the Vatican Palace and the villa had been terraced fifty years ago and a grand courtyard was still in the process of being completed around it.

As the appointment was urgent they rode out with a pair of guards, quickly entering the Vatican grounds and arriving at the southern end of Cortile del Belvedere.

"You will have to wait until the carousel practice has finished," an official informed them, denying them access to the courtyard itself. Pole looked past the man and could see a dozen or more riders with high-stepping Spanish horses practicing an elaborate equitation display in the lower courtyard.

Not wanting to delay, he led the group around the courtyard and through the sloping woodland beyond until they reached the side entrance to the villa. Leaving the horses with his guards, he entered with Alberto and sought Pope Julius.

Pleasant cooling breezes made the summer heat bearable and by the time he was shown through to the Holy Father he was cool and calm.

After kissing his outstretched hand, Pole launched into an account of the progress he was making to unseat King Edward and return England to Catholicism, fumbling for letters in the satchel and reading quotes from Gardiner on the recruitment of agents in the King's household.

Julius waved him to a seat and hushed him placatingly, having to get quite forceful when Pole insisted on continuing to justify his actions and declare his progress.

"My dear Cardinal I know you are making good progress on your mission, I have seen the reports on Edward's discomfit brought on by suspected poisoning. And of course I have prayed for his soul.

"But, that is not why I asked you here today."

Suddenly Pole was wary, and he stilled his body while his mind raced through possible indiscretions.

There was his dalliance with Isabelle Farnese the niece of the Duke of Parma, but that was innocent enough and was mostly finished anyway since her husband had returned from fighting in the war for the Papal army. No, it couldn't be that.

He had hired some men to steal papers from the secretary of another cardinal. They got the papers and almost got caught themselves, but finally escaped unrecognised, so surely it couldn't be that.

His men had whipped a baker's son nearly to death on his orders, when he thought the child was mocking him, but he had sent Alberto to pay off the parents so he believed that was hushed up.

No, it must be the team of Neapolitan horses he had purchased from under the nose of the Pope's own master of horse last week. He had bribed the sellers to ensure he got the four matching greys because he needed a good team for his carriage that he was expecting to be completed next month. He would not subject himself to being gulled into the carriage of Cardinal Guise again! The horses had been a rash act he realised now.

Julius walked over to a window and gestured for Pole to join him. Together they looked south over the gardens and down the courtyard where the carousel was still being practiced, to St Peter's basilica.

Julius took his elbow and leaned close.

Pole waited for the axe to fall.

"It is in regard to your purchase of that villa in Marino."

Pole felt his stomach lurch. *God's teeth. How did Julius find out about that?*

He had spent a third of the Pope's chest of gold purchasing a palazzo in the hills overlooking Lake Albano, about six hours south of Rome. Currently he was spending more of the gold on renovations and furnishings, and on the coach and horses to get there.

He closed his eyes in resignation, this was going to be bad.

"I am told you negotiated a really good price. I am looking at a property near there myself, as a summer palace. I was wondering if you could assist with the purchase and so help me get it for a good price too?"

His eyes snapped open. That was not what he'd been expecting.

They spent the next couple of hours poring over plans and contracts,

Pole relieved not to be censured and Pope Julius clearly excited about the prospect of another palace. At one point Innocenzo joined them with refreshments and Pole found himself warming to the charming young man, despite having been initially repulsed, although he still couldn't understand how the Pope expected to keep the relationship quiet and avoid a scandal.

Chapter 22 - Disarticulation

Saturday Evening the 4th of June 1552
Faversham, Kent

Black powder

Jack was still blinking away the searing red after-image of the flash of burning powder when he heard the whistle of the arrow. Instinctively he threw himself to the ground, shouting to the others, "We are attacked!"

Before he even hit the ground he heard the sickening thud of the arrow finding a target, and from the corner of his eye he saw Peter fall back under the impact, a look of total shock on his face.

Another whistle, then another. Crossbow bolts rained down on them from all sides. Stephen was hit in the shoulder and span round before falling face down in the dirt beside him. He risked raising his head a little to check on Peter, and saw to his alarm that the glow stick had fallen perilously close to the powder barrel which was now leaking a steady stream of black powder.

Realising he had but moments, he rolled away from the barrel and fell into a shallow trench made by cart wheels. The barrel exploded with a roar of sound and flash of flame, the pressure of it tugging wildly at his clothes, then all went black and he knew no more.

Two clay pots

"What the...?" Dee jumped up and ran to the window. He and Inkbold watched the tongue of flame pierce the darkening sky, knowing instantly that it could only be black powder.

Grabbing two clay pots from the shelf where Jack had previously spotted them he ran from the house shouting to Inkbold to fetch and arm the workers. As he ran toward the diminishing flames he saw figures with swords approaching from the edge of the property. Guessing that they meant harm to Jack and the others he pulled the string from one pot and threw it directly toward the biggest figure with all his strength.

Dee was no bowler, the pot was going to miss Pádraig by at least three feet, but in an instant the tall man reached out and caught it one-handed and stood looking at it bemused. Then it exploded in a shower of pottery fragments, blasting the big man to pieces and engulfing what remained in fierce fire and heat.

Dee's second pot landed well short of another attacker, who carried on running toward it obliviously, moments later it exploded sending the man cartwheeling through the air.

The other attackers dived for cover and Dee realised he was now unarmed, exposed, and facing the comrades of two men he had almost certainly just killed.

Luckily, at that moment, Inkbold and a half dozen workers emerged from the gloom and threw their hand bombs where Dee pointed, eliciting screams and shouts of retreat from the remaining attackers.

Carefully, Dee and the workers advanced. At one point Inkbold slipped on a severed arm, and almost gagged. They heard whimpers coming from a fallen man, and tried to ask who had hired him, but he died without talking coherently.

More workers came with torches that illuminated the carnage. They found Peter and Stephen, both dead from crossbow bolts and the initial explosion. Then, in a deep cart-track nearby, they found Jack. Luckily he had no serious injuries but they could not wake him.

"Master Inkbold, double the guards for the rest of the summer, and see that the families of Stephen and Peter are cared for. I will take Jack back to the inn where he will have to stay until fit to travel. Check on him as often as you can. I will have to leave at first light for London to report this attack to the King's councillors. Send a note to me in Kingston if you discover anything from these scoundrel's bodies tomorrow."

Turning to the unconscious Jack he said "Jack. I told you to keep my cap and cloak clean, and now look at them. They are ruined! You can buy me replacements when you wake up." The other men chuckled, the mood lifted just enough for everyone to perform their duties without despair for their fallen friends overwhelming them.

.

Part III

"Search while thou wilt; and let thy reason go
  To ransom truth, e'en to th'abyss below;
  Rally the scattered causes; and that line
  Which nature twists be able to untwine.
  It is thy Maker's will; for unto none
  But unto reason can He e'er be known."
                    - Sir Thomas Browne. Religio Medici.

Chapter 23 - Reorganisation

Tuesday the 7th of June 1552
Cecil House, London

Reporting to Cecil

Dee was tired and dirty after two days of driving the cart from Faversham back to London. He went immediately to Cecil House, where he had to wait for several hours before Sir William Cecil returned from a meeting of the Privy Council.

Finally he was taken to an office where Cecil and Sir William Herbert greeted him grimly.

"The messenger told me you had serious news, Brother. I came as quickly as I could. What has happened?"

"My lords. It seems our foe knows some of our plans and we are being hunted. My party has been attacked twice on the same day while returning from our inspection of the old abbey of St Augustine's in Kent."

"One attack would be bad enough, but twice you say?"

"Dottore Cardano and a servant were abducted from their inn by a troop of supposed soldiers, and have not been seen since. And a gang of mercenaries attacked my men and property in Faversham killing two workers and leaving my apprentice seriously injured."

"'S wounds," interrupted Herbert, "Were I there I would have given them a good thrashing."

"Thank you my Lord, but unfortunately you were not. We managed to drive the mercenaries away and left four of their dead in our wake, but still it is sore grievous. But I also bring some potentially good news, although there is a dark side to it as well."

"Go on."

"I have discovered information regarding an ancient gemstone. I believe it may be capable of healing. I thought, if true, it could be useful in our treatment of the King. However the clues to the location of the stone have been taken by the men who took the Dottore."

"A gemstone capable of healing? That sounds like superstitious papist mumbo-jumbo," said Herbert.

"It would seem to be very ancient my Lord. Perhaps even from pre-Roman times. It is certainly not a papist relic."

Cecil held up an admonishing hand to quell the brewing disagreement, then stroked his beard as he thought. "So you think it might help with the King? This last day he has seemed to be gaining strength again, but who knows if the poisonous humours will recur? It would be a good thing to have available to us, it could secure the realm."

"The clue to the location was only a short message in a jewel box. I remember the important details and I will be able to research it when I get back to my library, but…"

"But what?"

"But the attackers have it now, and may find the gem first, thus depriving us of it, whatever it is capable of. I think it best if we track them down and recover the message and Dottore Cardano at the same time. Perhaps that is something you could arrange whilst I do the research?"

"You speak wisely. I think we can arrange that, what say you, Sir William?"

"Aye, leave it with me, it will be my pleasure. The men of my household will scour the whole county if need be."

"Thank you sires, I will provide all the particulars I can to aid the search. I had to leave my assistant convalescing at the same inn in Faversham, because he had not yet recovered his normal health. Perhaps you could post a guard to look over him as well, in case the attackers return?"

What blasphemy is this?

Tomás went to the side door where the runner waited. He saw the filthy child with a note clutched in his grimy hands.

He cringed inwardly at the sight. Such poverty hardly existed in his home town of Seville, which was a booming metropolis of a hundred thousand souls, flooded with wealth thanks to a monopoly on trade with the Spanish Americas. Here in London, by contrast, the population was said to be a little larger but the population of beggars was vastly larger. There were many people with no jobs or who were unable to work and since the monasteries had come down there was no-one to provide even minimal care or alms, so many starved or succumbed to a deathly chill. *So much for using the plundered wealth of the church for hospitals! The nobles of England are greedy, miserable men. I can hardly wait to be finished with this mission and return home.*

Shaking his head he gave the boy a groat and dismissed him, taking the note to his master. Renard quickly read it, then summarised its content for Tomás.

"It is from our spy at Cecil's house. Apparently Cristóbal attacked Dee, but failed to silence him. Again. Indeed he might not even have survived this attempt himself as there are reports of several dead. There is more; it says Dee is on the trail of a *healing gem*. What blasphemy is this? But still, if they were to find such a thing they might heal the King and then our task will be so much harder. Silencing Dee is now no longer enough - we must get to this gem before they do."

Tomás stroked his beard to calm his anxiety, "Where is Cristóbal? If he needs our help we should set off at once. Perhaps our informant in Dee's household will know his location. For a little more gold he will tell us everything Dee knows and is planning."

"Sí. We should learn everything we can. Pay the spy - we need all the intelligence we can get. Then prepare a team Tomás, and be ready to go with them anywhere on this cursed isle, to find Cristóbal and this gem. Perhaps we can take it from under Dee's very nose."

The damned man

Sir William Herbert, Earl of Pembroke, sent his steward and twenty of his household men with unambiguous instructions ringing in the steward's ears.

"Organise a search. Have groups of men ride each of the main roads out of Faversham. Question everyone you meet for news of a group of armed militia with captives. I expect you to make quick progress as Kent is awash with observant soldiers, sailors and merchants thanks to the proximity of the Cinque Ports. Go now, and do not fail me."

Herbert himself rode with five remaining men to Rochester Castle, intending to meet the Lord Lieutenant of Kent, Sir Thomas Cheyne.

Cheyne was of similar rank having served on and off the Privy Council for several years. In theory they were colleagues, but the energetic Herbert had never warmed to the older man, who he thought of as slippery.

Nonetheless Herbert had to see him, as a courtesy, to explain why armed men of his household were roaming the Kentish countryside.

Cheyne welcomed him formally and suggested Herbert stay overnight and dine with him at the Keep, and insisted that on the morrow some of his own men would join the search, although Cheyne cautioned, "I cannot personally assist as I have to travel to Dover to oversee the muster of a band of pikemen for service in the castle there." Herbert managed to hide his surprise at Cheyne's unexpectedly generous response.

The evening meal in the Keep was attended by Cheyne's wife, Anne, their phlegmatic son, Henry, who hardly raised his eyes during the meal, and two dull older daughters from his first marriage. They were a dreary group and Herbert couldn't wait for the night to be over so he could join his men on the search.

The rest of Cheyne's household ate at lower tables in the great hall. They were a more lively crowd and Herbert reflected that he'd rather be dining with them. As his eyes swept the room he spotted a tall young woman in a green gown that offset her dark hair which was adorned with a sparkling hair net. After watching her quietly for a few moments he sighed and shook his head ruefully. He dared not get distracted by such a prize, however attractive, the rules of the Brotherhood were strict. Besides, his young wife Anne might hear of it and then no doubt she would feign headaches for several months like she had the last time.

Cheyne saw where Herbert's attention had settled and bristled automatically, *The damned man should keep his eyes to himself.*

Chapter 24 - Disinclination

Saturday the 11th of June 1552
Rochester Castle, Kent

Despair and self-loathing

At first light Cheyne and two dozen of his liveried men were already mounted in the castle courtyard when Herbert joined them.

Gesturing to half the men, "With your leave Sir Herbert, these will accompany you toward Faversham and undertake the search all along that route, thus letting you concentrate on the more likely coastal roads beyond. The rest will accompany me to Dover."

Thanking Cheyne for his assistance Herbert bowed, then leapt into the saddle with the agility of a young man. He waved for his own men to follow him, then wheeled round and trotted out of the gate, turning eastwards toward the Isle of Sheppey. Cheyne's men followed them out, riding in pairs and making an impressive looking entourage.

Thomas Cheyne watched Sir William and his men ride away and shook his head with a sly smile, "The impetuosity of youth," he muttered.

He dismounted and handed the horse back to his confused looking groom, "Take it back to the stables, I shan't be riding out today after all."

He jogged swiftly up the outer steps of the Keep, belying his own sixty six years of age. Servants scattered before him as he swept through the great hall and up to the gallery heading toward his private study. He was already mentally composing his letter to Bishop Gardiner when he rounded a corner and almost collided with a pair of young women of the household. One of them was the dark haired woman that had caught Herbert's eye the previous evening.

"Katherine, how fare you this fine morning?"

She curtsied, "I am well thank you. Agnes and I were watching from the window. You are not going to Dover after all?"

"Plans change, some urgent business requires my attention here first."

"'Tis a fine day for riding. Perhaps I would be permitted to take a ride out. Accompanied of course."

He chuckled, almost enjoying the sparring, "Maybe another day. There are rumours of brigands snatching people off the street, so we must all take extra care. Now, if you will excuse me?" He bowed briefly and walked smoothly past the women.

As he went to his desk, acknowledging his secretary Henry Tennent with a brief nod, he tried to examine his own feelings for the woman.

Just three short years ago, when she had been but fifteen, he had placed her with the other young ladies in his wife Anne's household at Shurland Hall, on the Isle of Sheppey. Ostensibly this was as a favour to Katherine's father, Thomas Arden, the Mayor of Faversham. She was a fine looking girl and he didn't have to delve too deep to recognise his own ulterior motives. However it had been a tumultuous time at court, with Kett's rebellion, and then the fall of the Duke of Somerset, and Cheyne's loss of influence as the Earl of Warwick took the reins of power. He had spent most of his time in London, rarely finding time to visit his family at Shurland. During a brief visit back to the Hall about a year ago he learned that Katherine had become a firm favourite of his wife's, and attended on her most evenings. This had given him ample opportunity to notice her developing womanly charms.

One evening, finding himself alone in the room with her, and fuelled by more wine than usual, he tried to press his attentions. She had dodged and wriggled and slipped away from his fumbling grip, slapping his face as a parting gesture. Her *coyness* as he saw it only served to inflame him further, and he had spent the next few evenings plotting how to get her alone again, this time without being the worse for drink.

However, before he could act out his carnal desires she vanished, fleeing the house without a word to anyone.

Anne of course had been distraught, questioning Cheyne about that evening and clearly not believing his version of events. However, within days they learned of a scandal concerning Katherine's family and so her disappearance was accepted as being related to that. As a Privy Councillor he had even had to make judgement on the accused in the scandal and had since almost convinced himself that this was why Katherine ran away, despite his failed attempt to seduce her.

There had been no contact for over a year.

Then, just a week ago, his secretary, Henry, had seen her entering Rochester on horseback, dressed as a rough adventurer no less. Henry, ever resourceful, had persuaded her to accompany him back to the castle, aided by a handful of burly young men.

Lady Anne had been delighted to welcome her back even though the young woman would say nothing of her absence, nor her reasons for leaving a year earlier.

Where she had been was a mystery, but now she was back Cheyne realised his own feelings were a jumble. He wanted her to stay because he still dreamed of dominating her, but the temptation and consequences were so great he also wanted her gone.

He sighed and hung his head, partly in shame and partly in despair and self-loathing. Then straightening his spine he pulled the parchment toward him and began to write to Bishop Gardiner.

Chapter 25 - Violation

Friday the 17th of June 1552
The Phoenix Tavern, Faversham

Forgive our trespasses

"Here Allie, take this broth up to the injured boy and see you feed it to him as best you can. That guard will be up to check in a few hours and we don't need no trouble from the powerful patrons that boy seems to have."

"Yes father, I'll do it now."

"And be sure you change the dressing on his arm and wipe his brow. Last time your mother checked after you'd fed him she said he was all sweaty."

Alice took the tray of food, a fresh poultice, and a clean cloth toward the back stairs that led to the room where the handsome stranger had lain for nearly two weeks now.

She trembled slightly as she climbed toward him, whispering to herself under her breath, "Holy Mary, Mother of God, hear my prayers. I am an unworthy sinner in my hour of need. Give me strength now that I need it."

As she entered the darkened room her heart beat faster and her mouth was so dry she couldn't swallow. She lay the tray to one side and tentatively stepped closer to the man who lay sleeping under the thin blanket.

She stood over him and gazed down at his strong chiselled features. He was her Odysseus, from the Greek stories, washed up on the shore of her private island. And she was his Athena - there to tend to his injuries and to his soul.

She knelt beside him and using the cloth she tentatively wiped the perspiration from his brow. He murmured at the touch, but did not

172

wake. She ever so gently pushed aside his wavy, shoulder length hair and mopped his neck and shoulders.

She paused and closed her eyes in another quick prayer. "Our Father, forgive our trespasses, as we forgive those who trespass against us. Lead us not into temptation but deliver us from evil. Amen."

Trembling, she reverently folded down the blanket revealing his chest, then she paused again desperately trying to avert her eyes, but stubbornly they remained fixed on the sculpted lines of masculinity that she had revealed.

Slowly, slowly she leaned forward, almost against her will, until her lips brushed his skin. She let out an anguished groan that was stifled by the very body she craved.

It is not too late - pull away before he wakes.

She ignored her inner voice and slowly pushed the blanket lower still as she laid fluttering kisses across his body.

If he doesn't wake, I will be able to stop, I am sure of it. Please don't let him wake. Please...

He woke.

"What? Where? I can't see! Kat, is that you?"

His eyes had been damaged by gunpowder they said, so had been bathed time and again with warmed goat's milk and were now tightly bound with soft cloth to protect them from the light. His wrists were tied to the bed to stop him clawing the bandage from his eyes if he woke...like now.

He struggled against his bonds, confused and a little delirious, the effects of the battle still preying on his mind. He never seemed to remember these episodes so she had grown bold over the preceding days.

Quickly, before the struggles became too violent, she whispered that "Yes, yes, it is Kat, I am here for you," and stroked his brow until he calmed.

Then she continued stroking and whispering until he became excited in other ways and again she succumbed to the temptation despite her prayers asking for strength.

As she rode him he called out in French and the only word she understood was "Kat."

Afterwards, as they lay exhausted, their sweat mingling, she felt their heartbeats gradually slow down in tandem and told herself that proved it was blessed by God.

Reluctantly, but hurriedly, she tidied up and while wiping his face and brow she was again tempted, but knowing her protracted absence would be noted she replaced the blanket, changed his bandage, and fed him. The activity had weakened him and he subsided again to a deep sleep. *A perfect angel,* she thought.

Rising, she kissed her fingers and placed them briefly on his lips, whispering "Jack, until tomorrow, my love."

Then taking a last look around the room to ensure no sign remained of her illicit tryst, she crept down the stairs and back to her mundane daily tasks.

Chapter 26 - Incarceration

Saturday the 18th of June 1552
East wing, Rochester Castle

Cunning Scottish reivers

Sir Thomas Cheyne put away his quill as his secretary entered.

"Henry. Come in. What progress with our prisoner?"

"I took Thomas in with me today as you suggested. He paced the room and glowered throughout the entire questioning, playing his role to perfection, but I fear Doctor Cardano is not as easily intimidated as we hoped. He still claims that he has no understanding of the message."

Cheyne banged his fist on the desk, "I need to know what the message means. And I need to know whether Dee already has the answer. These are simple enough things are they not?"

"My lord. He did offer one thing."

Cheyne waited for his secretary to continue.

"He said if you could supply suitable books he could research the matter himself, here, and deliver his results up to you. In fact he said he was looking for a new patron anyway, and was aware he was being treated well and could easily overlook the current loss of his freedom if he were taken into your household. He also said he was training the boy Matthew as his apprentice and he could help too. But that last is surely a lie, the boy cannot even read."

Cheyne paced the room, then turned back with a cruel smile. "Actually, that could provide me a way out of this mess. Yes. Find him the books he needs, and quill and ink, whatever he requires, within reason. Allow him some freedom of movement, but no mixing with the rest of the household. And ensure he is watched at all times. Tell him he has one month to solve the riddle and will be paid well if he leads me to the treasure. But if he does not…"

Henry's answering smile flickered uncertainly. He wished he was back at his accounts, controlling the running of the estates, not haranguing a man that they had no legal right to be holding as prisoner. He would never voice such qualms of course. He glanced at his master's face and saw the new resolve around this decision, and sighed inwardly. He would do his duty to his lord, and without mistakes if possible, after all, he didn't want to end up like the guard captain who had captured the wrong astrologer. That man was now demoted and guarding one of Sir Thomas' draughty northern estates, alternately shivering in a damp stone keep with minimal comforts, and riding the frozen hills and icy streams to chase down the cunning Scottish reivers and return the cattle they kept stealing.

Chapter 27 - Concentration

Late June / Early July 1552
Kingston, England

Chieftain of the Cimbri

Dee had written out the verse from the jewel box's parchment as well as he could remember it, and had pinned it to the wall of his library in Kingston.

The Bloodstone of Boiorix
Only the pure of heart will find it
Only the impure of body need it
Find the house of Justus
And four men will take yer
To the shrine of the baker

For days Dee pored over ancient scrolls and had eventually found references to Boiorix. He explained the story to the twins in an effort to cheer them up as they had taken the loss of Kat and Jack badly.

"Boiorix was a mighty chieftain of the Cimbri, a proud tribe who lived in the lands that we now call Denmark during the time of the early Romans. His people suffered hardships from flooding and so migrated to the south, where they had battles with the Romans, beating them soundly many times. However in a final battle the great General Gaius Marius led the Romans to victory and all but wiped out the Cimbri and their allies. The remaining fighters fled west to avoid capture and some finally arrived in England.

"Those few hardy survivors brought with them the great Bloodstone of Boiorix. This gemstone was as large as the egg of a hen, and captivated the eye of the beholder with its pattern of luminous red swirls. They said the stone had magical restorative powers and had healed the great Boiorix many times after his desperate battles against the tyrannical Romans.

"They presented the stone to the King of the Cantiaci tribe in Kent, and in exchange they were allowed to stay and live as respected members of the tribe.

"The Romans would not let them live in peace however, and eventually followed them into Kent, and after many battles finally conquered all the native tribes."

Ed was fascinated with the story and interrupted Dee excitedly, "Did the Romans steal the Bloodstone?"

"The Romans never found the stone, for it was well hidden. The ancient belief is that the stone would allow itself to be found again whenever the English kings needed its healing powers. The last king who wrote about the stone and hence is believed to have used it, is King Æthelberht of Kent who had an unusually healthy and long life. He converted to Christianity and founded a great Cathedral, in Canterbury, his most important town."

"So where is the stone now?" asked Hal, clearly getting frustrated with all the ancient history.

"It seems it stayed in Canterbury, perhaps always in the care of the Abbots of St Augustines, we may never know. Then the last Abbot planned to have it interred with him in the church of St Martins.

"But something happened at the last moment, some emergency they had not foreseen, and the stone was moved elsewhere with a hastily written clue being all that remained.

"Find the house of Justus

"And four men will take yer

"To the shrine of the baker."

"But what does that mean?" asked Hal again.

"Ay, well, that's the rub. I don't know. And yet I need to bend all my skill to deciphering the clue before the people who abducted Dottore Cardono figure out the answer."

Rousing the boys and encouraging them back to their tasks for the day, Dee returned to his labours, knowing that first he had to identify the mysterious 'Justus'.

Chapter 28 - Lamentation

Monday the 18th of July 1552
The Phoenix Tavern, Faversham

Vigenère

Walter, the guard posted by Sir William Herbert, wearily climbed up the inn's back stairs to check on Dr Dee's incapacitated apprentice. Just as he had three times a day, every day, for the last six weeks. The lad always looked healthy enough, but whenever he woke he always seemed delirious and no sense could be made of his words.

In his heart Walter believed that all this watching and caring was a waste of effort.

The lad will never recover his wits. We should put him out of his misery and have a priest provide the last rites.

Still, he wasn't the one giving the orders, so he trudged in and gave the lad's shoulder a shake.

No response. Oh well, at least it will be a quiet visit.

Looking down on the silent form he thought of his own boy, John, who would have been of a similar age if he had lived through the last sweating sickness that had taken so many from their town. His first wife had cried herself to her grave in the months following John's passing, refusing to eat, and denying Christ as the saviour.

A surge of anger swept through him; *no-one checked on my boy John, nor helped me tend to my wife Mary.*

Before he realised what he was doing he had reached down and slapped the lad hard across the face, dislodging the bandage from its place.

Jack's eyes sprang open and his calloused hand managed to pull against the restraint just far enough to catch the wrist of the man looming over him. Twisting and pulling at the same time he caused an astonished Walter to lose his balance and crash down beside Jack.

Jack hoarsely demanded, "Qui es-tu? Parle vite!"

Walter had no French, but even if he had he was too shocked to speak, merely babbling incoherently as he struggled futilely against the powerful grasp of the young man.

Almost as quickly as he had awoken, Jack's strength faded and he sagged back onto his pallet bed and fell asleep once more.

Walter levered himself painfully up to a sitting position, breathing hard, and held his sore wrist whilst trying to comprehend what had happened.

Gods he is strong, but still tired thank goodness.

I'm glad he is still tied to the bed otherwise he could have done more than wound my pride!

His wits are recovered though - I will have to report that to Inkbold and worse still to Sir Herbert.

Maybe the boy will remember that I hit him? That won't go well for me - I was supposed to be managing his care, not beating him!

But maybe, maybe he won't remember? Or will not know who it was? Yes, yes. I can always blame the inn keeper or his staff. He is probably still a little confused.

Calm Walter. Think!

First fetch the apothecary. And maybe the barber. And get some fresh food and water. See that the boy's waking moments reveal me as his saviour not his assailant.

Yes, that's the way.

He rushed down the stairs and up the street heading for the apothecary's store.

Walter stood with his beefy arms folded and an uncertain look on his face, as he watched the apothecary ply his trade. The barber stood beside him, fascinated to watch a fellow professional at work.

First he fully removed the bandage from the boy's head, and gently wiped around his eyes with a cloth. The swelling and burns on his cheeks and forehead had all receded now, although his eyebrows had barely started to grow back after being burned away.

He then mixed some powders in a little water and stirred the mixture for a few minutes, before scooping the resulting paste out on his forefinger and smeared it across Jack's moustache. Then he leaned back to wait.

Moments later Jack yawned and stretched. Walter braced himself, ready to spring and hold the boy down if he got violent, but there was no need. He merely woke as if from a normal sleep and croaked "Where am I?" and "Who are you?"

While the others explained his injuries to him, Walter cautiously untied the restraints, flinching slightly when Jack flexed his cramped arms.

Within a few hours, and against the apothecary's advice, Jack was sitting near the small window. The barber busied himself, darting around Jack, cutting and shaving, generally doing his professional best to make Jack look civilised again.

Walter fussed around and took pains to ingratiate himself by explaining his own attendance on Jack's health for the last few weeks.

Gazing out of the window Jack could see the courtyard with horses being led through to a blacksmith, chickens scratching in the vegetable patch, and beyond that a small church spire. The bells rang for noon and jarred a memory within him, and he looked uncomfortably around. He thought he remembered Kat visiting him while those same bells rang. Had she kissed him? Had she done more?

Nonchalantly he asked Walter, "Have any of my colleagues been to see me?"

"Nay, master. The Doctor returned to London and it has just been myself guarding you, the apothecary here visited occasionally, and the tavern owners have been providing your food and general care."

Jack coloured. He realised he had been incapable of looking after himself for many weeks and yet he felt....refreshed. And something more, nagging at the edge of memory. During Kat's visits... He picked at the edges of the memory trying to reveal it fully, but it wouldn't come, so shaking his head he left it.

"Please, Walter, I must go to the manufactory," he said.

The apothecary strenuously objected and even Walter thought this swift action would endanger his recovery, but Jack would not be gainsaid.

As they left the inn Jack made a pretty speech of thanks for his care to the old inn keeper and his wife, but said he had to leave urgently.

Walter guided Jack toward the gunpowder facility. Mostly he walked a pace behind Jack, so the lad could retain his dignity, but twice had to step up quickly and catch the young man as he stumbled, before rallying and continuing at a slower and slower rate.

As they reached the gated compound and were admitted by a pair of armed guards they heard an almost feral ululation of loss emanating from the town. They didn't know it, but Alice had returned from the market to find her god risen like a phoenix from the ashes and flown from the nest.

Glancing back as he left Jack and Inkbold together, Walter hoped the lad remembered no harm.

Inkbold greeted Jack warmly, still feeling responsible for the attack and the poor security at the compound. He offered some warmed Rhenish red to fortify Jack who looked grey and deathly weary.

Nervous, he drank two glasses of wine for every glass Jack drank, and soon his tongue was spilling a babble of stories, anything to fill the quiet and to dispel his unease.

Jack took the opportunity to rest and listen, and though he struggled to focus he learned more about the finances of the manufactory and the character of the owner Doctor Dee. Soon Inkbold was in full flow, earlier embarrassment forgotten, regaling Jack with family anecdotes, and even tales from his youth as an altar boy at the church in a nearby town.

Inkbold had just started telling the story of a heinous murder here in Faversham a couple of years ago, when Jack suddenly snapped his wandering attention back to the older man.

"Can you describe your time as an altar boy some more?"

Inkbold beamed. He rarely had visitors and certainly no one had shown such interest in his reminiscing before, and so he gladly launched into a more fulsome description of his responsibilities as an altar boy, and the architecture and history of the church.

Inkbold had started a new anecdote, this time about the Bishop, "It was during the Liturgy of the Eucharist you see. The old Bishop raised the chalice of wine over the altar, but clumsily stepped on his own robes, and stumbled, spilling the liquid over me and Joseph the other altar boy. Both our albs and the altar cloth itself were soaking wet and stained a ruby red colour! The Bishop reached out to stop his fall but only succeeded in somehow flinging the plate of unconsecrated host spinning through the air." Inkbold was chuckling at the memory, obviously still fresh after all these years.

Gradual realisation dawned for Jack. His smile broke out and just got bigger. Eventually he could contain himself no longer and jumped up interrupting Inkbold's own merriment, "Master, I need a quill and two sheets of paper as quickly as you can, for I must send a message to Dee at once."

Inkbold managed to look both confused and hurt at the same time, so Jack quickly placated him, "Your stories have given me almost divine inspiration Master Inkbold. Doctor Dee will be so grateful for your assistance."

Mollified, Inkbold bustled around the room collecting the writing supplies for Jack.

As Jack sat at the desk he asked, "What cipher do you commonly use?"

"Cipher? Why none. There is no need and so I have never learned."

Jack muttered as much to himself as to Inkbold, "Awkward. Dee and I had not expected to be separated, so we have not pre-agreed an encryption method. But I must use a cipher as this information is too vital to be written out plain where anyone could read it if our courier is intercepted.

"Dee taught me several methods for secret writing. The most secret relies on a grid of the letters of the alphabet written out many times, with a special keyword being used to encrypt and decrypt."

Jack's brow furrowed in thought, *But how can I let Dee know what method I am using and what the keyword is?*

Inkbold presented the quill, ink, and paper to Jack saying, "Here you are, young Master. Inkbold is a byword for efficiency in these parts you know."

Jack laughed out loud, and seeing Inkbold's face fall he explained, "Once again sir you give me the inspiration I need. I shall use a Vigenère method and your name as the key!

"Now first I must carefully create the grid. This may take a little while…"

He proceeded to write out the alphabet, then repeated the letters underneath it, then repeated again but with the letters shifted one place to the left, and so on until he had a complete grid.

```
    A B C D E F G H I J K L M N O P Q R S T U V W X Y Z
  A A B C D E F G H I J K L M N O P Q R S T U V W X Y Z
  B B C D E F G H I J K L M N O P Q R S T U V W X Y Z A
  C C D E F G H I J K L M N O P Q R S T U V W X Y Z A B
  D D E F G H I J K L M N O P Q R S T U V W X Y Z A B C
  E E F G H I J K L M N O P Q R S T U V W X Y Z A B C D
  F F G H I J K L M N O P Q R S T U V W X Y Z A B C D E
  G G H I J K L M N O P Q R S T U V W X Y Z A B C D E F
  H H I J K L M N O P Q R S T U V W X Y Z A B C D E F G
  I I J K L M N O P Q R S T U V W X Y Z A B C D E F G H
  J J K L M N O P Q R S T U V W X Y Z A B C D E F G H I
  K K L M N O P Q R S T U V W X Y Z A B C D E F G H I J
  L L M N O P Q R S T U V W X Y Z A B C D E F G H I J K
  M M N O P Q R S T U V W X Y Z A B C D E F G H I J K L
  N N O P Q R S T U V W X Y Z A B C D E F G H I J K L M
  O O P Q R S T U V W X Y Z A B C D E F G H I J K L M N
  P P Q R S T U V W X Y Z A B C D E F G H I J K L M N O
  Q Q R S T U V W X Y Z A B C D E F G H I J K L M N O P
  R R S T U V W X Y Z A B C D E F G H I J K L M N O P Q
  S S T U V W X Y Z A B C D E F G H I J K L M N O P Q R
  T T U V W X Y Z A B C D E F G H I J K L M N O P Q R S
  U U V W X Y Z A B C D E F G H I J K L M N O P Q R S T
  V V W X Y Z A B C D E F G H I J K L M N O P Q R S T U
  W W X Y Z A B C D E F G H I J K L M N O P Q R S T U V
  X X Y Z A B C D E F G H I J K L M N O P Q R S T U V W
  Y Y Z A B C D E F G H I J K L M N O P Q R S T U V W X
  Z Z A B C D E F G H I J K L M N O P Q R S T U V W X Y
```

When he had completed the grid he flexed his aching wrist and gratefully drank from his goblet.

Underneath the grid he wrote out his message in plain English script, starting with the salutation 'Doctor'.

"This is how I do it" he explained, "I look down the column that is headed by the letter I want to encrypt. I want to encrypt the letter 'D', so I start looking down the column for 'D'. I go down to the row that has the first letter of my key, 'Inkbold', so 'I' in this case. You follow?"

"Aye. I see that the row that starts with 'I' crosses the column that starts with 'D' to yield the letter 'L'."

"Exactly! And so we continue. The second letter of 'Doctor' is 'O', so

I look down that column until I reach the row for the second letter of my key 'Inkbold' which is 'N', thus the encrypted letter is … 'B'.

"The whole message may take me a few minutes…."

"Now I need to write out a plain introduction to my letter in such a way that Dee understands what key to use to decipher the rest."

> Greetings Doctor. I am here at the manufactory with Master Vigenère the manager of this place. Tomorrow I leave for Canterbury.
>
> LBMUCC, WPR VPQLWQBX PT EKM FDPBP LA EYDVPVBRB DOEKMQBBZ LW BUO TVCLVR YG KTOTVKN CQ SMEDI KSR ENC B PLNME, S TVLOT TY UVPUM AYX
>
> Jack.

Inkbold leaned over pointing out his mistake, "But Jack you have got my name wrong!"

Jack replied laughing, "Exactly. And that will draw Dee's attention to it, and hopefully he will guess to use your actual name as the repeating key to unlock the message. The name I have used 'Vigenère' is the type of code.

"I think there is little risk that our opponents will understand this code."

"But Jack. If the message is intercepted it is plain as day that it is in code and they can bend their will to decrypting it."

"You are right, but without the key they will make little progress. Can you send this by fast messenger to Dee today?"

"Of course, but it will take at least a full day. So you'll go to Canterbury tomorrow?"

"No, no. That is just more misdirection, to confuse anyone who intercepts the message. Dee taught me not to write anything of consequence in the plain text part of the message.

"Now, if you give me shelter tonight I will ride out west tomorrow, in the opposite direction to Canterbury. Can you write an introductory letter to help me when I arrive?"

Inkbold readily agreed and they laid their plans.

Chapter 29 - Observation

Wednesday the 20th of July 1552
Faversham, Kent

Missing from action

A message had arrived from his spy in Dee's household, so Renard knew almost as quickly as Dee, that Jack in Faversham had regained his wits and had written to Dee with the location of the gemstone.

Tomás had left immediately with a small troop of hirelings, and ridden through the night. They entered Faversham at a walk, their horses tired and covered in sweat.

Dismounting outside the Phoenix inn, Tomás turned to Big Red, "We need to confirm when the lad left here and started toward Canterbury."

Without a word the tall Englishman went to find the innkeeper.

Meanwhile Tomás brushed the dust from his fine riding clothes and toyed with the handle of his sword. A pretty barmaid crossed the courtyard and he thought her looks were spoiled by the red eyes as though from weeping.

Red reported that Jack had left two days before, accompanying Herbert's man to Dee's manufactory west of town. They retraced his steps. As they rode sedately through the town Tomás wondered where Cristóbal could be, or if he was even alive.

Again, Big Red did the talking. The guard answered his questions readily enough for a few coins.

"He caught a ride with a carter and headed toward Canterbury on Tuesday," reported Red.

As they turned east and took the road through the forest, Tomás sneered at the English for being such simple folk and so cheaply bought. He kept the men to a gentle pace as the animals were tired after their all-night ride, and he knew no haste would be needed to catch up with a lumbering cart.

Three hours later they passed over the river and under the imposing West Gate in the Canterbury city walls. They stopped for a much belated breakfast at the first inn they found. Grumbling, Big Red was sent to enquire about the carter.

They were eating the best pottage the inn had to offer when Red came back looking disturbed.

"It is the feast day of Mary Magdalene, and a dozen carts have entered the city already today. No one recognised Jack from my description, but that means little with so much traffic. Our best plan will be to search all the market stalls near the Cathedral, starting at the Bull Stake."

A Castilian oath escaped his lips as Tomás cursed their bad luck. He realised he had made a tactical mistake. They should have ridden harder and caught up with the carter on the road. Now they would have to search the whole city.

"Finish your food quickly, then we search in pairs. We meet back here at sundown. If you find the boy, keep a watch on him, and report back quickly."

Chapter 30 - Obfuscation

Historia ecclesiastica

It took Dee several weeks of dusty research before he emerged from his library triumphant.

He had focussed his efforts on the few ancient monkish books that he owned and had found an intriguing reference in *Historia ecclesiastica gentis Anglorum,* the eighth century account of the history of the church in England, by the venerable monk Bede.

It contained a reference to another book called *Textus Roffensis,* the Tome of Rochester. Dee had heard of this book. Supposedly, it contained details of early Anglo-Saxon laws, from the time of King Æthelberht onwards.

Dee felt sure he was on the right track, after all they had found the jewel case in the church of Queen Bertha, Æthelberht's wife.

But how to proceed? He didn't have a copy of the Textus.

A nagging thought stirred deep in his memory, and he scoured the shelves of his library until he finally found a 14th-century book called *Liber Temporalium.* This contained a few copied sections of the Textus, and there it was nestling in the middle, a copy of an ancient charter from King Æthelberht, dated 28th of April 604, that recorded a grant of land near Rochester to Justus' church. It was even signed by the King himself, and twenty other witnesses.

He shouted out in joy "'the house of Justus' is Rochester Cathedral".

Moments later, a shadowy form crept past the library door and down the stairs, exiting through the warehouse's side door, and merging with the afternoon crowd of townsfolk.

Rochester Cathedral

Dean Oxenbrigg had not been available when he arrived on the Tuesday, so Jack had spent the day learning the by-ways of Rochester, and preparing for the next stage of his journey back to Kingston.

However at noon on Wednesday he presented himself at the great west gate of Rochester Cathedral to meet the Dean.

While he waited he gazed up in wonder at the arched tympanum over the doorway, with its intricate carvings, surrounded by life-size statues. He marvelled that man could build anything so grand, and all in the name of a god that abandoned his people so readily.

A shuffling and huffing sound intruded on his thoughts.

Inkbold had said that Oxenbrigg was a short man, but he hadn't said he was nearly as wide as he was tall. As he approached Jack he seemed to roll from side to side. He was breathing hard and winced in pain as they greeted each other, and Jack wondered if the introductory letter from Inkbold would be enough to charm the man.

He shouldn't have worried though, because the Dean's face lit up with an expression of delight as he exclaimed "My old friend Tobias. We were altar boys together so many years ago you know." Jack said indeed, yes, he did know.

Oxenbrigg insisted on personally giving a tour of the cathedral, all the while patiently answering questions posed by Jack.

"Who founded the Cathedral?" asked Jack

"It was founded in the seventh century by Justus, a missionary who accompanied St Augustine to convert the pagans of southern England. Justus was made Bishop, and King Æthelberht granted him permission to build a church."

"Ah yes, I remember now, that is what Master Inkbold told me. It can justly be called the House of Justus then?"

Laughing at the pun and building on it, "Yes. Yes, it could be called just that. But you should realise that the building you see today is the result of massive rebuilding in the eleventh and twelfth centuries, after the Norman invasion."

As they walked down the nave toward the quire screen and organ they paused at the crossing, where the four arms of the cruciform-shaped church met, and the Dean pointed out which sections were original and which were of newer construction. Above them the roof included four distinctive faces of 'green men' carved in wood, and painted, mostly in green of course.

"Strange and slightly unnerving," muttered Jack, gesturing toward them.

Oxenbrigg replied, "Yes, each carved face is surrounded by leaves or ivy. I don't know the exact origin, but perhaps they represent our connection to nature, or maybe they're pagan fertility symbols. I understand that some other churches have them too, but I think ours are quite special."

Conspiratorially, Jack turned to the Dean and asked, "There is something else quite special, I think you have an ancient shrine here, don't you?"

Whispering, "Oh yes. We have one of the most important shrines in England, second only to Becket's shrine at Canterbury. But since the monasteries came down we try to keep rather quiet about it."

"I can imagine. But as I am directed here by your friend Tobias, would it be possible for me to see it?"

"Follow me," and he led the way into the north transept. In the centre of the floor was a large stone chest, with tall candlesticks holding fat yellow candles that burned with a low flame. The chest was intricately carved with both text and images.

Jack's palms were sweating. He needed time alone with the shrine.

"And could I possibly pray for my father, for a while? Alone?"

The Dean looked about him cautiously, even though no-one was around.

"Yes, of course. For a friend of Tobias, anything. Come and find me in the presbytery when you are finished."

As soon as he was alone, Jack fell to his knees. But not to pray. He shuffled over to the chest and peered closely at all the carvings. He wasn't quite sure what he was looking for. *Is there a secret compartment containing the stone? Or a mention of Boiorix chiselled into it?*

Some time later he had to admit defeat. He had been around the entire chest and closely examined every side. Some of the text was worn to the point of being indecipherable. Some of the carvings had been chiselled off, and many images defaced. The chiselling was probably the actions of commissioners during the iconoclasm brought on by the Injunctions for Religious Reforms. None of the remaining carvings were meaningful, at least not to his quest. And there seemed no way into the chest short of a team of men to hoist the huge stone lid.

He walked slowly back to the presbytery, head hung low.

The Dean turned toward the sound of Jack's approach. Guilt

embraced him as he saw how dejected he was, and he felt forced to ask, "Did you not get the satisfaction you sought, my son?"

"No," replied Jack, "It felt...empty, wrong somehow."

He saw the Dean blush a bright red, making his head look like a tomato, that newly imported fruit from the New World.

"Ah. Perhaps...but how could you tell? You see, the relic at the heart of the shrine was moved, to protect it from the commissioners of the Reformation. The actual reliquary is in the crypt beneath us, perhaps that is why your prayers were unsatisfactory?"

This must be it, he thought, there were often jewels embedded in the reliquary caskets, "Could I go down and pray beside it? It would mean so much to me."

Now the Dean looked truly uncomfortable. He cast around for reasons why not, but eventually acquiesced. Passing Jack a candle he led the way, unlocking the door and carefully leading them down worn spiral steps into the crypt. He led Jack to a far corner, where alongside a cold stone wall was a plain block of stone and atop it a decorated reliquary with some obscure bone fragments inside.

"Here are the remains of William of Perth, the baker, Saint of adopted children. I will leave you in peace for a while, may you find the solace you seek. But please...don't take too long."

It is not solace I am looking for, thought Jack, but he quickly knelt and bowed his head in prayer, until the flickering light of the Dean's candle had retreated back up the stairway and he was sure he was alone.

A quick glance showed that there were no jewels mounted on the casket and Jack chided himself for even hoping for anything so obvious. He shuffled closer. Fittingly there were many small mouldings that looked like babies, but also some that were just shapeless blobs. *Loaves of bread perhaps? Worn smooth by thousands of caressing hands?*

He shuddered, but forced himself to continue his detailed examination, running his hands over the frame and across all the decorations. It was quite heavy but he turned it around and continued examining the next side.

One of the baby figures had a strange shadow that wasn't being cast by light from his candle. He looked closer still and realised it wasn't a shadow at all, it was because the metal shape was ever so slightly raised from the body of the casket. He pushed and prodded, and then finally twisted the shape and heard a tiny 'click' and the moulding popped further out, with a grooved rod joining it to the casket base.

Eagerly but gently he pulled it out several inches. The groove was like a tiny tray, and resting in it was a rolled up scrap of parchment. With shaking fingers he teased the paper out and then slid the tray shut, whereupon the baby realigned itself with a gentle snap. He turned the reliquary back around and blew dust around the base to hide the disturbance he'd caused.

Gently he unrolled the message, read it, blinked in confusion, and rolled it up again.

Staring into unseeing eyes you atone
From the gift of the ferryman's daughter
Shielding the location of the stone
Or a chief gules taught her

Obviously this was not the Bloodstone itself, instead it appeared to be a second clue. Secreting the paper in his purse he took his candle and returned to the Dean.

"Thank you for your kindness sir. One more thing only I would ask. It is something I heard mentioned and it was puzzling for me, but to a man of your learning may be easily understood - do you know anything of a gift from the ferryman's daughter? No? Ah, well. No matter."

He again thanked the Dean profusely and promised to remember him to Inkbold. Then he tapped the side of his nose and said conspiratorially, "I was never here."

Dean Oxenbrigg thought that a great wheeze and winked back at him in an exaggerated way.

Jack bowed and then strode down the nave and out the way he had entered, through the great west door, and back into the warm July sunshine.

Tythes to B. Rochester

Cardano had read every book and every manuscript that had been made available to him. He had found nothing pertinent to solving the riddle, indeed nothing even remotely interesting. This wasn't surprising he thought, because the castle was a barracks not a place of learning, and scholarly material was thin on the ground. Henry, his gaoler as he thought of him, was a kindly man who had brought what books were available from all the leading merchants, clergy and scholars in the town, but it was to no avail.

Worried that a lack of progress would come with some loss of his already minimal privileges, or worse, he resorted to checking through the castle accounts. Soon he was well on his way to being bored to death by the minor fluctuations in the price of ale and hogs, and could tell at a glance which had been good harvest years and which poor - and there had been many more poor than good it seemed. He even found a trail of financial corruption in the accounts of one manor where a new man of business was clearly skimming the profits. He jotted a note to tell Cheyne.

He pulled over a dusty old ledger labelled 'Tythes to B. Rochester'. Opening it randomly he saw it accounted for all the tithes paid by the Lieutenant of the Castle to the Bishop of Rochester, presumably enthroned at the cathedral that he could see from the window behind him. Bored, he let the pages flick through his fingers, and noticed a little cartoon of a monk that someone had drawn in the corner of each page. He let the corners of the pages riffle through his fingers again, this time as many of the pages as he could, and laughed out loud as the figure bent over and lifted his cassock, before carrying a large cross and then the cross falling on him and crushing him. Clearly the castle comptroller had too much time on his hands.

He was still chuckling when Matthew rushed in without knocking and started babbling about Kat being pretty when she was clean and wearing a dress.

He stood stock-still looking down at the ledger that had stayed open on the first page, his mouth gaping open in shock. The page showed a listing of land leases to the castle including the name of the persons that had leased them.

The first name on the list was Bishop Justus in 615 Anno Domini.

He whirled around and leaned on the window embrasure, staring over at the cathedral which was only a few hundred feet away from him.

Could that be the answer? The House of Justus was Rochester Cathedral? And it was right there minutes away from where he had been kept these many weeks.

As he stared agog trying to wrestle control of his emotions, a figure exited the cathedral.

It looked like his friend Jack.

It was Jack!

He waved frantically, half leaning out of the opening, but it was no use, Jack had already turned and was headed further into town. Cardano tumbled into his chair and held his head in his hands. Was it a trick of the light, or his imagination? No, it had certainly been Jack. Which meant that *was* the House of Justus, he was right. He started to laugh, slightly hysterically.

If Jack was leaving the cathedral did that mean he had found the stone?

And where was Dee?

What to do now? If he could escape now perhaps he could meet up with Jack and they could escape together? They had done it before. They were a good team.

He became aware that Matthew was shaking him by the shoulder, asking if he was feeling alright.

A day late and a man short

The next morning Tomás and the team gathered dejectedly outside the inn, having spent the previous day in a fruitless search for Jack amongst the carters, drovers and market traders in Canterbury. They discussed widening their search, perhaps following the export route to the coast.

They all looked up when a rider galloped through the city gate directly toward them, sliding to a halt and splattering more than one of them with mud. He leapt from the saddle onto the street beside them. It was a long leap for he was a short man, so short that after making a brief bow he had to lean backwards to look Tomás in the face.

"Stumpy," acknowledged Tomás with a nod.

Too out of breath to talk, Stumpy handed over a sealed packet, then stood wheezing against the wall of the inn trying to catch his breath.

Tomás broke the seal and scanned the hastily written note from Renard. He muttered aloud as he read, "It is from Renard. We have been played for fools. We are to go to Rochester cathedral at once and intercept the boy there. There is no time to lose."

He cursed in fluent Castilian for a full minute, realising the oh-so easily bribed guard at Faversham had gulled him completely. He turned to Big Red and told him to ready the horses. Turning to everyone else he said there would be a bonus if they caught the boy this day. He told Stumpy to follow them tomorrow.

"No, no, Señor. Get me a fresh horse and I shall ride as far and fast, although maybe not as tall, as the next man."

The ferryman's daughter

Dean Oxenbrigg twisted and turned in his bed for what must have been the tenth time, pulling the thin blanket over his head in an effort to find sleep.

"By the Mass!" exclaimed his wife, "What on earth is wrong with you tonight? Normally you fall asleep as soon as your head is lain down."

He flopped onto his back and lay still. After a moment he sighed deeply and started his tale with the visit of Inkbold's friend, Jack, and his final strange question "Did I know about the gift of the ferryman's daughter?"

Then the tale took a darker turn. A posse of rough looking men rode into town and the tall red haired one had asked if he had seen Jack. Initially he had tried to deny it, but he was forced to comply when the man held a knife to his throat. He had quickly said that Jack had been interested in the architecture and history of the cathedral, and upon further pressing had revealed the parting question concerning the ferryman's daughter. Thankfully the men left without actually harming him, and he had settled his nerves with a slug of communion wine in the sacristy.

He had hardly resumed his duties when another group of men strode up the nave, headed by the Lord Lieutenant of Kent, who demanded to know what the younger man had wanted earlier in the morning.

"They must have been watching because they knew what he had been wearing and when he had left. I couldn't hope to deny anything, so I took them to the shrine in the north transept and told them what he had asked about the ferryman. I hope he will be alright because I fear he is in terrible trouble."

His wife made placatory noises and rolled over, but the Dean's head swirled with all the possible bad interpretations of the day's events, until resolving to write to Inkbold in the morning he finally drifted into fitful sleep.

New clothes

Jack sat in the gloom at the rear of the busy tavern nursing the last of his ale and wondered how best to proceed.

He closed his eyes and let his mind wander where it will:

Unseeing eyes and the ferryman's daughter.

Cardano being escorted into the cathedral.

The warmth of Kat's body.

A gemstone with swirling red patterns like a bloodshot eye peering at him.

Riding through forests for mile upon mile, seeing Kingston in the distance but never reaching it.

Snatches of other patron's conversations penetrated the fog of his mind;

"…if I had a penny for every time I was asked that…"

"…the price of wool is down again this month…"

"…they leave my shop in their new clothes and not even their mother would recognise them…"

He jerked upright, an idea forcing its way to the front of his mind. Finishing the last of his drink he left the inn by a back door, slipping out into the gentle evening drizzle, finally having a plan for how he could escape his own pursuers and rescue Cardano from his captors.

Chapter 31 - Deportation

Thursday the 21st of July 1552
Outside Rochester Cathedral, Kent

Market vendors

Market vendors were hawking their wares from temporary stalls they had erected in the square, between the castle wall to the west and the cathedral to the east.

At the south end of the square a troupe of travelling players were unloading their scenery and props from a cart, ready to perform a mystery play through which they would teach the audience about the mysteries of the bible stories.

On the grassy patch where the players' horse was tethered, a dozen children were kicking an inflated bladder around, pushing and shoving each other as they attempted to reach it.

A tinker slowly pushed his large handcart of knives and axes, complete with treadle-operated grinding wheel, through the cheerful late morning crowd, calling out in a peculiar accent "knives grinded, hand axes sharper" every few minutes.

A woman with a parrot on a stand was surrounded by a small crowd who ogled at its curved beak and green feathers, until it emitted a shrieking call "awwwwkkk, the lord's my shepherd". The crowd jumped back a pace, crossing themselves, then surged forward again to see the possessed bird up close.

Two armed soldiers emerged from the castle precinct, with a distinguished-looking bearded gentleman between them. Heading for the cathedral, they had to thread their way through the crowded marketplace.

As the soldiers reached the mid-way point an observant person might have seen the tinker pull on a string, and a hatch on the side of the handcart pop open.

Next moment a dozen rabbits hopped out of the cart and started running through the startled crowd. The children abandoned their ball game and raced into the crowd, weaving between goodwives and diving at rabbits, trying and generally failing to catch them.

The crowd surged as the children darted to and fro, separating the soldiers from their charge.

As the rabbits radiated away from their point of origin the children and even some adults followed and the crowd in the square thinned.

The tinker continued on his way, calling out his skills, past the half erected mobile theatre. The parrot screeched, and the traders called out their wares.

The soldiers looked around bemused. Their captive had disappeared.

One raced toward the largest group of children scattering them with the butt end of his pike, the other dodged between the artificial trees and billowing canvas of the theatre scenery. They met again in the middle and exchanged an anxious glance. After a hurried conference the younger soldier raced back to the castle to raise the alarm, whilst the other stood nervously scratching his head and gazing around, perhaps hoping the lost man would miraculously reappear. No such luck.

Behind a barn a few minutes south of the square, the tinker pulled his string again and simultaneously shucked off his tattered cloak and removed his grimy cap, passing them both to the stooped elderly figure that emerged from the barn. Money changed hands and the old man laughed heartily at the scenes he had witnessed. Meanwhile, Gerolamo Cardano, mathematician, astrologer, doctor of medicine, alumnus of the university of Padua, rolled out of the side of the cart onto the earthen floor strewn with damp hay. He sat with a look of absolute amazement on his swarthy features, until Jack jerked him upright and brushed the worst of the straw off him.

With a sketchy bow to the old tinker, Jack turned and steered Cardano to a waiting rowing boat on the riverbank. Within a few short minutes Jack had rowed them into the middle of the river Medway, where they bumped alongside a sailing hoy. A lone fisherman helped them clamber aboard, where they settled low down in the hull. A breeze plumped out the single sail and soon they were carving an easterly path toward the open sea, where they planned to round the headland and re-enter London on the river Thames.

Kat silently applauded the brazen rescue plan, as she watched it unfold from a window high up in the castle. At the same time realised her own plight was sealed. She had asked Matthew to take a message to Cardano, but apparently he had failed to give any credence to the boy and now he was gone.

Lady Anne called her back from the window, saying she would catch a chill. Seeing Kat's downcast expression she reminded her of their travel plans, "In a couple of days we will return to Shurland Hall, on the isle of Sheppey, which is altogether much more pleasant than this dreary castle."

Women and children thirst

"Master Jack, everything is ready as we have planned."

"I am in your debt Goodman Mullens. But tell me again please, are you sure no harm will come to you from this endeavour? My sister would not be happy if she thought I had placed you in any danger, even if it is in aid of her rescue from a rogue."

"Pshaw. You'll be long gone afore anyone even knows it. And if I am questioned I'll just say you cozened me, like you suggested," the man winked with a mischievous smile.

Jack was suddenly overcome with emotion at how this stranger had offered to help, and awkwardly embraced him. The portly man reddened and retreated into the inn, muttering that it was his pleasure and duty to help another Christian family in their time of need.

Jack lounged on the bench outside Mullen's inn, *The Creek and Paddle*, nursing his ale-pot of the inspiringly named, *Mullen's Best*. Another sip swirled around his mouth and he tasted oak smoked wheat and big hops flavours before smacking his lips in delight.

In front of the bench a gentle grassy slope ran down to a hitching rail and thus to the main road that ran from Rochester to the King's Ferry that crossed the Swale to the Isle of Sheppey.

He heard a fiddle start playing from inside the inn and the muffled sounds of singing and dancing. Taking a final sip he reluctantly put the strong beer to one side, thinking it best not to drink too much or too fast if he was to execute the plan successfully.

Throughout the afternoon several groups of travellers appeared on the road, and on full alert Jack would anxiously scan their faces before slumping back on his bench. Most groups would hitch their mounts and visit the inn for refreshments as it was well known as the last hostelry before the final hour's ride to King's Ferry and thus onto the Isle of Sheppey.

He was engaged in a conversation with a Flemish wine merchant about the unusual weather and how it affected the cross-channel shipping, when a richly appointed party rode into view. He glanced across to them, squinting into the lowering sun. Finally he saw the face he had been seeking and his heart skipped. Turning to the vintner he excused himself saying he needed to stretch his legs in the direction of the privy. He stood and faced the travellers, clearly visible to them.

Kat had been riding beside Rebecca since dawn when Lady Anne's entourage had left Rochester castle, and she was completely tired of her inanity. The younger woman had been in Lady Anne's household since she was twelve and knew nothing of the world except lace, lapdogs, and poetry, and her talk was confined to female frippery and gossip regarding which young ladies could recognise which young men merely by looking at their legs. So when Rebecca gushed about the handsome stranger standing outside the inn up ahead Kat initially ignored her and refused to even glance over at the building.

Undeterred, Rebecca called over to one of their escorts, a grizzled veteran of the wars, and intoned as imperiously as she could "This journey is intolerably dusty. The women and children thirst and need to stop for refreshments."

The old soldier indicated that they should wait while he checked, and he trotted ahead to ask his captain, who conferred with Lady Anne and then signalled that a short rest would be taken.

Frustrated at the imposed delay and the adolescent reason for it, Kat moodily glared at the inn. Staring right at her was Jack, who caught her eye, briefly nodded, and then casually sauntered around behind the building.

In shock, Kat allowed one of the guards to secure her horse, then she followed at the rear of the group of ladies and guards into the inn. Their group was immediately led toward a private room that the guard captain had apparently been offered, past the main bar area of the inn where the musicians were midway through a popular melody.

Various other patrons crossed their path, heading toward the dancing that had commenced amidst ragged cheers and laughter. A portly man wearing an apron bustled forward and with a surreptitious finger on his lips steered her by her elbow toward a different door, while Rebecca and all the others continued into the private room. The last she saw of her companions was a buxom barmaid taking tankards of ale into the private room and handing them out to the guards and ladies.

She glanced about in confusion, not afraid, but wondering where she was being taken. They passed down a dark corridor that reeked of stale beer, through a storeroom and out to the rear of the property.

She blinked as she emerged into the fading evening sunlight and Jack appeared as if from nowhere. He hugged her warmly, whispering in her ear that she should not say anything, then swirled a dark coloured hooded cloak over her shoulders.

With a nod of appreciation to Mullen, Jack led Kat across the courtyard through an arch in the wall and they disappeared into dense woodland. The well trodden branching path twisted and turned but Jack led the way surely and swiftly, never pausing or deviating from his planned route. They passed a host of others who were heading toward the inn, greeting them pleasantly but never slowing their pace.

"There is a free barn-dance at the inn tonight and all the locals are hurrying to partake of the festivities," explained Jack.

"Is it a local feast day then?" asked Kat.

Laughing, Jack replied "Aye. 'Tis now. Thanks to a bag of coin I left with the innkeeper. Our simple plan is that in the press of bodies no one will miss you for a while, allowing us to slip away."

Stopping suddenly on the path, with hands on hips she sharply retorted, "You think I am appreciated so little that they won't miss my pleasant company and ready wit?"

Jack fumbled for appropriate words to defuse her pique.

She let him flounder for a minute, and then gave a broad mischievous grin, saying "Nay, Jack I am only pulling your leg. I am a cruel and ungrateful mare am I not? Perhaps you should spank me soundly? But later methinks. Continue your gallant rescue and let us tarry no more."

Another few minutes of plunging along the path brought them to the marshy bank of a wide creek, with a row boat secured to a stump in the middle of the water.

Before she could think how they would reach the boat Jack swept her off her feet and splashed through the sucking mud and then through the icy stream. She nestled her head into his shoulder and cooed into his ear "Ooh Jack, you are my hero."

Even though he guessed she was being sarcastic again, her warm breath felt like it was caressing his ear and he blushed deeply, and had to force himself to concentrate on lowering her carefully into the front of the boat. He untied the painter and hopped in, settling onto the bench with his back to Kat he grabbed the oars and started rowing immediately.

They quickly built up speed and were soon gliding along the winding creek which ever so gradually widened into a serviceable river.

Kat pulled the cloak about her and relaxed for the first time in weeks. She watched Jack's powerful back muscles work smoothly beneath his shirt, as he sped them towards … well presumably to safety. She sat up. "Where exactly are we going Jack?"

"You'll see," he puffed, not even pausing in his labours.

They swiftly passed a broad marshland to one side and then emerged into a wide channel, which Jack said was between the isle of Sheppey and the mainland, and was called the Swale. Bobbing in the swell with just enough sail to hold position was a small sailing hoy. They pulled alongside and Cardano reached down to help her clamber aboard. Jack tied the rowboat to a cleat at the stern and a gnarled fisherman got them underway as they rejoiced in their reunion, and swapped tales of their individual adventures, although Kat still wouldn't talk about why she had disappeared in the first place.

Chapter 32 - Oscillation

Tuesday the 25th of July 1552
Middleton Regis, Kent & London

Fisherman friend

Several hours later they turned away from the sunset that was a baleful red glare further inland and docked at a jetty under the watchful artillery peeking from a large stone keep. The fisherman grunted that he'd see them at first light to complete their journey and limped off toward a large wooden inn called *The Three Cornish Chough's*, where a yellow light blazed from every window and muffled sounds of merriment could be heard.

Kat and Gerolamo followed Jack, who carried a lantern, as he strode confidently through the warren of small streets in the village. Some minutes later he stopped, seemingly perplexed, and scratched his head. Peering around he spotted the steeple of a small church poking above the house rooftops, and marched off toward it, turning into a lane on the left and ending at a blue painted door. "The house with a blue door, south of St George's chapel" was all he said by way of explanation.

After a rapid rat-a-tat-tat, tat, rat-a-tat-tat, knocking on the door he stepped back. Almost immediately the door was opened by an old, care-worn version of John Dee, who glanced at them and then peered cautiously left and right. Acknowledging the secret knock, he introduced himself as Rowland Dee, John's father, and invited them inside.

After Jack explained that they were on a quest to assist his son they were given all the courtesy that was possible in the simple home. They warmed themselves at the hearth, and Rowland's wife, Jane, provided a simple meal and a small serving of strong ale.

Kat seemed fascinated by the old man's appearance which in truth was nothing extraordinary, though even Jack could see the familial resemblance to their friend, John Dee. Rowland looked older obviously, and according to a whispered aside from Kat, "He looks more Welsh".

They recounted their tale, or at least parts of it, for Jack had been warned to say nothing of the gem as Rowland was apparently always short of money and such talk would only cause awkwardness. When they explained that Kat had been abducted off the streets by Cheyne's men, and Cardano had been pulled from an inn in Faversham, the older man become quite agitated and began pacing around the small room.

He explained he was in hiding here himself, with his wife's people, the Wilde's, and under the nominal protection of the eminent Wyatt family, but that he liked to keep a low profile and so wasn't especially happy to hear that they were on the run from Lord Thomas Cheyne, who had informants all through the county. Jack approached and mollified him smoothly, "Soft, soft. No one saw us arrive, and we will leave before first light on the morrow. I promise." He also slipped the older man a bag of coins, saying they were sent by John. One or the other of these actions had an instant effect and Rowland returned to his seat, asking if there was any other assistance they needed, to which they begged just to be allowed to rest and perhaps to have a little additional food to take with them next morning, which was all readily agreed. They spent a pleasant enough evening beside the fire, being regaled by Rowland with stories from the court of Henry VIII and his many wives. Rowland claimed to have been a gentleman courtier to the old King, but Jack wasn't sure whether to believe it or not. Regardless, the stories were funnier and more outrageous than any he had ever heard before. It was a good night.

Back on the sailing hoy next morning the fisherman was clearly tight after a long night carousing, so the trip upriver towards London was a quiet one.

Two hours later they stood on the quayside of London Bridge Wharf, and Kat effusively thanked Jack's fisherman friend.

Meanwhile Jack gazed at the approximate spot where he had last seen the *Stanislav von Danzig* back in February, and reflected on the changes in his life these past five months. Shading his eyes as he peered east down river he wondered where Jakob and even the cruel Georg were now. Seeing the wistful look on his face, Kat tugged kindly at his shirt sleeve and with a shake of his head he brought his mind back to their current situation.

The Aldgate tailor

When Jack had explained to Rowland, who was a member of the Mercers guild, that they were looking for a landmark in or around London, he had not hesitated, "John Stow. You need to call on a freeman of the Merchant Taylor's guild called John Stow."

Rowland went on to explain, "Stow recently set up his tailoring shop just north of the Tower of London, near Aldgate Pump. Yes, that is a perfect plan, and it is but a small deviation from your route back to Kingston anyway."

Standing on the quayside Rowland's words echoed in his mind, his soft Welsh accent still singing to him, *He is a queer little man he is, but as honest as the day is long. And he's a friend of our John, see. Well, more of a friendly rival really, if the truth be told. But yew won't find anyone else in the whole of London town that has half the antiquarian knowledge that he has. If the place you seek is in London, then John Stow will know of it. Mark my words, boyo.*

Jack reminded Kat and Cardano again of the full riddle.
"Staring into unseeing eyes you atone
From the gift of the Ferryman's daughter
Shielding the location of the stone
Or a chief gules taught her."

"We need to find the ferryman's daughter first," said Cardano, unnecessarily in Jack's opinion, but he kept quiet. "I said it yesterday and I'll say it again now: We have no chance at all," Cardano continued to gripe, "There must be thousands of wherryman and ferrymen in London. And most will have daughters. We should go to Kingston and lay it all before Dottore Dee. Maybe he can advise us and within a few days we'd have a useful answer."

"Well we are here now, so let's just go and talk to the good Master Stow, and see if he knows of the lady," said Jack, wondering why some people always saw problems where he saw opportunities.

As they headed off, striding north on Pudding Lane, Jack wondered about his friend Cardano. His attitude seemed to have changed during the few weeks they had been apart. He shook his head ruefully and put it down to tiredness, or perhaps some misuse during his captivity, of which he had spoken little.

Soon they stopped beside a bakery, tempted by the smell of fresh bread, their meagre breakfast seeming many hours distant although it was still early in the day. The sign swinging from the protruding first floor read *"Thomas Farryner. Master Baker"*

Kat was already haggling with the goodwife, and Gerolamo was gesturing keenly at the pies, but Jack saw the dirty iron stove with cheap brushwood fuel piled much too close for safety, and glancing into the rear he was disgusted by the sight of the slovenly baker who was wearing a dirty smock. He moved his reluctant friends further along the cobbled street, weaving between pedestrians and carts of offal coming down the hill from the butchers of Eastcheap toward the river. "That place was an accident waiting to happen. Let's find a better class of establishment."

When they reached Fenchurch Street the wider road had many more stores and all looked reputable, so they stopped for pie and ale at *"Angel's Bakery"*, where they all agreed the food was heavenly.

Gerolamo asked "Does Dottore Dee know of this new clue you found in the cathedral?"

Colouring a little, Jack replied "I was hoping that when we solve it we will have the stone and can go to him in triumph."

Kat looked thoughtful and said "What makes you think the chain of clues will end here? There may be another clue, or a hundred more clues! It feels like a fool's errand to me."

"I suppose you think that if we find the stone then you will be the hero, eh Jack? You will have secured your place in the team."

Kat glanced at Gerolamo her eyebrows raised, "Doctor Dee does not need heroics, only pure motives and honest effort."

Gerolamo squirmed under her gaze, then muttered something about using the privy and left the table disappearing toward the rear of the premises.

Kat reached over and laid a hand over Jack's, "Truly there is no need to seek further approval from the Doctor. He has already accepted you into the team, and you have proved your worth several times over already. Not least by rescuing me." She smiled coyly, "And for that at least you will always have my thanks."

Jack coloured again and stood up awkwardly, looking about and asked "Where is Gerolamo now? We need to get going if we hope to solve this today."

Kat smiled at his unease, but finished her drink and stood up beside him. As they waited her hand reached over and gently squeezed his, and he made no effort to disengage.

Gerolamo rejoined them a few minutes later and they hiked up Fenchurch Street for ten minutes or so, looking for the Aldgate Pump, near which they should find Stow's tailoring shop.

Kat saw it first. A six-foot high, stone obelisk with a leaden pipe emerging from half-way up and water flowing out and into a grate below. Obviously it ran continuously and was freely available for anyone to use.

Jack wetted a kerchief and wiped his face then tied it around his neck to keep it cool. He noticed the water had a slightly fusty smell. He scooped a handful and was going to taste it when he saw Kat shake her head, so he let it trickle through his fingers instead.

Cardano, oblivious, saw the shop of the Aldgate Tailor and pointed it out to the other two.

The window of the store displayed a number of fine looking cloaks, hose and doublets all hanging from a wooden pole.

When they entered the shop an apprentice accepted their enquiry and ducked into the back room, returning a few moments later with an earnest, bespectacled man, who introduced himself as the sought-after John Stow. He invited them into his home on the first floor. The stairs of the old building creaked mightily as the four of them ascended, but the room itself was surprisingly clean and airy for a bachelor's apartment, saving the mounds of manuscripts and parchments piled all over his desk and stools.

Clearing some papers away he invited them to sit and bid them tell their tale.

Jack quickly recounted their association to Dee, and how Dee's father Rowland had suggested they call on Stow, "'Tis said no one surpasses Master Stow for knowledge of the environs and history of London Town," flattered Jack.

The man was clearly pleased with the accolade however required no encouragement to assist them. If anything he seemed to relish the opportunity to be away from his trade and into his books.

Without divulging their quest they merely said they needed to find "the gift of the ferryman's daughter".

He looked at them through slitted eyes. Jack could tell he was considering what was missing from the story, but his antiquarian interest soon overcame his suspicions.

"I don't know the answer you seek," he said, pausing.

Jack's spirits plunged.

"But my memory is not always perfect which is why I write everything down. I believe I may have some notes somewhere about here that will help," he looked around, as did Jack, at the mounds of paper, "I believe there was an ancient story…something about a church…hmm…."

Kat looked sheepishly at Jack, "Do you have any of Doctor Dee's silver left Jack….I need a change of clothes."

Jack thought she looked just perfect as she was, in a well cut blue riding dress and the dark woollen cloak he had provided for her back at *The Creek and Paddle*, but he merely nodded and handed her the much depleted purse that he had received from Inkbold.

She glanced meaningfully at Stow and he instantly understood her intent, "By all means," he walked over to the stairs and called down to the apprentice, "Jeremiah, our customer needs your help if you please."

"Meanwhile, we can help you search your notes if you will allow us," said Jack.

For the next hour or so they searched for the information that Stow could barely remember, until triumphantly Jack held aloft a sheet of parchment where amongst the spidery handwriting a crude sketch of a church and the phrase "ferryman's daughter" could be discerned.

"Ah, yes. That's it. Well done, well done. Let me read it now…"

After refreshing his memory from the note he sighed, "How could I have forgotten, it is such an uncommon tale. You know, I heard it from the very lips of Bartholomew Linsted, who was the Prior of the Southwark Augustinian Priory at the dissolution." And he proceeded to tell them all that he knew.

He finished just as Kat returned. She was now dressed in dark green hose, white shirt with puffed sleeves and a well cut leather jerkin on top that accentuated her waist and chest, surmounted by the same long brown cape Jack had provided.

John Stow looked on in mild horror, and when prompted just muttered that he wasn't in favour of this ridiculous fad whereby some young women dressed in breeches.

Indeed she looked more like she had that first time they had met her, so many months ago in Richmond. She handed back a lighter purse, smiling, "Jeremiah is kindly arranging to send my other clothes on to Kingston for me by boat."

Expressing their thanks the trio trooped down the stairs again, the creaking seeming even louder now, and out into the street, waving and echoing their goodbyes to the diligent Master Stow.

Gerolamo stopped after a short distance and exclaimed, "That was thirsty work sorting though all that dusty paperwork. I need a drink. Could we stop for a small ale at that excellent bakery?"

"*Angel's Bakery?*" queried Kat, "Aye, if we are quick."

As they entered *Angel's* Jack immediately started salivating and bought himself another pie while the others sufficed with just ale. Gerolamo protested old age, and slipped off to the privy again, returning after but a few minutes.

Jack finished explaining their destination to Kat, "So we need to find Southwark and go to St Saviour's church."

Gerolamo took his time finishing his drink, insisting on telling the youngsters about the style of food and drink in his native Pavia, and how they were subtly different in Padua where he attended university, and yet different again in the larger and more populous Milan where he had become famous.

Eventually Kat almost had to drag him out of the bakery, "Pleasant as all this reminiscing might be, we should get going. If we return to the quayside, then a short distance west we can cross the river using London Bridge, and then reach St Saviour's quite quickly. Perhaps less than an hour all told." She chivvied the two men, especially Cardano, out of the bakery and on with their quest.

Perspective glass

Standing at the north end of London Bridge they looked in awe along its length, in fact it was so long and crowded that they couldn't see the other end.

The large gatehouse with its arched entryway was overshadowed by the buildings beyond it. Peering through the arch they could see the street was lined with imposing affluent looking properties. In the common style the upper stories often overhung the lower and so the top floors of some of the buildings almost met in the middle. Kat pointed out a couple of places where "they do actually meet over the middle of the street - see them blocking the view there. There are others further on where it is a single building that spans the entire width of the bridge, leaving only a tunnel over the roadway as the passage."

It was easily the busiest thoroughfare Jack had ever seen in his whole life.

They joined the long stream of people and carts that were heading south and marvelled how they generally kept to the left side of the road, whilst traffic coming toward them generally stayed to their own left, and therefore to Jack's right. A drover who was herding across a pair of oxen confirmed that this novel arrangement kept the people moving at a good pace and had evolved naturally through some unspoken agreement by the regular users of the bridge. Just as he told them this, all forward movement ceased and shouting and swearing could be heard from up ahead. "Probably some yokel taking up too much of the roadway and got into some altercation with the oncoming traffic. We'll be here for ages now. They should make it a law that you have to keep to one side."

"That'll never happen - they only enact laws that extract our money or our allegiance. Nothing that is ever actually useful to us little people," grumbled a nearby mercer leaning on his handcart. He looked like he was about to regale them with more of the world's grievances, so Jack acted decisively.

He managed to shoulder his way between the people ahead of him and although it took quite a few minutes he eventually came upon a chaotic scene. A high-sided cart had tried to pass under the centre of the arch of one of the tunnels through a full width house. Meanwhile a smaller cart loaded with freshly cut rushes had been coming from the Southwark end and its driver had tried to squeeze through the tunnel at the same time. The arch wasn't wide enough for both carts and their wheels had collided, breaking one completely off the smaller wagon so it now leaned against the larger cart. The drivers were furiously screaming at each other, while other pedestrians were calling both drivers the rudest names Jack had heard since his time in the galley.

As the drivers started throwing punches some of the Londoners started betting on which man would emerge triumphant and which would be beaten. Jack remembered being told that Londoners would bet on anything. No-one seemed inclined to help resolve the actual problem of the cart whose wheel had fallen off.

Jack stripped off his cloak and handed it to Kat who had just arrived beside him, then with his back to the cart he casually squatted and heaved the cart back up to horizontal, his chest and arms flexing but his face showing no strain. He turned to the driver and yelled, "You.

Get your cart wheel and reattach it. Now."

The startled driver was picking himself up off the floor where the larger man had just thrown him, and perhaps sensing a reprieve from a probable beating he scuttled over to the wheel and with the help of a couple of pedestrians realigned it with the axle and slotted it into place. As the driver hammered home a pin to secure it a hush descended on the crowd, then wild cheering and applause, mixed with a little grumbling from those who clearly felt the fight should have continued and that their bets were likely to pay off.

Jack let go of the cart, acknowledged the applause with a brief nod, and dusting his hands off he retrieved his cloak and proceeded to stride past the once stricken vehicle. Kat and Gerolamo hurried after him.

There was some open space in front of them so they quickly moved away from the scene and Kat said "Well that was impressive, but if we were hoping to travel incognito you just blew it big time. They'll be talking about that feat of strength in taverns up and down London all night, and by tomorrow they'll be saying you did it with just one hand."

Gerolamo looked with renewed admiration at his friend, and not without a little nervousness.

Finally they passed through the southern gatehouse and then past Bridge House where Kat said the bridgemaster lived who was responsible for maintenance, and onto Southwark High Street. As he glanced behind him Jack's gaze was drawn upwards to a ghastly scene. A dozen severed heads were stuck on poles and displayed above the gatehouse. He shivered involuntarily. Kat shrugged "They are the heads of traitors. They dip them in tar to preserve them from the birds and weather. A reminder to follow the King's law meekly and cause no offence. Of course, they wouldn't bother doing that to lowly folk like us, we would just be hung, or jailed at best."

Cardano pulled a face, "Barbaric country!"

Up ahead Jack saw two churches, "That smaller one on the left must be St George's, and the fine looking taller one on the right must be the one we want, St Saviour's. Let's hope the natives are friendly."

As they walked to the church he finished telling Kat the story they had heard from John Stow.

"Long ago, even before the Normans conquered England by beating King Harold Godwinson at Hastings in 1066, there was a woman called

Mary. She was the daughter of a ferry owner, and after his death she inherited the ferry and used the profits to found a nunnery on the south bank of the Thames here. Shortly after, in 1106, it was refounded as an Augustinian priory, and for over four hundred years the monks worshipped here. Then in King Henry's Reformation just a few years ago it was converted to a regular parish church."

They paused in the High Street and Jack turned to them, "Remember the clue:

> Staring into unseeing eyes you atone
> From the gift of the Ferryman's daughter
> Shielding the location of the stone
> Or a chief gules taught her."

"Alright, so this church itself is the gift of the Ferryman's daughter. So now we must stare into unseeing eyes and atone?"

Jack shrugged, "That's what it says."

As they started toward the church Kat suddenly grabbed their arms to halt them, then pulled them hurriedly to one side. "Did you see that horse? Tethered near the entrance?"

Jack scratched his head, "Yes, of course. Well … maybe. There are horses everywhere. What's so special about this horse?"

Cardano coloured, and Jack assumed it was because he hadn't seen the horse at all.

"The saddle pad was embroidered with the arms of Sir Thomas Cheyne - I would recognise them anywhere."

"What? How can that be? We left Cheyne back in Rochester."

"Well he is here now. Or one of his men is anyway."

Jack peered around the corner at the church entrance, "It would seem there is just that one. Let's get in quickly before any more arrive."

Kat quailed, "I'm not sure that's a great idea. I really don't want to be caught by him again. Gerolamo, surely you agree?"

Cardano nodded vigorously, but said nothing.

"Nonsense. We'll be fine. If it comes to it I'm sure I can handle whoever it is. I'm not giving up now!"

"You can't fight a nobleman's retainer, Jack. And certainly not in a church!"

"We'll sneak around - surely they won't be expecting us to be there. Come on." And with that he led them over to the church, where they peered inside.

They realised that the mid-morning service was still being celebrated. Standing near the back of the congregation Kat pointed out Henry, one of Cheyne's men, presumably the horse's rider.

As they quietly crept along the side of the nave, Cardano halted and pulled them over toward a niche. He pointed at a colourful green and red decorated tomb, on which lay a recumbent figure. A stone engraving identified him as a poet called John Gower.

"His eyes are closed," whispered Cardano excitedly, "They are unseeing eyes."

Kat leaned over the figure and stared at the face from different angles, then knelt down as if to atone, but from there she couldn't see the poet at all. Standing again she muttered, "This doesn't make sense, there is no way to stare into the eyes and atone."

"We need to find different unseeing eyes. Let's split up and keep searching. Stay away from Cheyne's man. We'll meet back here at the end of the service," said Jack.

Cardano sniffed, but couldn't fault Kat's logic, so wandered off cautiously checking the other statues and stained glass windows as he passed them. Kat circled around the other side while Jack wandered around the entrance. They couldn't get into the choir while the service was happening, if they needed to go there, they would have to wait.

Jack leaned against a pillar near the door and closed his eyes. He could hear the low murmur of the priest and the congregation's chanted responses. He could even smell some of the congregation: there was a fishy smell and overlaid on that there was an acrid smell from a tannery. Suddenly the ringing of the many bells cut through his concentration. He wondered how many bells there were as it was an unusually melodious peal.

Kat returned to his side, nudging him, and whispered, "We need a plan. This is a huge church, we could be here all day. Henry might know something we don't and could beat us to the unseeing eyes."

Jack replied, "I think we are missing something. The riddle said 'Staring into unseeing eyes you atone, *From* the gift of the Ferryman's daughter'." Kat looked blank. "Not *in* the gift of the Ferryman's daughter," he said, emphasising the word *in*.

He watched as people started leaving the church then stepped over to a church official and putting on a very French accent he asked, "Your bells, zey sound wonderful - better than any I 'ave ever 'eard in France. Is eet possible to see them, do you think?" The Deacon looked dubious, so Jack jingled his purse meaningfully, "I would of course make an offering to 'elp the poor of your parish." The Deacon's eyes lit up, and after some silver coins were placed in his hand he took them swiftly to the entrance of a stairwell at the base of the tower and handed Jack a small candle, "They're a long way up and the way is dark. But they are a beautiful set of eight matching bells it is true."

Jack and Kat started climbing the spiral stone staircase, which rapidly plunged to inky darkness, and the little candle was hardly enough to show the next step. They paused at each of the three main platforms on the way up, passed by the bells hung on their gigantic bell frame, and eventually emerged from a small arched door into the light on the top of the tower.

A chill wind whipped across the tower from the river and Kat hugged her cloak about her, "What are we doing up here?"

Jack looked around him. The view between the crenellations was magnificent. Rearing over London to the north was St Paul's with its immense spire, surrounded by at least a dozen smaller church towers and spires. But Jack brought his gaze closer, over the wide brown river, along the buildings on London Bridge, until they rested on the nearby gatehouse and its gruesome victims. The disembodied heads seemed close enough to reach out and touch.

"See all the unseeing eyes?" he asked pointing, then dropped to his knees in a position of atonement, only to stare at the wall of cemented blocks of stone. Feverishly he swung his gaze left and right. There! He shuffled over on his knees, until he faced a hole that had been bored right through the stone, almost wide enough to put his fist through. He peered through the hole and smiled. He could still see the gatehouse but the rest of the view was obscured.

Kat scrambled alongside him, peered though the hole and laughed out loud before hugging him joyously.

"Now," said Jack seriously, "the rest of the clue is, 'Shielding the location of the stone, Or a chief gules taught her.' Well the first part is simple enough, it is concealing the location of the stone. But the last part means nothing to me."

"Nay, Jack. The first part is not so simple," said Kat, peering through the hole, "Look again."

As he squinted to try to see some detail he had missed she asked "What do you see? Tell me everything."

He glanced at her and saw a smile cross her lips.

He looked again, "The gatehouse - with some ship's masts and rigging just visible beyond, presumably on the river somewhere. The gatehouse is a squat square tower with battlements atop. About twenty pikes jutting out at all angles from the top, most have a head stuck on them. Some of the faces still visible, ugh. Some are just skulls. Below that, a stone statue in a niche. It is too weathered to see any real details. On each side of the statue is a knight's banner, then a pair of shields. Below the statue is the keystone of the archway, the rest of the arch and the road."

He looked up again. Infuriatingly she just smirked, hands on hips.

Then it clicked for him. The shields.

He looked again, "All four shields are different. From the left: a large black cross on a white background."

"*Argent a cross sable*", said Kat smugly, "I know a little about heraldry, my father was obsessed. It means *White field, or background, with a black cross.*"

"Very impressive" said Jack, marvelling at her breadth of knowledge. "Next: Blue with a diagonal yellow band"

"Azure a bend Or", intoned Kat.

"These are starting to make sense," said Jack. "It is very much like my native French. First the main background colour, then the device and it's colour."

"The next is: a red background with a white chevron."

Kat replied, "Gules a chevron Argent"

"And finally," said Jack, "Yellow with a red banner across the top."

"Or a chief gules"

"That's it. That must be the one. The riddle said, '*Or a chief gules taught her*'. Sneaky!"

"We need a closer look at that shield," said Kat, "but it is hanging on a fortress wall, so I don't know how we will ever be able to do that!"

It was Jack's turn to smile. While Kat watched intrigued, he opened his satchel and took out a leather tube, about the size of his forearm. He unfastened a cap from each end, revealing polished glass in both, and then holding the two ends he pulled gently and the tube extended to twice its original length.

"I was taking this back from Inkbold at the compound, to Doctor

Dee, who had left it behind in his haste after the attack."

He squatted again by the hole in the wall and held the tube horizontally so that one end nestled in the hole in the wall, then he placed his eye to the other end so he could look through the tube, through the hole in the wall, and out at the gatehouse.

"Kat, you will not believe it. There is small writing on the yellow shield. Write this down, it is Latin," and he started to read. She stopped him after but a moment, with a hand on his arm, "Jack. I cannot write. Not English and not Latin. What if I read the words, and you write it down?"

Embarrassed, he swapped places and after a few moments to get used to the perspective glass, she started reading aloud.

"Sta in Triforium de Ecclesia rotunda ab Marescallus cum autem sol in Templum Domini vide 43:2"

Jack jotted down the phrase in a small book, which he then returned to his satchel.

"Jack," Kat had gone pale, "I will not be captured again."

"What is it? What's the matter?"

"Lord Cheyne is even now riding under the gatehouse towards us, with a dozen men at arms. Come we must make haste." She returned the perspective glass to him and he risked one quick look over the parapet before quickly replacing the end-caps and returning it to his satchel.

Kat was already racing down the spiral steps and he heard her cry out as she almost fell in the near darkness, their candle long since guttered. He closed the door behind him, plunging the stairwell into deeper gloom, the only illumination coming from an occasional cross trefly slitted window. They descended as quickly as they dared, not pausing until they reached the bottom, where they peered out into the nave. There was no-one in sight. No priests, no congregation, no Henry, and ominously, no Gerolamo. They crept under the crossing to the north transept, their footsteps echoing loudly in the vaulted space despite the care they took. Spotting a door they slipped through and found themselves in the vestry, where a startled priest was removing his stole. Apologising profusely they darted through another door, and finally were outside.

"I didn't see Gerolamo anywhere. He must have left already. We were a long time up the tower and missed our appointed meeting time with him," said Jack.

"Well, it is time we left as well. I really do not want to be at the mercy of Cheyne again."

They paused, uncertain where Cheyne and his men were, until, somewhat relieved, they heard the muffled sound of many hooves from the opposite side of the church.

Together they scurried across the yard and into a ginnel between some houses, soon emerging onto Southwark High Street where they hurried back under the gatehouse's archway and started across London Bridge.

"What was the verse again?" asked Lord Cheyne, as he cast his gaze around the rooftops of Southwark.

Henry repeated the rhyme to him and Cheyne immediately turned to the gatehouse with its ominous heads on pikes. His old but still keen eyes saw the shields and he grunted, "This game is not so hard. Look at that shield," he pointed to the one furthest on the right, "Or a chief gules. But beyond that I don't know. Come, let's go and rouse the gatehouse guard, they can take the shield down, perhaps there is a further clue hidden behind it?"

He turned to leave, then stopped and stared down into the road, "There they go, scampering like rats toward the gatehouse. Henry, quickly send some men to capture them now, they must not get to the shield before us."

A round church

They dodged through the traffic on the bridge for a hundred yards or so, frustrated by the amount of people blocking their path, then Jack pulled Kat aside and whispered, "I have been thinking about that Latin phrase. I can translate it, but I still do not know what we need to do."

"You understand Latin?"

"Well, I know a little, yes. The elders of our village church taught all the boys when I was young," said Jack, he was silent for a moment, lost to painful reverie. "Anyway, it means *Stand in the triforium of the church of the Marshal, with the sun over the Temple of the Lord, and see 43:2*"

"I am getting tired of this game," sighed Kat, slumping against the window of a shop.

"We could go and see John Stow again, surely he could help identify this round church?"

Kat glanced up sharply, "Round church? You didn't mention it was a *round* church."

"Did I not? Let me try again: *Stand in the triforium of the round church of the Marshal, with the sun over the Temple of the Lord, and see 43:2*"

"There is a famous round church here in London. It belonged to the Knights Templar, until the knights all died. Then the King took it - just like he took everything else."

"Really? Do you know this church? Is it close?"

"A short wherry ride, near to the inns of court where the black-robed lawyers have their chambers. Come on, back to the gatehouse where we can find the stairs to the river," newly energised she led the way.

Where the roadway narrowed under the gatehouse a knot of grumbling travellers had formed, blocking the path. Jack tried to force a way through the carts and people, until suddenly he stopped. Spinning around he grabbed Kat who was right behind him, and continued spinning several more times until the two stood face to face behind a tall hay wain.

"Well Jack, this is a bit presumptuous, I didn't know you cared so much," purred Kat.

"Cheyne is ten feet ahead, his men are holding the merchants back. That is why there is a crowd."

Kat stiffened instinctively.

A kindly matron smiled indulgently in their direction, whilst her merchant husband tutted at such a public display of affection. The matron nodded her head toward Kat in encouragement. Jack bent his head and whispered into her lips, "We are being watched. Pretend to kiss me." Without hesitation Kat's lips melted into his own and he tasted honey until his mind went blank and all he could do was respond in kind. When she broke the kiss he opened his eyes just in time to see hers flicker open too. He smiled and leaned in to steal another quick peck.

He became aware of his surroundings once more, and glancing over Kat's head he caught the eyes of the matron, who beamed her approval, whilst her husband had pushed forward to better see the action up ahead. Just at that moment the merchant called back to his wife, "Well that's all over then, they have entered the gatehouse to see the Constable."

The words sank in and Kat whispered, "Come on, now's our chance," and she guided Jack around the cart to the edge of the bridge seeking the stairs.

Kat found the entrance and they jogged down the wooden stairs that ran to the base of the pier, every twenty steps or so the stairs twisted at a platform to head down in the other direction until they twisted again. Four such sets of stairs they trotted down, until they reached the level of the starling upon which the pier rested. Jack whistled to a ferryman who gladly rowed the twenty feet from the shore to pick them up, and then with confident strokes took them rapidly upriver toward Temple Stairs.

Cheyne toured the gatehouse battlements while his men were tying ropes and clambering over the side to retrieve the shield. He paused and peered upriver. *Is that Katherine and the boy in a wherry? How…?*
"Henry!"

They huddled in the back of the wherry, their heads close together, whispering urgently.

"I don't understand how Cheyne found out about St Saviour's," puzzled Jack. "Surely the shrine only contained the single copy of the riddle that I found."

"We must have been betrayed by someone, but who?"

"We told John Stow very little, and he knows nothing of Cheyne's interest in the quest, so surely it is not he. Before him we saw Rowland Dee. And yes we shared some but not all of the riddle with him. Surely he would not betray us? Friends of his own son? And he did not recognise the phrase 'Ferryman's daughter', that's why he sent us to John Stow. Or at least he said he didn't recognise it."

"I agree it seems unlikely, and I hate to even consider it," said Kat, "but he did say he was hiding and that Cheyne had informants everywhere. Maybe he is one of the informants and that is how he buys his continued freedom?"

"Kat, there is one more possibility. I asked the Dean in Rochester if he knew what the 'Ferryman's daughter' was. He might have been forced to reveal our conversation by Cheyne and his men. I hope I did not place him in danger! We will have to be more careful."

"And faster! They will easily find the Templum Domini clue on the shield. We need to get to the round church and solve the clue today, we can't risk any delay."

Jack paid the wherryman and they strode up Middle Temple Lane, past a manicured woodland on their right-hand side. The area was teeming with black-robed lawyers going to and fro between chambers and court. Jack picked two lawyers who were in deep conversation, and followed close enough behind them to make it look like he and Kat were their clients. They went through an archway and across a genteel courtyard to the round church. They stopped in their tracks and gazed in awe at the church, the pale cream stone creating a perfect circle with numerous strengthening stone buttresses, and between each was a narrow arched window. Above this circular wall was another tier but of lesser dimensions, not very tall and topped with crenellations like a battlement. Attached to the eastern curve was a regular rectangular church body of the same stone, an entranceway clearly visible, but currently disgorging those who had attended afternoon prayers.

A serjeant with his white coif of rank clearly visible approached them and gruffly asked them their business. Jack gestured to the two lawyers ahead and mumbled something about a land claim, the serjeant grunted and waved them forward, rejoining "I shall have words with Brother Mortimer, he knows better than to let his clients loiter in the quad. Now on with you quickly." Jack, needing no further encouragement, bowed and muttered his thanks. They hurried after the robed figures.

After a quick glance behind him Jack pulled Kat into one of the market stalls that lined the church wall. The stallholder watched them suspiciously as they pretended to inspect the various baskets and sandals lining the shelves, all the while whispering half-baked plans about how to get into the church unseen. Eventually the woman tired of them and chivvied them out saying if they weren't buying then they weren't welcome.

Looking about them, fearful of the serjeant's return, Jack tried to formulate a plan. Too late he noticed a lawyer approaching, the man skewered him with a piercing glance, "So, you want to get into the church do you?"

"What makes you say that? We were just admiring the building."

"I know the look," he said cryptically. He furtively glanced around then taking Jack's arm he led them around toward a side door.

"Why would you help us?" asked Kat.

The man stopped amid a small crowd of matrons and leaned close, spitting out his tale. "These hypocrites. They threw me out of Commons for three months for cuffing the barrister who tried to get my brother arrested for being just a couple of months behind in his debt payments. And now I am let back in on sufferance only. They think themselves so high and mighty, but I will show them, if only through small gestures like this."

Kat made consoling noises and laid her hand on his arm, and gradually he calmed down enough to introduce himself. "Master Hugh Smythe. Barrister at law of the Inner Temple. It is as well I spotted you first. The serjeant usually ejects strangers from the precincts and arrests any that give cause. And you two stand out a mile, if you don't mind me saying so," he said with a grim smile.

"We had heard the church was magnificent and wanted only to enter and perhaps take in the view from the triforium."

He eyed them suspiciously, clearly sensing there was more to the story. "If that is all I don't know why I should bother helping you…"

"Soft. Maybe we need something from inside…" Kat suggested, a sly look on her face.

"That's more like it. Prithee, follow me, and stay close." Without further chatter he led them through the gaggle of women shoppers, over to the side door, and with a quick glance inside they ducked through and paused but a moment to let their eyes adjust to the dim interior of the entranceway, then into the nave where a blaze of light from the many windows in the tower nearly blinded them. He gestured across the nave to an archway with spiral stone steps beyond, "Up those stairs to the next floor, take the first door on your left and follow the corridor away from the sound of the organ music. That will put you in the triforium," he grinned slightly manically, "Good luck and send them to hell!" and with that he whirled round and strode out again.

Jack raised his eyebrows and muttered "Bizarre!", but Kat just shrugged and said "People have all sorts of motives for the good and bad that they do. Who are we to judge?"

Jack glanced admiringly around the circular space. There were warriors' effigies on the floor near them, and stone coffins beyond those. Beautiful fluted columns rose up supporting the inner wall that seemed to rise up and up to the sunlit heavens. Light blazed down through upper windows, making it impossible to see the top of the tower even when he squinted.

Kat, practical as ever, dragged him quickly over to the stairs and without pausing darted upwards, following Smythe's directions.

With the pattering from their shoes on the stone steps echoing up the spiral staircase ahead of them they raced up the steps and into the circular walkway that was the triforium.

They had brainstormed ideas during the wherry trip and believed they had a reasonable interpretation of the clue.

Stand in the triforium of the round church of the Marshal, with the sun over the Temple of the Lord, and see 43:2

Kat had said that the Templars had an important church in the Holy Land that had been known as the Templum Domini, or Temple of the Lord. So their plan was to stand in the triforium while the sun was over the Holy Land, meaning in the east, and see what happened. They had little enough time, it was already past high noon and the sun was swinging more to the south.

The triforium was a mostly enclosed circular corridor about half way up the circular tower. It had no outer windows, but had six open archways facing inwards, overlooking the middle of the tower. Leaning through one arch Jack could see the knights' effigies far below them. Light entered the triforium through these arches from the actual windows higher up in the tower, and made the triforium alternately light and dark as they walked around it.

They crept around to the archway on the west side, knowing that looking through the arch would orient them to the east and thus toward the Holy Land.

A brilliant shaft of ruby coloured light, presumably from a red patch of stained glass in an upper window, shone through the arch and pierced the dimness of the triforium. Kat turned to see if the beam illuminated anything in particular, and exclaimed "It spreads and shines on this whole bookcase," indicating a three foot wide shelf of books. Running her hand over the spines of the books she counted, "There are eighteen books here. It could be any one of these."

While Kat flicked through the pages of the first book Jack stood back and watched patiently for several minutes, "The beam is moving toward the edge of the shelf and then the wall further to the right. I think we have missed the moment when our true quarry was illuminated, because the sun is now to the south-east. But working backwards…" He traced an arc in the opposite direction to the current movement of the beam and stopped, pointing at a lectern with an open book. "I think the beam would have lingered here for several hours earlier this morning as the sun rose."

Kat stepped up to the lectern and examined the book. "The book is very old, being the minutes of the meetings of the Bench Table, whatever that is, but the chapters are not numbered like a bible, so our idea to find chapter 43 verse 2 will not work. Let me count the pages though…".

With deliberate care so that she did not damage the ancient pages of the book, she counted as she turned and at page 43 she stopped. Excitement evident in her voice, she looked down the dense script. "There is a paragraph, then a sketch, then another paragraph. It could be line 2 or paragraph 2." Reading to herself she shook her head, "Not line 2 surely, it talks of assigning people to the roles of officers for the upcoming Christmas season.

"Here, here, this must be it", with her finger pointing near the bottom of the page she looked up at Jack, her eyes shining with excitement. "It is a long paragraph, get your notebook and copy it down exactly."

Just then they heard voices echoing up from the stairwell. Someone was coming. No. Two or more people were coming, having a conversation about a court case with a stern judge.

Jack stepped up and to Kat's dismay he ripped the whole page from the book and stuffed it into his jerkin, then quietly closed the book so the tear was not visible. Grabbing Kat's hand he pulled her around the triforium further away from the voices.

As the debating lawyers ambled around the triforium discussing precedents, Jack and Kat stayed half a revolution ahead of them, pausing at every archway to carefully watch the lawyers stroll past the arch on the opposite side of the triforium. Thus they stayed well ahead of the lawyers until they had circled all the way around and were once again next to the stairs back down to the nave. As quietly as they could they returned to the ground floor. No-one followed them down, presumably the lawyers' debate was worth a second circuit of the tower.

They carefully looked around the church, and confirming that they were at least temporarily alone they examined the page in the flickering light of the nave's many candles.

As Kat had already said, the first paragraph on the page was a meeting memorandum from July 1511, concerning the lawyers who were being elected as officers responsible for the next Christmas festivities.

Then there was a sketch of a crypt.

Finally the last paragraph was again the notes from a meeting, but this time it minuted how the Inner Temple lawyers were taking responsibility for keeping some items secret and safe until demanded back by the inheritor.

"And there look, what does that mean?" asked Kat, excitedly pointing at a short phrase buried in the legal text "Bretwalda egg".

"It might be another name for the Bloodstone," replied Jack.

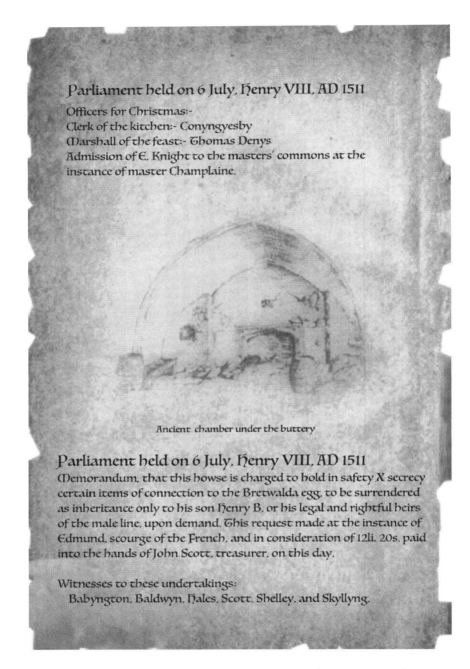

Parliament held on 6 July, Henry VIII, AD 1511

Officers for Christmas:-
Clerk of the kitchen:- Conyngyesby
Marshall of the feast:- Thomas Denys
Admission of E. Knight to the masters' commons at the
instance of master Champlaine.

Ancient chamber under the buttery

Parliament held on 6 July, Henry VIII, AD 1511

Memorandum, that this howse is charged to hold in safety X secrecy
certain items of connection to the Bretwalda egg, to be surrendered
as inheritance only to his son Henry B, or his legal and rightful heirs
of the male line, upon demand. This request made at the instance of
Edmund, scourge of the French, and in consideration of 12li. 20s. paid
into the hands of John Scott, treasurer, on this day.

Witnesses to these undertakings:
    Babyngton, Baldwyn, Hales, Scott, Shelley, and Skyllyng.

"Bret-wal-da egg" said Kat, sounding out each syllable in the strange word. "You're right. An egg, a gemstone, they could be just different names for the same thing. But who is Edmund, and...hey!"

Jack had folded the sheet and jammed it into his tunic again, pulling on Kat's arm.

"We need to go," he gestured up the stairwell where the sound of descending feet could be heard.

The pair moved carefully but quickly across the church to the side-door they had entered through. Opening the door a crack they peered out and saw the market was much busier with crowds of people visiting the stalls in the sunny early afternoon. Jack was about to make a move when Kat gently closed the door and pulled him back into the shadows. Leaning close she placed a finger on his lips. He inhaled her scent, a mixture of primrose and honey. His mind whirled. As he reached for her she gestured with her head toward the main body of the church. The two lawyers had reached the ground floor and were heading for the main exit. They passed the shadowy recess that concealed Jack and Kat without missing a beat, still debating their case. If Jack had fully opened the door the lawyers would surely have seen the daylight streaming in and would have investigated.

As the main door clanged shut Jack released the breath he hadn't even realised he was holding, bent his head and stole a quick kiss from the surprised Kat, and then pulled open the side door. They slipped out and strolled nonchalantly arm-in-arm across the courtyard retracing their path to the river.

Chapter 33 - Mortification

Tuesday the 25th of July 1552
London

Cristóbal's crystal ball

Cristóbal pulled the hood of his cloak lower over his face plunging it into deep shadow, and continued to force his weary body onward, along the last mile of dusty track that finally gave way to cobbled street.

The injuries he had sustained during the battle with Dee in Faversham pained him mightily, but not as much as the memory of total failure. That memory burned in him with every jarring step, and if truth be told had somewhat unhinged his mind. He muttered to himself as he laboured onwards, dragging his bad leg slowly as he leaned on the crutch he had carved from a broken bough. He still couldn't believe the ferocity of defence that he had engendered, and shook his head angrily, spitting out curses in three languages as he travelled. Other travellers crossed the road to stay far away from the crazy man, and when they thought no-one was watching they crossed themselves fearfully despite the prohibition against it under the new religion.

It was early afternoon as he approached Southwark, a ramshackle village on the southern bank of the river Thames, clustered around the entrance to the overbuilt London Bridge. He had previously looked down on the English who lived here, and despised even more those who frequented the brothels, animal baiting pits, and ale-houses that proliferated here. Now he craved what he would never have previously countenanced: some sort of occult verification of his future.

He entered a tavern. It was a grim dark place that even naive country-folk could discern was best avoided. Almost collapsing onto a stool he used both hands to straighten his bad leg out in front of him. He tossed a few coins onto the table and waited for the serving wench. Despite his weakened state no-one approached to cozen him from his purse. In fact a couple of burly patrons moved further away, and another left entirely, casting wary glances at the disheveled new arrival. Eventually a girl slouched over with some ale and scooped up the payment quickly, wrinkling her nose at the stench from his infected leg. Quick as a snake his hand shot out and held her wrist in a vice-like grip. "A sooth-sayer? Where can I find a sooth-sayer?"

The girl tried to pull away, but to no avail, finally turning and pointing to a back door, "Out yonder, left up the alley, four doors on yer right. Old Mother Warbley. She'll see your future for you, Mister. She is not cheap - but she is the best."

As he let go of her arm he called after her rapidly retreating back "And bring me some pottage, I am starved half to death," his Castilian lisp more pronounced than usual.

An hour or so later he struggled upright and hobbled out of the back door, his crutch catching on the uneven reed-strewn floor, and headed slowly in the direction the girl had indicated.

Leaning on the fourth door while he caught his breath, he almost fell inside the hovel when an elderly woman hauled it open from the inside. She quickly cast an experienced eye up and down, taking in his obvious poor physical condition but also spotting his high quality clothing and the ornate basket hilt of his rapier.

She gestured to a chair, and requested four silver shillings up front, an outrageous fee, but he spilled them willingly onto the table. Just as quickly they disappeared.

With a flourish she produced a dark, stained cloth, smoothing it out until it covered most of the table's pitted surface.

She cast a handful of powder onto the glowing coals of a small brazier that barely heated the room, and with a dull flash they vaporised and a heady scent assaulted his senses.

She handed him a beaker and commanded, "Drink to sooth your soul so it will converse with me."

Warily he sipped the liquid, and surprised that it had a pleasant sweet taste, he downed the lot.

"Remove your hood, seeker," she growled.

He shook his head, reluctant to reveal his disfigured features.

"Don't be afeared seeker, I have seen worse many-a-times after the sailors' brawls."

Reluctantly he pulled back the cowl, the rough fabric catching on the puckered skin and ragged stump of an ear.

She wasn't fazed. Indeed she leaned across the boards and peered into his eyes, perhaps sensing the self-loathing and embarrassment.

Clucking to herself, she stretched her arm up high and seemed to grab the fragrant smoke that hung over their heads. As she lowered her clutched hand it seemed to him that she pulled the smoke down to eye-level, her tattered sleeve obscuring her face for a few moments as more of the smoke wafted over him.

When her hand was finally laid flat on the table-top the room seemed to have darkened and Cristóbal had to squint to focus on her. He pulled back in horror when he saw her face again, realising it was as scarred as his, and half her hair was missing. *But she hadn't been disfigured when he entered the room, had she?*

Nodding to him, she swept her hand over the cloth and when he looked again he noticed there was a dark crystal globe resting there, smaller than his fist. It seemed to him that it pulsed with energy, in time with his heartbeat. And the pulses were getting faster.

The hag muttered some incoherent phrases, and Cristóbal caught glimpses of tiny fiery sparks swirling inside the globe. She leant forward and stroked the air around the globe muttering soothing words that held no meaning for him. The sparks responded by rotating faster until they were mere streaks.

When she spoke next, it was with a rich sultry voice that shocked him with its loin-stirring femininity. He heard it clearly and understood every word though he did not recognise the language.

"This very day you will find that which you seek. Not once but twice no less. Before the sun rises you will begin a long journey over water, where your future turns at the caprice of your own mind. Control your anguish young lord, and you shall receive your desires. Fail to heed my words and your fate is dark indeed."

Taking the crystal she turned and left the room quicker than he would have credited. He stood and had to hold the table for support as he swayed and his head throbbed mightily. After a few minutes he burst from the room into the cleaner stench of the alley.

All in all the messages had pleased him, and after pausing for a moment he launched himself forward on his journey back to his master and the house in Bell Yard.

Tomás leaned forward, staring hard toward the foot of the Temple

Stairs, where an unsteady passenger was being helped out of a wherry. The figure slipped on the wet planking and would have fallen backwards into the river but for the steadying hand of the boatsman, then without a word of thanks it limped away up Middle Temple Lane, lurching along with the aid of a rough cut crutch.

He shadowed the figure for a few minutes until there was no doubt in the identification, then, signalling to his compatriot to close in from the other side, he walked toward the shambling form. He made sure to call out from about ten yards distant, so that he didn't startle him, "Cristóbal. Is that really you?"

There was no reply. The man continued shuffling up the street.

As Tomás closed the remaining gap he heard his friend's familiar voice muttering disquieting phrases. He was apparently arguing with himself.

Initially he placed a careful hand on Cristóbal's arm, then immediately recoiled in some horror, repelled by a powerful stench of sweat, dirt, and much worse, decay. Steeling himself to help, and signalling his comrade to assist from the other side, he threw an arm around his waist just in time to help catch Cristóbal as his knees gave way and he almost collapsed.

As they supported his slumping figure, Tomás did a quick battlefield assessment. Cristóbal clearly had a deep suppurating wound to his leg, several other minor injuries that were bandaged with bloodied cloth, and terrible burning that had left vivid purple scars all down his cheek and neck. His clothes were badly burnt and possibly even melted onto the skin of his chest. He needed treatment quickly else he might not survive. Treatment could be arranged at the house in Bell Yard, but Tomás wasn't sure it was a good idea to let Renard see him in this state. But what choice did he have?

Cristóbal roused himself and supporting more of his own weight they trudged together up the street past the entrance to the Inns of Court. Jerking his head this way and that, like a cornered bird, he suddenly lunged forward pointing across the street, croaking hoarsely, "My nemesis, he is coming for me...", then his leg crumpled beneath him and he would have fallen full length if Tomás hadn't caught him.

Tomás looked in the indicated direction and saw perhaps a dozen lawyers, some robed, some not, and their clients, going in and out of the Inn's archway. No one was paying any attention to the crazy man, certainly no one was coming to get him.

Tomás shook his head sadly, wondering what had happened to his friend. Despite his qualms, he knew they had to report to Renard, so continued half dragging, half carrying him, towards the Strand, from where it would be but a few minutes to their house in Bell Yard.

The Angelus Bells

Kat stopped mid-stride, dragging Jack to a halt with her.

"The sketch on the page said it was an *ancient chamber beneath the buttery,* didn't it?"

"What sketch? Oh, yes. But what of it? We wanted the paragraph below, that mentions keeping items safe and secure."

Getting excited now she ploughed on, "What if the sketch is a clue to where the items are kept?"

Jack wasn't so sure about the link, but years as a slave had conditioned him to avoid disagreements, so he just replied, "Go on."

"Well the items could be hidden in the ancient chamber under the buttery. Why else show the sketch? Otherwise it was completely out of context."

"What is a buttery?" asked Jack, perplexed.

"It is a storeroom or pantry. Where you would keep provisions cool and fresh. Usually near the kitchens. And where do you think all these fancy lawyers are going right now? To their dinner that's where. If we follow them we will find the communal eating hall, and thus the kitchens, the buttery and then this ancient chamber."

A rough shout from a man across the road caught Jack's attention. He saw the man was being held upright by two others and yet he fell and almost collapsed in the street. Was he pointing toward them? Jack had an uneasy feeling, and decided that getting off the street was the safest option, so with Kat he turned and followed a stream of lawyers back under the arch and into the courtyard. The last he heard from the street was a chorus of angry voices shouting indignantly as a troop of riders forced their way through the afternoon crowd, then the gentler sounds of market vendors and murmuring lawyers engulfed him.

Four horses trotted down the lane heedless of the curses from those they splashed with filthy gutter water. Lawyers scattered before them like a flock of crows. The riders swerved around two men who half-carried their drunken companion up the lane.

The leader dismounted at the quayside. It was Henry. He quizzed the wherrymen.

"No. We ain't see no couple coming off the river. Nobody like that."

That was their response anyway.

Henry was street-smart enough not to believe them. But not smart enough to leave it well alone.

First he dangled his purse and promised to pay for the information, which just elicited silent stares. One boatman spat at the ground by Henry's boot.

Then he whistled over one of the guards that had accompanied him. The burly man dismounted and at Henry's instigation hauled ineffectually at one wherryman who hadn't yet moved from his seat on an upturned box. The man waited until the hauling ceased, then swiftly stood and took a pace forward so he was nose-to-nose with the guard. He easily matched the other man in height and bulk, and pushed him away with an oath. Other watermen materialised as if from the mist and clustered around. Although they were only armed with oars and boathooks soon there were two dozen surrounding Henry and his companions. They didn't say anything, but they didn't need to, besides, Henry wasn't a fighter. Retreating up the lane, Henry sent his men into various establishments but they always came out shaking their heads, *No one has seen anything.*

Kat steered Jack to the market stall they had visited previously, where she quickly bought a basket, and further along the line of stalls she bought two part-skinned rabbits tied to a stick, and at the next several small loaves of bread.

Jack was about to eat one of the fresh loaves when she stopped him and put it with all the other loaves under a cloth in the basket.

"Come on, we can get into the kitchens by pretending to bring these provisions, then get directions to the buttery."

"Oh. Yes, good plan. We probably don't need to take all those loaves though," Jack replied, eyeing the food hungrily.

It worked better than expected. They had hardly entered the hall on the south side of the courtyard when a uniformed servant saw them and rushed over whispering urgently that they were late and to take the rabbits to the kitchen immediately, with a non-too gentle push toward a door on the right hand side, "And next time use the trade entrance, churls!"

They bustled into the kitchen where a kindly matron waved them over and relieved Kat of the rabbits, and a liveried man paid them more pennies for the meat than they'd paid just a few minutes before at the stall. "Take the rest to the buttery my dears," she directed them to a door at the rear.

Kat curtsied and the matron smiled and said "No need for that, I'm no lady, now get along there."

The buteries were a set of four inter-linked rooms each one a few degrees cooler than the previous one. There were barrels and crates and bottles of all sorts arrayed around the rooms, in piles and on benches. A young girl came into the first room while they looked around, gathered up several bottles, then left again, barely even glancing in their direction.

They looked at each other and laughed, "That was easy!" said Jack, "Now we need to get to the chamber below."

A couple of minutes of searching and in the corner of the third buttery they found some ancient stone steps winding down into an unlit chamber. Jack left Kat at the top of the steps and returned a moment later with a torch, and by its flickering light they descended to a crypt-like space deep underground.

Jack took the lead, holding the torch as far out in front of them as he could, occasionally brushing through dusty old cobwebs. The steps were worn and in places broken, and they had to stoop as they went to avoid the low ceiling.

They paused at the bottom of the steps and Jack waved the torch to and fro. There it was, just like the sketch on the page. Ribbed vaults arched up, the walls made from solid stone blocks. Various old barrels and boxes lay discarded around the chamber.

Cautiously they started exploring, every step throwing up a small cloud of dust. Jack banged his head on one of the vault ribs and cursed in French.

"Over here," Kat mumbled through the cloth she was holding over her mouth. Jack joined her and together they looked at a real life fireplace that exactly matched what they had seen in the sketch.

"Let me have another look at the page you took, Jack."

Careful to keep it away from the flickering torch Kat looked closely at the sketch, then read the meeting minutes again.

"I've got it!" she blurted out suddenly, startling Jack so that he banged his head on the ceiling again. He reflexively lifted his hand to rub the sore spot and accidentally stabbed the torch into the low ceiling, guttering it. A few sparks flew and then it was dark. The only light now was a faint glow coming from the stairs to the buttery.

"Merde," said Jack, "I'm sorry. Stay here, I'll go and relight the torch." With that he started moving away toward the stairs. Kat grabbed his sleeve, "Don't be long, I have always had nightmares of being stuck for hours in the darkness."

A few minutes later he returned with the relit torch.

Kat, relieved, started babbling about the fireplace and the sketch. Jack calmed her down and asked her to start again.

She took a deep breath.

"Sorry. A little nervous. Look at the first sentence of the minutes again."

Jack read from the page, "*Memorandum, that this howse is charged to hold in safety X secrecy certain items of great import,*"

"We thought it meant 'safety AND secrecy', but I think that is a clue. Look closely at the sketch," she pointed at the small cupboard to the left of the fireplace, "There is a tiny 'X' marked on it."

"You're right. So you think the items are stored in that cupboard? That makes sense, let's see."

He tucked the page back in his jerkin and walked up to the wall, where he played the torch back and forth. "The detailing on this fireplace matches the sketch exactly. Look, here are the little carved shields and in the middle the angel holding the bigger shield. Those details all match, so this is definitely the fireplace from the sketch. So where is the cupboard?" He held the light to the left of the fireplace, but it was just a blank wall. "There is nothing here," he said.

Kat joined him and sure enough there was just a plain wall.

"But it must be here," the disbelief was evident in her tone, "unless there is another fireplace, she took the torch and did a circuit of the chamber, finally coming back to find Jack on his knees beside the wall.

"This is the only fireplace, it must be here," she said.

Jack was silent, one hand flat on the wall, slowly moving left then right, then up and down.

"I think it has been bricked up and mortared over. It is just *too* smooth," he said by way of explanation.

He sprang up, "Stay here," and before she could utter an objection he scrambled up the stairs again.

It was several minutes before he returned. "Look what I found in one of the storerooms upstairs," he grinned, holding up a hammer and chisel.

Kat immediately grasped his intention, "You can't use those. The sound will echo and dozens or even hundreds of lawyers in the building will hear you."

He smiled at her in a somewhat irritating way, and referring to the sketch he lined the chisel up with where the opening should have been. Then waited.

Kat paced nervously, "You're not thinking straight Jack. We'll be taken by that Serjeant for sure. Probably interrogated and imprisoned in some horrible gaol."

He just stayed smiling, hammer poised, head cocked to one side as though listening.

Then she heard.

A church bell rang out. Again. Again. Then quiet. She recognised the pattern of the Angelus bells, rung in the early evening. One, two, three, pause. She knew it would be repeated twice more for a total of nine strikes. Then there would be nine more, but this time in a continuous sequence.

Then it rang again, starting the second group, and as the second strike of the second group rang out, Jack hit the chisel, perfectly in time, then again with the third, then pause. Then three more times. A total of five strikes. The sound of chisel on masonry, though loud in the chamber, was lost in the peal of the bells.

The bell rang out to start the sequence of nine, then the second bell, on the third through ninth strikes Jack hit the chisel, quickly realigning it to make best use of every available bell ring.

A total of twelve strikes had almost been enough to excavate the opening, but not quite. Jack levered out the final mortar and brick, without having to actually hit the chisel again, each time deftly catching the debris and laying it on the floor.

Brushing away some final pieces of mortar he signalled Kat to bring the torch closer, and there in the exposed recess was a small trove of packages.

They beamed at each other.

Wasting no time Jack reached in and passed them one by one to Kat.

All told there were three irregular shaped packages, each wrapped in a kind of oiled cloth, no doubt to preserve them against the damp.

They put their haul in the basket in place of the bread, and covered it with a cloth.

They brushed each other down to remove any blatant mortar dust, and then brazenly walked out of the buttery and exited through the back of the building, down a short flight of steps to an empty quad in the gathering gloom of early evening.

Arm in arm they walked swiftly but calmly toward the river.

Ships in the night

Tomás reflected that Renard had every right to be as furious as his screamed insults had revealed him to be.

Not only had Cristóbal failed in all his attacks on the magician John Dee, but he had lost a troop of hirelings and spent much silver doing it, and surely revealed their identity and intentions to Dee in the process. Even worse, Cristóbal was now so badly disfigured and limping that he would draw instant attention to himself instead of blending into the crowd as was their mission. And of course he was alternately raving mad, then subdued.

They had paid a local wise-woman to treat his leg and sooth his fever, but he was still babbling about raining hellfire.

Renard handed over a small bag of gold and ordered Tomás to put Cristóbal aboard a friendly merchant carrack that was leaving on the next tide for the northern Spanish port of A Coruña.

Tomás knew what this meant for his friend: going home before the end of the mission, instead of being covered in glory he would be returning injured and disgraced, to be shunned by friends and family, having no honour. It was really a fate worse than death. But there was nothing he could do to help him now was there?

He volunteered to take him down river by himself, not wanting further indignity cast on his friend. So swaddling him in a voluminous clean cloak he walked him back toward the river, Cristóbal still limping but no longer in constant pain. They were crossing The Strand as the bells rang for Angelus. He should be going to prayer, instead here he was sending his long time compatriot to ignominy.

The wherryman started bending his back to his trade while they settled down for the short journey to the carrack at Wapping, just beyond London Bridge.

Suddenly the previously docile Cristóbal exploded in a frenzy of agitation. Jumping to his feet he shouted and waved his arms and seemed to be trying to climb out of the wherry despite being out in the middle of the river. Tomás stood and tried to restrain his friend, who fought back with the strength of two men. They grappled and swayed back and forth, Cristóbal with one booted foot on the gunwale, which dipped and rose, then plunged so far that frigid Thames water surged into the boat. The boatman cried out a very unchristian oath as his craft rocked violently beneath him.

Saving their breath for the struggle, the Spaniards grappled in near silence. A grunt; a slap of leather as a gloved hand grasped an arm; a tearing rip as clothing was pulled beyond breaking point; a deadly snick as cold steel was unsheathed from enclosing leather.

As quickly as he had started, Cristóbal stopped struggling. His eyes, suddenly lucid and calm, locked on to those of his friend Tomás, and his brow wrinkled in silent entreaty. As he swayed backwards his eyes lost focus and his hands lost their grip on Tomás.

A dull splash marked his entry into the Thames, his lifeless body floating for a few seconds before being claimed by the black depths.

Tomás staggered and almost followed the dead man over the side. A choked-off gasp was the only requiem for his friend of so many years.

He wiped his dagger clean on the tattered remnants of Cristóbal's cloak, before he dropped that over the side too, where it settled like a stain on the surface before following its owner to the bottom.

He sat down hard on the bench seat of the wherry and looked up at the astonished boatman who was staring at him with mingled accusation and surprise. His less than eloquent reply was an inarticulate shrug. *It was him or me*, he thought, but didn't trust himself to actually speak.

He pulled the bag of gold intended to pay for Cristóbal's passage to Spain, and tossed it to the boatman. It was weighed, found sufficient, and pocketed without a word.

The return to the stairs was quick, the wherryman departing with a conspiratorial nod.

Breathing hard, Tomás leaned against the wall of a small church, the enormity of what he had just done bearing down on his soul. There was no priest he could turn to in this cursed country, so a self-imposed penance was his only possible salvation. He crossed himself unobtrusively even though it was fully dark, and muttered a quick confession, *Bless me Father for I have sinned*. He resolved to ensure his friend's family were supported.

With a final groan of despair he hauled himself upright and stumbled away to find a tavern in which to drown his self-pity.

Jack and Kat were swaddled in their cloaks to ward off the river's chill, their basket of treasures tight in Kat's grip. They climbed aboard the barge, the last passengers of the night. It quickly pulled away from the well lit stairs and headed into the deepening gloom of the evening. The barge would take them quickly to Lambeth, where Kat said she knew the landlady of *The Black Prince* public house, and they would get a great meal and a room for the night.

Jack's keen hearing detected a splash and correctly interpreted it as a body entering the water a hundred yards or more behind them, but euphoric with their discoveries he paid it no heed.

Part IV

"Vanity, saith the preacher, vanity!
  Draw round my bed: is Anselm keeping back?
  Nephews—sons mine . . . ah God, I know not! Well—
  She, men would have to be your mother once,
  Old Gandolf envied me, so fair she was!
  What's done is done, and she is dead beside,
  Dead long ago, and I am Bishop since,
  And as she died so must we die ourselves,
  And thence ye may perceive the world's a dream.
  Life, how and what is it? As here I lie
  In this state-chamber, dying by degrees,
  Hours and long hours in the dead night, I ask
  "Do I live, am I dead?" Peace, peace seems all."
- Robert Browning,
The Bishop Orders His Tomb at Saint Praxed's Church

Chapter 34 - Conflagration

Wednesday the 26th of July 1552
West of London

Whoomp

A light mist drifted lazily across the river as the morning barge steadied against the Mortlake pier. Jack thanked the lead oarsman for letting him help, then clambered back to rejoin Kat, who melodramatically rolled her eyes and edged a foot away from him as he tried to sit on the bench beside her.

A prosperous looking merchant who was disembarking paused to help an attractive goodwife clamber aboard, earning him angry glances from his own rather plain wife. The goodwife promptly squeezed between Jack and Kat forcing them both to make more room, and sat there stroking the chicken that she carried.

"I call her Anne Boleyn," she said to Kat, "because I'm taking her to have her head chopped off, ready for our dinner," she laughed out loud at her own joke, and then she edged closer to Jack. Kat leaned around the woman and shot an angry glance at Jack, who felt compelled to defend himself from her opprobrium.

"It's been a while and I needed the exercise. I don't understand why you're so upset."

Kat just turned away again and hugged the basket to her chest.

The barge was already moving smoothly away from the pier under the power of the four regular oarsmen, one of whom had just enjoyed a break as Jack had volunteered his services in his place.

An uneasy silence descended on the couple, which the goodwife took as an opportunity to tell the whole barge all about her husband's health complaints. Leaning closer to Jack, she whispered huskily that her husband had various other limitations too, if he knew what she meant. Jack, feeling quite uncomfortable, tried to edge further away, but there was nowhere to go.

The next hour on the river seemed an eternity to Jack, who was still puzzling over Kat's attitude and verbally dodging the goodwife's increasingly direct suggestions. Thankfully she departed at Richmond, throwing a final longing look at Jack. Kat grudgingly allowed Jack to slide over and sit beside her.

"How long to Kingston?" he asked tentatively. Fortunately Kat was as keen to end the impasse as he was, "Only another half hour from here."

He struggled manfully with small talk, and then they exchanged whispered guesses as to the potential meaning of the items they had liberated, until thankfully up ahead they saw the familiar bridge over the river and a smudge of smoke on the west bank that indicated that the village of Kingston was just ahead.

He was about to say how hungry he was when he saw Kat's frown was back. "What is it?"

"Those horsemen galloping toward Kingston. I have a bad feeling about them."

He looked toward the left bank, and sure enough there were about a dozen riders, but he couldn't see any details at this distance, so he just made placatory noises, "Perhaps riding to see the King at Hampton Court, they need to use the bridge, so nothing to do with Kingston or us at all."

"Hmm."

By the time the barge drew up at the short pier they had lost sight of the riders, and Jack had already forgotten about them. He helped Kat disembark and they both gratefully stretched their legs and walked up to the market cross.

There was a tense crowd in the square, and they exchanged a worried glance as they edged forward to see what was happening. Jack's question yielded a hasty reply from a yeoman who barely took his eyes off the scene ahead of him.

"Yonder fancy lord rode up a few minutes ago with 'bout twenty men and surrounded that warehouse back there. Reckon they're goin' to break inside. Lookin' to capture someone I'd say. Must be mischief against the King."

The man suddenly shook his fist and shouted out "Hang the Frenchies!" nearly deafening Jack.

"Are there Frenchmen there?" asked Jack, puzzled.

"Must be, I'd say, 'tis always the French causing mischief is it not?" a moments pause, "Or the Spaniards o' course," he shouted out again, "Lock up the Spanish mongrels!"

Shaking his head at the bigotry, Jack looked back at Kat, and was alarmed to see her staring at the warehouse, her face was drained of all colour. Then he realised. It was Dee's warehouse that was surrounded! He kicked himself for being a slow idiot.

He stood on his tiptoes to get a better look over the crowd.

He recognised the 'fancy lord' immediately as Lord Cheyne, and he cast an incredulous glance over at Kat, "God's teeth that man is everywhere we go!"

The sumptuous fur-trimmed cloak easily marked out Cheyne amongst the group of retainers who surrounded him. He was conferring with a tall man who was facing toward the warehouse, so Jack couldn't see his face; *Something about him looks familiar though.*

At a signal from Cheyne the retainers split into two smaller groups and gathered at different entrances to the warehouse.

"I must go and help the Doctor," cried Kat as she frantically pushed past Jack. He quickly reached out and held her tightly so she couldn't go rushing toward the warehouse.

"Stop struggling, Kat. I won't let you go to certain capture. Just look at them; Cheyne is there and so are twenty of his men."

They both looked on in quiet desperation as Cheyne bustled about importantly.

Just then Cheyne waved a signal and the waiting men burst open the doors and charged into the building.

Kat gasped out loud, "It's Cardano."

Jack too saw Gerolamo turning to look toward the nearest breached entrance, following his conference with Cheyne.

Before they had time to react to the obvious defection of their erstwhile friend, there was a loud *crack* heard from within the warehouse, then a bone-shaking, unearthly, *whoomp* echoed around the square. Simultaneously a searing green fire exploded out of every window and door of the warehouse, the flames emerging twenty feet or more. Those closest to the building were thrown to the floor, including Cheyne and Cardano, everyone else shielded their eyes and took a few steps backwards. Jack felt a hand dragging on his arm and a moment later realised that a stooped old beggar was pulling both him and Kat toward the river where a dinghy waited with a small sail already flapping in the breeze.

As Kat started to remonstrate with the man, Jack looked down and saw a telltale buckle on his boots. "Kat, it's alright, let's go with him."

Still stunned they climbed aboard the dinghy and were underway immediately.

Looking back he saw the flames had already extinguished and a preternatural silence had descended on the crowd. But it was just the calm before the storm, because the good people of Kingston started shrieking and wailing and running to and fro in the square. Cheyne and Cardano had been helped from the ground by one of their entourage, but now were buffeted back and forth by milling townsfolk. As their dinghy gathered speed, Jack saw with some satisfaction that both men were knocked down for a second time, Cheyne's gorgeous cloak trampled into the mud beneath dozens of passing feet.

Chuckling, the beggar removed part of his disguise, revealing the smiling face of Dr John Dee.

They made good speed northward on the river, the breeze perfectly filling the little sail so the boat surged along the Thames creating quite a bow wave.

Dee, keeping one hand casually on the tiller and gesturing animatedly with the other, explained how he had discovered Roger eavesdropping and then passing on what he had heard to a shifty fellow out in the street. Realising that both his location and actions were compromised, he had decided to evacuate, after leaving an incendiary surprise for the intruders.

When pressed all he would say was that Roger was now *persona non grata* in their little clique.

Jack and Kat summarised their adventures for Dee, promising more details and an examination of the basket's contents after being fed, as both were quite hungry. Dee promised food within the hour and tightened the sail to get some more speed.

After a while the boat veered toward the south side of the river, and bumped alongside a simple wooden dock nestling inconspicuously amongst overgrown reeds. They all clambered ashore and Jack quickly tied off the painter. Dee led them through a pleasant orchard, the gnarled trees heavy with apples and pears, toward what he proclaimed was their new base, a large red-brick house.

Homecoming

The twins, Ed and Hal, raced from the house and launched themselves at Kat, hugging her and crying out how much they had missed her. She whirled Hal through the air, then Ed insisted on the same attention, so she fell behind Dee and Jack, who continued to stride toward the house. Dee glanced behind them, then said in a low voice, "Jack, thank you for bringing Kat back to us. Did you find out why she disappeared after Canterbury?"

Jack glanced back too, and confirmed that Kat was well out of earshot, "No. Not completely. She only said that she could not go to Faversham, and that you refused to consider any changes to the route, so she had no choice but to go her own way and hope to meet up with us later. But then she was captured by Lord Cheyne's men and held for a while in Rochester, before being escorted toward Cheyne's family home on the Isle of Sheppey. It was on that journey to Shurland Hall that I managed to rescue her."

"Well, well. You have done me a service Jack, I am in your debt. I would not want any harm to befall her, for all the wool in England. She has cares enough."

"There is no debt. I was more than happy to do it. I…I am fond of her."

"Let us say no more of't then. What is all this about Lord Cheyne, and being held in Rochester?"

"Of that I learned more. As a youngster she had been a maid to Lady Anne Cheyne at Shurland Hall on the Isle of Sheppey. As she grew older she realised that Lord Cheyne was watching her at every opportunity, his eyes lingering on her greedily. He even started making excuses to be alone with her, stroking her hand and smelling her hair, and saying how full grown and mature she was. It disgusted her. The other girls said it was just a matter of time before he did more than hold her hand, and being in Lady Anne's good graces would be no protection, indeed it almost seemed like a sacrifice that Lady Anne would be willing to make. So one day Kat secretly left the Hall, surviving off her wits, eventually meeting you and earning her place in your household."

"Ah, yes. And all that is a story for another day. Suffice to say that when she first met me she said she was running to avoid a powerful man. Now we know who."

Jack continued, "She says she saw Cardano being held in Rochester castle too, but they did not get a chance to talk."

"Ah. I see." Dee paused not seeing at all, "But I do not understand the original need to avoid Faversham, and hence her desertion, capture and necessity for rescue." A resigned sigh. "No doubt she will tell us in her own good time. And what of Cardano? You know him best."

"That is, how do you say it, l'énigme."

"An enigma?"

"Yes. An enigma. I am sure Gerolamo was aligned with us until Canterbury. But when I rescued him in Rochester he seemed….distant. Perhaps that was when he threw in his towel with Lord Cheyne?"

"Threw in his lot."

"Not his towel?"

"No."

"Well, anyway. That would make sense wouldn't it? He is tortured or persuaded, and decides that working with our enemy is no different for him. I am just disappointed that he so easily betrayed us. I thought we were friends."

A serious looking young man greeted them at the entrance, and introduced himself, "I am Nikolaus. It is my pleasure to meet you."

Dee said, "He is the new Roger. I will explain all later".

Dee excused himself and left Nikolaus to give Jack and Kat the grand tour.

At times Nikolaus seemed embarrassed at the condition of the building, and explained that Dee had asked him to effect the necessary repairs but that he didn't have the skills to do it himself and was afraid of engaging workmen for fear of spies learning their location.

In the room designated as the workshop they found half the floorboards ripped up. Nikolaus explained that the printing press was being transported from Kingston and would need a reinforced floor when it arrived in two more days.

Jack said he had some carpentry skills from his time on board ship where repairs to woodwork were often necessary, and would help, and Kat said she could arrange timber and trustworthy workmen. Nikolaus was visibly relieved.

Chapter 35 - Examination

Thursday the 27th of July 1552
Dee's new base of operations, Mortlake

A labour of Heracles

Kat carefully unwrapped the three packages they had liberated from the hiding place in the chamber beneath the buttery.

Unfolding the stiff cloth she extracted a decorated ivory staff, about a foot long and an inch or so in diameter. One end was flanged, like a pedestal, so she stood it upright. The top had a screw thread of two or three turns.

"But what screws onto the top?" asked Jack, as he snatched it up and twirled it in his fingers. It spun mesmerisingly, its colours and decorations beguiling to the eye. But it wasn't very balanced and it slipped away from Jack's hand. Kat lunged forward and caught the staff before it hit the floor. She glared at him and in return he shrugged in that maddening Gallic way he had.

While she unwrapped the second item, Dee carefully rotated the staff a few times so he could see the decorations all around it. He murmured something that she didn't quite catch and she turned enquiringly toward him, causing him to repeat himself, but louder, "The markings are fascinating are they not? I have never seen anything like them, and I am fairly well read."

Kat raised an eyebrow at the deprecation, but wisely chose to say nothing.

She placed a beautiful statuette of a horse beside the staff. Jack reached for it, but Dee was faster, "Magnificent. The paintings on it are similar to those on the staff. Partly plant-like and partly biological.

They seem somewhat mystical and at the same time erudite." Jack grabbed it and peered closely, his face displaying such an expression of confusion that Kat almost laughed out loud.

Unwrapping the final parcel yielded a book with stiff wooden covers. Kat gently opened it, revealing pages of flowing, arcane script, in a language she didn't recognise, and more of the same imagery, including sketches that they guessed were of plants, leaves, babies, women, castles and even a dragon. Dee picked up the book and flipped through the couple of hundred vellum pages. Stroking the pages and then rubbing one between thumb and finger he said, "Calfskin if I'm not mistaken. Look at this page. These are diagrams of stars, and this here is part of an astrological chart. I could interpret this for you…"

"And the rest?" asked Kat.

He placed the book on the table and turned the pages for a minute or two, before looking up at them both in turn and smiling.

"That, I'm afraid, is going to be a labour of Heracles for you two adventurers to pursue on your own," the twinkle in his eyes indicated amusement, and Kat couldn't decide whether it was because he liked puzzles or because he thought it would keep them quiet for a very long time.

Chapter 36 - Usurpation

October 1552
Hampton Court

Creeks and havens

Cardano struggled to keep pace with Lord Cheyne who strode confidently behind a royal page through the cloisters of Hampton Court Palace, his new cloak swirling behind him, occasionally snapping at Cardano's face. He allowed himself to fall another couple of feet behind to avoid it.

He glanced nervously at each uniformed guard that they passed, standing expressionless, and holding a long-hafted halberd at the ready. The blades looked wickedly sharp and were highly polished. He remembered John Dee's explanation of how light bounced off an illuminated object and travelled to our eyes and thus we could "see" the object. He glanced more closely at the next blade and sure enough saw his own pale face sweating and wavering ominously in the reflection.

He realised his mind was wandering, and tried to focus on the present.

Over Cheyne's shoulder he could see the corridor terminated in a pair of large oaken doors, studded with nail heads the size of walnuts. The doors swung open silently as they approached and a gaggle of courtiers in brightly coloured garb fell silent as they watched the pair enter. Finally Cheyne stopped his forward rush and after a perfunctory bow he conversed with one particularly elegant courtier with a serious face and long beard. The man's thick golden chain of office proclaimed a senior rank, but to Cardano's well travelled eyes he looked quite young.

He straightened his spine as Cheyne introduced the courtier. Sir

William Cecil.

As he bowed deferentially he searched his memory; *William Cecil, I know that name. He is a privy councillor and a patron of John Dee! This reception might be frosty.*

To his surprise Cecil was entirely cordial and proper, although there was little warmth in his greeting.

They had to wait some time, but were finally admitted to the King's presence chamber.

Apparently the King's morning lessons were concluding and Cardano realised with a start that the tutor was Sir John Cheke, the man that John Dee had introduced him to a few months ago and whose astrological chart he had drawn up. Unsure of the correct etiquette he nodded quickly to Cheke as he passed on his way out of the room. Cheke merely stared at him coldly, and said no words as he swept past.

Cardano shivered. Apparently news of his defection to Cheyne's camp had already reached Cheke.

Lord Cheyne was already making the most of his chance to talk to the King, promoting his efforts to secure Kent and the channel ports against possible French attacks, and delivering the King's justice to the locals. Cardano was amazed to hear Edward responding by asking about the defences at specific locations of specific rivers, and whether particular creeks and havens were dredged and how many ships they could now accommodate. *How does he know the names and locations of all these unremarkable places?*

As the talk of defensive preparations dragged on, Cardano took the opportunity to survey the room. He marvelled at the shelves full of books, clearly in several different languages, and on topics both scientific and religious. In pride of place were several astronomical instruments and an engraved quadrant, all of supreme quality as befits the possessions of a king, with gold chasing and ivory dials. He was sorely tempted to move closer and inspect them.

His wandering attention was brought swiftly back to Cheyne and the King when he heard his name mentioned, he tentatively stepped closer and bowed deep and long until he heard Cecil call him forward.

Sir William explained how the King was feeling the strain of caring for all his people, and was consequently not feeling completely healthy.

"Could you, Dottore Cardano, as a renowned physician and astrologer, discover the nature of the King's unease and cast his horoscope to foresee his recovery?"

Cardano had a flashback to the meal table in Dee's Kingston warehouse, now a smoking ruin thanks to his own perfidy. Back at that table Dee had explained the double-edged nature of casting a king's horoscope. Predicting illness or death was treason, and yet predicting health that was not actually attained could easily lead to imprisonment as a charlatan, or worse.

"Dottore Cardano?" Cecil's sharp enquiry cut through Cardano's mental turmoil.

"It would be my greatest pleasure, my lord. I shall pour the greatest part of my energy and all the skill that I hath learned at the feet of the mightiest European exponents of..."

Mercifully for all, Cecil cut him off with an injected question.

"His Majesty knows you will apply all your skills. Now he would also like to know if you have knowledge of the heavens for he would be glad of a few minutes distraction with talk of the fixed and wandering stars. If you know them?" Cecil's mildly raised eyebrow was akin to a gauntlet thrown down by a military man.

"Absolutely. Yes indeed. It would be my pleasure. I have travelled and held discourse with the greatest minds in Europe and know much of the planetae and...ow." Cheyne not so subtly kicked his foot, and caused him to pause his babble.

Edward leaned forward, one princely arm gesticulating toward the nearby stained glass window, his eyes glowing with intensity, "Dottore. I believe astronomy proclaims the works of God, from which He is revealed to men. For the skies describe in detail and reveal heaven, the invisible glory of God and His power over the whole world."

Cardano blinked, astonished. Again this fifteen-year-old was surprising him with his erudition.

With an encouraging nod from Cheyne he then engaged the King for a lengthy time on the nature of comets and the heavenly spheres. The conversation was entirely in Latin, and Cardano realised that Edward was as fluent as he was himself and had read widely and thought deeply about the nature of the heavens.

Together they read sections of a book that looked oddly familiar to Cardano, *De Revolutionibus* by Nicolaus Copernicus. *Doesn't Jack have a copy of this book?*

Edward asked him to think carefully about the author's premise and be ready to respond to it in a few moments.

To Cardano's surprise another physician stepped forward and quickly applied a watery preparation to Edward's eyes with a feather.

As he withdrew the physician explained that it was a tincture for sore eyes…red fennel, sage and herbs, ground peppercorns, white wine, three spoonfuls of honey and five of the water of a innocent man-child.

Whilst listening to Cardano's opinion on the matter of the sun circling the earth, or vice versa, Edward read more of the book, this time wearing a pair of spectacles.

A little later Cecil stepped forward and eased the conversation toward a conclusion, indicating that Edward had many tasks yet to complete this day, which was already growing old. Apparently there would be more opportunities to talk of stars and planets in the weeks and months ahead.

As Cardano withdrew he reflected on his meeting with the young King. Physically Edward was a little shorter than average for his age, pale-faced and with grey eyes. A serious face, but handsome in a way that the young ladies of court would surely fight for the attention of, whether he were king or no, when he came of age. He held his body a little tight and caused one shoulder blade to project a little. More exercise would do him good, he reflected.

"You did well Dottore. The King clearly enjoyed your talk of comets and such. You must make haste with the astronomical chart so we can keep up the momentum of this first audience," Lord Cheyne was upbeat and continued in an expansive tone, "Yes, this is a better plan than trying to catch that rat John Dee. We will make him irrelevant. The more influence we have, the less he has. When the Princess Mary is queen then we will finally deal with Dee and his nest of vermin."

Cardano was shocked and hurriedly looked around, calming only marginally when he realised no one was within earshot. Such blatant talk of the next monarch was surely treason? His shock was gradually replaced with a rare pang of conscience, he wanted power and wealth and more importantly wanted to keep his head, but didn't want to think through the consequences for those that he had previously considered friends.

Long life

For three weeks Cardano laboured to create an astrological chart for the King. Luckily the time, date, and place of the King's birth were known exactly: two o'clock in the morning on Friday the 12th of October 1537, in Hampton Court Palace. Cardano did not even need to ask for this information from the royal household because the whole country knew the details, as everyone had been so desperate for the queen to deliver a healthy son after the childbirth problems of Henry VIII's first two wives.

Edward's chart showed him as likely to be serious, mature, self-disciplined and practical, perhaps with a tendency to melancholy. He also showed promise as a diplomatic leader, with his Sun in libra and Saturn on the ascendant. Cardano sighed as he continued to think it through; *Unfortunately, the Sun is in the sign of its fall, so whilst he may aspire to avoid confrontation and to collaborate with others in order to ensure justice for all, he might find this difficult to achieve without considerable effort.*

He was unsure of the interpretation of the Moon being in detriment in Saturn's sign. It could mean Edward might appear somewhat cold, but also showed great ambition to create things of lasting value. *Ah, what I would give to have a second opinion from Dee, or just a conversation around the whole interpretation. Alas, that is out of the question now.*

As soon as he completed the work, Lord Cheyne took the horoscope and delivered it to Hampton Court himself, desperate to take all the credit. He hadn't even asked what it said beyond "long life and happiness."

Now the King had questions and had summoned them both back to the palace.

Cardano was nervous, he remembered again the comments made by Dee about the danger of providing horoscopes to royalty. He glanced across at Cheyne and experienced a frisson of schadenfreude when he saw the lord was sweating badly. *Let him suffer,* he thought.

Edward sat before them re-reading the manuscript. He pulled his spectacles off his nose and used them to tap the paper.

"Where you forecast illness for me in my thirtieth year, you do not specify the extent nor type of illness. Do you not know?"

Cheyne blanched, "Illnesses my Lord?" and looked accusingly at Cardano.

Gerolamo almost laughed with relief. *This is like a consultation with any client*, he thought. He paused as long as he dared, viciously trying to create more torment for Lord Cheyne.

Judging his timing perfectly he cut in a few seconds after Cheyne started babbling incoherently, "Your Grace. All men have illness at some time, yours will be mild I think. A skin condition, perhaps a slight fever, and in later years, a certain languor of mind and body. These are but normal complaints for men of accomplishment and responsibility, and will be nothing to hinder you. I had considered omitting them entirely but I thought with your greater wisdom of the heavens and understanding of the chart you would probably observe that Saturn, being the malefic contrary to sect and placed in the first house, may bring challenges to the body and health, as it also rules the 6th house of disease. Observing this you might wonder about my omission, and so think less of me."

Edward replaced his glasses and scanned up and down the manuscript, perhaps to find the details in the chart that related to Saturn. He paused a moment as though checking the details, then peered over the glasses directly into Cardano's eyes, and he felt the boy King's scepticism boring into his soul. His stomach did cartwheels. Cheyne blanched and looked decidedly ill.

Seconds passed, but they felt like hours.

Eventually, apparently satisfied, Edward nodded toward William Cecil, then carefully rose and limped from the room, one of his grooms rushing to assist him.

Chapter 37 - Preparation

Late December 1552
Cecil House, London

No good opinion of me

As he followed Dee along The Strand toward Cecil House, Jack felt a rush of excitement. *No wonder Kat and I have been picking fights with each other these last few weeks,* he thought. *We're both missing the thrill of the chase, cooped up doing bookish research in Dee's library. What are the column and the horse for? What do all the strange markings mean? Is the Bretwalda egg the jewel we seek?* He shook his head in silent frustration. *I don't know how we will resolve these questions.*

"Stay alert, Jack. Cutpurses and vagabonds are the least of our worries here. There are probably enemy agents combing the streets for us," Dee's admonition brought his attention back to the present, even though he thought he could detect some hyperbole in the words.

As they were admitted through the side entrance, Jack cast one last look around and his pulse raced as he glimpsed a dark figure slip out of sight behind a wall on the opposite side of the street. *Was that a spy or just a pedestrian?* Now he was jumping at shadows!

They waited in a chill room deep within the house. A high window provided the only illumination, revealing dark oak panelling, a portrait of a self-satisfied prelate, and some faded tapestries.

Dee nodded in the direction of the door, and Jack understood the silent instruction, returned the nod, and started toward it.

Just at that moment a section of panelling creaked open behind them and Sir William Cecil himself ducked through the low doorway it revealed.

"Ah, Dee, there you are. Come in here. Sir William and I have been waiting for your counsel."

Jack glanced past Dee as he went with Cecil through the hidden door, and got a brief glimpse of an elegant salon with comfortable furniture and colourful hangings. He recognised the old soldier, Sir William Herbert, in the background staring dejectedly into a roaring fire.

As the door closed softly behind them Cecil's grave tones were cut off and Jack was left alone in silence.

He slipped out the way they had entered and quietly followed the corridor around a couple of corners, trying to work his way around to where the secret room must be. He paused beside a slightly open door and listened for a moment. He was about to move on when he heard a floorboard creak inside the room. Without making a sound, he peered in and thought he could see a darker man-shaped shadow high up against the wall. He stepped back and looked around. The corridor was bereft of concealment, but there was another door opposite. He held his breath, opened the door and slipped inside. Luck was on his side, it was empty.

With the door open an inch he coughed once on purpose, the sound carrying easily in the otherwise silent house. A scrambling sound came from the room opposite and he silently closed the door just in time to avoid being seen by the servant who exited almost at a run. The man scuttled off back the way Jack had come, toward the busier part of the house. Jack made a mental note: shoulder length greying hair, dark green waistcoat, brown hose, limping on his left leg.

He crept across the corridor and into the other room, and stood on the chair where he'd seen the other man. He could see nothing in the dark, so felt with his fingertips. Wood panelling rose in regular squares up the wall. About head height each square panel was inlaid with a geometric pattern, and above that a final row of plain squares. Jack was about to abandon his quest in frustration, when one of the top panels gave slightly when his fingers traced their way across it. He pressed a little harder, and with a click the panel swung inward like a tiny door.

A beam of light shone from the opened panel. Peering inside he was amazed to discover that he could see through to the supposedly secure room beyond. Staying perfectly quiet he found that by moving his head left and right he could see any part of the other room and hear the occupant's conversations too.

Cecil, standing near the fireplace, was reading from a letter.

" '...*others revel but I took myself to my bed with weary body...no man scarcely had any good opinion of me.*' He goes on like this for several sentences, then *'John Knox has refused the appointment as Bishop of Rochester. I have decided to dismiss him because he is ungrateful and even had the temerity to question my religious views. I, who have suffered many dangers over the last few years for my support of it.'* "

From the ensuing conversation it was clear that the author of the letter was John Dudley, the Duke of Northumberland, supposedly the most powerful man in the realm - and yet apparently riven with insecurities. Jack filed away the information for later use. He gently pulled the hatch shut and gratefully heard a soft click as it latched back into position. He hopped down and replaced the chair at a nearby table and padded silently from the room.

He went in search of the kitchens, *the cook will know everyone that works in the household*, he thought, picturing the retreating grey-haired servant in his mind's eye.

Later, on the journey back to Mortlake, they stopped at an inn for refreshments.

In a reasonably good impression of Cecil's sonorous intonation, Dee shared the juiciest parts of what he had been told, the letter from Northumberland, "*Scarce anyone has a good opinion of me, so I took myself to my bed…*"

Jack, who had not yet had chance to tell Dee about his own adventures, butted in to complete that part of the story, "*And then I dismissed John Knox, because he refused the appointment to be Bishop of Rochester.*"

Dee gazed with astonishment, "Your accent is terrible Jack, but how…?"

Just then a young barmaid approached and placed bread, cheese and a pitcher of small beer and mugs at their table. Jack winked at her as he placed two pennies in her hand, causing her to blush from her neck to her hairline. She almost danced from their table with a beatific smile.

"Don't try to dodge my questions, Jack. How did you know what we discussed? Cecil assured me that the secret room was known only to himself and his most trusted servants, and that it was soundproofed as well."

Jack took his sweet time eating a wedge of cheese and then washing it down with an appreciative swig of beer, all the while enjoying Dee's mounting agitation. Finally he cracked and revealed his story, saying how he had prowled around as Dee had originally instructed, and found someone eavesdropping, and when they left he had taken their place.

Dee laughing with glee, gently punched his shoulder in admiration, then ordered another pitcher of beer from the barmaid, letting Jack once again charm her. And pay.

"So the head cook gave you the man's name? Excellent. Well all of this can go in my next report to Cecil. I wouldn't want to be that servant when Sir William discovers he has been betrayed!"

Chapter 38 - Facilitation

January 1553
Bell Lane, London

Ambassador Scheyfve

"You must control yourself Tomás. If you cannot control yourself I will have to send you to join Cristóbal, in disgrace, on a ship back to España. Our mission does not include revenge. When will you accept that? Dee has been sidelined. He is no longer important, he has no influence, and he has no access to the King or his councillors. Now it is all Dottore Cardano, and he is working for Lord Cheyne, who is working indirectly for the Pope. Your desire for revenge against Dee and his colleagues reflects very badly on you, and can only endanger our real mission."

Renard's short red beard bristled with indignation as he spoke, but eventually his furious fusillade abated, and muttering to himself he retreated to his desk, where he extracted various papers from a pile.

"Here is a report from one of our spies in the Royal Household:

'He spends much time in his chamber, often bedridden. I have seen bloodied handkerchiefs taken away and burned.'

"And another here from our countryman, Ambassador Scheyfve, although he is not always reliable:

" 'He sometimes struggles to draw breath, this I believe is caused by compression of the organs on the right side due to his right shoulder being lower….This is a visitation and sign from God.' "

"So you see Tomás, Edward is surely ill or poisoned, and he and his councillors will therefore be more receptive to suggestions of a reconciliation between Edward and his sister Mary. *That* is our mission. And when this sickly child has passed away we will be at Mary's right hand, positioned to help her steer this miserable, cold, wet country of ignorant godless peasants, back to the *true* religion, as our master desires."

Tomás realised some gesture was required, but he could think of none, his mind blank after the haranguing he had received, so he grunted and shifted his stance in what he hoped would be interpreted as affirmation.

Renard continued talking about how he would engineer the reconciliation and bring Mary back to court and ensure she was acceptable to the council when the time came for her ascension. Tomás felt himself growing angry with the arrogance of this cocky upstart who had come amongst them so recently, and who cared not about the loss of Cristóbal, nor about getting revenge against those who had caused it. He held his tongue as long as he could, but then burst out coldly, "You were not here for the last few occasions when Mary was at court, Señor. They did not go well for Mary or for our cause."

Renard cocked his head, intrigued, and waited for Tomás to continue.

Realising that his outburst was being treated as a serious comment, Tomás collected his thoughts and continued more calmly.

"In December 1550 Mary was at court to protest her right to hear Mass with her household, as had been previously promised by the Duke of Northumberland. She suggested Edward was too unworldly to make religious demands of her, while he insisted he was vested with the authority of their father. They argued, and both ended up crying. Over the next couple of months they exchanged letters, with Edward saying that of all his subjects the King's sister could not be tolerated to dissent from the prohibition against hearing Mass. Mary, for her part, continued to assert that he should suspend judgement until he was older."

Tomás paused to exhale in exasperation, before resuming, "In my opinion that was not a good tactic with a boy who is king."

Now he had started Tomás continued his outpouring, "Mary pleaded with our ambassadors for assistance and finally Scheyfve himself was involved, and ended up hinting to the council that they should ignore Edward until he was older, which earned him a strong rebuke and he was physically thrown out of the council chamber."

At this last comment Renard smirked, and Tomás realised that there was little love lost between the two men.

Renard was still attentive so Tomás continued his retelling of the events, "Mary apparently decided to confront Edward in person again, and so came to court in mid-March, surrounded by a large retinue of nobles who still cleaved to the true Church. She argued again with Edward and his councillors, assuming that those councillors were poisoning her brother's mind against her and the Mass. She had it backwards however, for it is Edward who is the zealot, as demonstrated when a letter was received two days later from Mary's uncle, our Emperor. Charles threatened outright war if Mary was denied the right to hear Mass. The councillors were all in favour of some conciliation for they feared war and the financial burden it would place on the country, but Edward refused to be swayed by such remonstrations, apparently saying, 'I would spend my life and all I have rather than agree to what I know certainly to be against the truth, for to allow a sin is a sin itself.'

"After this outburst the council did their best to mollify their young King, but still they ended up arresting two gentlemen and sending them to the Fleet prison because they were known to have heard Mass recently in Mary's household. Then a week later Mary's own chaplain was sent to the Tower.

"So when I say that Mary's last visits to court did not go well, I mean exactly that. She is stubborn, proud, and very aware of her own position, and while those qualities can sometimes be applauded, they can also lead to hot heads and failure of politics."

"Thank you for the lesson Tomás. So what do we learn? We learn that Edward loves his sister, and is respectful of her person. He opposes the Mass for Mary partly from belief but partly from good governance. So we will play on the respect and diminish the topic of the Mass. With Edward, and with the council. With Mary I shall advise more humility. You catch more flies with honey, no?

"Now, leave me as I have letters to write. Including one to that horse's behind, Scheyfve."

Chapter 39 - Navigation

January 1553
John Dee's house and workshop, Mortlake

Innamorati

The house was a whirlwind of preparation.

Jack had been assigned the task of arranging victuals, so he engaged the innkeeper from the local tavern, *The King's Arms*, to prepare food, a barrel of wine, and another of beer. Half a dozen staff from the inn were bringing in trays of bread and fruits to accompany the star of the show, roast wild boar with chestnuts. The aroma was drifting through the entire house already and several of the young apprentices had already tried their luck at charming the innkeeper's wife to get an early taste of the mouth watering dish. She was more than a match for them though, beating them off with a ladle.

Meanwhile Kat had the tricky task of procuring fitting entertainment. She had learned of a troupe of Italians who were newly landed in England and performed *Commedia dell'arte*. They were such a novel concept that as yet they had no license to perform in public from the authorities, and hence no work, so she thought they could be hired cheaply. This appealed to Dee who liked a bargain, and he encouraged her to travel into London and bring them back to Mortlake.

The troupe had arrived earlier in the day and were now preparing in the library, one of the largest rooms in the house. Kat complained that they had loudly demanded wine, but she was nervous of taking it in because they were getting unruly.

Casting a rueful backward glance toward the roast boar, Jack said he'd help.

Carrying a tray of goblets, he paused agog at the threshold of the rehearsal room. What had been a tidy library was now pure chaos.

Some players were fully dressed in bizarre costumes, some were half dressed with bulky padding being wrapped around them to make them look fat, their costumes still hanging from hooks on the ceiling beams. Many had strange masks over their faces.

Three actors immediately converged on him and took goblets of wine which they drank down greedily, clinking their glasses and bursting into song together.

A young actress approached with downcast eyes and thanked him shyly for the refreshments. She hovered near him taking sips of her wine. She laughed at the boisterous actors and leaning toward Jack she pointed out the characters in turn, "He is called *Pantalone*. He is a fat old merchant who will be the butt of many of the jokes. And that one with a hunchback and pot belly, he is named *Pulcinella* and is a social climbing buffoon."

She almost had to shout to be heard, so she moved right beside him and leaned in closer still, almost talking into his ear, "That third one over there, he is called *il Capitano* and is a swaggering braggart."

She laid her hand on his arm, almost stroking it, her husky voice close enough for him to feel the warmth of her breath on his ear, as she explained that she and two other younger actors played the *innamorati*, "Our purpose is being in love with one another, and with ourselves. We are completely sincere in our emotions," she cooed.

Just then Kat entered the room and looked askance toward Jack and the young woman who was leaning so close.

The inamorata saw her, and whispered one last entreaty, "Despite facing many obstacles, the lovers are always united by the end. Remember that Jack, and thank you again for the wine, I will find a way to repay you..." she glided away into the swirl of colour and bodies that was the troupe preparing to perform. Kat hovered protectively near Jack while he collected the empty glasses and they left the room.

The twins were responsible for preparing the main room. It was the largest room in the house, though Dee had claimed he wanted to get builders in eventually to enlarge it further. It had extensive wood panelling on three walls and a tiled checkerboard floor. They had assembled a collection of two dozen chairs from all over the house, and arrayed them in a series of arcs, facing a low stage.

While the twins arranged the chairs, Dee and Nikolaus were frantically working on completion of a set of strange maps. Even though he had learned the art of navigation on the Stanislav and had many months of practical experience, when Jack looked at these maps he could only recognise Hamburg on the coast of Germany, and Bergen in Norway. The rest of the coastlines and open seas were unknown to him.

The north-east passage

A deep chill still clung to the day as a seemingly constant stream of gentlemen and merchants arrived during the afternoon. Jack and Kat started playing a game where they had to guess the rank of the visitor based on whether they arrived by river or on horseback, and by how many liveried retainers accompanied them.

Kat was easily winning, but she admitted she knew who some of them were, so they abandoned the game and she just named them instead.

"See that man with the great nest of red hair? That's Sir Hugh Willoughby. He was knighted by the Earl of Hertford almost a decade ago, while in the field against the Scots. Then just last year he defended a castle against a joint attack by the Scots and the French. Rumour has it that since the Earl came down he has been looking for other adventures to raise his profile once again."

"And what about the old man?" Jack gestured toward an old man with a short forked white beard. He was sumptuously attired, wearing a thick dark-coloured robe with a fur collar, the robe sweeping the leaves along the ground as he approached from the river, his polished black walking stick sinking into the turf every time he leaned on it, "He seems very frail, but his entourage give him great deference."

"I don't know him, but mayhap we will find out as the day unfolds."

Another barge was jostling for space at the little dock, but with the crush of vessels it was several minutes before the guests could disembark. This time even Jack could recognise the visitors. Sir William Herbert and Sir William Cecil stepped off the barge together and ambled toward the house, heads together in a continuous conversation. As they entered they briefly acknowledged Jack and Kat, but didn't deign to speak to them.

Soon the entire ground floor of the house thronged with affluent visitors and their principal staff. Everyone in Dee's household was involved in victualling them. Jack found himself having to repeatedly name and describe the function of the many scientific instruments that were crammed into every room of the house, plus describe the many other curious possessions Dee had accumulated from his busy travels. The house echoed to the booming greetings between adventurers who heartily slapped each other on the shoulder, and the respectful greetings between merchants who surreptitiously felt the quality of the cloth of the other party as they embraced in greeting.

Quite the gathering.

At a signal from Dee, Jack went outside and lit the fuse of a small cannon, then rushed back inside so he could observe the effect of its detonation on the assembled crowd.

KABOOM.

Jack flinched even though he knew it was coming.

The crowd flinched too, but it only paused the conversation for a few seconds, then it picked up again at full volume.

Jack looked across the main room at John Dee and mouthed, *What more can we do?* Dee shrugged expansively in a Gallic manner he had picked up from Jack. Then just as quickly he held a forefinger aloft, he had obviously thought of something.

Dee stepped onto the low dais and turned to face his guests. No-one paid any heed. The next moment there was a eye-watering flash of golden yellow light accompanied by a low whooshing sound that seemed to suck the air and conversation right out of the room.

John Dee stepped out of a column of yellow tinged smoke and spoke into the sudden silence, "Friends, welcome to my humble home. If you would be so kind as to find a seat, I call forward our esteemed Principal, the exceptional, the venerable, the one and only, Sebastian Cabot. Sebastian, if you would be so good as to explain our proposal. Thank you."

A silver-haired man slowly made his way to the dais. It was the old man they had seen earlier. He was quickly flanked by two others.

Kat nudged Jack, "Well, now we know his name anyway."

"And beside him is the adventurer you called Willoughby with all his red hair. And who is that other?"

But before Kat could answer, Sebastian Cabot started talking, pausing for breath between every short sentence as old men are wont to do.

"Friends, colleagues, and most especially our exalted guests, ah. Most of you know me, and you know my story, um. I have navigated the wide oceans, having learned their secrets from my father who went before me, yes. Between us we discovered the most wondrous lands, ah. Sometimes in the service of England and sometimes, yes, in the service of Spain, uhum."

A disagreeable murmur rippled through the crowd.

Cabot held up his hand, to quieten his audience, then continued, "Many decades of experience upon the sea, ah, and yet a viable sea route to the hugely profitable land of Cathay and the Spice islands has always eluded us. Ahem. Until now."

Another murmur from the crowd, this time of interest.

"The north-east passage to Cathay will open up fast trading possibilities. English woollen goods in exchange for Cathay silks and spices, umm. Profit to be made in both directions, yes. Best of all the Spanish do not guard this route, indeed they do not know about it. Ah."

Immediately an excited murmur arose and merchants exchanged knowing looks with each other.

"Doctor John Dee, our host today," he nodded toward Dee, "Is known to many of you for his erudition and learning, yes. I am pleased to say he has been instrumental in the formalisation of the navigation aids and maps for this endeavour, yes he has."

Dee took a momentary step forward, gave a brief bobbing bow, then retreated to the shadows once more.

As his excitement built he seemed to gain strength and his pauses for breath receded.

"I, or rather we," he gestured to his companions on the dais, "are launching the most exciting subscription funded exploration in living memory. *The Company of Merchant Adventurers to New Lands.*"

As Cabot named the adventure, perfectly on cue, a dozen sconces around the room lit themselves and flared briefly with eye-wateringly bright white light, some whistling and some shooting short-lived sparks through the air. The overall impression was one of magic and adventure.

"This company will equip a fleet of ships and send them to Cathay by this new route. All the treasure we bring back is ours and all the glory is for England, King Edward, and Saint George." This last sentence had to be shouted in Cabot's scratchy voice, over the rising excitement of the crowd.

It was several minutes before the crowd became quiet enough for Cabot to continue, clearly straining himself to be heard. "Sir Hugh Willoughby will lead the expedition. He is of stout heart and is a formidable captain of men, known for his exploits in the barbarous northlands. Guiding the fleet day to day, will be Richard Chancellor, who has already piloted to the eastern Mediterranean." Both men stepped forward as their names were called and bowed, Willoughby with an exaggerated flourish and Chancellor with a more modest junior bow, his fashionable pointed beard bristling with pride.

"Gentlemen, I do not need to tell you to ready your purses, I can already see you doing that, and with good reason. However, an expedition of this kind needs political backing as well as financial backing. Therefore, it is with the greatest humility that I can tell you, that not only does this undertaking have the Duke of Northumberland himself as the principal backer, it also has the goodwill of his majesty, the King."

Dee gestured to Kat and Jack, who rushed to their places behind a massive oaken desk to the right hand side of the dais. Jack opened a ledger and inked his quill in readiness.

"We all show you our faith in this expedition, and demonstrate the equitable fairness of the arrangements, by being the first to pay for our shares. One share maximum per investor, for twenty-five pounds." And with that, Cabot, Willoughby, Chancellor and Dee all dropped bags of gold coin on the table, which Kat quickly counted and deposited in a chest on the desk, while Jack wrote names, amounts and turned the ledger for the subscribers' signatures.

There was almost a stampede of gentlemen and merchants behind them, as some brandished their purses whilst others pledged the amount before witnesses, and all signed the ledger. Jack had even purchased a share for himself, half financed by a loan from Cecil but the other half scraped together by selling his other liquid assets.

The principal investors worked the crowd, explaining in more detail the navigation challenges and solutions, which included Dee's loxodromic compass, and the best instruments, and the expected timings and financial arrangements of the expedition.

Within an hour Jack waved to Dee who leaned down and whispered to the seated Cabot who had been taking a much needed rest. Cabot stood and tried to get the attention of the crowd, and when he failed Dee gestured with a wave of his beringed hand and the sconces flared with a red-coloured flame accompanied by a deep rumbling sound. As the flames died away Cabot took the opportunity of quiet to make a final formal announcement.

"Friends, or should I say, fellow adventurers: our subscription for the Company of Merchant Adventurers to New Lands is now closed as we have the full two hundred and forty shareholders that were required. I congratulate you all on your wise choice of investment and am humbled by the confidence that you have bestowed on our plans. To those of you that have not managed to secure a share today I say this: opportunities like this come rarely and I am sad for you that you have missed out. Perhaps you can convince one of my fellow investors to sell his share, however," and here he chuckled, "I doubt they will sell cheaply."

At Cabot's comments a young nobleman standing nearby flushed deep red and stared fixedly at the floor. Jack nudged Kat and whispered, "I don't remember him coming up to the table and buying a share, perhaps he is regretting his tardiness". Kat said, "No wonder he is embarrassed, that is Guildford Dudley, son of the chief backer of this enterprise, the Duke of Northumberland."

The room darkened, although Jack knew the sun was still high in the sky outside, and then the dais lit up with a pearly glow, revealing Dee, who exclaimed in the lilting Welsh sing-song voice that betrayed his excitement, "And now we have some entertainment for you, fresh from Roma in Italia, The Zan Ganassa Players." As he bowed and backed off the dais the troupe of actors entered and began their performance.

As Jack and Kat carefully packed away the ledger and money the crowd roared with laughter at the antics of the troupe, and Jack had to continuously drag his eyes away from the beautiful young actress who had been overly interested in him earlier, as her suggestive performance seemed directed at him personally.

A distraction

As he locked the strongroom door behind him, now safely containing the ledger and chest of subscription money, Jack saw Cecil and Herbert abandon the entertainment and accompany Dee into another room. He only hesitated for a moment, then discretely followed them.

Loitering outside the room, he heard Cecil's chiding voice, "Brother Dee, I congratulate you on today's launch, but I hope *The Merchant Adventurers* is not proving too much of a distraction?" he continued without waiting for an answer, "The brotherhood's main concern is for the King's health. He continues to decline, just this week developing a hacking cough and taking to his bed. We need your assurance that you are putting all your energies toward that problem, our most urgent of problems."

"Of course, of course, I work on the matter day and night. Additionally my assistants are focussed on researching the matter of..." he lowered his voice and leaned conspiratorially closer, "the healing gem."

Jack grimaced. Despite the jewellery box they had found in the Bishop's cache, and despite the clues that he and Kat had solved whilst chasing around half of south-east England, and most especially despite the haul of hidden artefacts that they had retrieved from the undercroft of the Temple's refectory, he knew Dee still did not believe in the existence of the healing gem. He said such a fanciful tale was for children's bedtime stories, and could not exist according to any science he knew, and he was as widely read as was possible. Jack shook his head. *How could Dee not believe in the gem, and yet profess to foretell the future from the positions of the moving and fixed stars?*

Worse, he was now using the gem as a distraction with these two peers of the realm. Jack knew that Dee was not unsympathetic to the King's illness and the urgent need to find a cure for the good of the kingdom and the new religion. But he also knew that Dee secretly thought it a lost cause, and consequently wanted to focus his time and energy on other matters. Clearly he couldn't reveal that to Cecil and Herbert.

Herbert had been browsing amongst the curios in the room. He was holding a glass instrument up to the light and turned it first one way then another, presumably in some idle attempt to discern its purpose. He put it down clearly mystified, and chose this moment to enter the conversation.

"Brother Dee. What of the marriage of my eldest son Henry to Lady Katherine Grey. What do you advise?"

"Ah, my felicitations. When is the happy event planned for?" queried Dee, although to Jack's ears the interest was clearly feigned.

"On the 25th of May at Durham House in London," Herbert peered eagerly over Dees shoulder as the astrologer quickly sketched an astrological chart. Dee consulted several tables of figures, presumably to determine positions of the moon and other heavenly bodies, and marked the astrological chart with their positions. Muttering to himself he continued the forecast. Jack almost chuckled out loud, he knew how Dee hated having anyone watch so closely while he worked.

His hands were a blur as he used a straight edge to rule various intersecting lines across the chart.

"What do these lines mean?" asked Herbert, poking a meaty finger at the parchment while Dee was consulting a large leather-bound tome from the nearby bookcase. Dee scowled at the presumptuousness of the old soldier, then continued scanning the ephemeris in his hands.

His hands fairly flew over the diagram as Dee scratched some more marks and lines on the chart and then stood back from his work, one hand thoughtfully stroking his fashionable beard. Jack thought he had never seen Dee create a chart so quickly; *It must be an approximation and not a detailed reading*, he thought.

"Well?" asked Herbert

"I'm glad you consulted me sire, before it was too late," began Dee.

Herbert's head snapped up from where he had been studying the chart.

"It is not a good match, and not at a good time. No good will come from it. I strongly advise against it."

Clearly this wasn't what Herbert had wanted to hear and Jack watched in dread as his face turned first pink then suffused with rage it turned red, "How dare you presume to instruct me in what is a good match and what is not," thundered the Knight.

Dee, seemingly unconcerned about the eruption, continued in the same vein "Oh the marriage will go ahead, the chart is clear on that, but to undo the harm caused by it you will need to be swift and decisive in the following months, mark my words. It will cost you much treasure to unravel the deed. In fact, even that will not suffice. Your hand will turn against friend before you are safe in your position once more."

"You charlatan. You misbegotten oaf. *You churl*," this last accompanied by a spray of spittle that thankfully mostly clung to his own beard, though some also dripped onto Sir Cecil's gown as his friend's surprisingly strong arm sought to restrain William's motion. "This marriage will go ahead, I have already made the arrangements, and it will be successful. And Northumberland's boy Guilford will marry Katherine's sister, Jane, at the same time, cementing my ascendance."

"Oh yes, as I said," Dee was still unconcerned, "it will all go ahead. The stars confirm it. But you will regret it. So take my advice and be ready to reverse it within twelve months." With glorious nonchalance he started packing away his books and reference materials.

Cecil still struggling to hold Sir William back, so he could not launch himself at Dee, "William, you know the forecasts are not always precise, and yet even so, you shouldn't ask for advice if you aren't willing to accept it."

"Wise words, my lord," said Dee, with a brief bow to Cecil, "and now if you will excuse me I must see to my other guests." As he swept out of the room Jack thought to make himself scarce, but was not quick enough. Dee saw him and rolled his eyes in disparagement of his volcanic patron, and gestured for Jack to join him back in the main entertainment room.

Chapter 40 - Visitation

Friday the 10th of February 1553
Bishopsgate, London

Accelerate your plans

Renard sneezed, and reflexively calmed his horse even before it reacted, his childhood years riding the hillsides around his native town of Vesoul, east of Paris in the County of Burgundy, serving him well.

Despite wearing a thick fur over his padded jerkin he was shivering in the light rain that had been falling since early morning, as he waited with a hundred other riders and a crowd of townsfolk just inside Bishopsgate in the northern part of the London wall.

This gate had none of the ugly but unfounded connotations of Cripplegate, and smelled better than Moorgate, beyond which lay soggy moorlands with small pools of fetid water and malnourished cattle.

Impatiently, he ducked down so he might see under the sturdy stone arch of the Gate itself and up the cobbled street beyond, past an assortment of houses and workshops, and out into the countryside. As he craned his neck an icy pool of rainwater that had been gathering on his cap poured down his back, instantly soaking his shirt. He shivered again, more violently this time, and he had to move quickly to control his horse as it stepped back and forth in agitation. To his right, Jean Scheyfve, his supposed colleague the Spanish Ambassador, snickered, clearly delighting in his rival's discomfort. Renard, despising him as more of a merchant than a courtier, cast him a threatening black look and he quieted with a disdainful sniff.

He glanced around to see if anyone else was watching and judging him. However the richly caparisoned horses and brightly attired riders were not paying him any attention, instead they were shifting with nervous excitement, picking up on the mood of the less colourful but boisterous crowd of Londoners.

Tomás, mounted to his left, quietly informed him, "An advance rider says that Princess Mary is just five minutes away."

The waiting dignitaries included many adherents of the old religion, keen to see Mary and to be seen themselves. Many were noblemen, but others were rich merchants, burghers, and even some wealthy guildsmen. Around them all was an arc of heaving apprentices and poorer townsfolk. At the front of the crowd, waiting to greet Mary and her entourage, were leading men of the land, some of whom were accompanied by their wives, which was unusual. He could just see the Duke of Northumberland at their head, sitting squarely on a huge horse, looking more like the old soldier he was than a noble, for all his fancy clothes.

Renard smiled grimly to himself. *How hard had it been for Dudley to swallow his pride and lead this welcome party?* he wondered.

Arrayed around Dudley were several lords and leading officers of the privy council. Renard could see a bundle of furs that he guessed was William Cecil. *A most cunning mind and capable administrator. He looks as miserable and wet as I am.*

Despite the inclement weather he sighed contentedly, fully aware of how much work he and Tomás, and yes, Scheyfve as well, had to put in to make this visit acceptable to all parties. He, personally, had made more than a dozen visits to Mary's country house, each time taking a different message, sometimes real, sometimes invented, in efforts to get the headstrong but indecisive young woman to agree to visit her brother's court. The religious divide between them was deep, and the acrimony real, but beneath that there was a familial tenderness that could be tapped. Edward's illness had provided the opportunity for Mary to demonstrate her independence and yet her compassion, and not least to remind Londoners in particular that she was her father's child, and healthy to boot. Just in case. He grudgingly acknowledged that Scheyfve's task had arguably been even more difficult. Navigating the shifting patterns of allegiance and posturing at court, to align both the precocious King and his jockeying courtiers into not only agreeing to the visit, but to sending the invitation in the first place.

As Mary's liveried servants came into view a rousing cheer emanated from the waiting population, as was befitting for the leading Lady of the land.

Finally Mary herself, sidesaddle on a grey palfrey, bedecked in golden cloth, waving regally to the crowds, her attendants armed and attentive in case of some last minute trick by Dudley.

In the event there was no drama.

Dudley welcomed Mary on behalf of the King, and invited her to travel the rest of the way by royal barge. Then the Lord Mayor of London, George Barne, stepped up to present her the keys to the city. After the presentation he cast a wary glance toward Renard, who touched his cap in return. As the ceremony took place Renard acknowledged to himself that the man had successfully brought out many city dignitaries as he had said he would, so he turned to his companion, "Tomás, remind me tomorrow to send a letter to the Emperor recommending that the mayor Barne be allowed to increase his transport of cloth to Spain, and his import of wine back to England, for he has been of value to the Emperor's cousin, Mary."

As Mary's entourage rode on toward the waiting barge, accompanied by Northumberland, a cluster of courtiers, and a few paces behind them, by Scheyfve, Renard began plotting his next moves.

Ten days later Scheyfve came to Bell Yard to see Renard.

"You need to accelerate your plans, Renard. Things do not look so well for Edward, but Mary is not yet secure in her succession if my judgement is sound."

Renard waited for the Brabanter to continue.

"Upon the visit, Edward greeted the princess warmly and they chatted amiably for some time, and yet, all this was from his sick bed, which is where he lies yet. My informant John Banister, is a young physik at court, whose father is one of the King's doctors. Anyway, he tells me that the King has difficulty drawing his breath, especially when the fever is upon him. I have pointed out his physical defects to you before, his uncle the Duke of Somerset, was similarly afflicted if I recall." He continued smugly, "The boy will never do well with the lance. Indeed, this summer might see the end of his suffering altogether. Accelerate your plans, Renard!" He swirled his cape around him, the deep red lining flashing richly in the evening light, and marched out of Renard's office without waiting for a response.

Chapter 41 - Consideration

Monday the 10th of April 1553
John Dee's house and workshop, Mortlake

Of analgesics and inheritance

Kat respectfully entered John Dee's library, in the Mortlake house, now restored to order after the anarchy of the Zan Ganassa Players.

Dee was at his desk, immersed in his latest acquisition, a fat mathematics tome by Christoph Rudolff, who, Dee excitedly explained, "...had an interesting way of annotating *coss* or unknown things, and their relationships, and has invented a special character for the 'square root'."

Kat ignored the talk of mathematics, and reported that visitors were approaching, and gestured toward the window, implying the river beyond. She recognised his irritation as he set aside the book and his notes, and joined her at the large bay window. As they peered into the evening gloom she wondered at the contradictions in his character. One minute he was a man of action, the next he was a sagacious scholar of deep learning, and at times like this he seemed more like a grumpy old man preferring his own company to social interactions, and like old men everywhere he wasn't afraid to show his testiness.

Out of the evening gloom emerged a strange pair. A robed man leaning alternately on a tall staff and on the arm of a slender retainer who barely seemed up to the task. As they shuffled into the pool of weak light cast from the windows she recognised Sir William Cecil. "Presumably they travelled in the Master Secretary's barge," she ventured.

Casting a longing glance toward the discarded book, Dee sighed and turned to her.

"A jug of claret and two goblets, Kat, if you please, as quick as you

275 John Dee's house and workshop

like", as she hastened to the errand she wondered what Dee was up to, normally he preferred a rich vinho do Porto at this late hour, not the spicy dark rosé from Burgundy.

She returned only moments later but Dee had vanished, the room was completely empty. She blinked and looked around dazed: *Where has he gone?*

She flinched and almost dropped the wine when a section of panelling creaked open. She glimpsed his laboratory beyond, as Dee quickly stepped through the impromptu door and then closed the panel invisibly behind him. He had the grace to blush behind his short beard and shrug, saying "How did you think I moved around the house so quickly?" She sighed and kept her actual thoughts to herself; *Boys and their toys!*

He strode over to where she stood and without a word he deftly unwrapped a small twist of parchment and poured a finely ground dark powder into one goblet, then looked meaningfully at Kat, "For Sir William's joints. Might as well make our guest comfortable."

At her raised eyebrow he elaborated; "Willow bark, fenugreek, turmeric, ginger, cayenne pepper, and so on." He tossed the paper into the fireplace where it turned to ash and floated lazily up the chimney.

Moments later, Cecil, looking totally miserable, limped heavily into the room, and at a gesture from Dee, gratefully lowered himself into an upholstered chair near the blazing fireplace, and groaned. Dee sat opposite him, and nodded to Kat.

She poured the wine into both goblets passing one to each man, then retreated a discrete distance.

"God's teeth Dee my joints ache so, and are so very stiff."

Kat knew Dee was in his mid-twenties and Cecil was only in his early thirties, and yet Dee suffered from no similar aches. She idly wondered why Cecil suffered, and thought it was perhaps the strain of his high office, or waiting in draughty corridors and ante-rooms for the King to summon him.

She watched Cecil closely as he savoured a long draught from the glass, before putting it aside. *Ah. The strong claret is masking the taste of the powder. Clever.*

A few minutes later Dee leaned forward and waved his hands around in front of Cecil in an exotic pattern whilst murmuring softly to himself. Cecil jerked his head back, his eyes wide with surprise, and perhaps a little fear. Dee clicked the fingers of one hand drawing Cecil's eyes toward it, at the same time Kat saw a flick of his other wrist and realised he had discretely thrown something into the fire, before he concluded the incantation with a crescendo and what sounded like an appeal to Asclepius and Panacea for relief from pain. There followed a searing flash of light that briefly lit the room like a divine presence.

Blinking the glare from his eyes, Cecil stuttered, trying to ask Dee what he was doing.

Kat had to suppress a smile. The theatrical misdirection was all too obvious from where she stood, *off-stage*, as it were, and Dee's timing had been impeccable.

Dee sat back and took a long sip from his own goblet, and Cecil clearly shaken, mimicked by taking a deep draught from his own, though he had to use both hands to keep the glass steady.

Finally, Dee spoke, his first words since Cecil arrived. "I owe you thanks, my lord, for suggesting to the King my appointment as Rector of Upton-upon-Severn, and again for guiding the matter through Privy Council. I sorely need the funds that this appointment will provide."

Kat saw Cecil squirm in his chair. *Was the horse-hair padding loose? It can be prickly if it is, I should have checked it.*

"Ah. About that…"

Dee's eyebrows shot up enquiringly.

"Well. It seems that old Bishop Hooper, whose See includes Upton, firmly believes that only he has the authority to appoint the new Rector, and he will only do that for a priest not a layman and certainly not to someone who studies astrology."

Dee looked nonplussed.

Kat noticed Dee's reaction and grimaced ruefully. *Because you've probably already spent the annual income on more books, haven't you?* She trusted Dee, and would follow him anywhere, perform any mission, but she readily admitted to herself that his greatest failing was money management. It was usually spent before it was even received. *Now Jack,* she smiled as she recalled his many successful investments, *Jack can invest a shilling and recoup a half-crown before the week is out.*

Looking justifiably shamefaced Cecil continued, "But do not worry, do not worry at all. The council will set him straight, just a few weeks, you will see."

To give Dee time to recover his poise Kat noiselessly padded over and poured more wine, then retreated to her place.

Both men took long sips of their wine.

Cecil plunged into the real reason for his visit, "Tomorrow the King and his court will move to Greenwich. By barge of course.

"He is much weakened after attending the opening of parliament last month, but he did insist that he should go and be seen to be taking the reins of power. Now however his doctors are insistent, he needs to rest and he needs the cleaner air of Greenwich. Plus it will give the servants a chance to air out Hampton Court. Give it a good clean, you know, dispel any evil humours. And when he is feeling stronger there is the bowling green, the tennis court and even the tilt yard. The Palace of Placentia is as fine a house as any the King owns.

"The council has complete belief that he will recover and that all will be well...however..."

Here it comes, thought Kat.

"The prudent councillor must also think through all the possible alternative outcomes. Enemies of the realm, both foreign and domestic, might use his majesty's illness to cause mischief or even to launch surprise attacks against this country, thinking we will be in disarray. To prevent assassins hiding in plain sight we have doubled the guard at the palaces, cancelled all jousts, and postponed all unnecessary audiences with the King. To dissuade foreign powers from contemplating aggression, and to defend in case of it, we are very publicly positioning artillery to cover strategic points like the harbours and the river Thames. For example, there are now six more cannon at Gravesend. We have ordered the assembling of the navy and have authorised urgent repairs to any ships of the royal fleet that might require them. Anyone who can afford it is buying armour and personally I am only travelling armed and when protected by trusted retainers."

God's blood! That sounds pretty serious. Kat's mind raced. *Were they in any danger themselves? What could they do?*

Dee merely frowned, the Welsh lilt that crept into his voice the only sign of any anxiety as he asked in a sonorous voice, "And what is it you want from me, sire? I have no army, although Jack can probably hold off six strong men all by himself."

"I need you to cast another chart with all haste," and then he leaned forward and unnecessarily whispered, "and the Brotherhood wants to know what result of your quest for the Bloodstone." Before Dee could remind him of the unlikelihood of the Bloodstone ever being found Cecil made placatory gestures with both hands, "Yes, we know it is a long shot, but matters require us to follow every avenue."

Dee responded with a straight face "A decumbiture chart does not work in a situation like this". Kat realised immediately that this was a lie: *You can't risk casting an astrological chart predicting recovery when there is a strong chance that the King may die, and you can't release a chart that predicts his death because that would be treason. Lose-lose.*

"As for the search for the stone, my weekly reports have already informed you of most of it. To wit, we have a trove of artefacts that Jack and Kat found beneath the refectory of the Temple Church, and we continue to research what purposes they might have.

"My latest report only mentioned our guess of Oxburgh Hall for the stone's location, we did not explain why. The full explanation is based on who we think the personages are that are mentioned in the final clue…"

Dee handed the torn page from the Temple Church to Cecil, who had not seen the original before. Cecil closely inspected the paper and then, with a grunt, proceeded to read the key passage out loud.

"*…this howse is charged to hold in safety X secrecy certain items of connection to the Bretwalda egg, to be surrendered as inheritance only to his son Henry B, or his legal and rightful heirs of the male line, upon demand. This request made at the instance of Edmund, scourge of the French…*"

Dee leaned forward. "We think that 'Henry B' is none other than Sir Henry Bedingfield. And that 'Edmund, scourge of the French' is his father Sir Edmund Bedingfield, Knight of the Bath."

Cecil whistled as he leaned back in his chair, and appraised Dee coolly, "Sir Henry Bedingfield is a Privy Councillor. His loyalty and honesty are beyond reproach, although I have long suspected him of remaining a papist, in which he is far from alone. His father, Sir Edmund, was one of the bravest men to fight against the French in 1523 during Wolsey's invasion, and was knighted by Charles Brandon, brother-in-law to King Henry VIII, and leader of that invasion. You will need solid evidence that these men are involved in keeping something from the King before you can accuse them."

Dee explained their rationale, "Last week the news reached us that Sir Edmund had died in his bed at Oxburgh Hall, in Norfolk, after a long illness. Upon making discrete enquiries we determined he had indeed been called the 'scourge of the French' by his fellow knights.

"It seemed reasonable to assume he had secured the jewel somewhere, probably at Oxburgh Hall, and deposited these items with the lawyers as safeguards of some sort. Perhaps he didn't know of its power, or didn't believe the story, or was embarrassed by the nature of it. Either way we don't think he shared the story of the egg with anyone else. So we are not accusing him or his son of any intentional concealment, merely of ignorance. During his illness he has apparently been in and out of a fever and unable to communicate, and so we assume he couldn't tell his family about the items or the need to recover them. Nor about their purpose, and the egg."

Cecil had been nodding throughout the explanation, gently stroking his beard as was his wont when deep in thought.

"Yes, yes. It all makes sense. Sir Edmund was both trustworthy and Catholic, and so if you were a pious Abbot looking for a guardian for the stone he would be an excellent candidate."

"Now, sire," continued Dee, "our problem is that any enforced search at Oxburgh will surely aggravate the delicate tensions with the Catholic community who are already primed like a tinderbox because of the Council's prohibition of the Mass and the King's worsening condition. And of course we don't know the layout of the Hall nor indeed what we would be looking for. It's a dilemma."

"I checked with the brotherhood for information on Oxburgh…"

"Yes. And?" asked Dee eagerly, casting aside etiquette.

"And they told me of a master stone mason, John Adams, old now, who is the last known person to direct the alterations at the Hall that were permitted by Edward IV when he granted Edmund's ancestor permission '…to build towers, walls, and such other fortifications as he pleased in his manors of Oxburgh…'"

"Where is this Master Adams? Can we secretly question him?"

"That is why I risked a journey here today, even in such dangerous times. He is impoverished now, and held at the Marshalsea debtors prison for failing to pay back a loan of twenty pounds on time. Apparently his failing eyesight means he struggles to work and thus cannot raise the money to release himself from gaol. You could buy his freedom if he cooperates," and with that Cecil tossed a bulging purse to Dee, who caught it one handed, "Be sure to consult him quickly, Doctor, time is not on our side."

Cecil drained his goblet and rose easily from his chair. As he reached for his staff, Kat saw a surprised look on his face. He flexed his arms and legs, then cried out in joy. He turned back to Dee slack jawed, and danced a little jig. "Why, Dee! You have cured my aches. Is that what your pyrotechnics were earlier? Well, I'll be a Jesuit!" And with that he left the house whistling one of the more memorable tunes from the recent *Commedia dell'arte* performance.

Chapter 42 - Defenestration

Saturday the 6th of May 1553
Marshalsea Prison, London

The master stonemason

As they crossed London Bridge, Kat shuddered at the memory of only narrowly avoiding Cheyne and his men as they had searched St Saviour's church, "The gift of the ferryman's daughter", and then felt the heat rise up her neck and face as she blushed, remembering the long, arousing kiss with Jack while they were waiting to make their escape from the bridge.

They passed swiftly through Borough market where she kept one hand on her purse and the other on the hilt of her sword. Jack was very alert, scanning the crowd and at one point muttered that he thought they were being followed, but Dee urged them forward saying it was all in his imagination.

Finally they turned at a gateway in a brick wall, where a small sign fixed to one gatepost announced the place as "The Marshalsea Prison". She had been expecting something like a castle: formidable stone walls, guards, chains, and portcullis. But this...this was...odd.

They entered into a pleasant cobbled courtyard where she saw three different groups of reasonably well dressed men. One pair had stripped off their jackets and were playing a game of racquetball against the building's wall. The second group were animatedly discussing the prices of imported goods. The third group stood in the shade offered by a few fruit trees, and she heard them debating where they were going to have lunch today, in the prison restaurant or in a nearby inn.

Along the north side of the courtyard was a terrace of three storey houses adjoining an even larger building that was fronted by several Doric columns that provided a rather grand entranceway.

As they headed toward the entrance she asked Dee, "What kind of prison is this?"

He explained, "The Marshalsea is privately run for profit. The prisoners must pay rent and also pay for their food and clothes. If they can afford it they can have their own rooms, and even furnish the rooms to their own taste, at their own expense of course. I have heard that some of them even rent additional space from the prison operator to run small shops, and there is said to be quite a decent restaurant where meals can be obtained twice a day."

"And what if they cannot afford it?" asked Jack.

"Well, then their accommodation and overall experience is not so comfortable. As usual." He grimaced in distaste. "They are crammed dozens to a room, having to sleep in hammocks, with slops for food and rags for clothes. In that case they probably can't afford to buy the privilege of leaving the room to do some work and earn money, so they just accumulate debt due to their rent and food, thus owing more and more over time, and usually end up dying in the prison."

"But," spluttered Jack, immediately remembering his own time in captivity, "that's so unfair. The world is just a horrid place full of horrid people!"

Kat skipped over beside him and hugged his arm saying, "Calm. You're with friends here, Jack. You're safe with us."

Inside they were stopped by an officious porter who asked them their business. When Dee said they wanted to see John Adams the porter scratched his head as though thinking hard, "I don't think there is anyone here with that name sir."

Dee passed the man a silver shilling, and he suddenly exclaimed, "Unless you mean old Johnny Adams. Yes, he's here. If you will wait in the salon I will fetch him to you." He gestured toward the sweeping staircase, "The salon is on the first floor on the right hand side."

They climbed the stairs to the salon and Kat looked around awestruck, "It is like a palace" she said as she gaped at the lofty moulded ceiling and panelled walls with their tall windows.

Before they had chance to fully examine the room the porter returned, with a stooped older man in tow. Dee gave him another shilling and his eyes lit up, saying he would return with a pitcher of ale and some beakers for their refreshment. The old man squinted up at them from beneath his furrowed brow and exhibited the large hands and strong arms of someone who had spent a lifetime hefting heavy blocks of stone. He pulled a woollen cap off his head and introduced himself "John Adams, Master Stonemason, at your service."

Dee greeted him respectfully and made no mention of the man's embarrassing current predicament. "I am seeking intelligence concerning a house you worked on some years ago in Norfolk, called Oxburgh Hall. I need to know all the ways one could enter the house and also the layout of the rooms."

Kat blushed at the brazen request, thinking such information could only be needed for an attempted burglary.

Evidently John Adams thought the same, because he tilted his head to one side and looked sceptically at Dee, "That is a mighty strange request for a gentleman. Why not just get yerself an invitation to the home and ask for a tour?"

"You see right through me," grimaced Dee, "I am unlikely to be invited in. Nonetheless that is my request, and if you can help me in this matter I will pay off your debt," at this last he showed the bulging purse that Cecil had provided.

Adams blinked, clearly astonished at the possible turn in his fortunes. A couple of seconds was all it took before he smiled greedily, any reservations evaporating, "Now that was a few years ago that was, and of course I don't normally reveal client secrets. Old Sir Edmund was an excellent employer, and strong in the old faith as well, God bless him. A generous man...", Kat saw a crafty twinkle in his eye.

"Yes. Well he died last week, so I don't think he'll be giving you any more work," said Dee rather harshly, "Now I'll put your possible payment here on this table so you can easily be reminded of my generosity, if your answer satisfies me. Twenty pounds for an hour's work seems more than adequate payment to break your professional vow of confidentiality. So, do you remember the layout or not? Perhaps I should save my time and money and leave now?"

Realising his chance at freedom could evaporate as quickly as it had arrived Adams quickly changed his tone "Yes, yes I remember. Indeed I remember all my past commissions. We are agreed right enough," Adams spat into his hand and held it out to shake on the deal. Dee looked at the proffered hand with revulsion, "That isn't necessary, Master Adams. Now the layout of Oxburgh Hall. Quickly man."

Jack pulled over a few chairs and they all sat. John Adams started describing the house with such accurate details as can only be provided by a professional craftsman.

"You should understand that the Hall is first and foremost a gentleman's family home. It is not a fortress, although it is decorated with crenellations and such. It is not capable of withstanding a cannonade, but it is certainly capable of deterring casual entry. Will you be taking cannons?"

"Of course not."

"Well then. Surrounding the whole building is a square moat about 200 feet along each side, the water of which goes right up to the brick walls of the house. Inside the house is a square inner courtyard. To cross the moat there is only one bridge, made of stone and having three arches. It is on the north side and leads directly to a fortified gatehouse flanked by tall towers that rise in seven tiers. The gatehouse is three stories tall and houses the guards' quarters and the armoury, and of course has machicolations. If you were thinking of entering though the gatehouse, think again."

"What are machicolations?" asked Jack.

"Openings in the vault above the gate through which the guards will drop burning oil onto your head, lad," replied Adams before continuing his exposition, "So all in all, the gatehouse is not a realistic entry point for you.

"There are windows in the outer walls of the house of course, but they are not easily reached from the water, whether you were to swim or use a boat. Anyway the walls are very slimy and slippery thanks to the water in the moat. So if you were tempted to enter that way, think again.

"The moat is twenty feet wide and the surrounding grassland is trimmed short by grazing sheep. So if you were thinking of climbing a tree and dropping into the Hall from an overhanging branch or something, think again.

"On the ground floor of the house the rooms in the north side are all used by servants: kitchens, storerooms and such. The rooms in the western side of the square include a dining hall, stairs and further hall. The east side is all stables, feed stores, smithy, armoury, and so on. Oh yes, and the brewery, a mighty good ale was brewed there by an old monk they keep for that reason. On the south side you have the library, grand salon, and chapel.

"The first floor has servants' quarters above the kitchens, retainers and visitors are lodged on the west side, and family bedrooms on the south and east sides."

He proceeded to explain the layout of corridors and connecting galleries, the number of staff as best that he could recall and what types of staff they were. All in all the detail of his recollection was amazing.

After a while Jack interrupted him, "But Master Adams, how can we gain entry? You said it wasn't a fortress but it certainly sounds impregnable."

"Well this is where I really earn my wages, young sir. You see, Sir Edmund was worried about the lack of exits in case of attack, so he had me engineer a tunnel from the stables, under the moat, to a folly in the grounds. That tunnel took some digging I can tell you, for it is deep and long and mostly through solid rock. Only Sir Edmund and I know about the tunnel. And now you three. So that's your way into the Hall."

He sat back with a smug look on his face.

Dee rubbed his hands together with glee at the news.

Kat glanced over and saw that Jack was sketching with a piece of charcoal on a sheet of parchment. Adams peered over and tutted mildly, "That diagram is not bad based on my description lad, but if you wait here a moment I will fetch for you my original plans for the alterations, I have them in my room just above this salon. I'll be back in a moment." As he ambled away they helped themselves to some of the weak ale left by the porter, pouring one ready for Adams' return as well.

Kat wandered over to the windows overlooking the courtyard and could see that the racquetball game had ended and only the merchants remained outside. *Still discussing the price of wool and cloth no doubt*, she thought.

Just then a scream pierced the amiable silence of the precincts, and before she could react a body fell past the window not three feet in front of her, its arms windmilling crazily. She dropped her beaker and sprang back in shock, but not before she had glimpsed the horrified face of the man falling. It was Adams.

Thud.

She stepped over to the window and looked down to the courtyard. The body spreadeagled with the limbs at unnatural angles and a pool of dark red blood spreading from the head over the cobbles.

Numbly, she turned to her colleagues, "That was Adams. I think he's dead."

Jack wasted no time and sprinted for the door almost knocking down the porter who was hurrying into the salon.

"Which room is Adams'?" but the man was too shocked to answer. Jack shook him by the shoulders until he finally replied, "Top floor, fourth room on the left."

Jack ran up the next flight of stairs with Dee hard on his heels. Kat drew her sword and followed just a few steps behind them. Counting the doors out loud as they passed, Jack hurtled into the fourth room.

It had probably been a clean and tidy room before someone had ransacked it. Now there were torn papers on the floor, a prayer book cast aside with a broken rosary near it, the beads scattered everywhere. Even the thin mattress had been shredded spilling straw all around.

Kat was last to arrive and skidded to a halt in the doorway looking around aghast, quickly taking in the mess and the shattered shutters where presumably Adams had been thrown out. Then she was pushed hard from behind and almost stabbed Dee in the leg as she stumbled forward. She caught herself and span around lunging her sword into the corridor, just in time to put two inches of steel into the arm of her assailant who was fleeing. He cried out in pain and blood sprayed over the wall, but he managed to pull his arm free and kept running after his accomplice who was already exiting via a back stairwell. She gave chase but a door was thrown shut blocking her access to the stairwell. Frustrated she turned and just had time to step aside as Jack came careening down the corridor and threw himself shoulder first at the door, only to yowl in pain as he slid to the floor, the solid oak door unmoved.

Dee joined them, helped Jack to his feet and turned back for the main stairs. As all three emerged into the courtyard they knew they had lost the assailants because the merchants were all pointing toward Borough high street and talking in excited tones. All except the porter, who had by now covered Adams' body and most of the blood pool with a piece of old sacking.

As they exited on to the high street Dee suddenly remember the bag of gold and frantically turned to retrieve it. Jack caught his arm and handed over the gold. "Don't worry, I never misplace money."

Chapter 43 - Triangulation

Wednesday the 10th of May 1553
Deptford, East London

Cannonade

Jack felt exhilarated as he and Kat waited on the quayside at Deptford, just east of London.

Anchored midstream they could see the three newly built ships that belonged to the Company of Merchant Adventurers to New Lands.

Kat asked him "I know your twenty-five pound share in the Company was more than you could afford, Jack, do you think you will make a profit?"

"Oh, I know I will"

"Why so sure?"

"Because I already sold it for forty five pounds to Guildford Dudley, the son of the Duke of Northumberland. You remember him? He was embarrassed at missing out on getting a share. From that money I paid back the loan I had arranged with Sir William Cecil and so I have already made twenty pounds. That's eighty percent profit in four months."

"Well, I'm….but that's amazing! So now I suppose you are worried you will miss out on all the riches the adventure will return?"

"Kat, I have sailed in the northern waters myself, they are not always gentle. This adventure will be going much further north than the Hanse regularly sails and then it will go east, in an attempt to find a route to Cathay and the spice islands. If they succeed then yes the profits will be enormous, but the risks are great. So I think I can safely say that twenty pounds profit in my purse is worth far more than even one hundred pounds profit that I might never actually make."

They had to step aside as two longshoremen rolled barrels of fresh water to the edge of the quay, ready to be lowered to a small boat that would transfer them and other last minute provisions to the ships.

The final loading and boarding preparations were increasing the excitement of the watching crowd, who were getting noisier by the minute. Jack declined refreshments from a vendor who was wheeling his handcart through the assemblage, hawking his locally brewed ale, while Kat paid a youngster a ha'penny for a cone of freshly roasted chestnuts, rolling her eyes dramatically at Jack as she savoured the first one "hmm, delicious, and a bargain too."

Jack replied, "An enterprising fellow, I'm sure he will go far." He refrained from pointing out the old woman with the brazier who was doing the roasting over hot coals, and who was selling the same cones for a farthing, half the price the boy had charged. *The lad has just doubled his money in a few minutes, a profit of one hundred percent. So who is the better investor, him or me?*

Jack shifted his duffel bag on his shoulder and followed Kat through the crowd toward the large awning that had been erected to shelter the principal Company investors from the already hot sun. The canvas provided shade, but Kat wrinkled her sensitive nose in disgust and said it smelled like stale sweat.

They approached Dee and Cecil just as they concluded a conversation with Sebastian Cabot, who as Governor of the Company seemed to be in high demand for handshakes and backslaps.

Cecil turned to them, "I know you understand the importance of your mission, but know this; time could be short, so if you do find the gem remember that my resources and contacts stand ready to expedite your return to Greenwich with all haste, where Doctor Dee and I will meet you in the hope of using it to the benefit of the whole realm."

"No pressure then," quipped Jack.

Cecil merely raised an eyebrow, then passed Jack a rolled parchment, "Take this warrant and show it to anyone who questions your authority."

Dee looked like he wanted to hug them both, but restrained himself, and merely said "Take the next supply boat, for soon Willoughby will be ready to depart and to avoid speculation you should not be seen leaving in the same dinghy as him. You take our hopes and prayers with you. Go now and return safely and as swiftly as you might. "

They clasped hands with Dee, bowed to Cecil, and turned away quickly to the quayside to hide a sudden upwelling of emotion. They flashed their warrant and descended to the dinghy that quickly headed out to the bigger of the three ships, Willoughby's flagship, the Bona Esperanza.

Jack looked wistfully at the crew as they busily prepared for the voyage, and felt Kat's restraining hand on his forearm. He remembered her frostiness when he had helped the ferry crew row them upriver a few months ago, and the fact that he was on a mission for Cecil and Dee, and so didn't give in to his desire to climb the rigging and help out.

Willoughby himself arrived shortly after and within minutes a calm descended on the ship. On the quarterdeck a drummer boy struck up a rousing tattoo, and a moment later a cannonade was fired from the quay, the smoke drifting lazily down the shoreline and out toward the sea. The tension on board could be cut with a knife, then Willoughby boomed, "For King Edward and for adventure!" in a shout that no doubt carried across the water to those watching from the quayside, as it was probably intended.

Immediately the anchor was lifted and the topsails unfurled as one, and the ship gently moved off to cheers from the watching crowd.

Jack looked behind them, and saw that the two other ships of the little flotilla were following, the Edward Bonaventure and the Bona Confidentia. He knew the chief pilot was Richard Chancellor, and that he sailed on the Edward Bonaventure which was captained by a dour man called Stephen Borough. The other captain was Cornelius Durforth, a quietly competent man who Jack remembered from the launch party at Dee's house in Mortlake.

Deptford slowly receded as they travelled down river. Even so it only seemed like a few minutes before the order was given to prepare to salute the King.

Jack introduced himself to the master gunner, "John Brooke. Pleased ter meet yer, young fella."

Brooke was closely observing a gun crew, as they readied a big bronze culverin cannon.

"Master Brooke, I have never seen a cannon fired," said Jack, "what is the method?"

Brooke looked pleased of the opportunity to explain.

"First the crew rolls the gun carriage inboard as far as the breech rope will allow - the rope is fastened to the hull, you see?

"Then one gunner uses a wet sponge on a rod to clean and dampen the barrel. That is to extinguish any sparks remaining from the previous firing, but of course here we are just doing it for a training exercise.

"See that parchment bag that young Tom has? Full of gunpowder it is. Tom will ram it down the barrel, then quickly follow it with cloth wadding."

Jack noticed that while Tom rammed the wad home, Brooke passed a quill to the gun crew's leader. Turning to Jack he said, "That quill is sharpened at one end, and gets poked down through the touchhole at the rear of the barrel, so it pricks the bag of gunpowder that we just rammed down there, so the gunpowder is exposed."

Another gunner mimed placing a cannonball into the cannon and followed that by miming the placement of a second set of wadding. Together the four man team hauled on the gun tackles to run the gun out so that its carriage was hard up against the bulwark. The leading crewman sighted along the barrel and yelled for a wedge, which was quickly hammered into place thus angling the barrel slightly higher.

Finally Brooke passed across another quill, which was pushed into the touchhole and left there. Then the gun crew stood back from the culverin and waited, panting from their exertion. While they waited Jack risked asking about the second quill.

"It's hollow and full of the finest priming powder," replied Brooke, "When we light the exposed end the flame will instantly burn down the quill and light the powder in the pricked parchment bag. Then Boom!" he waved his arms to simulate the explosion, much to the merriment of the gun crew, "The explosion will shoot the ball, or in this case the wadding, across the ocean."

Jack idly wondered whether the priming powder had come from John Dee's manufactory in Faversham. He knew from first hand experience that that powder burned very fast indeed.

Several minutes dragged by. Then as Greenwich Palace hove into view off the starboard bow, John Brooke yelled "fire", and the leading crewman touched a smouldering match to the quill and instantly the cannon roared, firing its wadding harmlessly across the river, the carriage recoiling back fast until arrested by the breech rope. It was followed by echoing cannon fire from both the Edward Bonaventura and the Bona Confidentia.

Jack thought he could see the tiny figure of the King waving from a window high up one of the palace towers, but maybe he was imagining it.

I haven't the foggiest

He awoke on the fourth day, Sunday, to an eerie silence. *Becalmed.*

Without waking Kat he noiselessly padded topside. Every sailor he passed looked downcast, and he knew why. Even before he climbed the final ladder to the deck he could feel the moisture in the air getting heavier and more oppressive. *A sailor's worst fear, well one of them anyway. Thick fog and no wind.*

He paused on deck, momentarily disoriented, then instinctively sniffed the air, picking up faint traces of fenland and cattle. They were fairly close to land he thought, but could be anywhere off the Norfolk coast as it was all much the same.

Blindly, but confidently, he walked toward the stern of the ship where the quarterdeck was, found the wooden ladder and almost jogged up it. He crossed behind the steersman at the wheel, careful to call ahead of him so he did not surprise the fellow, and entered the Master's cabin.

Around the chart table stood four men, all looking ill-at-ease and barely illuminated by the two lanterns whose fat yellow candles burned valiantly but ineffectually.

Willoughby, the Captain-General of the little fleet, was talking in an undertone to William Gefferson, the Master, who was leaning on the chart table with both hands, staring hard at a map of the Norfolk coast, but giving the definite impression of someone who no longer understood what he was looking at. Behind Gefferson two of the merchant adventurers who were accompanying the crew were exchanging worried comments.

They all looked up with hope, saw who it was, and immediately returned to their dejected states, except Gefferson who recognised a fellow sailor when he saw one.

"Jack, welcome. As you see we are becalmed in this thick fog. I'm afraid we will not be landing you at King's Lynn this day as we had planned."

"Is the flotilla still together?

"Aye. The Edward and the Confidentia are both seaward of us. Or they were an hour ago. We dare not attempt to close on them as we have so little headway we cannot steer very well."

"I assume we are safe? No shoals hereabouts?"

"Aye, we are still in the open sea, and taking soundings every quarter hour in case of drifting."

Gesturing to the map, "Show me, sir, if you would, your best estimate of our position."

"Well, I haven't the foggiest. Not exactly anyway." Gefferson tapped an area of the map, off the coast of Norfolk, "Here somewhere, maybe twenty miles north-east of the Wash."

Jack traced his fingers across the map, tapping on a wide inlet at the top of the hump on the coast that was Norfolk, "The Wash is this wide bay and estuary here, isn't it?" He continued without waiting for an answer, "If I remember rightly, the current runs toward the Wash ever stronger as you approach it. If we can move west a few miles we should be able to insert into that current and be carried on it toward King's Lynn, agreed?"

Gefferson hesitated, then confessed, "Aye lad, that's probably true. But I can't move us at all in this calm."

"I sailed with the Hanse for several years. In and out of King's Lynn, Ipswich, and other ports even as far north as the Humber estuary. I am familiar with these waters. I have seen this calm before.

"Get seven of your strongest rowers to join me, and another man to take soundings, and we'll go out in the ship's longboat and tow the ship. Have another seven rowers warmed up and ready to rotate with the first crew every 30 minutes."

"What about you? Don't you need rotating out?"

"I'll be fine, I can pull an oar all day long."

Jack led the oarsmen for 4 hours, never tiring, rowing the longboat and thus towing the Esperanza westwards, until a slackness in the tow-rope confirmed that the ship had caught the current and was now moving faster than them. The Master waved to them to confirm the current was carrying the Esperanza into the Wash and the river Great Ouse, toward King's Lynn.

When Jack re-boarded the Esperanza the crew cheered and threw their caps in the air, clapping him on the shoulder in gratitude. He smiled with glee. *It is good to be back with a crew of like-minded fellows.*

Kat was watching from midships, a wry smile on her lips. "You just couldn't resist could you?"

He just shrugged happily, "It was an emergency, what could I do?"

That evening they finally docked at King's Lynn, about twelve hours later than planned. The crew bustled around on orders from the quartermaster who was hurrying to procure more fresh water and vegetables before the town closed down for the night.

Meanwhile Jack and Kat were preparing to disembark, Jack with his duffel bag, Kat with her sword, when Willoughby approached them, with Gefferson behind him.

"Gefferson says you saved us almost single-handedly, for which I give you this ring as a token of my thanks," he pulled a large garnet ring from his finger and clasped it in Jack's fist. "Are you sure I can't persuade you to continue with us to Cathay? We could use another good man. And Kat, you would be most welcome to stay as well."

"You are too kind, but as you know we are on a mission for Sir William and cannot delay. But I thank you for the consideration."

"In that case I will send a letter to Sir William recounting your services to the Company and also your loyalty to his mission. Bid you good day and God Speed." He bowed and left them.

Gefferson clasped his hand warmly, "And my thanks as well, Jack. You saved our bacon back there. If you ever need help, I am in your debt."

"You have already been too kind, ferrying us here like cargo without even asking why. There is no debt. Fare you well and see you on your return."

A few short minutes later they headed down the gangplank and into the town that had been called Bishop's Lynn until the King took ownership of it.

They walked quickly to the marketplace, where Cecil's contact had been told to meet them. It was deserted. Cecil's man must have long departed.

"What now?" asked Kat, "We have nowhere to stay tonight, and nobody to help us." She sat dejectedly on the steps of the market cross.

"We will have to improvise. Use our own contacts and arrange our own travel plans." He reached down and pulled her up, "Come on, I know someone who can help."

The King's Lynn Kontor

Jack guided them through the evening gloom a short way along the quayside in the direction of a tower that he told Kat belonged to St

Margaret's church. Just before the church they arrived at a long, two storey brick building, the upper storey of which was overhanging the cobbled lane by a foot or two.

He paused, reminiscing, and hoped there had been no changes in the leadership in the time since his last visit.

Beside him, he sensed Kat shivering in the growing evening chill, and shook himself from his reverie. He reached up and banged on the door with his fist three times, then paused and banged twice more.

The door was opened by a teenager who was dressed according to the style Jack had seen in Hamburg on a previous visit. The youth's question seemed to confirm his suspicion "Ja? Was willst du?"

"Guten Abend junger Meister. Ich würde gerne mit Andrus Mierjewski sprechen, wenn Sie bitte."

The boy looked surprised at the German response, then his face lit up and he smiled, "Sicherlich. Folge mir bitte," and opened the door wide to allow them to enter.

The warmth and smells of the building hit them instantly: Wood smoke, cinnamon and beer, with the beer dominating.

They followed the young man, who introduced himself as Joachim. He led them past a dining hall where a dozen sailors were noisily haranguing each other over fried vegetables and roast meats, accompanied by large tankards of beer. Jack's stomach grumbled, he hadn't eaten all day.

Climbing a narrow stairway to the second floor they doubled back past numerous sleeping quarters. Respectfully Joachim knocked and waited outside a blackened door, "Komm herein" came the gruff reply.

Jack saw Kat's worried look, and smiled to put her at ease.

Joachim waved them in and stepped back into the corridor.

Jack entered and instantly recognised Andrus, who was almost the twin of his mentor Jakob. Andrus looked up and cried out joyously "Jacques, is it really you?" He lurched out of his chair and hurried round his desk and crushed Jack in a bear hug. He pulled away and inspected Jack critically nodding his approval, before greeting Kat politely and ushering them both to seats. He leaned out of the doorway and called out to the retreating Joachim, ordering food and drink to be sent immediately.

While they ate Andrus chided Jack for a lack of correspondence, confiding that Jakob sorely missed his young protégé. He then proceeded to quiz Jack relentlessly on where he had been and what he been doing since leaving the *Stanislav* and the Steelyard. Apparently Jakob and the Stanislav had been in King's Lynn just two weeks ago, but were now on their way back to Gdansk. Could Jack stay until it returned? No? Jakob would be disappointed to have missed him.

Gradually, Jack was able to explain their urgent need to travel inland, in the general direction of Ely.

Andrus gesticulated with a partly eaten kielbasa, "These are not good times to go travelling cross-country by yourself, Jacques," part of the flavourful Polish sausage broke off and fell onto a pile of papers on his desk, Andrus quickly scooped it up and ate it, but not before it left a greasy stain on the topmost bill of lading.

He continued, "There are a lot of nervous people about, and nervous people are dangerous. The latest rumour is that the King has been poisoned and that the Duke of Northumberland is setting himself up as ruler in his stead, and will impose the new religion much more harshly."

Jack tried to interject that it was nonsense, but Andrus continued by talking over him, "I know, I know. All very unlikely. But people believe this, because they believe Northumberland to be a greedy man. And let's not forget, he did order the execution of the Duke of Somerset, the King's uncle, who the people loved."

He paused just long enough to bite more sausage.

"Many of the great lords in this part of England are religious conservatives and are preparing in case of a possible protestant campaign against them; the Earl of Sussex, Sir Richard Southwell, Lord Henry Mordaunt, and even Lord Wentworth. They are believed to be stockpiling weapons and supplies. Their retainers roam the countryside in groups stopping travellers and demanding to know their business, taking them into local custody if they are not happy with the responses, which is often the case."

"How do you know so much about what is happening, Andrus?" asked Kat, between mouthfuls of a delicious pierogi that she said tasted of juniper.

Andrus was licking his fingers having just finished the sausage, so Jack responded to the question "Merchants from all over the east of England come to trade here at the King's Lynn Kontor, Kat. They have a drink and gossip like old women. In fact they gossip whether they have a drink or not."

Andrus nodded sagely, "And of course we are happy to sell supplies to anyone who wants them, including the merchants and the great houses."

"So how can we travel without risking capture?" asked Kat slightly panicking.

"Hmm. If you really must go, then I suggest you go in the company of a known merchant who has good reasons to be travelling, and who is sympathetic to your cause. I'm sure I can find somebody to help if you are really set on this plan. Rest here for a couple of days while I ask around."

By Wednesday afternoon Kat was getting frustrated with the delay, "Sir William told us to hurry, that's why we begged passage with Willoughby. Yet here we are stuck in King's Lynn with no sure way forward. What are we going to do?"

"Andrus says he is meeting someone today who might be able to help us," Jack shrugged, "he is very reliable. Let's see what he comes up with."

That evening Andrus called them into his office. Sitting with him was a priest, clearly very nervous. Andrus introduced him as John Hullier. "Master Hullier is the vicar of Babraham, a village about fifty miles south of here, near the town of Cambridge."

They had agreed that Kat would do most of the talking, because Jack's French accent sometimes slipped out and could easily make a reluctant accomplice even more nervous.

So, at a nod from Andrus, Kat explained their predicament, and that they were on a mission for Sir William Cecil, and ultimately the King.

The priest looked seriously at Kat "I would be pleased to help you whatever the circumstances my child, but how can I know that you speak the truth?"

Jack handed over the warrant from Cecil, and Hullier's eyes nearly popped from his head as he read it. "Well of course I never doubted you at all, but one can't be too careful in these dangerous times. The magnates here in Norfolk are asserting their power and detaining anyone they feel might be conspiring against them or the Lady Mary."

Kat agreed. "So you understand why we need your help? Would you be able to help us travel inconspicuously to Oxburgh?"

The priest rested his chin on his steepled hands and looked thoughtful for a few minutes. Nodding slowly, more to himself than to them, he seemed to come to a decision.

"Yes. Yes, I think I can. This coming Sunday is Whit Sunday of course, and I will be leading special prayers for the King's health, here at St Margaret's church. I trust that I will see you in the congregation?" He stared hard at each of them until, guiltily, they promised they would be there.

"After that I planned on travelling back to my village which is a three day journey...but..."

He looked at each of them in turn.

"...what if...what if I invented an excuse to travel to Bury St Edmunds instead? It is not so far from Babraham, so it entirely reasonable that I should do this."

"I don't understand. How will that help?" asked Kat.

The priest's eyes twinkled, clearly starting to enjoy the thought of subterfuge. He asked for paper and quickly sketched a map of the county of Norfolk, bulging into the North Sea.

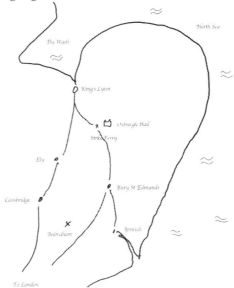

"The road from here to Bury St Edmunds passes through the village of Stoke Ferry, which is very close to Oxburgh."

Kat's eyes gleamed, "So if we get stopped on the journey we say we are travelling to Bury St Edmunds and thus don't alert the Bedingfield family at Oxburgh Hall?"

"Exactly my dear," said the older man.

Jack looked from one to the other confused, "But what reason would we have to go to this Bury St Edmunds place? And why would it not arouse suspicion?"

The priest raised a finger and grinned, "The Bishop of Winchester is a prisoner in the Tower of London because he is a religious conservative and opposes some of the King's reforms. His name is Stephen Gardiner, and his father is a cloth merchant in Bury St Edmunds. I know this because he supplied material for my cassocks last year. Did you know they say his mother is an illegitimate daughter of Jasper Tudor? No? Well, no matter. So this is my idea: we say we are travelling to Bury St Edmunds to deliver a letter from the good bishop to his parents. No one aligned to the old religion would obstruct such a mission. All we would need is an official looking letter in case they ask to see it, they wouldn't dare open and read it of course."

"That is a wonderful idea," gushed Kat, "rather than being detained by the local lords they would probably help us on our way!"

Andrus clapped his bear-like hands and guffawed, saying he could provide a letter fit for a bishop with a fake seal and everything.

So the plan was agreed.

Chapter 44 - Convocation

Thursday the 18th of May 1553
Palace of Placentia, Greenwich

Placentia

Sir John Cheke idly watched the river traffic from a third floor window in the Palace of Placentia.

The river was sluggish at this time of day, but there were still dozens of vessels of all sizes, mostly long ferries and wherries. Three ponderous merchant ships drew his gaze, as they gracelessly manoeuvred in line-ahead formation past the last marker buoy. They reminded him of the expedition to Cathay, and he wondered how Jack and Kat were faring.

Squinting, he discerned ant-like movement in the rigging as the topsails were furled and the ships slowed to a halt before wallowing in the languid current. A single masted pinnace deftly glided alongside the lead ship. Someone, probably the Trinity House appointed pilot, clambered down to the boat before it peeled away smartly and headed for the far shore. Moments later the ships' mainsails were deployed and instantly rippled in the wind before snapping out rigidly and accelerating the ships eastward on their journey. *Bound for the Netherlands mayhap, or perhaps Calais,* he thought.

He noticed that several wherries were aiming for the grand river steps in front of the palace gatehouse. *They will have a long wait, there is a great crush of barges and wherries there already.*

Someone had told him just last week, *was it John Dee?,* that there were now nearly two thousand wherries operating on the river in London, each being used by one or two watermen in shifts to earn their living. *That is one wherry for every one hundred inhabitants,* he thought smiling, *I can do mathematics too, John.*

He tried to see who the passengers were, and cursed his poor eyesight as he strained but couldn't recognise the blurry faces of the huddled figures. Nonetheless he could guess who they were.

The King's rheum cough, that had plagued him on and off for over six months now, had kept him in his bed again yesterday. He had confided to Cheke that he believed he may never be cured and so he needed to make preparations, starting with an order that the Brotherhood should convene immediately.

Cheke knew that not all the Brotherhood could possibly join them today, but there would certainly be a quorum. The archbishop of Canterbury, Thomas Cranmer, was already at Placentia of course, attending on the King. The two Sir Williams, Cecil and Herbert, plus himself were already present for meetings of the Privy council. *That makes four.*

Remarkably, John Dee had arrived unbidden yesterday, saying he had felt drawn to the King's side. *That's five.*

Cheke leaned out of the window, partly to get a better view of the gatehouse which he thought architecturally delightful, and partly hoping to see the disembarkations, but his view was obstructed by one of the many towers along the front face of the palace. *Five members of the Brotherhood is enough, but I wager one of those wherries is bringing the Duke of Northumberland. He would not miss a summons from the King even if the hounds of hell were before him.*

He scanned the river one more time before reluctantly turning back to his work preparing for the convocation.

It would be the first time they had met in Placentia. Previously their meetings had been in Hampton Court or Westminster Palace. *Ah yes, and just once in the crypt beneath St John's college in Cambridge.* He shivered at the memory, *that had been creepy!*

For Cheke the location was no trivial matter. He was responsible for secrecy and so had to choose the meeting room carefully. He had initially suggested the crypt beneath the chapel, which had but a single door and good stone walls, but he had been warned in no uncertain terms by the King's physicians that they would no longer be responsible for the King's health if he were subjected to such unhealthy and stagnant air. Next best was this third floor room, normally the dining room for visiting nobility. It had fresh air and river views, and was at the far eastern end of the palace so access could be carefully controlled. He had even gone so far as to evacuate the rooms immediately below, in case anyone thought to listen through the ceiling.

As he personally finalised the room's preparations he mused on all the history this building had already seen since being built some fifty years previously by the old King Henry, the founder of the Tudor dynasty.

His son Henry, the eighth king of that name, had been born here, as had Henry's own surviving female children Mary and Elizabeth. Edward, however, had been born at Hampton Court. *I wonder if there is something in the air that encourages male births at Hampton Court and girls here at Placentia?*

He silently berated himself, remembering how Henry VIII's sisters had been born at other palaces: Margaret at Westminster, and Mary at Sheen. The three siblings were all long since dead of course, leaving Edward and the two princesses as the direct Tudor legacy.

Swear another oath

The ritual opening of the convocation was announced by Cheke himself, the King feeling too weak to do it.

"The Brotherhood of the Red Rose is an Order of worthy disciples dedicated to supporting and defending our Evangelical Realm of Christ. We use scripture as our sword and shield against idolatry, greed and heresy."

When Cheke had finished, Edward leaned forward, resting an arm on the table, and looked each of the Brothers in the eye, one by one.

"You have already sworn to work tirelessly to create the Realm of Christ for me. But today I will ask you to swear another oath."

Edward looks ghastly, thought Cheke, *I wonder if he has the strength for this?*

The room was totally silent. A final tally of twelve Brothers, not all male of course, had arrived in time, and all sat, robed in red, attentive to their master, Cheke amongst them.

"You must swear to deliver the Realm of Christ, even after I am gone, regardless of the sovereign that governs you. Consider though, before you take this oath. Your allegiance to this oath could be strained by the duty you will owe to your new prince. That will require you to walk a narrow path to ensure you do not break your pledges."

There was a murmur of disquiet. Cheke felt sure it was not the difficulty of maintaining two possibly competing oaths that was the cause. Rather it was the very act of being forced to contemplate the King's death, which was treason at any other time. He wasn't comfortable about it himself, even though he knew Edward was ill and had known what he was going to propose.

Chapter 45 - Illumination

Monday the 22nd of May 1553
Oxburgh, Norfolk

Hullier than thou

Jack and Kat set out on a crisp Monday morning with Hullier. During the Whit Sunday service they had discovered he was quite the firebrand when the spirit moved him. He spent much of the ride south railing against the wickedness and greed of the old Catholic church and its priests, "Especially the bishops that sell so called *indulgences* for the early release from purgatory to parishioners who have almost no money anyway. They should be stripped of their positions and forced to live in penury in some remote and obscure place. Somewhere like Criccieth. That's so deep into Wales it is almost in the sea, I think. Then they could provide solace to whatever parishioners they can convince to attend their services." He continued in the same vein for several miles, only quieting when another group of travellers joined them for safety.

By early evening they reached the small town of Stoke Ferry, which was just west of Oxburgh. They halted outside an inn, where a faded sign creaked ominously as it swung in a gentle breeze and proclaimed the establishment as *The Ferryman's Arms*.

Kat sniffed, "It looks a bit run down."

Jack thought so too. But it also looked like the only option in town so reluctantly they decided to stay the night. Their horses were taken by the ostler and they trooped inside. They settled near a roaring fire and slaked their thirst with a surprisingly good ale while they waited for an evening meal to be served. As they drank Jack outlined his plan.

"I will go to Oxburgh tonight, enter the house and start the search. I will be back before daybreak. If we need more time then perhaps John can feign a minor injury that needs to be rested and we can stay a few more days."

Kat was indignant, "I'm not meekly staying behind while you take all the risks, Jack."

They quietly argued for several minutes while John Hullier discretely busied himself with a tasty rabbit stew that the innkeeper's wife served.

Kat slammed her ale on the tabletop and hissed at Jack "This is not *your* mission, Jack, it is *our* mission. You have no right to exclude me, or to coddle me, and if you thought you did you are sadly mistaken. We go together or we go separately, but I am NOT staying behind."

Jack was left with no choice so he mumbled an agreement, wondering why he even tried to keep her safe, when she was so determined to run toward danger.

It was fully dark when Jack and Kat knelt in the undergrowth and stared across a wide open greensward, across the moat, to the vertical walls of Oxburgh Hall. Just as they had been told to expect, it was a big square brick and stone built house with crenellations atop the walls. Impossible to sneak into but not a castle by any means. Kat pointed to a light coming from a window in the north-west gatehouse tower, but as they watched it flickered and went out, and then all was dark.

Jack insisted they stay still and observe for another thirty minutes or so. Finally satisfied, he gestured to Kat. She lithely stood and was ready to move off, but had to wait while Jack shook the cramps out of his legs before he could walk. She waited patiently with her arms folded, a told-you-so smile adorning her face.

Together they crept as quietly as possible toward the woodland of mixed oak and chestnut trees to the north.

They easily found the folly. Jack circled around it to fully appreciate its size. From the north it looked like a huge rock protruding from the gently sloping hillside, covered in patchy moss, and almost as tall as the trees. The south side was slightly downslope, facing the Hall, and contained a deep depression or cave. In front of the rock was a small reed-choked pool.

Clever carving around the cave entrance gave the impression of a column on each side and a triangular pediment surmounting them, like the entrance to a Greek or Roman temple. The figure of a woman wearing a simple stola and holding an amphora was skilfully chiselled in the rock face, positioned so that an emerging trickle of water seemed to pour from the mouth of the amphora and run into the pool. In the silvery moonlight it looked like a goddess pouring wine into a bathing pool.

Jack wrinkled his nose, *It's a pretty effect, but unfortunately this bathing pool is full of slimy reeds and is stagnant from neglect. It needs cleaning out before anyone bathes in it.*

Stepping between the fake columns and into the cave he banged his shin on a stone bench. Kat shook her head in mock disbelief and made a point of carefully stepping over the bench, then walked past him. She immediately started feeling the wall of the cave, seeking the crevice they had been told about. He shuffled forward still rubbing his shin and banged his head on the back wall and had to resist the urge to cry out. Kat rolled her eyes and continued feeling her way across the cave wall.

"I've got it," she whispered, and before Jack could say or do anything she had turned sideways and disappeared inside it.

Jack had to admire the way it was concealed, no doubt in the daylight it would just look like a crack in the rock, or maybe not even be visible at all. He shook the duffel bag off his back and stepped into the slim gap, the rock walls scratching at his doublet as he sidled into the unknown.

He stepped forward blindly, right into Kat, grabbing her waist to ensure he didn't knock her over. "Stop fooling around and light the torch" she said.

He groped around in his bag for a moment, then struck his flint and lit their torch, immediately noticing that everything was exactly as described by John Adams: a tiny platform at the top of a crude staircase.

Water trickled down the walls, pooling on some of the steps, making the descent quite treacherous as he led the way. About twenty steps down it levelled out and the tunnel began. Rough hewn walls stretching before him as far as the flickering light could illuminate.

Kat took the torch from him, "Finally we're making some real progress," and marched off down the passage.

Jack hustled to catch up, but Kat's dancing shadow made it difficult to see his footing and he stubbed his toe on a rock. He hopped about in pain for a few moments, before gritting his teeth and limping determinedly after Kat, muttering under his breath. He slowly fell further behind and when Kat abruptly turned a corner it threw him into almost total darkness and his progress slowed even more.

From up ahead he heard an ominous grumble of grinding rocks, followed by a pattering of falling stones. Then silence.

Quickly rounding the corner he blinked against the sudden flare of the torch, and looked in shock at the ragged pile of rubble that completely blocked the passage. *Where's Kat?*

The torch was jammed between two stones, and to the right of that was a gap between some of the bigger fallen rocks. A muffled grunting and scraping was coming from the gap. He peered inside and could see Kat's boot squirming from side to side. Suddenly, it stilled.

Holier than thou

Jack wedged the torch into a different crevice so its flickering light was cast more fully into the hole where Kat's leg emerged, then he grabbed her foot and tugged at it.

"Oww."

He stopped.

"Jaaack, is that you?" Kat's voice quavered, followed by a cough.

"Of course it's me. Are you hurt? What are you doing?"

"I crawled into this gap beneath the rockslide but I must have dislodged a stone and some more rocks slid down and pinned me in. I think I'm stuck."

"Can you wriggle back out?"

"What do you think I've been trying to do?"

Silence.

"Can you see my feet?"

"One of them yes. I'll pull you out."

"Aargh. Stop. You're making it worse. My hip is stuck fast against a boulder and my dagger is digging into my belly. You'll have to make the hole bigger."

Jack stood back and looked critically at the rockslide. Part of the roof and left wall had tumbled in, totally blocking the passage except for a small gap at the base of the right wall, where Kat had crawled in.

Why would you risk crawling in there, you must be insane!

It was like an elaborate puzzle, each rock resting on several others.

He tentatively pushed and pulled at a couple of key rocks to see if he could move them. He could, just barely, but as he did so another rock further above groaned and threatened to fall down. And there were several other rocks above that in a cascade. If he wasn't careful Kat would be crushed, or trapped forever. His mind whirled in panic.

A muffled cry, "Jaaack. Hurry, please. "

He knelt in the gap and moved the torch to see more clearly, looking for other rocks that had some potential to move, but everything was compressed under the first rock that he had instinctively pulled at.

He sat back on his heels and thought desperately. A memory came, unbidden, of the burnt-out bookstore in Gdansk and the angled timbers that had been used to prop up the walls.

"If I move any rocks the ones above it will fall, and perhaps more as well. I need to prop them up before I start. I will be as fast as I can, but I need to go back to the wood and cut some lengths of timber."

"Don't leave me in the dark!"

"I will leave you the torch. I'll be as fast as I can."

He made sure he had his dagger then dropped his duffel bag, turned and scuttled down the passage as fast as he could, before his resolve left him.

He careened off the rock walls several times, scraping the skin on his hands and banging his head several times. Finally he tripped on the bottom step, falling against the rock stairway. He paused for breath, then scampered up and through the crevice into the nymphaeum.

The minimal moonlight that filled the woodland was like the brightest sun after the absolute darkness of the tunnel. He immediately started searching for straight, stout branches.

His dagger wasn't made for woodcutting so it was slow going.

After what seemed an eternity, but was probably only a half hour, he had half a dozen thick branches of different lengths. He gathered them together and dragged them back to the grotto, where he struggled to push and pull them over the bench and through the crack. Once back inside and down the steps he risked shouting down the tunnel to Kat, hoping she would hear and be heartened, "Kaaat. I'm coming."

Chapter 46 - Congregation

Thursday the 25th of May 1553
Durham Place, London

Till death us do part

John Cheke gazed fondly at his wife. Wearing her best dress and adorned with her brightest jewels, Mary Cheke was fairly vibrating with excitement. Maybe she felt his gaze for she beamed up at him before returning her attention to the wedding vows of the three couples getting married that day at Durham Place, the Duke of Northumberland's palatial house in London.

Cheke himself felt numb.

He well knew that the Duke's fourth son, Guildford, had known Jane Grey since childhood, and really the match wasn't such a surprise. However the timing was terrible. Even to Cheke it looked like Dudley was consolidating his power-base around the ill King, by marrying his own son to the King's cousin Jane. *What is she, fourth or fifth in the line of succession? The people have no liking for Dudley as it is, this will only make them even more suspicious of him.*

"Doesn't Guildford look ever so handsome in that silver and gold doublet and cape?" whispered Mary.

He looks as dull as an ox, thought Cheke, uncharitably. *And Jane is so well-read and learned. The poor girl will be starved of intelligent conversation.*

But all he said was, "The robes were a gift from the King himself." This tidbit of information was welcomed by Mary, and presumably stored away ready to be exchanged during the wedding feast for equally thrilling gossip bartered by the other wives.

Cheke could easily recall Jane's quick wit during doctrinal debates when she had joined Edward for tutoring with Cheke, whereas rumour had it that the only quick thing about Guildford was his temper when thwarted, which was often.

By now, Guildford's twelve year old sister, Catherine Dudley, was exchanging her vows with Henry Hastings, the Earl of Huntingdon's son, "Till death us do part."

She has remembered her lines well considering that she is but a child, thought Cheke, not approving of the marriage of a girl of such a tender age. Behind the couple a large window revealed a view of a well manicured lawn running down to the River Thames, so Cheke contented himself with watching the river traffic, which he found soothing for his spirit.

Soon the third couple were arrayed before the picture window ready to swear to live together in harmony till death do us part.

Cheke was truly excited by this match and managed to dispel his gloom and look on with genuine happiness. The groom was Henry Herbert, the son of his friend Sir William Herbert, and the bride was Lady Jane Grey's younger sister, Lady Katherine. He had often tutored Henry for the pleasure of it, knowing him to be a well mannered lad with a good work ethic, an enquiring mind and a special interest in heraldry.

The fact that Herbert was consolidating his power and position at court by marrying off his son to a prepubescent girl, just like Dudley, did not strike Cheke at all ironic or distasteful.

After the ceremony the guests were mingling prior to partaking of the wedding feast, when Cheke saw Sir William Cecil talking with the French ambassador. Cecil looked like a cornered goose, so Cheke decided to rescue him, sweeping a low bow and claiming Cecil needed to accompany him to the Duke's presence. The ambassador gave up his quarry reluctantly. Cecil heartily thanked Cheke for the deception as they exited to a private chamber where they could talk undisturbed.

Cheke, who had only returned to London the previous day, related the latest diagnoses of the King's illness. For his part, Cecil wondered aloud why Herbert had allowed the match of his son to proceed in the face of John Dee's warnings against it. Cheke had not heard this before and eagerly squeezed every last drop of information from Cecil, knowing that his wife Mary would thank him lustily for it later that night.

Chapter 47 - Infiltration

Thursday the 8th to 15th June 1553
Stoke Ferry, Norfolk

A secret passage

Kat threw aside the crutch that she had been using for over a week now, and stormed around the room.

"I am perfectly well, Jack, and need no more coddling. I'm fit enough to travel, so we should get back to the Hall and find that gem."

Jack sighed. Kat's increasing impatience was clear testimony to her regained mobility. But he also knew that mobility was not the same as complete recovery.

Initially her leg had been so badly bruised that they had feared it broken. It had swollen to twice its normal size, and was an ugly purple and yellow colour. The pain when she tried to put weight on it was so intense it had made her cry.

Hullier had already left for Babraham, so Jack asked around the village himself and found a local woman who rented them this one-room cottage, and more importantly was clever with herbs. The woman provided a herbal paste to be applied daily to Kat's leg, and a sweet infusion of spices and healing plants to drink every evening to ensure a deep healing sleep. Gradually the combination had worked and now Kat was fighting fit.

Realising he could not force her to convalesce any longer he capitulated, "Tonight we will go back to the Hall. So lets get our gear ready," said Jack.

Pleased to have triumphed, Kat was giddy with excitement, and started packing their equipment.

That night they stumbled through the undergrowth in almost total darkness, the moon was but a faint silver crescent. When they reached the folly Kat pulled up short and admitted to Jack that she was afraid to go back down the tunnel and crawl through the rockfall, "I'm sorry, Jack, I don't think I can do it. I just can't. I thought I'd be alright, but all that rock hanging over me, I just can't do it."

Jack cursed himself for wanting to keep it a surprise, but they'd come this far so he thought that for a few more minutes he would keep his secret. He held her in an supportive embrace and whispered that it would be ok, "Trust me".

He had never been more proud than when she swallowed her fear and followed him into the tunnel once more.

As they shuffled down the tunnel Kat gradually became more and more agitated. As they turned a corner she stayed close behind him but still didn't hesitate. They continued, rounding yet another bend, this time to the right.

"Wait Jack, there is something wrong. Where are we? Where is the rockfall? I thought it would be in that last stretch of tunnel but obviously it was not. Is it ahead? I'm confused."

"That's my little surprise for you, Kat. While you slept through every night I have been coming to the tunnel and have cleared it, and reinforced the walls back there. We can go all the way to the Hall itself, no more obstructions," he beamed at her in the dark, proud of his accomplishment, which truth be told had been an immense amount of work.

He was unprepared for the anger that erupted from her as she started pounding both fists against his chest and arms. "You inconsiderate great fool. You callous oaf. You should have told me. I have been petrified for hours and you could have just told me."

Eventually she calmed down enough to cease striking him, and stalked ahead in the tunnel, taking the torch with her.

He stood still, in shock. Dumbfounded.

What just happened? Why is she so upset? I thought she'd be pleased and excited.

I should have told her before we got here and it would have avoided the fear...but there would have been no surprise!

Mon Dieu. I turned wine into vinegar - idiot that I am.

Jack kicked the tunnel wall in frustration at his own mistake, then hurried after Kat trying to explain and apologise, but his entreaties fell on deaf ears. They progressed the last few hundred feet in silence, eventually reaching the foot of a chiselled staircase.

Kat turned and looked at him, and said in an even voice, "Please don't ever do that again, Jack. I'm glad you cleared it of course, and I realise it must have been a lot of hard work. But please, no more surprises. Now let's put it behind us and find this jewel."

Chagrined, Jack pulled out his diagram of the Hall from an inner pocket, and they peered at it in the flickering torch light.

Kat pointed up, "These steps should exit through a trapdoor into the storeroom at the north end of the stables."

"Yes, and we agree that the most likely resting place of the gem is somewhere in the chapel, so we will go there first, assuming we can get into this corridor here," Jack stabbed a meaty finger at the plan between the stables and the smithy.

Jack carefully folded the plan and returned it to his pocket, then climbed the steps and gently pushed on the trapdoor overhead. It didn't budge. He was fearful of rousing the household, but Kat just said "put your back into it, go on."

So he literally put his shoulders against the trapdoor and slowly straightened his legs, pushing against the stone steps. Some dust fell down revealing the outline of the door, then with a tortured squeal from the hinges it sprang open, showering Jack and Kat in musty hay and dust. Jack froze and strained his ears for approaching footsteps or voices raised in alarm, but there was nothing.

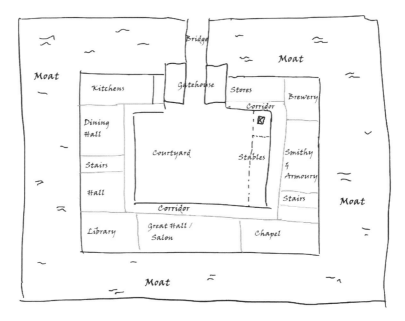

He clambered through and hauled Kat up beside him. They were in a dusty and evidently rarely used storeroom. Several sheaves of old hay had been piled on the trapdoor which, together with the rusted hinges, had caused the difficulties opening it. Kat kept watch at the door for the next few minutes while Jack surveyed the interior, only finding old sacks and a few rusting tools. He closed the trapdoor, grimacing at more squeaks from the hinges, then pulled some hay over to obscure it from casual inspection.

Kat had cautiously opened the door a few inches and had observed the courtyard for several minutes. "It seems safe. Totally dark, no dogs, no people."

"What about possible doors into the corridor?"

"One at the corner of the gatehouse, but surely there will be guards in the tower and we would be overheard."

"Anything else?"

"I can hear the horses in the stables to our left. They seem to be open to the courtyard, which makes sense. There might be a door providing easy access from the corridor. That's what I would build anyway."

Jack went first, sidling along the wall ten feet or so and disappearing into the stables. Kat followed quickly, finding Jack stroking and whispering to the nearest horse, a huge charger suitable for the tilt yard.

Kat's guess proved correct, at the back of the stable they found a door that gave onto the corridor. They cracked open the door and peered through, and were alarmed to see the corridor illuminated by a lurid red light. The dull glow was coming through a doorway opposite, which they realised led to the smithy, where presumably a low fire still burned in the forge.

The corridor was straight, and unobstructed, for at least fifty feet. In the previous weeks they had debated endlessly how to safely traverse it and had settled on a brazen plan.

Jack lit a candle, and they walked hand in hand steadily down the corridor, as if they had every right to be there. They had prepared an excuse in case they were spotted, but in the end there was no need because everything was quiet.

They slipped into the chapel and lit another candle. In the sparse light the chapel was smaller than Jack had expected; *that will just make searching it so much easier,* he thought.

Their candlelight twinkled off large silver plates and ostentatious golden goblets that were arranged on the small alter.

They split up.

Kat searched the tiny vestry. Immediately drawn to a cupboard where she found communion wine and more silver platters perhaps for the host, but no secret compartments and certainly no large gemstones.

Meanwhile Jack completed a detailed examination of the altar, an ornate altar screen that had the initials EB engraved into the lattice, and some wooden chests that were stacked against the panelled rear of the chapel, but came up empty handed too.

They swapped places and searched again.

Jack looked around the vestry. He could see nowhere to store or hide anything, unless one of the bricks in the wall was false. He traced the mortar with his fingertips until he was used to the texture and thickness, then scanned the walls desultorily. There was nothing obvious, and hundreds and hundreds of bricks, no hope of finding anything here.

Faint fingers of impending dawn glimmered through the chapel windows and jerked Jack out of his stupor and back into action, he called to Kat as loudly as he dared "we should leave quickly, the servants will be up and about soon."

"Wait, I think I have found something," whispered Kat. She was standing on one of the wooden chests, reaching high up and pressing against the panelling with both hands.

Jack looked up and smiled, admiring her curves that were emphasised as she exerted herself against the panel.

"It gives a little, there must be something here"

He leapt up behind her and reaching over her head he pressed the same area of the panel. There was a click and it popped open.

They jumped off the chest and Jack dragged it away from the wall. As he did so a large section of panelling swung open.

"I've found a secret passage!" said Kat excitedly.

"Quickly then, we don't have much time," he grabbed a candle and they plunged into the void.

A spiral slope took them deep under the chapel, until they emerged into a large fan-vaulted crypt. Both sides were lined with shelving ready for coffins, four tiers high, although only a half a dozen spots were occupied. A low stone bench ran along the middle of the crypt, and on it lay an elaborate coffin.

Jack thought it looked fairly new, and when he looked closer he realised why. "It must be the coffin of Edmund, scourge of the French. Remember he died recently. Look, here are the initials EB chiselled into the lid." He wrinkled his nose at the faint smell of decay that assailed him.

Beyond the bench was a narrow wooden cart; *for carrying the coffins down the slope*, he thought.

"This whole crypt has been well planned," mused Jack out loud.

"But its not the sort of place you would hide a healing gemstone, so let's get out of here," observed Kat, already heading back up the slope.

They retraced their steps without incident, clicking shut the crypt door, and repositioning the chest. They almost jogged back up the corridor, and slipped noiselessly through the stables and back to the storeroom. Jack wedged open the trapdoor using an old wooden bucket he found and contrived to balance some hay on it, then they slipped through and pulled the bucket through after them, leaving the hay to hopefully obscure their secret access.

Every night for the next week they returned through the tunnel, and slipped unseen into the Hall. They searched the salon, the reception and dining halls, even the brewery. To no avail.

The library was the only ground floor room they had failed to search, because the door was always locked. They dare not search the sleeping quarters upstairs and so vested all their hope in the library and became convinced it must be the hiding place.

"It must be hidden in there," muttered Jack, "that's where I'd hide a healing jewel if I was lord of the castle."

"Well that's what you said about the chapel," snorted Kat, "anyway, it might be upstairs. Perhaps in Sir Edmund's bedchamber, where he died?"

"That's possible I suppose. But surely he would have hidden it whilst he was healthy? And then delivered those clues to the lawyers of the Inner Temple for safe-keeping until his son or heirs had need of them. If he was still healthy then the hiding place could be anywhere in the Hall, but most likely the library, his private room for documents and deeds and such."

Kat made no reply.

"We should send a note to Dee or Cecil, letting them know our progress."

"Or lack of progress," Kat muttered morosely.

Jack was dejected too, and so they let it lapse.

Chapter 48 - Medication

Thursday the 22nd of June 1553
Palace of Placentia, Greenwich

Seville oranges

Sir William Cecil watched John Cheke stride from the King's bedchamber, the heavy door swinging fast behind him, and only the swift action of the chief gentleman Thomas Worth prevented it from banging loudly shut.

Cheke strode on, head downcast, past the groom, Christopher Salmon, who tried but failed to catch his attention, and past Dr Owen who was waiting to return to the King.

He could see that Cheke's face was ashen even from the twenty paces that still separated them.

As he drew near, Cheke grasped Cecil's arm and pulled him along, through a plain door into a small ante-chamber that was empty now, but usually used by visiting ambassadors and nobles. Once inside, Cheke threw himself into a chair and cast his head into his hands, his body shaking violently as he finally succumbed to tears that now ran freely down his face and into his beard.

Cecil didn't have to ask what was upsetting him, he could guess readily enough. Instead he poured Cheke a goblet of strong wine, then thought better of it and poured one for himself as well. He sat next to Cheke and clumsily reached over to console his friend, tentatively patting his shoulder. They stayed like that for a few minutes and he let himself believe it was comforting.

As the sobbing subsided he forced the glass into Cheke's hand and encouraged him to drink. Then he waited patiently. He was good at that; waiting patiently. *A much underrated skill*, he thought to himself.

To give Cheke more time to recover he allowed his mind to wander, his eyes idly roaming the room. *This suite is so dreary, it does not display our Court to good advantage. It is almost embarrassing even. We should have it redecorated. Perhaps some lighter colours and gilding of the acanthus leaves on the decorative columns. And that gloomy rain-drenched landscape will have to go, perhaps we can bring in something modern. I will talk to the court painter, Levina Teerlinc. Hmm, but she is stubborn, she prefers to paint those damnable miniatures, and regardless of how good they are, one of those would be of no use here. We need something big and bold. What a pity Hans Holbein died before his time, he would have jumped at the opportunity to create a statement piece. Maybe If I get Mildred to talk to Levina...*

Cheke started to speak, but it came out as a mumble that Cecil couldn't understand, so he encouraged him to repeat himself.

"I said," sniff, "Edward is in such pain. He lies in bed constantly now. His legs are swollen to twice their proper size and his skin is a ghastly bluish colour. His beautiful golden hair is falling out, and even his fingernails are coming loose."

Cecil tried to ease Cheke's anguish, "His pain is eased by Dr Wendy. He gives him twelve grains of opiates nightly. It soothes him and lets him sleep."

"But don't you see, that is just it. He cannot eat properly, nor sleep without the drugs. And with them, his mind cannot focus fully. We used to have such complex and deep discussions on everything from the new religion, to astronomy and geography, and now he struggles to remember what we are even talking about. Ah, what a king we are losing."

"He will get better, you'll see. This is just a ... a setback. His doctors are the best in the land," Cecil didn't believe a word of it himself, but what else could he say?

"Pah. These doctors know nothing. Do you know what Dr Owen said to me? He said *'there is a full moon in three days and it will tax Edward's strength to the limit, possibly beyond.'* What nonsense. Even Dee doesn't ascribe such powers to the moon. Anyway, that is not the worst of it," Cheke choked and couldn't continue for a couple of moments.

"His Majesty said to me...he whispered to me, *'I feel so weak and can resist no longer. I am done for. I am glad to die.'* "

Cecil was so shocked he could think of nothing to say.

Cheke went on, "And god help me but I had to turn away, for the stench of his breath was too much to bear, I nearly lost my lunch. I turned away from Edward in his hour of need. I am not worthy to be at his right hand."

"Come now, John. That is not what the King believes. He made you joint Secretary of State just a couple of weeks ago, and since then you have been a tower of strength getting the signatures of all the nobles, judges, and officials onto his *devise*. His devise might be the last act he performs on this earth, and he turned to you for your help and steadiness to achieve it. How many signatures have you rallied now? Eighty?"

"More than a hundred."

"Well there you are then. More than a hundred worthies have signed his devise and that is mostly thanks to you. If the King should, you know, not recover, then his wishes are clear and known by and supported by over a hundred leaders in his land. Mary and Elizabeth are declared bastards, and his cousin Jane Grey will inherit the crown and keep strong his reformed religion. And this is his greatest wish, as we both know.

"I am expecting a delegation from the French. Here to see Northumberland and myself. You stay in here a while and recover your poise. I will go and see to them.

"I already know they are going to press for closer diplomatic union. My spies tell me they will promise to support Jane's succession, as if their help was necessary. Ha. They do not know of the hundreds you have helped rally to support the succession already, with signatures and oaths, not mere diplomatic promises.

"Although, I would sorely like to know who told them about Lady Jane being named to the succession. I will have to turn my hand to that, it is supposed to be a state secret. I expect that in exchange for their support of Jane they will demand England aids them in their ghastly war against the Spanish, which is the last thing we need.

"Then the Spanish will no doubt come a-knocking next, with their condolences and offers. A basket of Seville oranges and promises of Spanish ladies if we just keep our noses out of it and don't aid the French. And if they try reminding us that the French are our natural enemies one more time I might just lose my patience.

"Argh. It will be wall-to-wall foreign ambassadors for weeks to come."

Chapter 49 - Exploitation

Saturday the 24th of June 1553
Stoke Ferry, Norfolk

Positions at the Hall

A sudden banging on the cottage door interrupted their increasingly fractious and yet circular strategising. Jack paused before opening it, while Kat drew her dagger and hid behind the door.

It was the wise woman, their landlady.

She bustled in without waiting for an invitation, and Kat hurriedly sheathed the dagger.

"Young master Jack, I 'ave news of some work that might interest you and your lass. Where is she now? Oh there you are, my dear."

"I'm not really looking for work right now," began Jack.

"Up at the Hall they're needing extra servants cuz they're hosting some great assembly of the nobility next week."

"What? Really? Well actually that might be...", he started to reply, "How do we get the positions?" interrupted Kat eagerly.

"I heard they will be recruiting tomorrow morning after communion, down at *The Ferryman's Arms*. Able-bodied, presentable, good Catholics, that's what I heard they're after. Of course I thought of you two right away, and I put in a good word with Mistress Corkdale at *The Ferryman*. You need to earn a living if you're to go on renting my cottage, now don't you?" her eyes gleamed avariciously.

"Indeed, and we thank you mistress. We will be there tomorrow, never fear." Jack led her out, confirming that they'd pay the next week's rent as soon as they had the positions.

"Well, that is the best luck ever. A legitimate reason to be in the Hall, roaming the corridors, maybe even getting into the upstairs bedrooms."

"What kind of work were you thinking of applying for?" Jack's eyebrow arched and a lascivious grin appeared on his face. "Ow," he rubbed his arm after she playfully swatted it.

The next morning they both attended communion. Jack hoped nobody else could hear Kat's teeth grind as she endured the old religion's rites. Back at *The Ferryman* they stoically endured being picked over by the clerks of the different household functions. In the end Jack was picked by the cellarer, who commented that he should have no trouble carrying the casks of wine and ale, while Kat was snapped up by the clerk of the ewery who had responsibility for all the linen, because she was well presented and clean.

The household comptroller handed them each a shilling in advance wages, saying they'd get sixpence per day, and no days off for the next month. If they performed their duties well there was possibility of a permanent position but no guarantee. They were to report at dawn the next day at the kitchens where they'd be fitted for livery and start their training.

As they walked back to their cottage Jack complained about the miserly wages saying it was exploitation of the common people, but Kat reminded him they were in the middle of fenland and there wasn't much employment except for farm work which paid next to nothing, so they should be grateful to have got the positions at the Hall.

Royal bastards

Over the next week Jack and Kat were worked hard and long.

Learning the rhythm of the Hall and the expectations of the household they were rushed from pillar to post, fetching, carrying, cleaning, and delivering.

Each evening they made the trip back to Stoke Ferry, walking with the other villagers along the forest track. Most were happy to be employed and even happier to have a full belly as the Bedingfield's kept a good table and the servants were permitted any uneaten food.

Kat pointed out how several of their new colleagues were feeding their entire families from the leftovers they carried home with them.

Jack noticed one shy little lad who kept himself slightly apart from the adults, but always travelled with them. During the week he gradually encouraged him to talk. His name was Thomas. His mother was too lame to work and was caring for her two young daughters anyway, his father had died of the sweating sickness three years ago and there were no other relatives. They received alms from the church and charity from the other villagers, but mostly the family relied on Thomas for food.

After befriending the lad Jack occasionally slipped a package of bread and meat to him, claiming he wasn't hungry but the boy could use it and grow up strong. Kat admonished him, "Jack we can't take in all the waifs and strays. And anyway we'll be gone soon and you'll break his little heart. Look how he watches you now, like a puppy watching its master." But Jack didn't care, he remembered only too well what it was like to work all day long and still have an empty stomach.

That Sunday they reluctantly returned to church, fearing that someone would report them to the household if they didn't.

They were glad they did because on the way they overheard a messenger telling a maid how he had heard a rumour that the King had been seen at a window in the palace at Greenwich, and so the rumours of his great illness must be exaggerated.

Kat pulled her cloak around her as the interior of the church was far colder than the temperature outside. Again they endured the service until they were pulled from their reveries by a surprise omission that brought a gasp from the congregation. Unusually there were no prayers said for the King's sisters, Mary and Elizabeth. Some minutes later they were even more shocked when the priest read out the announcement that the sisters were now considered royal bastards.

As they walked from the church to the Hall they exchanged hurried whispers about this unexpected turn of events, only to realise that everyone else was talking openly about it. Most of the servants were scandalised and one even went so far as to squarely point the finger of blame at the Duke of Northumberland, loudly opining, "He is killing the young King with poison, and now he is making sure that the princesses won't inherit the throne when he dies, instead he is setting his own son up to take the crown and he will become the power behind the throne."

One older woman contradicted the general feelings by loudly proclaiming that when Edward was dead then Mary would be queen and would bring back the old religion for good. Jack noticed that many of the servants seemed to agree that would be a good outcome.

The following day Jack was called over by the elderly cellarer, Bart, who placed a fatherly hand on his arm as he said "take a barrel of ale over to the dining hall, Jack my lad, there are thirsty men who'll be wanting a drink unless I'm mistaken."

On his way to the brewery in the northeast corner of the Hall he glanced at the stables and saw at least a dozen extra mounts being sponged down as though after a long ride. He rolled a barrel out into the yard, and easily hoisted it onto his shoulder and dodged between servants in unfamiliar livery as he crossed to the dining hall. A half dozen young noblemen cheered as he entered and grappled for the barrel, quickly uncorking it and pouring ale for themselves. He received a couple of grateful backslaps and was quickly forgotten, so he busied himself with straightening chairs and moving mugs from table to table. All the while he tried to eavesdrop on their conversation, with only limited success.

That evening he relayed his information to Kat, "This is Sir William Drury's household, he travels with a dozen young men of his retinue." And she countered with her own, "They are the first of several groups expected. This is why we were hired, to make sure they would be well served during their visit. Apparently they are staying for a couple of weeks then continuing their journey."

"We should take advantage of all these new people in the Hall and complete our search. If the rumours are true the gem is urgently needed back at Greenwich."

The next day, Tuesday, Jack was returning along the south corridor after delivering wine to the main dining hall. He often took this route as it afforded him a view of the library door, which he had noticed was shut this morning as usual. Ahead of him he saw Kat, loitering near the brewery. She gestured that he should follow her and she led the way to a private nook where she giddily told him about a secret she had discovered.

"Upstairs, near the main bedrooms, is a storeroom for clean linens. Hidden inside that room is a secret door, behind which a stairway leads further up into the roof space of the Hall. Alice, one of the other maids, tells me it leads to a secret room where the old Lord, Edmund, used to take young maids for secret trysts without the Lady Grace finding out about it. Apparently he especially liked French maids, none of them were safe from his passions, for he developed an attraction for them when campaigning in France during the war."

"Do you think the Bretwalda egg is stored up there?" asked Jack, confused.

"Well no, that's not very likely. But I thought it was interesting that the house has secrets. Maybe we should be looking for other secret doors and passageways?"

Just then the cellarer's other assistant came jogging past, saw Jack and called to him, "We're needed right away Jack, a fresh delivery of supplies for the brewery has arrived on a wagon that is now waiting to be unloaded in the courtyard."

Chapter 50 - Sequestration

Thursday the 6th of July 1553
Oxburgh Hall, Norfolk

Heist and seek

Jack was in the corridor outside the brewery, gently thumping the wall in frustration. *It's been almost two weeks already. Are we ever going to get into that library? Maybe we can create a diversion and sneak in for a quick search? How long would such a search take? Maybe ten minutes?*

There was a rapid pattering of feet behind him and he span around alarmed. Thomas, the lad he had befriended on their walks back to Stoke Ferry, sprinted down the corridor, and skidded to a halt beside him.

"Sir Henry has gone into the courtyard to await the arrival of Sir John Mordaunt's household," he breathlessly announced.

"Why tell me this, Thomas?"

His face a picture of innocence he continued, "Sir Henry left the library door open when he rushed out into the courtyard."

Several thoughts quickly raced through Jack's mind.

The library!

This is a diversion just like I was hoping for!

Oh no, another household of Catholics traipsing around the house!

How on earth did Thomas know I wanted to get into the library?

Deep thought wasn't needed, it was clear that this could be their only chance.

"I need to find Kat," he said, turning on the spot.

At that moment Kat appeared around the corner carrying a pile of folded linens. Seeing the alarm on his face she ran to him.

"The library door is open and Sir Henry is in the courtyard and will be there for several minutes," blurted Jack.

"Then get your bag and let's go," she replied unhesitatingly.

Her decisiveness spurred him to action and he sped away, quickly returning with his bag. All three hurried through the corridors toward the library.

Jack surreptitiously checked for occupants, and finding it empty he dashed inside. Meanwhile Kat dropped her pile of linens on the corridor floor and pretended to be picking them up again, whilst actually keeping a lookout. Luckily the whole household seemed to be excited by the prospect of the new arrivals and had flooded into the courtyard.

"I want to help," said Thomas.

Kat didn't want to endanger the boy, but he had already done that all by himself, "Quickly, go around the corner and watch the other corridor, if anyone approaches just whistle."

Jack had already started searching. As they had agreed he called out everything he saw in case Kat recognised the importance of something that he didn't, "Big wooden desk. Ledger with household accounts. Lots of scrolls on the desk, farm yields and such from the local villages. A suit of armour, a shield, and two broadswords. A small wooden chest on the floor. I can't open it, it's locked…I can't see a key anywhere obvious. Panelling on the north wall. Books on a shelf fixed to the panelling. Wait. Here's something. A candlestick at one end of the shelf, with decorations…"

"That must be it," shouted Kat excitedly, dropping the linens again and rushing in to help.

Jack examined the candlestick "yes, the symbols are similar, maybe even exactly the same as the staff we found. But it is fixed to the shelf, I can't move it."

Kat started clearing books from the shelf, piling them haphazardly on the corner of the desk. "Jack, look!" she fairly shrieked.

As she pulled the last thick tome from the shelf it revealed the base for a second candlestick.

Jack shrugged his bag off his shoulder and quickly extracted the staff that they had spent so much time and effort examining. The thread at the bottom screwed neatly into the candlestick base that Kat had revealed, and the flange that they had previously been standing it on was the drip-tray for the candle itself.

"Now what?" asked Kat nervously. She ran to the door and peered down the corridor then shaking her head she returned to his side.

Jack paused and stared at the shelf supporting the two candlesticks, one at each end. *What is so important about a second candlestick? More light? More weight?*

"Hurry up Jack…think of something…"

Slowly, without any conscious plan he walked toward the shelf. He paused, then reached to his left and grasped the screwed in candlestick, then stretched to his right and gripped the original candlestick as well. He was at a comfortably full stretch. *This feels right.*

He tried to twist the shelf clockwise then anti-clockwise. Nothing.

He pushed both candlesticks. Nothing.

He tried tilting both sticks forward then backward but they didn't budge.

He pulled both sticks toward him, away from the wall….and there was a sharp "click" sound, and Kat yelped as a whole section of panelling popped out of the wall as though on a balancing mechanism.

Kat pushed the edge of the panelling sideways and it slid noiselessly aside, allowing them to peer beyond it, "It is similar to the chapel, a secret space behind the panelling. But this one contains…"

"…an altar," finished Jack.

They stared almost mesmerised, gazing at the golden altar and precious objects on and around it.

Kat picked up a small, handsome book and flicked through the pages, they glimmered with gold leaf and bright blue ink. "It's in Latin I think," she said.

Meanwhile Jack was running his hand over the altar-top itself, muttering to himself. "Is it made of gold?"

He stroked the smooth richly coloured surface, "No, it is painted wood, I can feel the grain. But beautiful nonetheless." His fingers traced up spiral carved columns that supported a little roof over a carved figure of the Madonna cradling a baby Jesus. To each side of this central piece was a richly carved scene inlaid in the backplane of the altar, containing hand-sized figures in flowing robes. Each figure brightly coloured and adorned with symbols.

He realised there was a six inch gap. "The horse statue" they exclaimed in unison.

He reached into his bag and extracted the statue that had so vexed them for the last six months, and gently placed it in the niche, the hooves fitting exactly into tiny carved hoof prints.

As the weight of the statue settled onto the altar they both clearly heard the gentle "snick" of a catch releasing, and a shallow panel flipped open below the biblical scene.

Jack's hand darted forward and emerged with a gem the size of a hen's egg. It was a deep ruby red but streaked with silver that seemed to swirl with a life of its own as they gazed at it.

"The Bloodstone of Boiorix!" exclaimed Kat.

"Jack! Someone's coming," squealed Thomas from the doorway.

Jack pocketed the gem and leapt backwards quickly reaching to slide the panel back to position, then stretching wide he pushed gently on the candlesticks. The air seemed to sigh out of the niche as the panel clicked back into place.

"The books!" said Kat, indicating the piles she had placed on the desk.

"No time, let's go."

They sprinted out of the library, Thomas stood with his arms full of the linens, and followed them as they darted down the length of the corridor, covering the distance to the next corner in record time, before turning and pausing, panting as they regained their breath.

Kat beamed at Jack, and his heart skipped a beat. He leaned forward and kissed her warm lips. First triumphantly, then more tenderly.

He realised Thomas was tugging at his sleeve, "Sir Henry and his secretary have seen the mess you left in the library and are calling the guards. We must go. Quickly!"

"Thomas you go back to the kitchens. If anyone asks, you never saw us alright?" he nodded, returned the linens to Kat, and left at a jog.

"Follow me Jack," Kat led him quickly and surely to a stone-built staircase and up to the next floor, which was luckily deserted. As they strode down the corridor Jack noticed the furnishings and tapestries became more and more sumptuous.

"Are you sure we want to come this way? These look like the family bedrooms."

"They are. Now quickly, open that cupboard." He flipped the catch on the door she indicated and revealed a reasonably large storeroom full of linens. Kat dumped the ones she was carrying in the shadows at the back of the room, before returning and pushing against the inner panelled wall causing a narrow door to pop open. She smiled at him, "This is the secret entrance to the attic that I was telling you about."

Jack closed the main cupboard door, cutting out most of the light, and gingerly followed Kat through the little door and up a steep, narrow stairway, the wooden treads squeaking with each step. "Walk at the edges of the treads, not the middle," she admonished, "else they squeak."

The attic had a small round window, like a porthole on a ship, that gave just enough light to see. The room was surprising large and in the middle was a rudimentary bed complete with dusty blankets.

Jack knelt down near the inner wall of the room, "I can see down into the corridor from here," he said, squinting through a knothole in the floorboards, "it looks like the whole household has been roused to search for us, I can see guards and servants frantically going both ways."

He turned back toward Kat to find her sat on the edge of the bed, leafing through the book she had picked up from the altar. Sensing Jack's gaze she shrugged and said slightly embarrassed, "We were in such a rush to leave I forgot to replace it."

She laid it aside and stretched out on the bed. Jack joined her and sidled over until they lay in each others arms and listened apprehensively to the commotion in the corridor below.

Kat's breath caught in her throat every time the footsteps were at their loudest and Jack could feel her tense up. He tried to imagine what he would do when the storeroom door was flung open, the panel popped, and aged wooden stairs squeaked beneath the feet of armed guards coming to search the attic. His mind was blank with apprehension and he felt the muscle in his left arm twitching uncontrollably.

Despite the anxiety they fell asleep, Jack cradling Kat protectively, and she resting her head on his shoulder.

Some time later Jack woke, perfectly content. If anything he pressed his body closer to Kat. His mind wandering aimlessly as he breathed in the fragrance of her hair.

With a panicky jolt, he remembered the egg, and the dozens of people searching for them: *What hour is it? It is completely dark - so it must be night.*

Are they still looking for us? How will we get out of here?

Garrr. I should have had a contingency plan, idiot that I am. How did I ever think we would be able to just walk out at the end of the day like normal, with a precious jewel burning a hole in my pocket?

His mind cycled round and round, most of his thoughts being dark and promising little by the way of a good outcome.

He felt Kat move, then finally waken, "I think I fell asleep."

He smiled despite everything. *Indeed.*

"All is quiet below. We should prepare to leave."

"But how will we escape? We had thought we would sneak in, find the gem and sneak out. We didn't expect them to even notice anything was missing, and certainly not to think that it was us who took it."

"I suppose we could have pretended to join the searchers and just brazened it out," said Jack, "but we didn't, so here we are. Anyway, I have another plan. Here, take the egg and hide it on your person. If we do get caught they are less likely to search you. Now, come on, follow me, but quietly."

They carefully edged down the stairs, only ever using the edge of the treads so they stayed silent. Jack popped open the hidden door and then inched open the main cupboard door. He watched the corridor for several minutes before declaring it safe to proceed.

"Back down the stairwell to the ground floor," he whispered.

They exited to the corridor without a sound, then boldly walked side by side northwards, their eyes accustomed to the near total darkness.

"There is the red glow from the forge, coming under the smithy door."

The glow flared brightly as the door was suddenly opened. A hulking silhouette suddenly filled much of the corridor, both Jack and Kat sprang silently to the side wall and pressed tightly against it. After a breathless moment the figure disappeared and the door closed again.

Heart pounding Jack whispered, "Luckily we are just deeper shadows in a dark corridor. Nonetheless we should move on quickly," gesturing toward where the apparition had been, he sensed more than saw Kat's hesitation, "Come on, we can't stay here."

They continued, taking even more care to be silent.

Finally they drew level with the smithy. Jack turned his back to it and tried to open the door to the stables, "I can't open it, its locked!" he whispered.

"It can't be, it doesn't even have a lock," hissed Kat.

"Well it won't budge," he could sense the edge of panic entering his voice, and forced himself to continue more calmly than he felt, "We'll have to continue to the exit by the gatehouse."

"But there will be guards awake for sure!" Kat said, alarmed.

Jack led them up to the end of the corridor with more confidence than he felt, and with the brewery to their right they peered around the corner to the left, seeing only a lonely flickering torch at the far end.

Behind them the cellarer, Bart, stepped out of the brewery, his eyes wide as he looked directly at Jack. He was about to cry out in alarm when Jack leapt forward and slapped his hand over the portly man's mouth, his momentum propelling them both into the brewery. Kat followed them in and shut the door quickly.

Jack was whispering rapidly to Bart.

His eyes flicked from Jack to Kat and back again a few times before he nodded and Jack tentatively removed his hand.

"I don't rightly know what's going on, Jack. Sir Henry gathered the entire household in the courtyard and said there was a thief in our midst. Then Osborne the comptroller noticed that you two were missing, and because you are both new to the Hall Sir Henry said you were probably the culprits, and everyone was sent searching for you. He was fuming mad I tell you."

"We have done nothing wrong I swear to God," Jack lied vehemently.

"Then give yourselves up. I will vouch for you," Bart was almost pleading.

This kindly man doesn't know how great the stakes are, thought Jack.

"I cannot," Jack glanced at Kat and then back at the cellarer, "I do not trust Osborne the comptroller, nor Norwood the head of the guards. They have both been pestering Kat and trying to lay their hands on her person. I think this is all their doing."

He glanced at Kat, and she played along, blushing innocently and yet managing to look violated at the same time.

"Aye, they never leave me be. One time the two of 'em cornered me and t'were not for the arrival of Lady Jane I dare not think what would have happened."

"The scoundrels! I had no idea. But I still think it best if you come to Sir Henry with me. We can sort it out, I promise not to leave your side, Kat."

"No, I'm sorry. We cannot do that," said Jack, thinking furiously. What he needed was to get safely into the courtyard, particularly the stable area. "If you really want to help us, just lead us round to the stables. Everyone is looking for two people, not three, so if you are with us we should be safe."

"What? Help you escape? You must think me mad. If I did that then I'd be as guilty as you."

"We could tie you up and when you are found you can say we forced you at sword-point. Things can't get worse for us, so you can blame us entirely."

"I don't know Jack, I'm not very good at lying, it doesn't sit well with me."

"Just do this for us, and then we'll be gone. If it will help your story we could knock you out when we tie you up."

"Now hang on a minute. I don't think we need those extremes. Tying me up should be enough."

"So you'll do it?" gasped Kat breathlessly.

"Oh, I suppose so. It looks the only way. Though how you'll get past the guards and through the locked gates I don't know. I can't help with those."

Jack opened the door a crack and after a moment turned back to them saying, "Well now is as good a time as any, let's go."

They strode down the dark corridor toward the gatehouse door and the exit to the courtyard, with the cellarer leading the way. As they passed the guardroom door he leaned in and waved in a friendly fashion, "Alright, lads? I'm just stretching my legs but maybe you'd like me to bring you some warmed mead later?" A chorus of acceptance floated back, and the cellarer withdrew into the darker recesses of the corridor again before heading out to the courtyard, "Let's cut across the corner here and look sharp about it."

As Jack steered them to the storeroom beside the stables Kat realised his intent, "Of course".

The cellarer sat compliantly on the dusty floor as they found a length of rope and tied him comfortably but securely to a post.

"Thank you for helping us, you are saving our lives," said Jack. "And doing your King a service too," said Kat. Jack looked at her in alarm as she realised her own mistake. Jack bent down and punched the cellarer once, hard, on the temple. The man's head bounced back against the post and he lolled against his bindings.

"I thought you weren't going to hit him!" said Kat.

"It is for his own good. He will have a headache tomorrow but his story will be more believable. Now quickly, to the trapdoor and into the tunnel."

Flight of fancy

They part jogged and part walked back to Stoke Ferry and arrived before dawn. Jack quickly negotiated rental of two horses at the inn, saying they needed to go to King's Lynn urgently. They mounted up with just the belongings they had with them and galloped north.

As soon as they were out of the village they turned left off the main road and headed into the woods and then circled back around the village and emerged south of the village, near the ferry over the river Wissey.

"Ho, ferryman. How much for us two and the horses?"

"A ha'penny for each leg young master, so that's sixpence in total."

As they tethered the horses, Jack made small talk, believing that being friendly was the most reliable way to get and keep others on your side.

"I was told there was a bridge here, was I told wrong?"

"No, sir. There was a wooden bridge over yonder, but the Abbot of Ely had it burned down he did."

"What?" exclaimed Kat, "Why would he do a thing like that?"

"Because he gets the tolls from this ferry as income, miss, that's why."

"That's outrageous"

"Yes, miss. The Hundred Court thought so too, and they have demanded that he rebuild the bridge from his own purse, but he is mighty slow doing it."

Jack broke a small dry loaf in two and gave half to Kat, seeing the ferryman watching he broke his own piece in two and shared with the man, "Mighty kind, young master, I missed breaking me fast this mornin' I did, and a bite will keep me going."

Kat broke her bread too, and gave it to the man with a shy smile, his gap-toothed smile returned an eloquent thank you.

As they disembarked Jack whispered to Kat, "Should we bribe him to keep quiet about us?"

"No. That would just offend him. He won't want to help authorities, instead he will probably remember us fondly and keep quiet without even being asked.

After a morning of hard riding, they reached the small but bustling town of Thetford.

"Jack can we stop here for some food? I'm half starved," Kat gestured to the *Bell Inn*, standing proudly beside the Little Ouse river.

While the innkeeper's wife fussed about, bringing small ale and a hastily assembled meal, Jack wandered over to the fire and pretended to warm his hands, while trying to overhear the conversation of a nearby group of patrons. The clientele was a varied mixture of merchants and guildsmen, exchanging gossip and trading concerns for the market on the morrow.

A stout man with an unfashionable beard burst into the inn and looked around desperately, then spotted the artisans who were standing in the small group near Jack.

With that faded old apron, splattered in wet clay, he is surely a potter, thought Jack.

The potter rushed over to join his mates, grabbed a tankard from the hand of one who looked similar enough to be related and was too startled to stop him, and downed the ale in one long draught.

A very thirsty potter, if I'm not mistaken.

"Hey Robert, that was my ale, you donkey!"

"Never mind that brother, listen to this tale I have and you'll be buying me ale for the rest of the day," replied the potter, wiping foam from his mouth with the back of his hand.

He had the full attention of the group and puffed himself up to inflate his importance as he blurted out his story. "I was just getting a bucket of water from the well beside my workshop see, when this finely dressed fellow stops his horse and asks me if I have a vase fit for a queen. Well, as you all know I have a good reputation for my vases as I have perfected the making of fine pottery for ladies chambers and..."

"Get on with the story you dull braggart," shouted one of his audience.

He looked aggrieved but continued, "Anyway, I bring him a shapely vase that was painted all nice by my Joan and it has that clear gaze that I make so you can see the painting. I start telling the gent about the workmanship and the time it takes to perfect the consistency of the clay and so on. He interrupts and offers me a decent price for London, near triple what I'd call a good price here. But nevertheless I haggle a bit, you know, to make him think he has a good deal..."

"Get on with it you windbag."

"Hmmph. So he ends up paying me a shilling more than he originally offered, which is not too much for fine craftsmanship like that. You can't get quality pottery just anywhere, you know. Anyway, as we exchange coins he tells me the vase is a gift for Princess Mary who is staying at the Priory that was and is now the house of his grace the Duke of Norfolk. So he says he *was* the goldsmith to the Princess, and I ask him what happened if he is no longer her goldsmith. And can you guess what he tells me?"

"He tells you you're a blowhard who can't tell a story in less than a day," came the laughing shout from one of the many other patrons who had gathered around the group. An indulgent chuckle came from the original listeners.

Despite the insult, Jack thinks the potter looks smug.

"He says that now he is goldsmith to ....the *Queen* Mary....because young King Edward died the night afore!"

The crowd erupted with questions and shouts of disbelief.

Jack's thoughts were in turmoil, his mind racing;

Edward is dead? We are too late with the Bloodstone!

Mary to be Queen? But she is fervently Catholic. What will become of the new religion and all of its supporters like our friends, Dee, Cecil, and Herbert?

We stole the stone from the secretly Catholic Sir Henry Bedingfield, a privy councillor under Edward, and who knows how powerful under Mary?

We must leave here quickly, rejoin our friends, and plan for the future.

Damn these people pressing in all around me - I can hardly move!

Kat paused in the doorway and glanced back toward Jack.

He was trapped within a jubilant crowd, the press of bodies hindering his actions. Both behind him and beside him she recognised the watchers; cold, hard men, willing to commit any atrocity should it be ordered. Jack's handsome face showed his rising sense of panic as he no doubt realised he had no freedom of movement.

She longed to stay with him but deep in her soul she had known this time was predestined. A time when her own dark past would reclaim her. The tugging on her arm was insistent and reluctantly she yielded, allowing herself to be pulled out into the afternoon drizzle that heralded a dour new future for them all.

Epilogue

"…Come, my friends,
  'T is not too late to seek a newer world.
  Push off, and sitting well in order smite
  The sounding furrows; for my purpose holds
  To sail beyond the sunset, and the baths
  Of all the western stars, until I die.
  It may be that the gulfs will wash us down:
  It may be we shall touch the Happy Isles,
  And see the great Achilles, whom we knew.
  Tho' much is taken, much abides; and tho'
  We are not now that strength which in old days
  Moved earth and heaven, that which we are, we are;
  One equal temper of heroic hearts,
  Made weak by time and fate, but strong in will
  To strive, to seek, to find, and not to yield."
  - Alfred, Lord Tennyson. Ulysses.

I forgive thee with all my heart

Implementing the terms of Edward's will, called his Great Devise, the royal councillors announced Lady Jane Grey as Queen. This bemused much of the population who had assumed Mary would inherit the crown. It also stirred cynicism and unrest because Jane Grey was the Duke of Northumberland's daughter-in-law, having recently married the Duke's youngest son, Guildford, therefore many people assumed she would be Northumberland's pawn.

At the request of the councillors, Northumberland took a small army to capture Mary before she could flee the country and perhaps raise sympathy or even an army abroad. Northumberland was an ex-soldier so he was deemed the best person for the task. Through a mixture of desertion and bad luck the force evaporated as it neared its quarry. Eventually Northumberland himself was overtaken by events and arrested.

During Northumberland's absence the will and cohesion of the councillors soon crumbled and descended to plotting to keep their own heads. After a mere nine days they emerged at Cheapside in London, and heralded Mary as Queen. The group included more obvious Catholic adherents like Lord Cheyne, but also William Herbert and John Cheke. Even William Cecil quailed and tried to make it seem like he only briefly supported Jane because he was pressured.

A scrabble of courtiers tried to gain favour with the new regime in order to keep their heads, by swearing oaths of fealty and by cleaving back to the old Catholic religion.

On the 1st of August Sir William Herbert went so far as to throw his daughter-in-law Katherine Grey (ex-Queen Jane's sister) out of his house, despite or because of the recent marriage to his son Henry, no doubt regretting tying his family so closely to the now doomed Duke of Northumberland and his impossible dynastic plans.

On the 8th of August 1553, over a month after his death, Edward VI's embalmed body, sealed in a lead coffin, was lowered into a vault of white marble and so laid to rest in Westminster Abbey. The Archbishop of Canterbury, Thomas Cranmer, led the service according to the rites of the new religion. It would be one of his final acts before being replaced.

With Edward's passing England had lost a King of enormous potential, but one who had also displayed a high degree of religious zealotry. Of course we will never know, but if he had lived, England's history could have included absolute intolerance of Catholicism, civil war, and even invasion by a foreign power.

On the 18th of August the Duke of Northumberland and several others were tried and found guilty of treason for supporting Queen Jane, despite the fact that those passing judgement had also supported Queen Jane's ascension.

On the 22nd August the executioner's axe ended the life of several of the previous regime's leading men, including the Duke of Northumberland and Sir Thomas Palmer.
The Duke, presumably in a desperate attempt to save his life, repented on the matter of religion, heard the Mass, and claimed to regret many of his actions, all of these statements being a welcome propaganda coup for Mary.
Sir Thomas Palmer did not. He leapt onto the scaffold and threw his cap into the crowd. I leave you with a snippet of his final speech to the eager onlookers:

> "God give you all good morrow!…. in the Tower I had a vision of Christ sitting at ye Right hand of God the father in glory and majesty…whose power is infinite….
> The world is altogether vanity, for in it is nothing but ambition, flattery, foolish or vainglory, pride, discord, slander, boasting, hatred and malice"

and then to the executioner:

"Come on, good fellow - art thou he that must
   do the deed?
   I forgive thee with all my heart."

Check the author's website, http://www.jadownes.com, for news about other novels in the *Predestination* series, and for conversation with the author about the locations, characters and events mentioned in *Predestination*.

Printed in Great Britain
by Amazon